Ordering Information:

Quantity sales. Special discounts are available on quantity purchases by book clubs, corporations, associations, and others. For details and/or LCCN number, contact the publisher at: director@vanvelzerpress.com

The characters and events in this book are fictitious. Any similarity to real persons, living or dead, is coincidental and not intended by the author. Please note our style of punctuation is comma and hyphen lite — we are very consistent with this on-purpose style.

Cover design / Van Velzer Press

Author Page Photo Credit: Florence Rodale

Edits & Layout & Publishing via Van Velzer Press

ISBN: 978-1-954253-13-1 (paperback)
ISBN: 978-1-954253-17-9   (ebook)
ISBN: 978-1-954253-18-6 (hardback)

10 9 8 7 6 5 4 3 2

Printed in the United States of America

VanVelzerPress.com

Red Dragon's Gambit

C.R. Buonanno

Dedication

This book is gratefully dedicated to the Communist Party of The People's Republic of China (CCP) for saving countless American soldier's lives during the Vietnam War by their self-serving duplicity in pilfering superior Russian war material passing through China by rail en-route to North Vietnam ... and substituting their own inferior, relabeled munitions in their place.

The above CCP policy saved this author in the early morning of January 13th 1968 when a shell landed next his hut and failed to detonate. There were other personal incidents in which Chinese intervention saved this author's life; and he would be glad to tell these tales if asked for an interview.

Chapter 1

Vox Non Incerta

Valentine Fountain Parrott lay in a catatonic state. Her body was shrouded in a blackness devoid of dimensions—no depth, no width, no length; nor did she experience any queasiness symptomatic of spatial disorientation—that trick of the inner ear that traps unwary pilots into losing ground reference to plunge their aircraft into an unrecoverable death spiral. Parrott felt none of these sensations. She was simply unable to move a single muscle. Then came the noise. Undulating at first, even mesmerizing, until the sound level expanded. An acoustic anomaly with the resonance of a steam piston in its unrelenting kinetic cycle of pitch and drop. As the sounds came louder and closer, a mental apparition began to emerge. A behemoth form in the shape of a ship's bow began bearing down on her as she lay motionless. At the base of this approaching apparition was a geyser of white water foaming violently. At the point of being overwhelmed by it, its vortex inexplicably carried her upwards. As she ascended, Val slowly began to visualize two large eyeholes with massive anchors suspended from either side of this towering bow of steel. Loud buzzing and whirling noises assaulted her. This apparition now completely dominated her subconscious. Parrott found herself staring down the long, flat expanse of an aircraft carrier flight deck. The spinning propellers of antiquated bi-planes, held together by vibrating guy-wires with menacing torpedoes slung between high braced landing wheel struts, confronted her. Oil-blackened engines with exhaust pipes belching flames and smoke were being run up to maximum performance preparatory to launch. And they were pointing straight at their unseen observer! The first bi-plane started to roll forward and quickly picked up speed. Still frozen in a catatonic state, the lower wing just missed decapitating her. As the antique aircraft groaned into the air, Val could make out a goggle-faced pilot with a flowing scarf and someone in the rear seat. On the side of the fuselage was the insignia of a big blue rondel with a smaller red one inside. Underneath the tail in stenciled letters was *HMS Illustrious*. A second bi-plane quickly followed, then a third … then several more in quick succession. After that she lost count. Unable to even close her eyes, the whirling propellers were slicing the air inches from her face. The diminishing resonance of the propeller screws churning the waves of the apparition was again solitary, then fading. Suddenly it was replaced by muffled explosions of thunder and lightning from the distant horizon where dark clouds were momentarily highlighted by a bright orange glow. Buzzing around the backlit clouds were the bi-planes, resembling fierce fireflies engaged in an intense aerial combat. They were dropping flares, bombs and launching torpedoes upon the silhouettes of battleships and cruisers anchored in some harbor. Searchlights swept the air trying to catch the menacing fireflies. Randomly, red darts of anti-aircraft tracer rounds found their mark. A fabric covered bi-plane was struck and caught fire. Out of control, a tail of orange flame arched across the dark sky. The plunging debris of burning men and wings came crashing down directly upon the terrified Valentine Parrott. Just at the moment of flaming impact she found her voice!

"Swordfish! Swordfish!"

"*Cheri!* Wake up! Wake up! You're shouting in your sleep!" a voice with a strong French accent called out to her with a gentle touch on her shoulder.

Val abruptly sat up turning toward her husband, then fumbled for the bedside lamp as she tried to relax. "It's alright, Claude I'm … I'm sorry for disturbing you."

"You really frightened me, Val. That must have been some *cauchemar* you were having."

She struggled to collect her thoughts. "More like a premonition."

"Now I'm even more concerned. Premonition frightens me more than you shouting in your sleep."

"That damn nightmare was bizarre beyond belief. First, I'm almost rammed by an aircraft carrier, then attacked by antique airplanes." She took a few seconds to gain control over her breathing. "I know it's preposterous—but goddammit, I have this feeling it was a real premonition of sorts."

Claude tenderly brushed back light brown hair from her forehead. "Did you eat any of that left over Roquefort? I warned you it was off."

"No *cherie*. It's not bits of undigested cheese aggravating my stomach. It was much more *real* than any dream I've ever had. Anyway, there's no need to dwell on it. It's over, please go back to sleep Claude. I'll check on the kids, see if my yelling woke them up." She slowly slid out of bed and put on a robe, then closed the bedroom door behind her. She went quietly across the second floor hallway toward the room of their twelve year old daughter Corinne and peeked inside. *Sleeping like an angel. Now I'll go spy on the devil.* It was the same result for ten year old Charles also sound asleep. *Hell must be a quiet place tonight,* she thought chuckling.

About to turn around and head back to bed, she hesitated. Instead, she descended the carpeted stairway to the living room. Downstairs, she ducked through the side kitchen door, opened the refrigerator and poured a glass of milk. With glass in hand, she headed for the living room instead of returning upstairs. In total darkness, yet with faultless familiarity, she selected a green bottle with a pair of black and white Scottish Terriers on the label. Using a tried and true elixir of pouring a measured shot into milk and stirring just once, as the smartest man she ever knew taught her, she lifted her glass—*To my mentor in this hard world, Robert Adair Alastair Brown—Slan-ge-var!*

After that solitary toast, Val went back upstairs and spent the rest of the night dreamless, snuggled up to her adorable husband.

"Welcome to the breakfast of champions, *mon papa*," said the precocious ten year old boy, and the only other male sitting at the kitchen table.

Claude Regnault smiled at his family gathered around the table. Valentine received the first affectionate kiss. Then he gave a tender peck on both cheeks to his daughter. For Charles, there was only a rub on his forehead with feigned scrutiny. "Those little horns must have receded during the night. Maybe I should check for a tail?"

Corrine started to giggle. Her brother reacted by spitefully tapping his spoon on top of her soft-boiled egg.

Their father intervened at once. *"Tu arréte, Monsieur Charles. Discipline, s'il-te-plaît."*

The boy instantly obeyed. He felt he was the luckiest boy in the world to have a French professor for a father and a spy as a mother; it was like living in a movie. To Claude's relief the school bus was winding its way through their Georgetown community.

"Okay kids, kiss your mother good-bye and get your school books."

Brother and sister didn't need to be told twice, and were out the door rushing to meet their classmates. Quietly pleased this morning went so smoothly, Val poured herself a cup of coffee and entered her pin into her iPad to get the morning news.

Claude was now hiding his face behind a physical copy of *Le Monde*.

Val decided to tease him a little. "Ah, the French government's official mouthpiece. Still crying that if the US State Department only deferred to the ministry of foreign affairs on the *Quai d'Orsay* the entire world's problems would be over in half an hour?"

"No, my Valentine, not in half an hour," he teased back, "but in seven days, most surely. *Bien sûr*. All things are possible under the call of *Liberté, Égalité, Fraternité*. Unfortunately, what's missing is—*Réalité*. Believe me, my adopted state department officials remind me of a bunch of *Simile Sartres*. How boorishly they preach American altruism over a diplomatic luncheon of big macs and fries. *Incroyable!"*

Val laughed. "That was Clinton and Trump; fast food lovers for sure and Biden was always out to lunch. Our current POTUS is more likely to just serve Champagne and Cognac courtesy of his Radcliff First Lady."

The conversation slowed as each read a little, ate a little and talked a bit about the childcare center that their daughter loved but their son was finding ways to constantly get time outs. They would have to come up with a plan B in case he was kicked out. If he could just hold on until the next school grade, then they could get a high schooler to come to the house and babysit them in their own home.

Val went to the hallway closet and put on a blue government windbreaker with the US Army Corps of Engineers turreted castle emblazoned on the right side. She then grabbed a clothing bag off a hanger and picked up her empty briefcase, also embossed with a turreted castle, and headed for the door. It was a show for the neighbors, performed each workday. For self-evident reasons, they couldn't advertise - *Spooks live here*. Wrapping her arms around Claude, she gave him a passionate kiss in the best traditions of a *Parisienne*.

"Valentine, promise me you'll stop listening to that spaghetti man, Mr. Brown. The one who is constantly repeating anti-French clichés. I can always tell his influence on your words."

Val was about to spoil the moment and remind her husband that spaghetti man was her boss. Thinking better of it, she simply returned a deeper kiss. "I'll see you tonight, my love," said Val as her hands reluctantly slid from his body. This was indeed an issue; being in the agency, Val's personal life was fair game for not only her immediate boss, but anyone in the higher levels of government. And with a French born husband, anyone could stir up trouble for her, although Claude became a US citizen well before their first child was born. As if rising in the ranks was not hard enough, she had to push against an old-boys' network and suspicion about her husband's loyalties. Meaning she had to walk a thinner line than anyone else to keep advancing in her career.

Walking out the back door to the driveway, she spotted their 96 year old neighbor, Luther Naill. Luth was the last president of the old Chesapeake and Potomac Bell Telephone Company before it morphed into the conglomerate now known as Verizon. Lost in thought, the old gentleman was pruning roses.

"Good morning, Luth. You're up early."

"Hey Val, got to leave a reasonably attractive garden behind for the family that eventually acquires my home after I'm gone."

"Luther, it is my firm belief you'll achieve the century mark without breaking a sweat."

"Oh God, I hope not. By the way Val, from what I've read lately, your boys have their work cut out in the Louisiana delta. Those earthen levies are as old as I am."

"Not if they make me chief hydraulic engineer…" Val tried to walk off fast before things turned political.

With the speed of lonely old men, Luth was able to keep eye contact and tried getting a conversation going to fill his empty day. "Hey Val, what do you think of China buying up multiple blocks of oil leases in Alaska? I was under the impression there was a world-wide oil glut. Those Reds are up to no good if you ask me. I fought them once in Korea, a long time ago."

Val gave a flippant response, "Still reading The Wall Street Journal, Luth?" Uncomfortable with this particular topic, she didn't wait for a response, and just waved as she got into her car, which also prominently displayed a turreted castle decal on the rear window.

Driving across R Street, Val took a left turn, heading south on 35th Street, which lead straight to the on ramp of the Francis Scott Key Bridge. Once across, she continued along Interstate VA-123 to McLean, Virginia. Val's mind began to dwell on two unrelated but disquieting matters. Making the required stop at one of several security booths along the private road, she displayed a green badge that hung around her neck to the security guard. The next required protocol was to place her left hand against a flat screen attached to the side of the booth. Once the palm print came back positive, a three foot high barrier was lowered and meshed with the road. The overhead red light went green and Val zipped into her assigned parking space in the hierarchy of this governmental institution. Mentally switching from Val to professional Parrott, she took off her decaled windbreaker and tossed it in the backseat with the empty briefcase and took out a gray suit jacket from her clothing bag. Low but fashionable heels clicked along as she headed for the main entrance of the six story original headquarters building, OHB as it was referred to in the agency. After passing through a revolving glass door, she stepped across the floor mosaic of an eagle's head, symbolizing the strength and alertness of the Central Intelligence Agency. The blue shield and 16 point compass star underneath the eagle head was meant to lend credence that the agency was all encompassing.

Once again, she flashed her green badge, this time to a somber group of mixed civilian and uniformed personnel behind a raised reception desk. Parrott took an elevator to the 3rd floor. Once there, she walked down a nondescript hallway. With an encrypted keycard, Parrott opened an unmarked door. Among the maze of cubicles that filled the room, the most striking feature was an enlarged photo that covered the entire north wall. It was reminiscent of the classical age of 1950s roadside billboards like Smokey the Bear warning *only you can prevent forest fires*. In this version the image displayed an ash-blackened New York City fireman in torn bunker gear with the admonition: ONLY YOU CAN PREVENT ANOTHER 9-11.

Val Parrott sat at her workstation among rows of other identical ones. She reached underneath to spin the combination dial to a personal safe and removed a stack of portfolios and a collection of color-coded books. She then switched on her computer and selected the slate colored book assigned for Fridays. She crossed referenced the shackle sheet of numbers and letters. This gave her the correct sequence of key strokes, supplemented by her assigned password and was able to access the CIA's mainframe data base firewalled to her security level. She typed in the word Swordfish. A color image of a World War II canvas-covered bi-plane popped up. Last night's image exactly. *That's disturbing, how did I conjure that up exactly right?* As she scrolled down, a large aircraft carrier filled the screen. While reading the description, Parrott realized the head of strategic analysis was behind her.

After a span of 40 years, Brown's prep-school Latin was still on the tip of his tongue. "*Vox Non Incerta*–No Uncertain Voice. That was the motto of *HMS Illustrious*, the British aircraft carrier now on your screen."

Chapter 2

Leviathan

Somewhere in the dark blue expanse of the south Atlantic, a three ship convoy of supertankers was plowing through the lower latitudes marking the Tropic of Capricorn. If anyone of these gargantuan curved shapes of steel were upended, each would dwarf the Empire State Building. They were of the 554,000 dead weight ton Batillus Class which certified the vessels as ULCC–Ultra Large Crude Carriers. Due to the absence of the 4,000,000 oil barrels they had the capacity to carry in their 41 separate tanks, it gave the illusion that three mountainous islands had broken loose from the Azores archipelago and were rapidly floating south. These ships, *Leviathan*, *Zeelandia* and *Antilles*, charged forward. Their enormous bows powered by six bladed 70 ton propellers with a 38' diameter churned aft at 90rpm driving them along at 16kts. The hull displacement of each supertanker cut such a deep trench into the south Atlantic it rivaled the Red Sea parting.

More incredible was that these steel objects could be sailed by a computer student with average skills. Satellites and ground positioning systems were displayed on 70" monitors located on the command bridge, mapping their exact position anywhere on the globe.

* * *

Months prior, in the Norwegian Fjord of Hammerfest, the crew was first mustered aboard for the backbreaking work of de-mothballing these supertankers after a storage layup of years due to a world-wide oil glut. A paycheck was a paycheck, so nobody questioned the work. For the most part, the problem was not the labor intensive work anyway. It was the unorthodox arrangement of assigning two captains and crew from two different countries to each ship. The primary crew of Danish and Norwegian sailors had been contracted for a small fortune and started the work first; then were forced to have a secondary crew of all male Chinese, who were paid much less, assigned to each ship.

At first, the arrangement was a novel distraction from the daily shipboard grind of welding, painting and rewiring endless miles of electrical cable. Every Scandinavian crew member had a Chinese co-worker, every assignment was done by this twin set. After 17 months of this drudgery in a gloomy fjord under an endless midnight sun, followed by a stretch of complete winter darkness, morale hit bottom. The culture clash and close quarters had given each twin set the feeling of constantly being watched.

Even after 19 days at sea, just less than half way to their undisclosed destination, the unease remained unabated. Only the forfeiture of all bonus pay maintained discipline. The pejorative term of *mirrors* was picked up by each homogenous crew; used toward the other set of sailors along with spitted complaints about foreigners. Yet in international waters, with an undetermined client, heading to an unknown port; who should be calling whom a foreigner?

* * *

Captain Pieter Voss peered out into the predawn mist over the African continent. He knew the coastline was 200 nautical miles out, at 90° relative due east of *Leviathan's* current position. Growing sunlight began to drive away the night's dampness and reflected off his thick blond hair and well-groomed beard. There were competing opinions as to Captain Voss's being a gentle giant. No crewmember ever recalled hearing him raise his voice in a reprimand. There was, however, a persistent rumor of a colorful incident during a layover in Rotterdam years ago. It involved a number of captains and officers engaged in an all-night drinking binge. One foolish engineering officer persistently taunted Voss about the origins of his Christian first and rarely mentioned middle name. That being Pieter Stuyvesant, the fabled wooden legged governor of New Amsterdam. Not getting a satisfactory answer in keeping with the animated atmosphere, he went so far as to playfully kick the captain's right leg to feel if it was wooden or not. Before he knew what was happening, Voss hoisted him up by his collar and belt, and sailed the offending officer along the full length of the bar. His skull shattered half a dozen beer bottles and as many shot glasses. The two patrons sitting on the end stools were the last barrier this Flying Dutchman encountered that night. The inquiry about names was never raised again.

Despite the breathtaking beauty of blue skies and white, whale-shaped clouds above the sea's horizon, the tall man who paced the huge port bridge wing was not happy. Formally a senior captain in the Royal Dutch Shell maritime division, Voss didn't relish selling himself for wages. A glance at the masthead flag reinforced his considerable loss of self-esteem. Flying the red square above a red star, and a blue star above a blue square told the world that his ship was of Panamanian registry—a whore of the sea. He was now sailing a French built, Dutch operated, Chinese owned and mirror operated, Panamanian registered vessel. Such a registry made it legal to flout every maritime safety code. The most egregious cost-cutting issue Voss had been forced accept was the deliberate refusal to take industrial X-rays of the main oil tank support brackets welded to the lower deck, right above the ship's keel. Potentially, if any of those brackets failed under any of the 41 separate, internal tanks, a catastrophic collapse could plunge the tank through the hull. Moreover, the design of a supertanker was to transport crude oil. Yet for reasons unknown, the main deck intake and discharge pipes were left sealed and their structural integrity never calibrated to an atmospheric pressure test.

Incredulous at such blatant disregard for safety and operational protocols, Voss was mystified why his Chinese paymasters insisted that all three tankers be ready for sea in record time. Normally, even under optimum conditions, overhaul required a minimum of two years to bring a ship back to life. And with the worldwide oil glut, he couldn't fathom the rationale of why the Chinese government purchased these sea going dinosaurs in the first place. At least he was spared the indignity of having to affix his signature to a bogus maintenance document. Nor bribe port officials to falsify quality control documents. The dubious honor of having to bribe the harbor master of Hammerfest fell to *Leviathan's* second master—the owner's representative: Captain Zhao Ju Phong of the People's Republic of China.

As this co-captain left the wheelhouse, he too walked the 55' length of the port bridge wing to approach his opposite number gazing meditatively in the direction of South Africa. This was the expected landfall reference before the convoy would swing 90° to port, passing the Cape of Good Hope. At the convoy's maximum speed of 16kts, and with no predictable weather deterioration and a following sea, they were to transect the 20° longitude meridian in two days. That was the secondary navigational waypoint of Cape Agulhas giving passage into the Indian Ocean.

Captain Voss turned away from the seascape to face the man who was half his size but equal in resolute determination. Captain Phong exhibited the air of a grandfatherly sage, complete with the long chin beard of a Confucian scholar. It was even a flowing white color. But underneath that benign look, Phong possessed the survivalist instincts necessary for a long and successful career within the Chinese Communist Party regime. The CCP was not very forgiving. Nor was it very communist any longer. It was run by elite party members intent on keeping their positions as family legacies.

In addition to the deep furrows of a weather beaten seaman's face, Phong's black eyes were alert and keen. He professed to having no friends except a manifest loyalty to the party. On the mainland, his many rivals referred to Captain Phong as *Shuì bào*–Sleeping Leopard. A sleeping leopard which, if provoked, could change more than its spots if the occasion required.

After a measured pause Phong asked, "Did you order the Chinese government's official interpreter off the bridge yesterday, causing him to lose face?"

"Qu Xing is a very clumsy interpreter. Very confusing to my officers. He's setting the stage for an incident. A critical miscommunication on the command bridge could be catastrophic. Besides, we both prefer to converse in English. It's neutral."

"That's true, Captain Voss. The People's Republic of China has the largest English speaking population in the world, and you Dutch seem to enjoy using it for your leisure activities."

"What if I arrange for Qu Xing to give Mandarin classes to my off watch crews? Will that be face-saving enough?"

"An excellent idea. You're a diplomat."

"However, for my crews to show the right amount of enthusiasm, they should be paid to attend."

"A bad idea, Captain Voss. Now you're a pirate."

"Paid enthusiasm would go a long way to salve Qu Xing's loss of face."

"You do realize, Captain Voss, for this one contracted voyage alone, China is paying you more money than my total accumulated wages from thirty-eight years at sea? But I'll see what can be arranged. Now for new business. Captain, our ships must purge tanks before we round the Cape."

"Purge tanks? Our tanks are empty!"

"With seawater. I have orders to deliver our ships in pristine condition, without the slightest residue of crude oil sludge."

"You're ordering me to flood all our tanks? That will take thirty hours to fill, and twice that much time to purge back out to sea. Providing none of the ballast pumps fail on any of our ships while playing with two billion pounds of seawater."

"My orders come directly from Beijing."

"Do your orders contravene the Paris environmental accords about polluting the world's oceans? To which your country was a signatory, I may add."

Phong remained unfazed. *You have no idea of the circle within a circle of all the accords we are about to blow apart. Yes, you just worry about the whales you fool.* "Captain Voss, I realize this could slow our speed and conceivably add three or four sailing days to your already generous contract." *Which you will never collect.* "That should make you the richest man in—West Friesland–wasn't it? Please join me on the command bridge, captain."

As Captain Phong turned to leave, Voss's first mate, Hendrik Van Het, came forward. Both gave a nod of respectful recognition as they passed each other. Het, waiting till Phong was out of earshot, asked, "What did Captain One Ball Hung Low have to say?"

The remark severely tested Voss's gentle giant image. He glared down at his first mate. "First Officer Van Het — as long as you're aboard my ship, you will not disrespect any fellow sailor. Furthermore, that man has been commanding ships since before your own testicles dropped."

"Sir, with all due respect, Phong is a die-hard communist. If he ever received instructions from his Beijing masters to heave us all over the side with anchors tied to our feet, he'd carry out his orders with alacrity."

"That's enough, Het. Follow me to the wheelhouse. Now!"

The first officer persisted. "You know Captain Phong's first mate — my mirror? How do you pronounce his name?"

"I've given explicit orders to the crew that term was not to be used. Your Chinese counterpart is First Officer Wei Jing Hua."

"Well, this Hua is a dying man. Haven't you noticed his fatigue and confusion on the bridge? He frequently leaves his operating station to go to the head so he can vomit in secret. Plus, that vial of pills he carries around. Don't tell me you haven't noticed those red spots on his neck?"

Out of patience, Voss stopped and glared. "What's your point, Hendrik!?"

"We're on a bizarre mission to transport three supertankers to the other side of the world. They weren't properly overhauled and we're under the command of a captain old enough to have sailed with Noah's Ark. And, whose first mate is less than thirty and looks like a walking dead man. And what is going on around the communications deck? Chinese only radio operators? All our family ship to shore messages have to go through a censor for approval. All watched over by armed guards!"

"I advise you to think more about what you're going to spend your generous salary on, courtesy of these Chinese you detest. Therefore, until we reach our port of call, suspend your attitude. That's an order."

Back on the command bridge, Captain Voss surveyed the assembled ship's officers which included his Dutch first and second mate, together with their Chinese counterparts. He was relieved to see a Dutch seaman at the helm. The interpreter Qu Xing was somewhere else. Voss now focused his attention on the large square dial indicating a speed of 16kts. *Leviathan* was within its safety parameters. Slanting to port and back to starboard within 6° or less was acceptable. Next, he inspected the glass domed compass on the flat navigation table, making sure it pointed south-southeast at 1-5-3°. This was verified by an overhead green colored monitor display. After a glance at the chronometer, tracking 06:05 hundred hours Zulu Greenwich mean time, and 07:05 hundred hours Alpha local time, all data readouts were entered into the ship's log. Satisfied, Captain Voss gave a nod to his first mate.

Van Het picked up the ship to ship transmitter. "This is *Leviathan* calling *Zeelandia* and *Antilles*. Recommend your captains repair to the bridge and standby for orders."

A minute later the overhead speaker came alive. "This is *Antilles*. Captain Zwaan standing by."

"This is *Zeelandia*, Captain Ochssee here."

"Gentlemen, this is Captain Voss speaking. Our ship owners have ordered us to flood tanks for one last purge before we enter the Indian Ocean. We shall commence flooding in four hours. Any questions?"

Only static was heard for about ten seconds. "Hope to Christ your mirror knows what he's doing!"

Captain Voss recognized Ochssee's acerbic tone. Not turning to Phong to catch his reaction, Voss simply requested the two ships notify him when their tanks were flooded, then placed the transmitter back on the navigation table. It was then he notice Captain Phong smiling at him.

"No need to apologize for your secondary captain's apprehension. After Rotterdam, nobody questions the orders of the Gentle Giant. Your leadership and fortitude is why the party esteemed you entirely worthy of confidence to be convoy commander. Tell me, do you think we just pulled your name out of a fortune cookie? Only Americans engage in that childish stupidity."

Phong was quite free with his words, knowing that the other two Chinese officers in earshot knew not a word of English. And with Interpreter Xing absent from the bridge none of his words would ever come back to be reviewed for deviation against party orthodoxy. With plenty of remaining time before executing the order to flood tanks, he wanted to practice his conversational English. "Are you married Captain Voss?"

"Yes, I have a wife named Simone, and a seventeen year old son."

"My wife's name is *Sheng-Kai*. It roughly translates into Flower Blossom. A literal rendering would be Snapdragon. Home from the sea after thirty-eight years, my retirement upset the rhythm of her daily life. I've become a piece of unwanted furniture. She has taken to calling me a dead refrigerator after reading about divorce statistics among the aging Japanese retirement class. I don't really blame her, though. This is not a conspiracy of Asian women to gain more personal freedoms. My gullible little Sheng-Kai is an unwitting victim of a revanchist plot perpetrated by the Americans to undermine our ancient customs—to literally destabilize China right from under our feet."

"If I should hazard a guess, it sounds like your wife may be spending too much time on social media," said Voss.

More bitterness was evident in Phong's tone. "I have a grandson who recently graduated from Tsinghua University. One of the top ten engineering universities on our mainland. Generously paid for by our party's benevolence. Now his only ambition is to go to Hong Kong and become a web designer and go clubbing all night. Thoroughly unlike his father, my son, who is the hard working port director at Lu-Shun. It's China's most strategic port, located between the Yalu River and the Yellow Sea. The main separation point between the avaricious Russian devils at Vladivostok and those ungrateful North Korean creatures living in their fool's paradise. I was overwhelmed with joy when the party recalled me from my agonizing retirement. In fulfilling my new duties, I'll not only atone for my grandson's selfish behavior, but it will provide me with a happy excuse to have a joyous reunion with my son, whom I haven't seen in years."

The normally stoic Dutch captain was completely caught off guard, picking up on a clue probably not meant for him. "Phong, you just said, you hope to meet your son? I understood this convoy was heading for Shanghai. Now you're suggesting our port of call is Lu-Shun? As you are well aware, it's for vessels of three hundred thousand dead weight tons or less. What's changed? What's going on?"

Phong himself was momentarily stunned into silence. It was not his co-captain's inquisitional tone, but his own words that unsettled him. His mind raced to re-examine everything he just said.

Captain Voss was now upset with himself as well. Realizing that ever since he took command of this convoy he was an unwitting pawn in some Chinese plot. He was too much of a professional seaman to be obsessed with international intrigue for long, but wished he hadn't given away that he caught that clue. Voss needed a moment alone. He needed a break from the command bridge. He formally excused himself to all, then left the bridge to descend into the netherworld of the engine spaces. Voss told them he needed to monitor the oil tank purging operation first hand. As he descended, he stretched his arms outward to take a firm grip with each hand on the yellow safety handrails. The last thing he needed was to lose his balance and go tumbling down and end up with a broken leg or worse.

Voss passed through the wardroom. Below that, kitchen smells of onions, fish soup and rice wafted up as he came upon the organized chaos of the mess deck. The ship's cooks and galley stewards were in never-ending preparations of feeding three meals to three different watches for two distinct cultural palates, three time a day.

At the bottom of the third deck was the crew's quarters, where he replaced his captain's white cap for a pair of industrial strength green ear protectors and heavy duty safety goggles. As soon as he undogged the hatch to descend to the fourth deck, a roaring blast of escaping air and machine noises rushed up to meet him. Air conditioning compressors and fresh water evaporators were producing hurricane sounds well in excess of the 88 decibels of human tolerance. Descending further, he wedged himself in between rows of hydraulic power pack systems and immense auxiliary diesel generators. The engine room crew was on the fifth deck. The sight gave him a much needed moment of levity. The physical contrast of the taller and mostly blond Dutch sailors contrasted with their Chinese counterparts. It was striking, despite the grime and sweat which covered their shirtless torsos.

Once he reached the sixth deck, he could see the propeller's massive cylindrical drive shaft rotating at 90rpm. Partially exposed in an open steel trench, it was fenced off by a row of waist high safety handrails. Voss was now standing just above *Leviathan's* keel. Below that was 27,000' to the bottom of the south Atlantic. Overhead, a line of caged red lights guided his steps along a grated catwalk. On both sides of this catwalk were the ship's electrical dynamos, each the size of an amusement park carousel. Next were giant oil/water separator tanks, in tandem with three story high suction pumps. All were interconnected by a labyrinthine arrangement of green, red, yellow and white painted cross-sectioned piping, all attached to even larger piping for the uptake ventilators. Each piece had its own individual console board of rounded analog and elongated digital instrumentation in color-coded light emitting diodes to reassure the crew that the entire system was working as designed. At the end of the catwalk, Voss entered a sealed double outer door compartment, similar to a space station airlock. Once inside the relative safety of the noise cancelling space, he removed his goggles and ear protectors, then opened the last inner door.

Leviathan's nerve center was a hybrid between a nuclear power plant console and a television network control room. A vast array of multiple screens and dials of all shapes and sizes with flickering needle movements produced a constant stream of data that required round-the-clock monitoring by operators. Order was the prime directive for successful operation of a ship of this size. Choreographed under Chief Engineer Maarten, *Leviathan's* engine room machinery ran as efficiently and precisely as the finest Swiss watch.

Voss walked past a long row of beige circuit breaker cabinets. As he approached the main console, he was dismayed to see a dour portrait of Chairman Mao. He was further dismayed to see the obnoxious interpreter distracting his engineering crew and generally making a fool of himself. Then he came upon Maarten, sitting at his operating station. Maarten had his own national icon displayed. Framed above energy graph scales was an 9x12 photo of a 49 year old King William-Alexander of The House of Orange. Maarten stood up quickly. "Good morning, captain."

"Good morning, Johannes. You're familiar with today's operational orders?"

"First Mate Van Het notified me as soon as orders were transmitted to *Antilles* and *Zeelandia*. We flood tanks at ten hundred hours Zulu."

"Correct. We have a few hours to prepare. In the meantime, I need to relax. That's why I've come down here for a special cup of your engine room coffee."

"Our shaft alley coffee? Coming right up. A strong Dutch brew with a dash of salt and lots of Suriname sugar," said the chief engineer with pride.

To kill time before the operation, they had a long discussion of family and home. It was just what Voss needed. After a while, their discussion strayed into their reasons for contracting themselves out to China. Mindful of the Chinese crewmembers within earshot, they continued to speak in guarded terms. When Captain Phong became the topic, Maarten sarcastically complained about overloading a ship and the song about the *Edmond Fitzgerald*. Voss thought the relaxing talk was becoming dark and cut it short.

"It's time. Are we prepared to go Maarten?"

"You staying here captain? Once we start flooding tanks, and if the pumps runaway on us, well, the Atlantic is pretty deep."

"You're the chief engineer, Johannes—you tell me!"

"Kindly have another cup of coffee and make yourself comfortable," he responded with a soft smile. Then he swung into action, assembling his engineering staff and their counterparts. Orders were issued non-stop. "Second Engineer Embrech—you are to immediately muster crews to positions at all standby emergency cut off ballast intake valves. Third Engineer Finnsson—you are to physically liaison between all emergency valve crews and this station. I want verbal status every thirty minutes. First Engineer Horbach—do not leave my side." He then turned to face his captain. "Any further orders, sir?"

"Yes. I want the next off watch crew on full standby. Inform your men our Chinese owners will sign off for all overtime. Full forfeiture of bonuses of any crewmember who refuses to report." It was then Voss noticed that Xing was still milling about. For some inexplicable reason he felt a need to show the diminutive man a small courtesy, and offered him a cup of strong Dutch coffee. The normally tea drinking interpreter eagerly accepted. The sight of the most powerful man aboard *Leviathan* deferentially serving Xing in the presence of the

Chinese engineering crew was more than adequate to restore his loss of face. Voss then settled back in his chair and focused on the sweep of the phosphorescent minute hand on the overhead chronometer.

With ten minutes to execute, First Engineer Horbach began lifting the red safety lock catches on the double row of 12 ballast pump handles. Five minutes later, the automatic engine room telephone rang, informing Maarten that all crews were at their emergency manual valve cutoff stations. A minute later, Finnsson reported in person to give his verbal confirmation. Voss gave a nod and the ballast pump handles were turned and activated. The sealed control room cancelled out any noise except for nascent interior vibrations that made it evident titanic kinetic forces were now in play. Five minutes later the neutral white pipe schematic displayed on screen slowly turned bright green. *Leviathan* was forcing the Atlantic Ocean through its opened ballast vents. The displaced seawater jet-streamed directly into the uptake pipes. From there it shunted to the overhead intake system. It then sub-divided among the crude oil tanks. For stability, it was necessary to uniformly flood each tank at the same time to the same level. As long as the pipe joints on the monitor didn't flash red, and the un-X-rayed load bearing tank support brackets didn't fail, there was no cause for alarm.

Thirty minutes later, with the initial tension behind them, Captain Voss insisted on making a fresh pot of coffee himself. He didn't want any of the crew to leave their stations. The first hour ticked by and the monitor screen was still an eye-soothing green. A second hour showed no change.

The third hour started well.

AAW! – AAW! – AAW! – AAW! – AAW! The emergency sound of the telephone cut short the relaxed atmosphere in the engine room. Captain Voss yanked an oversized black receiver from its heavy cradle. First Mate Van Het's voice came in loud and agitated. "Recommend the captain repair to the bridge—radar reports fast approaching aircraft sixty miles out—intentions unknown!"

Voss slammed down the receiver and dashed for the double air lock doors without a word to anyone. In record time he crossed the lower sixth deck catwalk and bolted up the companionway ladder to the fifth deck. On the stairwell between the fifth and forth deck he began to get sluggish and falter. His central nervous system was shutting down. Even the most robust of men can't endure a high intensity noise level over 88 decibels for long. In his haste to return to the bridge, he had left his ear protection behind. Machine noises were attacking him from every direction at once and blowing out his eardrums.

He was at the point of blacking out when the illusion of a frogman appeared. It was Xing wearing oversized green goggles and large heavy duty ear protectors. He quickly placed a lifesaving set of ear protectors over Voss's head. Then handed over a pair of safety goggles as well. With his strength slowly reviving and with the assistance of the diminutive man, both made their way back up to the command bridge.

Their arrival went oddly unnoticed. The entire compliment of Dutch and Chinese officers had staked out their own individual portholes or were spread out across the ship's two bridge wings to scan the horizon with binoculars. Voss picked up an extra pair laying on the chart table.

With ears still ringing like church bells, his eardrums were further racked with pain by the thunder clap of a sonic boom by a jet aircraft that made a low level pass over *Leviathan* from bow to stern. The flyspeck that made so much noise disappeared over the horizon. Seconds later, it came back around for a second pass. This time it came in low and slow, for a positive identification of the ship which also allowed Voss to study it. The small, mid-fuselage delta wing and unmistakable pronounced barrel nose with a protruding needle cone and tiny tail fins confirmed it was a MIG-21. NATO code: Fishbed.

Captain Phong answered the question everyone was thinking. "It's a Chengdu J-7. A Chinese built version of the Mikoyan-Gurevich-21. A far superior aircraft than the Russian original. It's one of twelve we sold to Namibia. He flew all the way from the Skeleton Coast to take our picture. No cause for alarm gentlemen, I assure you. China is building a brand new port facility for the Namibians at Walvis Bay."

Whether there was cause for alarm or not, on its third and final pass it kicked in its afterburners to jump back to Mach speed and shake *Leviathan* with a second horrendous sonic boom. The anti-climax to this was the now empty sky and calm sea matched by the utter silence on the bridge. For two whole minutes no one had said a word—in Dutch, Mandarin or English. Voss felt he needed to say something. Either because of the constant ringing in his ears or a sense of foreboding on how that Namibian pilot somehow knew this convoy was under the protection of China. *If such a remote African country knows our destination and mission, who else does? What if Namibia is not so Sino-friendly as Phong thinks? What if their intentions are hostile?* Despite the ice pick sharp pain inside his head, Voss also needed to hear the sound of his own voice. He needed to know he was not going deaf.

"Captain Phong, I recommend we change course to get ourselves under the cover of South African air space as soon as possible."

"Not necessary, but I concur on the side of caution, captain," answered Phong.

Voss wasted no time. "Helmsman, change course one-two-three degrees east-southeast."

The helmsman turned the ship's wheel to port until the compass aligned with the new course correction. It was simultaneously relayed to *Zeelandia* and *Antilles*. Captain Voss once again excused himself from the bridge but this time gave no reason.

* * *

Four hours since activation, the incoming satisfactory status reports on the ballast pumps on all three ships was welcome news. During that time, Voss discreetly visited the Dutch medical officer. Results showed he had suffered a 20% temporary hearing loss, narrowly escaping a career ending diagnosis of tinnitus. Voss rested in his stateroom, but continued to monitor reports. *Leviathan's* 41 tanks were ⅓ full. There were no anticipated problems taking on the remaining 800,000,000 pounds to full capacity. Deck and engineering watches were rotated. A quiet routine settled in throughout the ship. A solitary Dutchman rode a bicycle from the superstructure to the bow and back again for exercise. A group of Chinese practiced Tai Chi. Official sunset was over two hours away. By sunrise the convoy would be under the protective umbrella of South African airspace which no Namibian or other foreign aircraft would dare enter. All was well until the overhead ship to ship loudspeaker blared to life.

"This is *Zeelandia*. Namibian gunboat approaching our port quarter. Coming up fast. Intentions unknown." Captain Von Ochssee's voice showed his irritation.

Besides the command bridge, that alarm was transmitted below decks into the officers' wardroom. All officers hurried to the bridge including *Leviathan's* co-captains. Every officer swept binoculars port and aft. First Officer Het scrolled an ID program on a monitor and gave a rapid report. "Captain–it's one of those hundred fifty-two foot Brazilian built Gra-Jan class patrol vessels. Her main armament consists of one forty millimeter cannon and two twin fifty caliber gun mounts. Personnel is four officers and forty-two men. Us three Goliaths against one David. Advantage us."

There was silence on the bridge. The Dutch officers didn't appreciate Het's humor and the Chinese didn't understand the translation.

The speaker added to the mounting apprehension with a veiled warning by an African voice who spoke with clipped self-assurance in an upper class English university accent. "This is Namibian gunboat NS *Erongo*. Captain Brendan Homba commanding. This Panamanian convoy is to stop their engines immediately. Heave to, and be prepared to be boarded. I repeat, you are to stop all engines immediately."

Captain Phong reacted swiftly. He pressed a button and gave an order in Mandarin over *Leviathan's* secured internal intercom system. On cue, his order brought down the Panamanian flag and a very large red flag of one dominant yellow star and a semi-circle of four smaller yellow stars was run up the masthead in its place.

Zeelandia's impatient captain now added racial slurs to this confrontation over the ship to ship open frequency for all to hear. "Voss, are we shutting down in mid-ocean for this Kaffir boy or not?"

Despite the gravity of the situation, Voss couldn't resist. He pointed a finger toward the overhead speaker while looking directly at Phong. "Now that is a Dutch Afrikaner! And now you know the difference between us." He picked up the handheld transmitter. "This is *Leviathan*, Captain Voss speaking.

If you check your satellite GPS you will confirm this convoy is in international waters. By what right are you challenging this convoy's freedom of navigation?"

"This is Captain Homba of NS *Erongo*. I guess your Chinese status is under the protection of English speakers with Dutch accents. Flying false flags on the high seas is an act of piracy. You have five minutes to heave to or you will be fired upon."

Captain Von Ochssee's ill-temper finally got the best of him. "You're the pirate Kaffir boy! You just want a shakedown tribute for your pissant country! Go loot your own treasury like the rest of you Kaffir boys do!"

For once Voss found himself in agreement with the old Afrikaner. This was definitely a floating Namibian toll booth. If he was still sailing for Royal Dutch Shell, the Namibian's tribute check would have already cleared the bank before the convoy left their Norwegian harbor.

Suddenly, the echo of a far off explosion was heard. A 40mm shell had exploded off *Leviathan's* enormous bulbous bow. The tiny water spout it made in proportion to the supertanker's size was like a dolphin at play, but the intent was clear. The last thing Voss needed was to have the wheelhouse raked with 50 caliber machine guns. As a teenager, his grandfather had told him gruesome stories from World War II: that if you had to get hit with a 50 caliber projectile, you will wish it was one with an exploding head instead of a solid armor piercing one. Better to get it over quick instead of thrashing about in excruciating agony for however long it takes to lose consciousness.

Resigned, Captain Voss was about to press the transmitter button and comply when Phong approached him. He yanked out the transmitter's black cable from its console plug. Nobody had ever heard Captain Phong raise his voice before. What he shouted into the ship's intercom made all the surrounding Chinese officers shudder. The lockjaw expression on Qu Xing's face made him utterly useless for the translation. Voss understood only a few words of Mandarin. Phong had shouted *Hong-Jan* three times—Red Arrow.

The Chinese began staring down below to *Leviathan's* main deck. All of them seemed to be waiting for something. Suddenly the main port hatchway at the base of the island superstructure burst open. Running out onto each tanker was a team of four men each. Each team seemed to be carrying a coffin. In short order the teams opened them. One man from each team lifted out a thick, 4' sand-colored tube that appeared to have an oversized black collar ring at both ends. The first team member supported by a second, mounted one of these tubes on his shoulder. They bore sighted on the Namibian gunboat. The ship to ship speaker box was again activated.

"This is NS *Erongo*! I order you for the last time to stop all engines or be fired upon! This is your final warning!"

Simultaneously, and unobserved by *Erongo's* gun crews, *Leviathan's* team with the sand-colored tube mounted on one man's shoulder fired off a *Hong-Jan--12* aka Red Arrow: a high explosive anti-armor missile. The weapon contained a dual kinetic projectile with a two stage detonation, so the first exploding projectile packed a secondary exploding punch right behind it. Initially, it looked like the supertanker and gunboat were instantly connected by a burning cable line. The first part of the charge penetrated *Erongo's* main superstructure. The second detonation erupted inside the command bridge and blew out all 12 portholes that were instantly replaced by burning, flaming orange tentacles. Agonizing shrieks were broadcast over all three of the tankers speakers before *Erongo's* microphone circuitry melted down.

Then … static.

In sequence, a second team fired off their Red Arrow-12 directly at the base of the 40mm gun mount. The explosions blew the entire ball shaped gun turret 75' into the air and ripped apart *Erongo's* bow. With the same precision as the first two teams, a third delivered the *coup de grace* firing into what resembled a small floating volcano of red glowing metal and hissing scalding steam. This projectile struck the burning wreckage and gutted whatever was left inside the gunboat's charred hull. In less than eight minutes the pile of twisted metal, with her crew of 46 cremated ghosts, descended to the bottom of the south Atlantic with not so much as an oil slick to mark her grave.

The Dutch officers were staring dumbfounded at Captain Phong, whose defiant glare prevented anyone from challenging his course of action. Never would he allow the sacred red banner of China, now proudly flying at *Leviathan's* masthead, to be disrespected by a bunch of pirates from a third world country. *Shuì bào* had been provoked! The awakened leopard placed his hand in his breast pocket and took out a little red book and held it for all to see.

"Chairman Mao says, *'One man, one problem! No man, no problem!'*"

Chapter 3

The Four Wise Men

Robert Adair Alastair Brown was a proud Scottish-American. Not one of those lower Shenandoah Valley Ulster Scot-Irish, but of Edinburgh heritage stock. He could trace back his restless ancestors to those who fought in every historic battle from that seminal uprising of Culloden Moor to the Plains of Abraham against the French in Canada.

One of the those descendants of Clan Brown now occupied the third floor corner office in the strategic analysis department of the CIA. As the senior head of that department, Robert was reputed to be a very intelligent man. Some of his staff considered him the smartest man they ever knew and admired his delicate precision when sliding a bow across a Stradivarius.

Regrettably, his overarching intelligence did not make him popular with the ladies and this left him a rather lonely old man who was prone to take out this frustration in verbal lashings. This stemmed from his childhood sweetheart having tragically died of cancer after only four years of happy marriage. A morose sadness overshadowed all other interactions with women he felt any interest toward. None approached the allure of his lost love. Drawing upon his interpretation of primitive anthropology, he was not circumspect about letting women know their primary role in the grand scheme of human evolution was to procreate and accept their ancillary function in the nuclear family. During cocktail parties, for which he was receiving fewer invitations, he could be aggressively anti-social. Feminists were particularly singled out by Brown, especially if they made some obnoxious remarks about his Neanderthal male behavior. Brown was quick to point out that Neanderthal families were hunter-gathers and not sedentary farmers. This constant mobility necessitated the

Neanderthal mother to nurse her offspring on the average for about three years. A hefty pair of mammaries were needed for that function. Therefore, all full figured females were throwbacks to Neanderthal heritage. Needless to say, after that exchange, nobody went home with the widower.

As an anthropologist, he had been trained as a keen observer. So when he noticed a British Swordfish biplane and the aircraft carrier *HMS Illustrious* on Val Parrott's computer screen, it sparked color to his day. After Brown's initial translation of the ship's motto *Vox Non Incerta*, he was interrupted by the third senior member of their analytic department.

The former Marine Colonel Manus McMackinaw approached them leaning heavily on a cane. The injury was from a 1983 Beirut bombing that left him with a shattered leg, a shattered command, and a shattered military career. He oftentimes boasted that he carried more shrapnel in his leg then Ernest Hemingway's 237 mortar shell pieces from *A Farewell To Arms*. Such bravado didn't conceal that the experience left him a bitter old man. While he pulled up an extra chair to join them, he released some flatulence in the narrow confines of the cubicle area.

"Don't you have something less pronounced to contribute to this morning's brief?" asked Brown.

Ignoring the jab, McMackinaw stared at the screen. "Interested in model airplanes, Parrott? In the 1990s radio controlled models were the precursors of today's drones. Our largest subcontractor was the IRS. They used them to fly over rich people's homes in the Hamptons to see if they had any in-ground swimming pools. It put them in a higher tax bracket if they did."

Valentine played off the crusty old man against the middle-aged one like a violin. Since she was married and made it clear happily so, it took off some of the tension found when these men worked with other women. That alone wouldn't have gotten Val this far; she also pushed back on them as good and as hard as they pushed on her and she never, ever, brought up anything from a past disagreement. That and her always grey suit somehow had put her in the category of 'just one of the guys.' Yet it was not the cut of her suit that had seemed to do the final trick, but just the color, or lack of it. Val's suits were often tonal masterpieces of subtle embroidery or would have textured fabric patterned into the design. They were modern and stylish, yet always in shades of serious grey.

Just as she was working up a snark about the stench, a fourth analyst came over and pulled out a chair as well. Johnny Cirrus, a full-blooded Navajo from Lake Powell, Arizona, and a graduate chemical engineer from Texas A&M, at 26 years old was the youngest member of this team. He carried a stack of sealed briefing folders, all time-stamped and color-coded in levels of priority. "Did I miss anything?"

"Johnny-on-the-spot saving us from more nostalgic babble," remarked Brown.

"You despise me, don't you Robbie?" said McMackinaw, the only member of the team to dare address him so informally.

"If I gave you any thought, I probably would," Brown retorted.

Parrott just shook her head. "Gentlemen, if you please," she interrupted before they got any further.

"What's your interest with the British Swordfish?" asked Brown.

"That dream I mentioned while waiting for the ancient pot to drip our coffee. I went to bed cleared-headed, no drinks. Can this mean something?" answered Parrott.

"Nah—I bet it wasn't Pearl Harbor. Anybody here ever studied the 1927 operational war archive files on Plan Red? It's where the US invades Canada and the whole of the British Empire comes to their rescue with Australia making a surprised troop landing inside the bay area of San Francisco," stated McMackinaw.

Val normally ignored Manus, but this statement sent shivers of recognition and 'rightness' down her spine.

"Not quite, colonel," said Brown. "The planes were British all right, but the battleships were Italian. In Ms. Parrott's confrontation with her subconscious, she was re-enacting the Battle of Taranto where the British navy executed a surprise attack and crippled the Italian fleet with torpedo planes. It was eleven months prior to Pearl Harbor. No one in US Naval Intelligence connected the dots, but the Japanese Admirals Yamamoto and Fuchida certainly did."

"You know, right up until the day my father died, I used to drive him to navy veteran reunions. There would always be one old fucker off in a corner rambling on about FDR having had prior knowledge," said McMackinaw.

"Some of my tribal elders were code talkers. Half the Japanese intelligence officers in the Pacific committed *seppuku* in frustration trying to decipher our Navajo language. More to the point, I heard those same FDR/Pearl Harbor rumors repeated by our tribal veterans. But once I became a man of science, I could no longer abide conspiracy theories," said Johnny Cirrus.

"A man of science, huh?" remarked the colonel. "Cirrus? How is that an Indian name?"

"The honor of naming everyone born in our tribe belongs to our chief, Sun Eagle. Our Navajo, not Indian, chief, names every new born child for the first auspicious encounter of the day. The clouds were prominent in the sky the day I was born."

"The first auspicious encounter of the day, eh? Well, I guess Cirrus is better than being baptized Johnny-Two-Buffalos-Mating."

Johnny had been expecting some jibe like this from Manus for months now. He actually felt a bit relieved that it was about to come to a head. He was pulling in a breath to unload on the old fart when his boss cut in.

"Please excuse the colonel, Mr. Cirrus. His enlarged prostate is making him testy," said Brown. "Now, back to our discussion of Parrott's oneirology." None the three team members had the remotest idea of what their department head just said. So he addressed their blank expressions. "*Oneirology*—dream analysis—a study of dreams and their interpretations. Please continue, Ms. Parrott."

"More than a dream, it really seemed more like a premonition of sorts," she answered.

"Very commendable, it shows you're working so intensely that all the data you're analyzing is seeping into your subconscious. The details are deep inside your memory palace. You'll probably need an external trigger to reveal the full meaning to the light of day. I'd like to raise one more discussion point on Parrott's *cauchemar*. And yes, I know your husband hates me," he said with a straight face. "The reason why the British attack on Taranto was so successful was first and foremost: deception! The British had littered the Mediterranean with every essential and non-essential ship available. Italian naval intelligence was overwhelmed and confused. Their early warning detection technology didn't have what approximated our radar systems. The Italians relied upon long range listening devices and air reconnaissance. Every needle movement on an analog dial listening set, every radio message intercepted, every visual sighting, and every written report filed, indicated British ships going everywhere and nowhere. In the end, the British navy just waltzed in the front door, destroyed the Italian fleet for a loss of only two obsolete Swordfish biplanes. Watch word: *deception!*"

"Well now," interrupted McMackinaw, "how about we channel our individual memory palaces into some effective soul searching. Since nobody in pre-war US Naval Intelligence connected the dots between the surprise attack on Taranto and Pearl Harbor—it stands to reason our latter day intelligence services is ditto for the eight years, six months, and 15 days between the first World Trade Center attack and the second."

That sent Brown into a lecture about aircraft and safety and hijackers.

To change the subject, Parrott stood up and shook open the front page of The Wall Street Journal. That drew all their eyes. The headline buoyantly exclaimed that China was planning on purchasing billions of dollars' worth of exploratory oil leases in Alaska. More billions were going to be spent on right-of-way easements to lay pipeline to Anchorage and Point Barrow. The lower page article featured a story about the supermarket chain Finest Food Emporium opening up a few satellite stores at selected locations for a marketing test in China. In the last few lines of the article, it reported the Chinese government was further saving FFE several thousand dollars by not requesting relabeling of all products into Mandarin. The team as one looked over Val's shoulder as she flipped the pages. On a page six article, it noted the Chinese had purchased several large oil tankers in Hammerfest.

Poking the paper with a teal colored nail she said, "Now ask yourself for what purpose? The Chinese have a long term reserve of nearly 5,000,000 barrels in Jin Zhou Province and a short 90 day reserve in Shandong. Does anybody anticipate a deception here? Are there enough ships at sea to confuse us? Do these newspaper articles warrant further investigation?"

"The Wall Street Journal is the only newspaper I read," interjected Cirrus. "If you always follow the money, the truth is never far behind. And that's a lot of money to shovel on the fire in a worldwide oil glut. Why are the Chinese sharing with us?"

Brown gave his analysis. "As I see it, providing the articles are genuine and not a plant by some financial entity to artificially depress crude oil prices on the spot market, the Chinese are handing us their Yuan Renminbi for an uncertain futures market. Now ask yourself—why does a guy lavish expensive gifts on a lover? Therefore, I shall task you for a credible motive regarding their cornucopia of largesse in lowering America's national debt. As for the Finest Food Emporium not relabeling, I see two reasons. The first is simple. It's an enforced English lesson on China's lower classes. After all, China is the largest English speaking country in the world. Then again, once you start educating the lower classes, and they start to interpret events outside their censored totalitarian prism, you'll never get that genie back in the lamp. The second reason is a bit more complicated. Back in the early 1990s, one of my Cornell professors gave us a modern example of the law of untended consequences. There is never a literal translation of mores in cross cultural cultivation. A prime example was the marketing campaign of the now defunct Montana Mountain Soup Company. At the time, they were producing a hearty beef and vegetable stew. Called Big John's. The label featured a Paul Bunyan type lumber jack holding an axe. All went well until the soup can crossed the border into bilingual Canada. Market strategists were not happy with the literal translation from Big John's to *Grand Jean.* It just didn't resonate that big hardy outdoor flavor the label was meant to convey. So the soup company changed the name to the more masculine sounding *Gros Jos* and printed five hundred thousand labels and stocked the food shelves all over Canada. Unfortunately, in Québécois Patois—*Gros Jos* translates into big tits. Therefore, who knows what insulting nuance could be misconstrued from a naked translation of English into Mandarin. The Chinese could conceivably wind up eating dog food and thinking it was a can of hash. Those are the only two reasons I can fathom for the moment. Well, maybe to assuage their guilt over letting Covid-19 out into the world. Lastly, the page six article about the purchase of mothballed supertankers is obviously related to the first part of this conundrum, or as Parrott's premonition raises the prospect, it's all part of some nefarious deception by China."

"I once knew a man who ate dog food for three days and died of a broken neck. He fell off his sofa licking his ass," laughed McMackinaw.

"Why do I find that not hard to believe about someone you knew?" replied Brown.

To get the team finally started on the day's business, Cirrus broke the seal on the red portfolio binder he was holding. "Guys, let's start. I have the newly revised GPS satellite locations of the terrorist group The Islamic State of The Levant oil storage depots used to finance their activities throughout the world. The majority of oil is supplied by Iran then supplemented by occasional oil truck hijackings in Iraq and Pakistan. Then the terrorists sell the oil to Afghanistan, Yemen, Somalia and as far afield as Samarkand and Tashkent. All well below market value. If we're all agreed, we should pass this on to DOD for their B-2 and drone strike missions."

"For Christ's sake!" interrupted McMackinaw. "Isn't there anything else on today's threat board besides fucking oil? We know where they are! We should just go in and nuke them! Turn all those Wogs into shadows and fuse their desert sand into one big sheet of glass!"

"You mean thermite meld all their desert silicon dioxide into one big solar reflector," dryly responded Cirrus using his precise chemical knowledge to push back against the old fart. *Anyone over 60 should be fully retired and brought in just for consulting. This grump is completely out of touch with the real world,* thought Johnny. *If the public got wind of the things he says, we would all be up for review and probably fired.*

"Let's stay on point," said Brown starting to get annoyed. "Inverse priority order."

Cirrus broke another seal on a slate colored portfolio. It contained transcripts of radio traffic intercepted by the NSA at Fort Meade. Incidental chatter about an overdue and incommunicado Namibian patrol vessel along the

Skeleton Coast. The group discussed it, wondering if the NSA had any real-time satellite photographs available in that part of the south Atlantic. Parrott said she would personally follow up.

Next, a seal on a green portfolio was broken. This report was on the long standing maritime border dispute between Costa Rica and Nicaragua. Isla Portillos, at the mouth of the San Juan estuary, was occupied by the Nicaraguan army; 30 kilometers of Costa Rican territory was unlawfully and belligerently annexed. Costa Rica disbanded its army in 1948. They made an urgent appeal to the UN and the Organization of American States. It also made a special request to the US to send a Littoral class naval ship up river in solidarity. As yet there was no response from the state department, but state wanted to know if the CIA had any active field agents in the area. Brown let it be known that anything involving the DOS was his exclusive domain.

The last seal was broken. The orange color indicated it was second highest priority. This brief contained a flash notice from the Pentagon about a missing aircraft. The USAF reported one of its Fairchild Republic A-10C Thunderbolt II aircraft, from the 355th Tactical Training Wing, stationed at Davis-Monthan maintenance and regeneration group in Arizona, went missing during a live fire exercise. As the team was handed their individual orange coded copies, they all read in silence. It stated both plane and pilot were still missing. The report went on to say the missing pilot was Captain Krystafen Rizk, an exchange officer from the Egyptian Air Force. The exchange pilot's training officer, Major Sewell, recalled that before the two aircraft reached the firing range, Captain Rizk inexplicably switched off his rotating beacon and navigation lights. Then he shut down his emergency locater-transmitter and transponder so his aircraft could no longer be picked up by radar. It then banked left and dived into a cloud layer. The major claimed he attempted multiple calls to Rizk without result. Sewell elected not to pursue because the A-10 is designed solely for close air support not all-weather navigation and the flight area was in mountainous areas around Tucson.

The team looked up to see Brown lost in thought, staring at the 9-11 poster on the north wall of their office. Fixated on it, their team leader spoke without turning his head. "Was this Egyptian exchange officer just starting his training cycle, in the middle, or nearly finished and what was his stated religion?"

Cirrus answered for the team. "According to this brief, this was his last exercise of a three month course. Captain Rizk was due to be rotated back to Egypt next week. He was a Coptic Christian."

"Read me the specifications on the aircraft's primary armament."

"The Thunderbolt II, also known as the Warthog, is armed with a General Electric GAU-Eight-A Avenger seven barrel hydraulically driven Gatling style auto cannon. About the size of a Volkswagen. From its effective firing range altitude of four thousand feet it fires a thirty millimeter caliber of depleted uranium, armor-piercing projectiles at a three thousand nine hundred rounds rate per minute from a link-less feed system that has never known to jam. It will shred anything within a forty foot radius of an intended target, be it a main battle tank or reinforced bunker. This same auto cannon is also mounted on US Navy ships as a last line of defense against incoming missiles. Our navy calls them phalanx goal keepers." Johnny finished with a small curl of a smile on his lips.

"If this pilot isn't an imposter masquerading as an Egyptian Coptic Christian—then I'm as Irish as Paddy's pig," declared the Scotsman. Brown turned away from the large wall poster and the fireman's accusatory stare. "Cirrus—I want you on our Gulfstream this afternoon. I want you to personally investigate this matter on site. Especially if a crash site with a body, which I doubt, is discovered. You're the chemical engineer. If the Air Force shows you wreckage, use your metallurgy skills to match up the debris to the mill specs of Fairchild Republic specs. If they show you a body burned beyond recognition or not, amputate the right arm midway from the elbow and bring it back ASAP. All Coptic Christians have a four pointed cross tattoo on their right wrist. I need to know if the tattoo is temporary, recent, or years old. Get back to Davis-Monthan; you'll be contacted by our operatives who will render any assistance you may require. Since Arizona is your home state, you'll be officially on vacation."

"Mr. Brown, I assume this will be a sanctioned CIA operation? Missing domestic aircraft fall under the purview of the FAA and the transportation board. If foul play is suspected, the FBI will have priority. What I mean is, frankly, you're ordering me to commit interstate felonies and employ third party operatives to assist me in them."

"Mr. Cirrus, your concern is misplaced. Just cast your mind's eye to the destructive havoc a terrorist at the controls of a fully armed A-10 aircraft could do to an American city, a nuclear power plant, or a government building. To expiate your presumed legal transgressions, you'll be provided with valid US State Department credentials with the express purpose to contain a diplomatic *faux pas* with the Egyptian embassy. You'll be unquestioned and untouchable. Since it was probably some state department's misguided concept of international cooperation, and not the Air Force, to invite this imposter through our front door, DOS will neither confirm nor deny your existence." Then Brown turned to face Colonel Manus McMackinaw. "You're going with him!"

"What!?" he stammered.

"I sense a national emergency here! You think you're just going to continue flatulating around here until your diamond jubilee? I need you to run interference for Cirrus and keep Air Force base personnel off his back. Excuse me, I mean I need you to hobble off any interference."

"You elitist son-of-a-bitch!"

Without skipping a beat, Brown played his septuagenarian subordinate like one of his violins; a tool Val had learned from her mentor/boss and was honing her own mastery of this technique. She kept any expression off her face as she admired the manipulation.

"I'm promoting you to brigadier, pay raise effective immediately and pension revised. Screw this up and I'll reduce you in rank to lance corporal and shred your personnel records. You'll end your days as a carping old man on a park bench railing at passersby about how the CIA erased your life and made you an unperson."

Appearances to the contrary, McMackinaw was not a fool. "Pay raise retroactive to last month's pay cycle."

"Fine! Mr. Cirrus, help newly promoted Brigadier General Homo Tri-Habilis up on his third leg. Vehicle transport will be waiting downstairs to take you to the airport. By the time you both land in Arizona your credentials and mission brief will be hand-delivered by special courier."

Parrott waited until the they were out of ear shot gathering their things. "Why do you keep him around?"

"For luck. But that's a story for another time."

"I don't see the wisdom in having Cirrus drag him along."

"I sent McMackinaw for the waters."

"Waters? What waters? He'll be in the desert."

"I guess I was misinformed."

"Tell me, Brown, what brought you to the CIA? I like to think you enjoy having people killed—it's the romantic in me."

"Romantic!? I'm Shocked! Shocked! To learn I have a black widow on my staff. Does *Monsieur* Claude know what gets into bed with him every night? Now go do your job and analyze those satellite photographs and see if you can find me a missing Namibian patrol vessel."

Parrott bit her tongue and waited until her boss walked down the narrow passageways between the endless rows of cubicles to shut himself behind the closed door of his corner office. The 'romantic' in her contemplated waxing her boss' steep cellar steps all the way down to the concrete floor. Then she settled in to scrutinize week old satellite images. Collating them with the real time ones provided by the NSA from the West African coast, she scanned for patterns and clues.

After several hours of non-stop eye strain over high resolution photos, a stop action motion of three large ships in convoy sailing around the Cape of Good Hope into the Indian Ocean caught her attention. All three were easily identified as Batillus class by the design of their superstructures and 1,358' length. Two anomalies presented themselves. First, a much smaller vessel consistent with the missing patrol boat appeared to intercept the convoy. It manifested a brief heat signature corona then disappeared. *Most likely it was rammed and sunk by the lead ship and they're keeping quiet about it. What else could have sunk it? Supertankers are unarmed.* The second was that once in the Indian Ocean, these same tankers were leaving comet tails of darkened water in their wakes. Obviously purging seawater against maritime law. Whatever the case, it was not the job of the CIA to be the environmental police. NSA could deal with it if they cared to. Parrott began printing out her report with attached collated photographs in a time lapse sequence. Then she included all material in a portfolio brief, duly signed and time stamped. Finished, she got up and walked to Brown's office and knocked. From outside the door Parrott heard a World War I tune emanating from an antique victrola:

Another Little Drink –
Another Little Drink –
Another Little Drink –
Wouldn't Do Us No Harm –

Things must be going well, thought Parrott. *At least today he's not playing that resigned to death French one* Adieu La Vie. The record playing stopped and she was called to enter. She internally laughed reading a sign behind his desk:

BE RUDE TO FOOLS

The first thing the man behind the large desk did was to reach over to the beautiful photograph of his deceased wife and place the frame face down. After that he continued to dip into his leather tobacco pouch and spread a measured amount onto to rolling paper. He licked it sealed, then struck a match. As senior head of the strategic analysis department, there was no one to tell Brown to put out his cigarette. Val waited to be addressed.

That moment came right after Brown swept aside a stack of files with distain. As the sound of them swooshing on the floor was fading he said, "Ninety-nine percent of these incoming field dispatches have all the relevancy of a socialist position paper on agrarian reform."

Ignoring the foul mood, she said, "Here's your missing Namibian patrol vessel. Nothing to worry about. Not our problem." She instantly regretted that last sentence. A rebuke was brewing. "Where shall I put this report?"

"Just hand it to me. Would you like a scotch?" Brown opened a lower desk draw and produced an expensive bottle of 30 year old Macallan and two tall glasses. His deft wrist movement poured exactly the correct measured shot for each glass. He then went over to his ornamental Russian Samovar and turned the spigot to release a drop of tepid water into both drinks. A necessary additive to bring out the bouquet and prevent burning the taste buds from numbing the flavor. "*Slan-ge-var.*" And their glasses clinked.

As Val sat opposite to the smartest man she had ever known, she felt too ill at ease to enjoy the expensive scotch; she respected her mentor, yet still, he was, well, difficult in many ways. "You mentioned earlier that you keep MᶜMackinaw around just for luck?"

Brown crushed his cigarette in an ashtray. "Correct, for luck. Finish your drink. The luck of the Irish and the legacy of unintended consequences is why I keep that superannuated Leprechaun around." Brown emptied his glass, then gave his staff member his undivided attention. "You're now free to go. One more thing, Parrott, if you ever again hand me a brief and presume to tell me there's nothing to worry about, you may presume the end of our beautiful friendship, and persuade me to arrange a letter of transit to our CIA black ops base in Brazzaville. A place where I'm sure *Monsieur* Regnault will be happy to converse with the locals in his native tongue."

* * *

On the way home Valentine drove back across the Francis Scott Key Bridge and turned onto 35th Street. During that time, she wondered if Brown's veiled threat of transfer was serious, if her aggressive confidence finally eroded the sexless way they interacted; it was all such a delicate balance and the maintenance if it seemed to be all on her shoulders. During her first five years with the agency she had resigned herself to middle level status. Parrott knew full well the upper echelons of the CIA were the legacy of political appointees; as well as an inner sanctum fraternity. A degree in Franco-American political studies from Louisiana State University and a sterling letter of recommendation from Senator, now Vice-President, Francis Lejeune cut no ice in this unique entity beyond entry levels. Moreover, she didn't play golf, tennis or squash. The best she had hoped for was to ride Robbie Brown's coattails to the 6th floor. Now that was feeling tenuous. She needed more than surreal nightmares of historical events to be entitled to an expensive glass of scotch with this rogue intellectual. A quick glimpse at herself in rearview mirror, then in a flash, she lashed out, *I'll be damned if I play Miss Moneypenny to that middle-aged armchair James Bond!*

Driving home faster than she should, Val turned onto her street and squealed her breaks when parking. Letting herself in the backdoor, she heard the melodious tones of Jacques Offenbach's *Barcarolle from the Tales of Hoffmann.* As she quietly stepped into the living room, the music teacher sub-vocally kept time as Corrine tenderly played the keys. The proud moment of soothing rapture evaporated the minute her eyes met the expression on Claude's face. Staring back at him from the opposite side of the room, she motioned for him to go to the kitchen. Once they both met, she gently embraced him for a kiss but was rebuffed which was unusual and unexpected.

"Look at this!" her husband demanded. On the kitchen table was an open box of yellow and orange mums. An angry Claude handed the card over: *A Claude Regnualt avec amities de Spaghetti Homme.* "Val! Is he tapping our phones? How does he know I call him spaghetti man?! And I can take the flowers as a sign of disrespect that you make more and have a more important job than I do. Another thing, your damn boss knows we French use mums exclusively for funerals!"

Embarrassed, she could never admit what she revealed about their personal life with co-workers; mostly as a tactic to fit in rather than a desire to share. Val frowned, shrugged; then just put her index finger to hers lips and pointed in the direction of the piano music. This gave Val a slight reprieve to think up a plausible way to explain the painful need to fit in with the male team. When the final stanza was played, and they both heard the word *Brava* from the music teacher, the couple walked into the living room. Claude gathered up the mums into a bouquet for the surprised piano teacher. As they exchanged pleasantries, Val seized the opportunity to escape upstairs.

Looking for a safe space, she ducked inside Charles' room. Her precocious son made a mildly surprised face, then returned to the open books on his desk. His only concern was to ask if his sister was finished banging on the piano keys so he could concentrate on his homework. Feeling hurt that her son didn't care to have his own mother around for companionship, she got up to leave. Suddenly her mind was changed after spotting a large book titled *The Illustrated*

Ships of The World resting on the desk. Instead of leaving, she curiously watched him flip through, then study the page with a large internal diagram of a Batillus supertanker.

She spoke in an almost demanding tone as her nightmare tickled her backbone. "Why are you reading a chapter on oil tankers?"

Sensing an abrupt change in his mother's usually supportive tone, Charles answered plainly for once. "It's for our environmental class. We're studying the long term environmental damage to the Earth's oceans from oil spills like from *Exxon Valdez*. It grounded on a reef and spilled eleven million gallons of crude oil in Alaska."

"I remember that. It happened in 1989 when I was as old you are now. They said the captain was drunk. But the third mate was at the helm and their radar had been out of commission for a year."

"Mom, I don't understand. Why do these big ships have to carry just oil? Why not transport fresh water to drought areas? Or carry tons of meat and vegetables to famine areas? Or turn them into floating hospitals with plenty of doctors and nurses? They're big enough to move whole communities of people all over the world."

"What did you just say!?"

"I said, why do these giant ships have to just carry oil? Why not—"

"Love you. Get ready for dinner." Val rushed to her own desk to write down some thoughts before family time.

Chapter 4

Navel of the World

Unlike the two unambiguous symbols of the American flag where the thirteen stripes represent the original colonies, and the fifty stars represent the fifty states, the flag of China has four that serve as an index of its ideology. The first is a blood red field that symbolizes revolution. The second symbol is one dominate yellow star, closest to the flagpole side, emblematic of the Communist Party of China. The third symbol is the yellow color of that star, it implies that China belongs to the Chinese people, a yellow race. The fourth is symbolized by the semicircle of equidistant four smaller yellow stars personally defined in a moment of egomaniacal flamboyance by Chairman Mao Zedong. These smaller stars represent the four social classes of modern China. This flag was first raised at the founding of The People's Republic of China in Tiananmen Square on October 1st 1949.

One of those red flags was flapping in the icy winds of a remote part of the barren Himalayan mountain range to enforce its belligerent claim over The Navel of The World. That claim was being defended by the People's Liberation Army (PLA) garrison at Wujang. Situated below the slopes of the Tibetan plateau, it marked the tenuous boundary with the Indian state of Himachal Pradesh.

Sullen and inattentive about his duties, Lee Ji-Nan was just another artillery gun bunny marking time until his obligatory 24 months were up. In his 16 months of service, Private Ji-Nan failed to demonstrate the proper attitude toward his battery commander, and more important, his regimental political officer. Twice denied the honorific service ribbon of the Red and Yellow Star of Loving The Chinese People, he had lately been reprimanded with the accusation of *Thinking for Himself*. Lee Ji-Nan did have a dissident attitude.

First, he grew up in the cosmopolitan city of Shanghai. A city known since colonial times for its fast and loose lifestyle. Ji-Nan was a mechanic and limo driver before his mandatory time in the military.

As a teen, his first activity after school was acquiring a proficiency in English so he could read pirated reprints of Scientific American and Popular Mechanics magazines. While working in his father's garage, he took apart old fashioned carburetors and rewired car radios while watching a bootlegged copy of *FNF: Tokyo Drift*. That movie was the reason he wanted to be a mechanic and a driver. One day he went to school with his party neckerchief stained with engine oil. A teacher opened a file starting a life-long record of reprimands. Luckily, this was 21st century China. Multifaceted skill sets and a profitable family business kept him out of real trouble. His father amassed a small fortune maintaining a fleet of limousines for the high rolling party officials of the national bourgeoisie.

As Lee Ji-Nan grew into manhood, his wages, and tips to keep his mouth shut, grew exponentially. Mechanic's pay and chauffeuring also taught him how the rich and elite party members lived. Driving CCP members to night clubs, European style restaurants, first class bordellos and the occasional diplomatic gala event, was a revelation. Eventually, he came to realize that in the Chinese classless society, not every Chinese person was in the class.

Exposed to an intoxicating atmosphere of life beyond his own lowly status, it only took one affair with a middling rank party official's mistress to land Lee Ji-Nan in his present unenviable circumstance at coldest outpost China had.

Such drama so early in life only explained the first part of his maladjustment to military life. The second part resulted from Ji-Nan serving in a peacetime army. There was simply no enemy; no way to relieve boredom or express anger. The army was comprised of regionally and ethnically diverse ranks of functionally illiterate enlisted men. None of the few women in the PLA messed up bad enough to be assigned to this frozen hell. Even under one national banner, 22 provinces and 56 ethnic groups were all foreigners amongst themselves. Unit cohesion was tenuous. Unsurprisingly, when young soldiers were placed in a remote spot with nothing going on, the habit of military discipline gradually broke down.

There was nothing for Ji-Nan to channel his bitterness and hostility towards except his fellow soldiers. Sergeant Woo Haung hailed from the Province of Yunnan where the people boasted, *Even our slaves have slaves,* and fancied himself a warrior. Another peasant from Yunnan was the fawning Private First Class Han Yi, Sergeant Haung's informer. Then there was Mongolian Private Ba-Hui, who boasted his cock was bigger than their 155mm Howitzer's gun barrel. Preying eyes in the communal shower lent some credence to that claim. An ethnic Vietnamese, Private Danh Nguyen Diem, from the southern border province of Guan Gxi, had the best looking girlfriend with a photograph to prove it. The last of this motley team was a pig farmer from Ji Lin Province, stupid Chu Yu-Shu. He earned that 'stupid' during a live fire exercise as secondary ammunition handler, packing the breech of their Howitzer with a torn propellant bag, and in the process spilling lots of little squares of potassium nitrate all over the firing mechanism. Luckily the danger was spotted in time by Corporal Ku Sheng Wen who physically prevented Haung from pulling the lanyard. His quick action prevented a breech flare explosion that would have blown the Howitzer and all seven of its gun crew *To a mountain so high, no bird can fly over,* as a Himalayan legend foretold.

By no small coincidence Corporal Ku Shen Wen was the smartest man on the gun crew, and the only one other than Lee Ji-Nan who knew how to program the laser technology that enabled the Howitzer to perform multi-target engagements. He was also from Shanghai, and the only member of the gun crew Ji-Nan called a friend. Wen's former status as a senior accounts manager of the Shanghai Maritime Investment Bank designated him the only member of the gun crew who could claim to be of the urban bourgeoisie class.

Conspicuously absent from gun mount 2, or any other organic unit in the PLA, were members of the class of bureaucrats who inhabit the corridors of power in the party hierarchy. When asked by Ji-Nan why he abruptly quit his lucrative bank job and joined the PLA, Wen's only response was a Confucius quote, "*A man who does not think and plan long ahead will soon find trouble right at his door.*"

The pair was in total agreement feeling not the slightest sense of loyalty toward the cabal of party leaders who now ruled China. Sitting on cold boulders around their gun, these two confided their grandfathers' stories about the Korean War. Gruesome tales of how only one in three soldiers were issued rifles during wave attacks against the American army. There would be plenty of spare rifles lying about from comrades who took a bullet for others to continue the attack. And then, as now, the omnipresent political officers, with constant exhortations to never hesitate to sacrifice for the love of the Chinese people; how to imitate the fleetness of the long-legged water crane to tip toe through minefields; what you had to do when caught in rows of double apron barbed wire as American bombers dropped burning stick-to-the-skin red paste on you – hope to die quickly! Then came the medical teams with bailing and grappling hooks to pull away the dead and badly wounded, hoping to deny the foreign devils an accurate body count. They both agreed, they were having none of that! If America wanted to invade China and enforce a national constitution like they did to Japan after World War II, both men would be happy to sing Yankee Doodle Dandy in Mandarin from the walls of the Forbidden City.

On designated cleaning day, Corporal Wen was in charge. Their boss usually avoided such drudgery and happily wandered off. It was rumored he liked to ingratiate himself with the battery commander by volunteering to polish his boots. Sergeant Woo Haung was not missed.

Ji-Nan vigorously turned the azimuth wheel counter-clockwise on the side of the Howitzer to drop the gun barrel to its lowest negative declination so the rest of the crew could insert the equally long and cumbersome cleaning rod into the muzzle. With the remaining four members of the gun crew straining to swab out the grooves of the barrel, Wen leaned close toward Ji-Nan and whispered, "Tell me again, how did that party fool discover you fucked his mistress?"

"I've told you a dozen times already. When she called me into the back seat of the limousine, she already had taken off her panties and raised her legs straight up. I was in such a rush I didn't even bother to take off my chauffeur's cap. But the stupid woman forgot to remove her shoes. Her high heels punctured two holes into the roof padding of the limo. When that pig bureaucrat spotted the two holes in the overhead padding, he wasted no time beating the truth out of her the minute he got her alone. So here I am."

"Every love story is beautiful, but yours is my favorite," laughed Wen.

"Screw off!"

"Was she beautiful? Worth the risk?"

"White as cream, skin as smooth silk to the touch," he said.

"Love is like a spice. It can sweeten your life; it can spoil it too." Wen was laughing again.

Ji-Nan could tolerate a lot from his fellow Shanghainese, but being the butt of jokes was not one of them. "Perhaps you can tell me why a rich banker gives up a huge salary and joins the army? Even turns down officer school—but of course, you did it all for the love of the Chinese people! Though I heard the People's Court of Revolutionary Justice tends to forgive a laundry list of crimes if the criminal forgoes a public trial and accepts rehabilitation by serving a tour; like here on a frozen mountain top."

"Hold your voice down fool!" Wen snapped.

Their banter caught the curiosity of the rod crew. Stupid Yu-Shu spoke out, "What are you two chattering about? You strutting peacocks practicing your English again? Come on, say something in the foreign devil's tongue!"

Ji-Nan obliged him. *"Yu-Shu, tie my shoe!"*

Wen made the translation back to Mandarin for everybody—everybody laughed, except for Yu-Shu. He immediately stomped over to fight Ji-Nan. The quick thinking corporal stepped in and defused the situation. "We were discussing a soldier's desolation—from women." He turned to Diem. "Please show us that beautiful picture of your girlfriend."

Private Diem unbuttoned the top left breast pocket of his green camouflage jacket and removed a color photograph from its protective plastic folder. "Her Vietnamese name is *Chau Mai*. The closest to a Mandarin translation is Pearls of May. Her parents insisted on giving her a name from their homeland though her family now is considered Chinese."

The entire gun crew crowded around Diem for a closer look, except Private First Class Yi, who snuck off. The crew took no notice of his absence. Everyone's attention was fixated on the longhaired woman with large and not so Asian eyes. She was wearing a traditional Vietnamese floral *Ao dai* tunic. The young men at this isolated military outpost were drooling.

"She looks almost western," said Ku-Hui.

"Eurasian—a touch of French ancestry," mused Wen.

"Yes—you're right! One of her paternal grandfathers was a French colonial soldier from Vietnam's first war of liberation," answered Diem.

"I heard stories Indian and Thai mixed women are out of this world," added Ku-Hui.

"I'd like to cross the border to India and discover that for myself," answered Wen.

"Do you know why party members prefer western blond women for mistresses? Because they don't want to fuck a woman with the same hair color as their wife!" joked Ji-Nan.

"Well, you ought to know, since you were the party pimp in Shanghai," mocked Yu-Shu.

This time Wen was not quick enough. Ji-Nan landed a full-force closed-fist to the stupid fool's solar plexus. He went down hard, making gasping sounds like a man whose lungs just collapsed. Ji-Nan didn't hold back. He threw himself on the downed man in an unrestrained frenzy and worked off months of pent up frustration. He pummeled his victim with a succession of facial and body blows. It turned into a melee when the largest man of the group, Ku-Hui, failed to pull Ji-Nan away and Wen joined the struggling pile of flailing arms and kicking legs. Diem's only concern was the preservation of his precious photo.

"Stand at attention!" shouted Gun Captain Sergeant Woo Haung. All eyes looked over to see their furious sergeant and his pet informer. "What is going on?" Sergeant Haung was fully informed, yet felt no small satisfaction in seeing the bloody face of Yu-Shu. After a pause, he harangued his crew. "Assistant Gun Captain Corporal Ku Sheng Wen! Why is that cleaning rod hanging half out the barrel like a rake inserted in a cock to scrape out gonorrhea pus?"

"Sergeant, I was in the process... "

"Shut up! Indian artillery could rain down on us at any time and we would be unprepared to do our duty! You're all traitors to the motherland!"

Wen spoke his mind. Always a questionable act when speaking to a superior in any army, and which carries deeper ramifications in a totalitarian one. "Sergeant Haung, we don't have any ammunition anyway. The arsenal will take over three hours to honor a requisition for shells and propellant for effective counter-battery fire. By then our gun mount position, and the rest of Battery 8, would be pounded into shale stones. The only shells we have for immediate use are practice rounds, and you still need propellant charges to fire them. We're sitting around waiting to get blown apart, waiting for written permission from Beijing to commence return fire which we then would be incapable of doing."

Seething with contempt at the fool who dared to say out loud what everyone knew was true, Sergeant Haung stood stone silent for a full minute before addressing his gun crew a second time. Meanwhile, he slowly undid the left breast pocket of his utility jacket and removed a little red book and opened it to a well-worn page. "The Chairman says, 'Execute one—Educate one hundred.' Are there any other traitors who want to shout classified information to the Indian listening posts across the frontier? All of you *Pi Yang* smiling soldiers are aware that the party charges the cost of bullets wasted on executing traitors to their families. In your particular case Wen, if it was up to me, I'd stuff you down this barrel and fire you all the way back to Shanghai! Along with your friend!" He glared at Ji-Nan. "And that goes for you as well, you stupid saboteur, Private Yu-Shu. Stop bleeding all over my gun mount and report to the infirmary at once! Tell the medics you tripped over a stabilization rail. Private Ji-Nan! Escort this pig to the infirmary! The rest of you traitors get that cleaning rod out of the gun barrel and button up this cannon immediately!"

* * *

Ji-Nan was sitting at attention along a 25' table in the mess hall with the rest of Battery 8, about 80 officers and men, minus the one earlier escorted to the infirmary. Besides being gun cleaning day, it was also psychological warfare and counter insurgency training day. It actually meant a day to learn rudimentary English skills for field application. English being the unifying language of their

Indian border enemy and all the foreign devils arrayed against the peace-loving PRC. Thus, in place of their usual noontime meal of steaming bowls of vegetable dumplings in rainwater broth, multiple cans of unknown contents in colorful but confusing labels were stacked in front of them. Chopsticks were substituted for western utensils. Even the sacred communal teapots, traditionally provided at each table to instill fraternity, were replaced with tawdry plastic cups. The table configuration was changed as well. The standard parallel seating arrangement was squared off to resemble one large rectangle with a center empty space. Four elongated silk screens signs were suspended from ceiling rafters. Each sign displayed only five words. Each word was individually presented in simplified Mandarin Han characters then in its English equivalent.

Underneath it all, inside this giant rectangle stood the regimental political officer: the dreaded Major Jiao-Long Tone. A man who looked exactly as one ought to look whose job it was to inspire fear and indulge in its consequence. A captain was guarding the major's left. A funerary silence pervaded the mess hall. Major Tone scanned the many faces staring intensely back at him before he spoke. An old trick to convince a captive audience they are all being addressed individually.

"Soldiers of the People's Liberation Army, our ancient military strategist Sun Tzu teaches us: *Knowing only your own capabilities but not that of your enemy— for every victory you will suffer a defeat.* Today's important lesson is to improve our capabilities to sustain ourselves on the battlefield and by doing so fulfill our sacred duty to the Communist Party, which is the eternal bulwark of our Motherland. Are you patriotic soldiers of the glorious artillery regiment of Battery Eight, ready to do your duty for your Motherland?"

The commander blurted out, "Major Tone, as the Communist Party's most trusted representative, kindly convey to the Politburo, their loyal soldiers of the glorious Artillery Regiment of Battery Eight, stand ready and willing to carry out their sacred duty for the Motherland."

All 80 men stood up with right fist in the air and shouted, "Long live China! Long live China! Long live China!"

With their full throated enthusiasm noted and approved, Major Tone motioned the regiment to be seated. The lesson now began in earnest. Every soldier understood the practical application of being able to scavenge from an enemy's captured stockpiles. The smartest soldier sitting in the mess hall, Corporal Wen, was also sure he knew something very unsettling indeed. It was plain these cans were regular food with no resemblance whatsoever to American military rations that might be retrieved from a battlefield. *He* thought, *what army in the world puts commercial labels on their field rations?*

The soldiers began to examine the various cans. They simply trusted the depiction on the label to match its contents to get on with things. This worked fairly well with vegetables and fruits. Corporal Wen reached for a red and black square tin depicting a mermaid with the English word Sardines.

Next to him, Ji-Nan, in a flaunting motion to exhibit his knowledge of English, held up a large can with a sea-green label for all to see. He spoke with a straight face and in a carrying voice. "I love fish. This is really good. Everyone should try this one."

As Lee knew he would, Sergeant Haung took the bait and snatched the can out of his hand. Haung vigorously began removing the lid with a can opener. He lunged his fork at the silver-flecked mush, and quickly downed several forkfuls. He would have emptied the can if he had not caught sight of Ji-Nan's mocking grin.

That expression abruptly stopped Haung's enthusiasm so he put his nose where his mouth had been. The smell needed no translation. The humiliated and furious sergeant threw down the can with such force the entire assembly stopped tasting. He lunged at Ji-Nan and grabbed him by his collar. "As of this minute you're on hand grenade training! We just received a new batch of university reservists and you know how dexterous they are! Report to the grenade pits immediately!"

"Take your monkey feet hands off me, poleman!"

It was a sneering reference to ancient peasants who used a long bamboo pole to balance a heavy load at each end. It was the worst insult on another's pride. The angry Haung brought his free arm around to give the offending private a closed fist blow to the side of his head, but it was effectively blocked.

Haung was thrown off balance and tumbled onto the nearest bunch of nearby soldiers.

"You two soldiers! Stand at attention!" shouted their commander, whose loss of face before the regimental officer was irredeemable.

Before discipline deteriorated any further, Major Tone intervened with a pre-arranged hand signal. From a side corridor seven men in starched blue, grey and dark green camouflage uniforms burst in. Each had a red and gold emblem of crossed daggers over an anchor on the front of their caps. All were armed with a QBZ-95 Bullpup assault rifles capable of firing 650 rounds per minute from 30 round clips. The seated soldiers were as surprised as they were confused. Where did these marines come from? Swiftly surrounded, both sergeant and private were secured with their arms pinioned behind them and unceremoniously frog-marched out the mess hall doors.

Private Han Yi bolted from his seat and scrambled to retrieve the half-eaten can off the floor that started all the ruckus. He made a showy presentation of clicking his boot heels together to come to attention as Major Tone accepted it from his hand. No one ascends to political officer status in the PLA without superior English skills. Tone carefully scrutinized the lettering on the green label:

> **Whiskers will wish for**
> **A Feline Fish Fillet**
> **A Cat and Cat Lovers**
> **Dream Team**

The entire compliment of junior officers, non-commissioned officers and remaining ranks were stunned to hear a deep sustained laughter echo throughout the mess hall.

* * *

About an hour after lights out Ji-Nan sauntered back into his darkened barracks. His only regret was that his slumbering gun crew would have to wait for reveille to admire his newly sewn on corporal stripes. For the first time, he felt some small satisfaction serving in the PLA. He also had the satisfaction of having Major Tone personally authorize his promotion and a transfer of Sergeant Haung to the university reservist training unit. He thought about staying awake all night standing in front of Han Yi's bunk so he would be the first thing that little ass wipe saw in the morning. Maybe after that welcoming surprise, he'd head over to the infirmary and encourage Yu-Shu to return to duty as well. Ji-Nan could not believe how his luck had changed.

Gradually, the day's excitement began giving way to fatigue. He first unlaced his boots and then unbuttoned his green utilities. He placed them on a hook assigned below his name tag, and shoved his boots under his bunk. Within minutes he had slipped underneath the coarse blanket and closed his eyes. Within seconds they were wide open in alarm! An unseen hand pressed down hard over his mouth.

"Quiet—it's me!" hissed Wen.

Relieved that no one was trying to murder him, Ji-Nan cracked a joke, "You know the PLA frowns upon homosexual activity. That is, except for our women soldiers."

"Don't be a Pi Yang puppet clown! You committed two acts of assault in less than twelve hours. The last one against a senior non-commissioned officer! Why aren't you in the stockade!?"

"Sergeant Haung attacked me first. I was defending myself! But most important of all, Major Tone likes me. He says keeping soldiers with a knowledge of English in the ranks is of paramount importance to party initiatives. His words, not mine. Oh, by the way, Major Tone promoted you to sergeant. You are officially Senior Gun Captain of number Two Mount."

"You mentioned my name to Major Tone?"

"I didn't have too. He seems to know all about you. And is quite familiar with your activities at the Shanghai bank. He dropped hints that you're a very rich man——in Luxembourg."

"Major Tone mentioned Luxembourg? Then he must be in on it too. All the smart money people in China have hidden numbered accounts there."

"What are you talking about? He's a political officer. Major Tone is probably setting a trap to help ensnare all the economic criminals of the state."

"Exactly! That's why he promoted me to sergeant. All of a sudden, newly promoted Corporal Ji-Nan has selective memory loss of the behavior he witnessed as chauffeur of our party officials?" Wen furtively looked over his shoulder at the snoring men for any sign of movement from a light sleeper who might take an undue interest in his words. "Listen to me, you simple-minded fool! Yes, Major Tone is a political officer! Who best to know everything? He knows China's economy is a house of cards on the verge of collapse. When the old Soviet Union came apart in '91, yesterday's party elites became today's Russian billionaire oligarchs. We need to be prepared for the same."

Ji-Nan became visibly nervous and began to stutter, "I – I – don't believe it."

"Believe it! China is riding a bike she can't get off. Have you forgotten our great road and belt initiative? We've used up all our credit by building highways and bridges for people who can't afford to buy a car. Finance went into construction and equipment without the demand to meet it. Bankruptcies have begun to surge all over China. All due to hidden, non-performing, over-extended government loans. Look at my bank. The party insisted we extend credit to the navy to purchase a fleet of retired supertankers in Norway. The navy requested that they only be certified seaworthy, nevermind about the interior oil tanks or pump mechanisms. All bank personnel from director down to purchasing agents made small fortunes in kickbacks and bogus quality control bribes, including me! When the government audits our books … well, economic crimes in our land of compulsory joy is punishable by death. I got out just in time and have been hiding out in this shithole outpost ever since."

"Why does the navy want to transport oil?" asked Ji-Nan.

"Not oil. I've heard rumors they're going to use them as troop transports to invade Taiwan to stave off our inevitable economic collapse by annexing a dynamic and vibrant territory we have always claimed as our own."

"Invade Taiwan?! The Taiwanese would resist to the bitter end. And the world would help them."

Wen nodded. "And the very infrastructure China desperately wants would be destroyed."

After a pause, Ji-Nan kept up his questions trying to grasp why Wen was nearly melting in fear. "Taiwan speaks Mandarin, same as us. So what's all this bullshit with the English cans? The nearest English speaking country is Australia. Is China planning to invade a country that is one big fucking desert? We have our own useless Gobi Desert—do we need another, bigger one?"

"Name me another English speaking nation?" quietly suggested Wen.

Ji-Nan blurted out, "That's insane!"

Just then the barracks lights flickered on. Ji-Nan thought spies had ensnared him for his treasonous words and Wen for his economic crimes. Instead, loud diesel engines erupted to life outside the barracks. Blinding halogen headlights shone through the windows. Heavy 2½ ton trucks were lining up in convoy fashion. A squad of marines rushed in, brandishing automatic weapons.

"Stand at attention in front of your racks!" shouted a marine.

Those who were still half-asleep or slow to respond were encouraged with a few rifle butt strokes.

The menacing officer in charge began barking orders. "Soldiers of the 312th Artillery Regiment, Battery 8—there has been a reported earthquake in Sichuan Province. Your entire regiment has been seconded to a special engineering division tasked to rescue and recovery. Pack immediately! You are to take canteens, blanket rolls, all the extra uniforms you have, and first aid kits only! No weapons! You'll be issued special rubber bullets when we arrive on site to control looting! No cell phones! Sergeant, collect all cell phones and get me the name of any soldier who fails to comply. You have your orders— Now MOVE!"

While hastily packing, Ji-Nan heard Wen muttering under his breath that if there was actually an earthquake, he was Pu Yi—the last emperor. Then Lee watched Wen slip his cell into his underwear! Something was wrong.

The once orderly barracks became chaotic. As soon as a soldier slipped arms through the loops of a backpack, he was escorted roughshod out the door and onto the back of a waiting canvas-covered truck. When Ji-Nan's turn came, he managed to secure a rear bench seat to avoid being sardined. This gave him an unobstructed view out the back. From this vantage point he witnessed something puzzling. Wen was calmly making a path through the crush of mustering soldiers until he came upon a parked Mengshi personnel carrier, a virtual clone of an American Humvee. Unchallenged, he opened the driver's side door and got behind the wheel. Even more puzzling was Major Tone, immediately recognizable by distinct red party tabs on his lapels, occupying the front passenger seat. The Mengshi started just as two Marines shut the rear canvas flap and blocked his view.

* * *

The Indian army held the high ground 17,000' above the mobilizing Chinese in Himachal Pradesh. Ensconced on a mountainous ridge, protected on all sides by impenetrable and unmapped shifting crevasses, was a warfare school for difficult terrain. Strategically located on the Solon Gorge defensive line separating India and China, the school was a series of acclimation shelters up to the summit and elevation training centers. With an average snowfall of 300' per year and wind speeds between 75 to 110 mph, sneak attacks by the Chinese were not envisioned, therefore base security tended to be lax.

The school's commanding officer was becoming enormously irritated to the point of violence. Previously sound asleep on his cot, cocooned in a thermal sleeping bag, an incessant bell ringing was piercing his eardrums. Overhead lights were now burning his eyes. Worse still, somebody had entered his personal quarters and was rocking him back and forth.

"Colonel Sab! Wake up, sir! Wake up!" said the anonymous voice.

It was his orderly. He unzipped his sleeping bag and planted both feet on the ice cold floor. Though they were encased in double pairs of heavy woolen socks, it felt like he was stepping on the pointed ends of upside down icicles.

"Answer that bloody telephone!"

The orderly picked up the receiver from a bulky hand-cranked telephone. It was one of those World War II models, capable of operating at high altitudes and low temperatures. "Acclimation school headquarters. Who is calling?" said the deferential orderly. It was Captain Norris reporting from the frontier border outpost, claiming he had a most urgent report to give.

It seems that two Chinese deserters crossed the frontier. They drove right past their own border checkpoint unchallenged, as if they were VIPs. They came across in a lightly armored personnel carrier. When questioned they spoke back in English saying they were a major and enlisted soldier and started to give an unbelievable story.

As the commander listened intensely to the details being related to him from 10,000' below, he literally felt his jaw drop.

"Stop! Listen to me exactly, Captain Norris! Requisition all the soldiers you need, regardless of rank, and protect those two Chinese at all cost! And get their vehicle out of sight! Depending on road conditions, I'll be down mountain in less than two hours, if my fool of a driver doesn't take me over a cliff." As soon as he heard 'Yes sir,' he slammed down the bulky receiver, wound the small bell generator crank through several clock-wise turns and picked it up again.

At battalion HQ down mountain, the duty communications operator plugged in a transmission jack just below the flashing white light on his call-board to acknowledge the incoming signal to connect it to Mumbai.

Chapter 5

The Sandman Riddle

Sweating like a beast under the desert sun, CIA Senior Analyst Johnny Cirrus felt the heat burn up through the soles of his shoes as he paced an isolated stretch of asphalt along I-10. *Damn it's good to be home,* he thought as he paced the Arizona blacktop looking for clues. His starting point was the section of highway where a dozen or so telephone poles had been deliberately cut down and were now being replaced by utility crews. He was in between Tucson and Davis-Monthan Air Force Base. Officially called the 309th Aerospace Maintenance and Regeneration Group but universally known as the boneyard. Since the end of World War II it served as an above ground cemetery for obsolete aircraft. The arid desert climate would preserve these relics of propeller bombers and cold war era jet fighters well into the next millennium thus ensuring the US thousands of tons worth of emergency scrap metal as a strategic reserve. Despite its ramshackle appearance, the base had one active unit that kept it alive. Surrounded on all sides by multiple rows of long dead aircraft, that isolated duty station was billeted to the 355th Tactical Training Wing and called The Flying Zombies. One of their zombies was missing.

Despite the searing heat, Johnny kept his jacket on to keep up the charade that he was a state department official to facilitate his investigation without airmen taking a dim view of another government agency poaching their territory. It did seem to be a moot point however, for the two air force escorts who trailed behind him were themselves deep cover agents, assigned to assist and protect him. They were what the agency euphemistically called Jekyll and Hyde operatives. The captain and the tech sergeant, in perspiration stained khaki uniforms, were regular truly career military air force personnel; unknown to their commanding officer, they had also been recruited into the CIA and given extra training and an extra paycheck. The CIA had these types of covert personnel in every branch of the military, with the exception of the US Marine Corps; some claimed this was because they had the aggregated lowest IQ of all the services so were incapable of complex multi-layered missions. Others claimed it was to keep a presidential oath: *Semper Fidelis*.

Cirrus had some lingering thoughts about leaving McMackinaw at the base. The old fart thought it amusing when he suggested Cirrus put on a loin cloth and pair of moccasins before acting as lead scout for this hunting party. Racist humor notwithstanding, Johnny's Navajo training was not dormant. It guided him towards the spine covered arms of a 15' high saguaro cactus. It grew beyond the downed telephone poles marking the landing site of the stolen plane. This point of the investigation now required more modern skills.

Priority one was to confirm that the unique pattern of skid marks which appeared out of nowhere were actually from a Thunderbolt II. It was clear the three swerving tire tracks embedded in the asphalt were the signature of a heavily loaded aircraft. When he crouched down to take spacing measurements, a disturbed diamond back rattler made its presence known.

"Careful sir, whoever was responsible for cutting down these telephone poles didn't get away scot-free." The late warning came from Tech Sergeant Mark Hornbeck, pointing to several used glass ampoules of anti-venom a few feet away from the restless snake who, disturbed again, decided to slither further away from the gloriously warm asphalt.

Cirrus eased away from that side of the highway. As expected, the tire imprint was just the right size. Due to the cannon placement there was a nose/wheel offset that put it closer to the right main gear than the left one. Satisfied he had a match, Cirrus stood up and turned to face his two escorts.

"We've walked past seven poles newly replaced. With five still under repair at one hundred and twenty feet between each, that comes to one thousand four hundred and forty feet. Can an A-10 make a successful short field landing within those parameters?"

"Sure—with full flaps and wing spoilers, a good pilot can grease her in just under a thousand feet. Under the right conditions, sometimes even less," replied Captain Layton Ryedell.

"So, where is this thirty thousand pound aircraft with a fifty-three foot wingspan?" asked Cirrus.

Hornbeck answered the obvious. "A good mechanic can get the wings off in four hours. With an experienced team, three. Look at all those other tire marks. Somebody brought in an eighteen wheeler and hauled it away. It could be just stored up in the desert around here or hauled across the country by now. Maybe even in the hold of a ship."

Cirrus frowned. "Just out of curiosity, and if I'm not violating any agency confidentiality clause, how were you two regular air force personnel recruited into the CIA?"

Both men exchanged glances before Ryedell decided to speak. "We just went through the normal background checks. The agency likes to weed out applicants whose family history includes genetic lunatics, blacklisted Cold War commies or Anabaptists. The latter are considered too doctrinaire to carry out unquestioned orders. Then we took the standard CIA ethics exam—multiple choice."

The three agents smirked at each other.

Leaving their Humvee behind, the CIA men continued on until they approached the two utility repair crews. The first truck was white with Verizon black and red markings. Shirtless with helmets, safety goggles and work gloves, they were installing new creosote coated 40' telephone poles. The second crew was huddled in the air-conditioned crew cab of a blue and white striped truck from the Tucson City Eco-Friendly Electric Company waiting for the first crew to finish before they mounted the high voltage wires across the top.

After introducing themselves and asking for some water, Cirrus and the two airmen each gulped down a drink and caught their breath. Since morning, Cirrus guesstimated he had sweated out two pounds of water. The foreman waited patiently then finally asked, "Are you government folks investigating this as an act of sabotage?"

"No, I'm a defense contractor. We're searching for an air-to-surface missile a fighter pilot accidently pickled," lied Cirrus.

"A missile? Are we working in a potential minefield?" The foreman was visibly alarmed.

"No danger, I assure you. The arming mechanism is inert," answered Cirrus.

"Good. By the way, these saboteurs, or Mexican cartel smugglers, or whoever the hell they were, paid the fucking price for their handiwork. Look over there," he said walking them behind the Verizon truck where he pointed to scrap wires from the downed poles and high voltage electrical conductor spools. The foreman told them to examine one very closely.

"See those little bits of brown specs stuck to the wire? They're pieces of clothing and human flesh. It's where our fuck-head with the chainsaw got the shock of his life. That's police evidence, so my men won't move it until the forensic team arrives–God knows when."

Cirrus' only thought now was how to get a sample without raising suspicion. He nodded to the airmen who returned a furtive acknowledgement. Then Cirrus abruptly walked back around the large utility truck speaking to the foreman, causing him to walk fast to catch up and take no notice the airmen who stayed behind. Captain Ryedell wasted no time scraping samples of what little remains he could bag and tag. Hornbeck stood with his back to the captain and placed his right hand atop of his unlatched holster, just in case.

An approaching figure from the Tucson electric truck was smiling. "Is that Johnny Cirrus?"

Shocked to hear his full name, Johnny took off his sunglasses. It took a moment for him to match a name to the face. Bobby Clearwater, a fellow tribal member and a classmate from Lake Powell Reservation High School. They'd never been close friends, but in the presence of white men it would have been an egregious insult to rebuff another Navajo. Both Native Americans peppered each other with the same words at the same time–*What are you doing out here?*

Clearwater answered first. "I'm the foreman on this job. I've been working for Tucson electric ever since we graduated. The tribe lost all track of you after your scholarship to Texas A&M. Your dad threatens to beat the shit out of anyone accusing you of going *apple*: red skinned on the outside but white on the inside. Luckily, nobody takes him seriously anymore, ever since he started drinking every full moon. Come to think of it, it's every half-moon, quarter and moonless night as well."

Johnny Cirrus didn't flinch. The insults delivered in a joking way were an admonishment for leaving. However jocular, insults were still insults. Once upon a time a tribal member could forfeit his tongue for such words. It was true his father was an alcoholic, sloppy drunk. But only after his mother passed away. He did feel a little shame in neglecting his father; there was no excuse for it except selfish ambition. This was neither the time nor the place for a personal reckoning or engaging in macho banter. He acted servile to get this day over with faster.

"Bobby—my apologies, you're right. I've been one ambitious SOB these last couple of years. I'd like to make amends. Can you smooth things over for me with the tribal elders? I'd like to visit the reservation tonight and convey my long overdue respects."

"For you? The tribe will have a perfect excuse for a joyful council fire. Lina will be glad to see you. My sister's grown into a woman and still refuses to date. Perhaps you can change her mind?" Clearwater's tone had altered from angry jealousy to fraternal tribal mate. When he saw the men armed with pistols walking over, he became wary. "Are you the chief scout for these whites?"

"I'm twenty-five percent Oklahoma Comanche my red brother," growled Hornbeck.

"And what twenty-five percent is that?"

"My fucking ass—you want to stick your red beak up there and sniff out a smoke signal?"

"That's enough sergeant! My apologies. We've been out in the heat all morning. It's starting to take its toll," said Captain Ryedell as he stepped in the middle of the pissing contest.

"No apologies necessary captain, besides our twenty-five percent magenta skin brother here knows it takes ten Comanche to kill one Navajo."

"I think you got that legend ass-backwards boy," said Hornbeck.

Cirrus rolled his eyes. This was just the kind of time wasting banter he hadn't wanted drawn into. At any moment he expected Brown to call demanding immediate updates. Neither plane nor pilot had been found. Cirrus notice a coyote pack scratching around off in the distance. That mound of sand was going to have to be investigated.

"Bobby, we do need your help. Do you have any of those manhole respirators?" asked Cirrus. "The kind you use to investigate nitrogen dioxide accumulation?"

"Sure, anything for a brother, including my twenty-five percent one." He went to the storage compartment in the back of his truck and returned with a large cardboard box. He removed three opti-fit butyl rubber gas masks. He knelt down, broke the sterile seal on the round canister filters and screwed them on to the left side of each mask. Then gave a quick demonstration for a proper fit. As a bonus, he handed out three pairs of heavy duty construction gloves for protection against snakes, cactus plants and any jagged metal pieces he assumed they were hunting for. Clearwater also assumed the rocket propellant from the lost missile was toxic–thus the request to borrow the gas masks. In any event, that was the explanation Cirrus gave him when they had a chance to speak privately on a few personal tribal matters. Clearwater watched the men help themselves at the portable water cooler for a second time before they walked back to their Humvee. When they were halfway down the road, he called after him one more time. "Johnny–when you're finished, make sure you return those gas masks. They're three hundred and seventy dollars apiece. I'm signed out for them. See you on the reservation tonight. Don't disappoint the tribe."

"Fuck you and fuck your sister too." Cirrus murmured to himself as he waved to Bobby Clearwater for a parting he hoped would be the last one in this lifetime.

The expletives were overheard by the others, they said nothing. Finally, Hornbeck's 6th sense got the better of him. "I have a bad feeling about these gas masks. Do you expect we'll be walking into a floating cloud of sarin gas?" he half-joked.

"If that happens," Johnny tried to relax his angry face as they rode toward the sand pile, "I'm certain these rubber masks won't dissolve, but your skin layers probably will. Not to worry though, right before that happens your bronchial tissue will liquefy. The active chemical pathogens will cause you to— sorry that blast from my past put me in a bad mood. Can this Humvee handle the dry gullies and desert scrub? We're headed to that mound of sand where some bodies might be decomposing, *that* is what the masks are for."

"As long as we don't drive over an IED the bad guys may have buried," answered Ryedell.

Hornbeck had the air conditioning going full blast. Cirrus had offered the comfortable front passenger seat to Ryedell who refused; he insisted on the rear bench hemmed in by multiple radio sets. The bulkier ones were for monitoring air traffic and base housekeeping transmissions such as weather forecasts and hourly situation reports from perimeter security patrols. The equipment was all USAF standard issue. The smaller, more expensive ones used encrypted bandwidth. The first one had a direct patch to a CIA operational handler at Langley, Virginia. The second was an emergency call-on radio to activate the Dr. Jekylls from their regular air force sleeper cell duties into operational Mr. Hydes back at Davis-Monthan, should that exigency be required. Captain Ryedell took off his white garrison cap and replaced it with a military green headset. Before driving off the road, Hornbeck pressed the black sand-mud-snow button on the dash for optional tire pressure. The lower inflation was necessary for soft ground conditions. This also automatically engaged the double-wishbone suspension. Once Hornbeck turned onto the pebbly loose soil, the drive was comfortable, smooth and short. A horn blast scattered lizards and possible snakes, Hornbeck hoped.

"Well, let's go do some dirty work," said Cirrus.

Both he and Hornbeck put on their gas masks. Cirrus took off his jacket and tie, Hornbeck left the engine running and unclipped his pistol holster draping it over the driver's seat. Ryedell remained comfortably ensconced on the back bench, monitoring a constant stream of radio chatter. Hornbeck went to the rear of the Humvee grabbing two entrenching tools and handed one to Cirrus.

To no one's surprise, the site turned out to be a shallow grave. Soon exposed was a dried wrist bone stump where a hand had been chewed off, probably by a coyote. After an initial hesitation, both men pitched in with their short handle spades. There were already signs of warm leaking enzymes and putrescence. The body that was emerging was male, less than 6' in height, and past the state of rigor mortis. Cirrus cursed inside his mask when he realized the missing hand belonged to the right wrist. The coyotes had gnawed his clue down to the bone. When the body was shoveled free from its sandy grave, lattice lines of burnt shirt fabric and scar tissue convinced Cirrus this corpse wasn't the missing pilot. It would have been impossible to land until the telephone poles were down. The poles were cut first and whoever did it got electrocuted in the process. The pilot and/or others had buried this corpse.

Ditch digging beneath a scorching desert sun takes its toll. It was time to hydrate.

They jammed their shovels in the sand then inserted straw tubes connected to their gas masks into a canteen so they could sip water without removing them. Cirrus crouched down and took a long look into the facial features of the dead man. He quickly concluded there was no discernible way to positively ID it here; it would have to be by dental forensics back at Langley. Hornbeck rummaged around for a standard issue human remains bag leaning in a side door of the Humvee.

Ryedell suddenly emerged with wide eyes. "We've got to get the hell out of here now!" Alarmed, Cirrus and Hornbeck rushed over. The captain held up his hand and shouted again. "Get back there—bag'em and tag'em—and let's go! I've got no time for explanations!"

When they returned to the Humvee with their package, Ryedell took in a deep breath and rushed over to help lift the body bag, placing it alongside the vehicle getting ready to heave it up to the roof. As an afterthought, Ryedell gasped in a breath, tucked in the samples from the electrical wire with the body then zipped it tight—no leaks. Up it went. Hornbeck then lashed it down like a hunting trophy causing a flat gurgling sound. Only then did everyone remove their gas masks and slime-stained work gloves, tossing them onto the hot sand;

Bobby could come get them or take the hit to his paycheck. Another round of water was chugged down as Ryedell filled them in.

"Your Brigadier General McMackinaw got arrested for assault. However, his cover hasn't been blown yet. Base authorities don't know who the hell he is, so they want us to detain you for questioning. I radioed back we already dropped you off at Tucson International and your flight departed hours ago. Now the Provost Marshal wants me and Hornbeck to report back immediately or they'll start looking for us."

"I bought us some time," interrupted Hornbeck sliding into his seat with an actual laugh. "This Humvee's original GPS tracker is now planted on your Navajo brother's work truck. Ryedell and I didn't ace our CIA field training for nothing."

Cirrus gave an appreciative snort then asked, "What do you mean assault charges? The man is seventy-one!"

"He evidently took exception to being challenged on drinking privileges at the officers club and wacked a lieutenant over the head with his cane. It's pretty serious because there was a titanium barrel inside of it with a 12 round magazine!" Ryedell rolled his eyes.

"What?!" exclaimed Cirrus.

"Do you know who the victim is?" asked Hornbeck.

"First Lieutenant Henry Blakefield."

"The commissary officer? Wasn't he the one who tried to get Master Sergeant Tomkinson court-martialed for giving him a salty salute with a cigarette in his mouth? The same Master Sergeant Tomkinson who was loadmaster on a C-130 and got severely burned single-handedly putting out a cargo fire after his aircraft took Triple-A over Afghanistan?" questioned Hornbeck.

"Yup. They awarded him a DFC for saving the craft and crew. I heard Colonel Mooney showed Lieutenant Blakefield the door when he first presented the insubordination charges," said Ryedell.

"I heard Colonel Napalm Mooney dropped kicked him out the door," added Hornbeck.

"Well guys, that's a very colorful story, but I need a resolution for McMackinaw. I can't face the wrath of my boss if I simply abandon him. Luckily, we're in the middle of the desert nowhere near a cell tower site so I can't be contacted for updates. Has Langley contacted us on your secured radio yet?"

"No," answered Ryedell.

"What's our Plan B?" asked Cirrus.

There was no immediate response. Instead, Ryedell chose to gaze out the window at passing green cactus plants. For the moment, he was more concerned about the trail of dust being kicked up from the desert floor by their speeding Humvee. Easy for search drones and helicopters to spot from miles away.

"Is there any Dramamine in the first aid kit?" Cirrus asked feeling the bounces from speed and some left over stench on his clothes.

"You just gave me an idea. We'll do a Sandman Ops!" exclaimed Ryedell. "You mentioned your general is seventy-one. How's his heart?"

"How the hell should I know? I guess normal for a man his age," replied Cirrus. "What's a Sandman Ops?"

"That's my Plan B! Since he's being held in only light detention, not the stockade, we can have one of our Mr. Hydes slip him something to induce symptoms of cardiac arrest. Then our second set of covert operatives disguised as a medical trauma team rush in and grab him. Transporting him as a medical emergency out of harm's way. The agency also employs Sandman Ops for the involuntary collecting of people the agency deems a threat, real or imagined. So, is it a green light? Or do you want Plan C? Injection with the deluxe version. In which case there's no lingering after effects and the Air Force is left with a General John Doe." Ryedell waited for an answer.

"Plan C is appealing for the SOB but above my pay grade. What about your real time back channel to Langley?"

"Yes. I can submit a disposition in real time. But I won't get an answer fast." Not waiting for Cirrus to make up his mind, Captain Ryedell did it for him. "Agreed. We'll green light a Sandman Ops–Bravo. Instruct your Gulfstream pilot to expect a three hour departure delay. I'll make sure the extraction team uses the mobile desert ambulance for transport to Spanish Wells. If I had twenty-four hours advance notice, I could have conjured up a Blackhawk medevac helicopter. So, blame the snafu on McMackinaw who put this shit storm in play."

"Just promise to return the old man with a beating heart. My chief, the White One back at Langley, will be flipped over mission failure to locate this A-10 aircraft and it's pilot, let alone the death of his general," said Cirrus.

Ryedell was already issuing operational orders into his headset. At that same moment, Hornbeck gave a thumbs up as he drove over the threshold of a lengthy asphalt runway, painted over and disguised with interwoven patterns of desert beige and sage green. He drove down the full length of the uncharted runway guided by a perimeter line of cone-shaped infrared landing lights. Their illumination was generated inside specially modified flight decks of CIA aircraft, enabling a three-dimensional runway hologram. It provided an all-weather display for pilots during clandestine landings and takeoffs. Armed guards signaled the Humvee to pull alongside a Gulfstream G-450 covered in desert camouflage netting.

"Welcome to CIA Airbase Spanish Wells!" announced Sergeant Hornbeck. "Can't get more desolate then, this. Wouldn't know we've arrived unless the GPS told us. The agency sometimes uses this base for intercepting and eliminating Mexican cartels runners, or for doing business with them."

Hornbeck turned to face Cirrus. "By the way, I've been meaning to ask you. Do you have any idea who that body is on the roof is?"

"One desiccated Asian man," responded Cirrus.

* * *

Unknown to any department, all of whom were engaged in their own independent investigation into the missing aircraft, a semi-trailer with California commercial plates (belonging to the Ottomanelli moving company though not yet reported stolen) drove through the gates of the decades closed Ramapo Valley Airport in northern New Jersey.

There, it pulled alongside an abandoned hanger. The overgrown field still had a useable runway. By car, the airport was a 30 minute drive from New York City.

For a twin jet engine Fairchild Republic, A-10C Thunderbolt II aircraft, even with full combat ordinance load, it was no time at all!

Chapter 6
Port of Call

Captain Voss sat in his stateroom chronicling his voyage, not in the ship's log, but in his own personal journal. He glanced up at an oversized calendar with circled days and crossed out weeks. The convoy was 38 days out from Hammerfest, and two days inbound to their now confirmed port of call, Lu-Shun, in the northern province of Liaoning. In 1904 this port was where the Imperial Japanese navy made a surprise and undeclared attack on Imperial Russia, 37 years before their surprise and undeclared attack at Pearl Harbor. For a variety of somber reasons, this destination didn't sit well with Voss. Yet for money he was speeding his convoy to Lu-Shun.

Twenty days had passed since committing an undeclared act of war on the high seas. The sinking of the patrol vessel was on his conscience. Captain Phong may have given the order, but he did nothing to intervene before or after the event. His voice was the only one on all the recorded ship to ship transmissions, damningly supplemented by that racist Captain Van Ochssee. Should charges ever be brought, such an inquiry would never dare to indict Captain Phong and hazard the lucrative largesse of the deep pockets he represents. The sooner he signed off as co-captain of this convoy—the better!

A brass chronometer mounted on the wall chimed five bells–02:30 hundred hours in the morning. His 30 minute break from the bridge was over. Voss had deliberately assigned himself to the graveyard watch from midnight to 04:00 hundred hours to ensure minimal contact with Phong. He took one last comforting gaze at a picture of his cherished wife Simone with their teenage son, then switched off his desk lamp. As he got up, he noticed an upward movement on the latch handle of his stateroom hatchway. A barefoot figure pushed open the oval hatch and furtively let himself in. Once inside, the silent figure quickly dogged down the hatch for a secure seal. The figure then turned. Interpreter Qu Xing stood still as a statue, holding his index finger pressed against his lips. *A bit melodramatic,* thought Voss, *considering my wall to wall carpeting will soften any noise.* The short man was visibly nervous but unapologetic for the intrusion. Voss went to his desk and pressed the top button on his multiple call directory in-house ship's telephone.

"This is Captain Voss. My return to the bridge will be delayed. Keep me apprised of any change in ship's routine." He stared directly at the interpreter. "You obviously have something very important to tell me." Voss motioned for Xing to sit in front of him.

Xing diffidently accepted the offer. "Do you mind if I smoke Captain Voss?"

Voss nodded and retrieved an ashtray from inside a glass door of an empty bookcase. Placing it on the desk between them, he sat down again. Xing took out a square pack of Players Navy Cut cigarettes and offered one to Voss. To keep this situation relaxed, he accepted.

The interpreter was pleased when the large bear of a man leaned forward to accept his light. "These English cigarettes are my one indulgence. Do you know why we Chinese say the reason Englishmen wear monocles? *So that they would not see more than they can understand.*"

"Our great Dutch Admiral De Ruyter taught the English more than they could understand in 1667, as well," chuckled Voss.

After a few relaxing puffs, as if he was building up steam, Xing launched into a low key, rambling account about the trials and tribulations visited upon the mainland Chinese people since Mao Zedong came to power in 1949. The interpreter ticked off a list of party catastrophes. He ended by bemoaning the deaths in the 1989 Tiananmen Square suppression.

Voss listened in rapt disgust to this tragic history lesson given by a party functionary. The words reminded Voss of a cold-blooded observation from Stalin—*One death is a tragedy; a million deaths are a statistic.* He began to sense a dark motive for the interpreter's tale of woe.

"Captain Voss – for what purpose are you and I aboard *Leviathan?*"

"Aside from the obvious one of money, pure folly."

"Exactly, pure folly. We both know in their present state, these ships are incapable of transporting a single barrel of oil. You must realize by now they were never intended to do it. Captain Phong was called out of retirement. He is competent enough, but old and expendable. First Mate Wei Jing Hua is dying of leukemia, convenient. The other ship's officers, especially that snake Second Mate Liu Bohai, aren't fit to navigate a sampan on a narrow tributary. We also have a platoon of Chinese marines disguised as crew members. They were the ones firing those missiles that sunk that Namibian gunboat. Lastly, as you said yourself, I'm a terrible interpreter. In English I can hold my own. I just can't translate your Dutch rolling R-sounds into Mandarin."

Perplexed, Voss crushed his cigarette in the ashtray. "So then, for what conceivable reason did your government spend a small fortune to purchase these sea going dinosaurs?"

"To throw all the mahjong tiles on the table and hope it doesn't end up being China's greatest folly of all."

"I'm afraid you are making some inference that leaves me as unsure as before," said Voss.

"Let me be blunt, Captain Voss. No more deceptions; except Sun Tzu's greatest deception of all. *When using our forces, we must seem inactive—when we are near, we must make the enemy believe we are far away.* However masterful and clever that may sound, that tactic may well end up being China's greatest disaster. My government intends to use these supertankers as the vanguard of an amphibious landing force."

"Invasion force?" said Voss, taken aback.

"To capture its perceived rightful territory of Taiwan. Concealing soldiers in the modified holding tanks converted for short term human habitation, an invasion force of ten of these supertankers could overwhelm the island. The key is surprise Captain Voss. Before the US Navy's Seventh Fleet can intervene. China is attempting to occupy and hold Taiwan so fast there will be no way to stop it. That's Beijing's great mahjong gamble." Then he too crushed his cigarette stub into the ashtray.

Voss was totally incredulous. Yet Phong's unconventional order to purge the ship's tanks mid-ocean now made sense. That would certainly make them habitable for a short duration. The idea was feasible. Was it plausible? "Why are you telling me secret war plans?"

"I am imploring you to help me save China from itself."

"How do you think a Dutch sea captain can single handedly save your country from a mission in full action?"

"Captain Voss, I judge you to be a man of high moral integrity, with the reserve strength of a *saladang*, I might add."

"A what?"

"A *saladang*—a Malaysian water buffalo, one of the strongest and most dangerous animals on the planet."

"I've been called many things in my life, but never one of those."

"Nor do I believe you are a greedy man. One who wouldn't hesitate to sacrifice his bonus to avert a destructive superpower war between the United States and China. The world will owe you a debt it could never adequately repay."

"Yes, but I have no idea what I could do to stop this now."

Qu Xing's voice began to get animated. "You must call out and expose this mission called *Lóng Pán*—Dragon's Coil—before it's too late!"

"And just how do you suggest I do that when our communications are controlled by the Chinese crew?"

"You must somehow be the one to alert the Americans. When we reach port in two days' time, your crew will be transported overland by train to Shanghai for their final contract payout. They'll want you all in person at the Shanghai Maritime Investment Bank for contract closure, and give inexplicable reasons why air transport is unavailable. The party will then ensure you and the other captains have an accident before you reach the bank, the fate of your crew is still being discussed. Captain Voss, our only hope is for you *not* to get on that train for Shanghai. Your best course of action would be to stowaway aboard one of the many foreign vessels anchored in Lu-Shun. Though I would advise against boarding a North Korean one. Best to try for one of those visiting Russian trawlers that are always spying on us. The Russian psyche is very susceptive to conspiracy theories."

"Come with me. So, we can make our case together."

"Captain Phong watches me like a hawk. Besides, Lu-Shun port authorities, namely Phong's son, would certainly not recognize my request for political asylum if I attempted to flee, especially with my operational knowledge of *Lóng Pán*. They would forcibly remove me from any ship regardless of the flag it flies and execute me in front of everyone on the pier. Even if I managed to escape, how could I live in a foreign country with a price on my head, constantly looking over my shoulder for the rest of my life? I want to save my beloved China, not be its traitor giving lecture tours ridiculing my country's fallibilities on talk shows all across America."

"And what of *my* family? I don't fancy ending my days as some incognito barge captain on the Nooderhaven Canal in West Friesland—waiting for my day of reckoning motoring under a low drawbridge with a tampered gear lock. Can you guarantee me that the Chinese people are of such a forgiving nature that if I cause them to lose face on the world stage, my family and I won't suffer retribution?" The interpreter was at a loss for words. Shoulders slumping, Voss resigned himself to the course of action already predetermined for him, his conscience would allow no other. "Tell me this then–how much time do I have?"

"Kindly inform me of the sailing time to Taiwan," said Xing.

Voss rose and walked over to the large Pacific Ocean wall chart opposite his desk. He picked his fixed point 6" navigation dividers, then made several hand over hand movements from the top of the chart to its midpoint. He made the calculation that Taiwan's only deep water port, Kaohsiung, had to be the intended invasion point. The dead reckoning between the two ports had a 1,029 nautical mile separation; with the convoy steaming at 16kts, transit time was a mere two days, ten hours. His expression betrayed his shock. *What the hell am I supposed to accomplish in two days,* thought Voss, *post the Chinese invasion plans on social media?*

Xing saw the despair on the captain's face and offered further details. "I have it on unimpeachable intelligence that *Lóng Pán* will be ready to embark twelve weeks from the day we dock at the port of Lu-Shun. So, with your estimated two days sailing time as part of the twelve weeks of logistical preparation and tactical lading–that's our given timetable."

"This will certainly be the most momentous decision of my life. Nevertheless, I make no promises. For both our sakes, let's not say another word on this matter and separate now. I have to resume my duties on the bridge. Qu Xing, I shall forever be in your debt for saving my hearing. A deaf sea captain is not very marketable."

The Dutchman and Chinaman shook hands for the first and last time. Voss switched off all the lights in his stateroom so his barefoot visitor could slip away unnoticed with no backlighting. He then started to follow him out. As he was about to close his bulkhead hatch behind him, he had the uneasy thought that Xing might have noticed his private journal laying open on his desk.

* * *

The bridge lookouts aboard *Leviathan* logged in their first visual landfall at 03:26 Zulu Greenwich Mean Time, 11:26 local time. Two hours later, First Officer Van Het reduced engine speed to a dead slow to allow the harbor pilot's gig alongside. Although the transversal propulsion thrusters provided precision maneuvering around the harbor marker buoys, rendering the pilot's job largely obsolete, no ship freely enters China unsupervised. On *Leviathan's* bridge, and no doubt on *Antilles* and *Zeelandia* as well, the arrival in Lu-Shun was greeted with the traditional end-of-voyage elation by all. Even Chief Engineer Maartan ascended from the bowels of the machinery spaces to partake of the mood. Their captain, usually in his stateroom during his off watch periods, also made an appearance on the bridge. Voss took a pair of binoculars off the navigation table and strode out to the farthest end of the starboard bridge wing. He thought the harbor pilot was bringing *Leviathan* in excessively slowly; deliberately taking more time to berth her. Perhaps the pilot wanted to prolong the privilege of maneuvering one of the largest ships in the world.

The port of Lu-Shun was nothing as expected. It resembled a gargantuan sunken aircraft carrier with sea level just below the landing deck. With its long, flat, recently completed, pier extending out into the Yellow Sea it seemed intentionally designed to be a hazard to navigation. The port served as an unintended showcase of what modern China had become: a soulless shape of functionality, completely without character. Still staring through his binoculars, Voss counted seven other supertankers. The name of the first ship the pilot was attempting to berth *Leviathan* behind was the *Queen Wilhelmina*. Voss was mildly amused.

The entire pier was a hive of industry.

Monster whirly cranes, so named for their ability to whirl around a full 360°, were extending their gantry hooks in non-stop lifting and loading of material from the pier to the main decks of the many tankers. Facing the northern side of the pier, Voss saw a row of fishing trawlers flying Chinese, North Korean and Vietnamese flags. Off by itself, deliberately anchored upwind of those foul smelling fishing vessels, was an immense Russian icebreaker whose beige superstructure seemed to squat on a bulbous hull.

In the center of all the harbor bustle three sets of railroad tracks extended the full length of the pier. Only one was occupied by a line of freight cars, and that was closest to the berthed tankers.

In all that frenetic labor, what caught his attention, and left him mystified, were metal protuberances being welded to *Queen Wilhelmina's* gunwales. They resembled high back chairs. For all Xing's talk of deception, the Chinese government was putting on quite an industrial show for the small community of nations anchored on the north side of the pier. *Secrecy in plain sight*. Voss put down his binoculars and looked directly below the bridge wing as the green sea disappeared under the hardwood framed pier which was layered in reinforced concrete and steel. The sensation in his feet from the ship's unrelenting engine vibration of 40 days suddenly stopped.

First Officer Van Het opened the starboard bridge hatchway and called out. "Captain, *Leviathan* is docked and all lines are secured, sir."

Without acknowledging, Voss returned to the command bridge. At the already opened ship's log, showing the current date, time, and port of call, Captain Voss signed his full name and duly relieved himself of all responsibility on *Leviathan*, as well as *Antilles* and *Zeelander*. He turned to his one-time counterpart, Captain Phong, and uncharacteristically showed contempt by bending his head down to speak to emphasize his height. "The ship is yours," he said bluntly. "I'm going to pack my things." Without ceremony, Voss simply quit the bridge and retired to his stateroom.

* * *

On the afternoon of the third day of his self-enforced confinement, Voss finished the last paragraph in his private journal. It was to be his unvarnished account as convoy commander shepherding three Batillus-class ultra large crude carrier supertankers the 3,718 nautical miles from Norway to China. *Maybe someday,* Voss mused solemnly, *my future grandchildren will read about their ancestor's adventures in the south Atlantic.* He closed the journal slowly.

Het knocked on his hatchway. Once again, he invited Voss to join the farewell party in the wardroom. This time Voss accepted. Voss stuffed the journal deep into the recesses of a bulging suitcase. After dressing in his black uniform jacket with four gold stripes on each sleeve cuff, he carefully adjusted his tie then walked the passageway toward the sounds of revelry. He was chagrined to see Captain De Zwaan of *Antilles* laid back in a lounge chair, drunk. De Zwaan's distinguished white Van Dyke beard pointed upwards. Being over 70, he was excused as an old sea dog who could no longer hold his liquor. De Zwaan's age was balanced with the youngest officer, Third Engineer Finnsson, who had passed out under the long dinner table, while another unseen officer was heard vomiting in the wardroom head. Captain Von Ochssee of *Zeelandia*, his collar open and black tie askew, staggered towards Voss, just managing to hold upright two fluted glasses of champagne. As soon as he saw Voss's sullen expression, Von Ochssee's demeanor changed as well— from a jovial drunk to a nasty one.

"Still brooding because Phong sunk a boatload of Kaffirs?"

Voss refused to dignify the Afrikaner's outburst with an answer.

"How many years have we sailed together, Voss!?" he angrily demanded. "I can read your mind! We both know what's going on with that big fucking Chinese fire drill down on the pier! There's a reason why these slopeheads are welding chairs with holes to shit through on the gunwales. I only hope the country they're planning to invade has enough pesticides to counter the swarms of yellow locust that will descend upon them!"

The wardroom camaraderie was stunned into silence by Von Ochssee's alarming rant. All eyes, sober and drunken, were cast on their senior officers.

"I advise you to guard your words!" growled Voss. If this bullheaded Afrikaner could see through Beijing's machinations, the time for circumspection was over.

"Well speak of the devil," Von Ochssee said while craning his neck over Voss's shoulder.

The subject of their conversation just made an unannounced, and uninvited, entrance. Captain Phong, accompanied by a middle-aged party apparatchik, entered the wardroom. Von Ochssee stood there awkwardly, still holding two glasses of celebratory champagne. Instead of offering them to the uninvited guests, he downed them both in quick succession. In the meantime, Voss ignored them as well, and retired to a corner in a chair. He suspected Phong was keenly satisfied about this guest witnessing the undignified spectacle of inebriated Europeans.

"Gentlemen, may I introduce my son, Zhang Wei, the port director of Lu-Shun." The man with a fixed smile in a business suit, carrying a construction helmet under his arm, bowed stiffly. "Unfortunately, my son's English is lacking. Therefore, I shall speak for both of us. We are here to wish you all a good voyage home and a soon to be happy reunion with your families. Now, it is my pleasure to report, or rather my son's, that your private luxury train will arrive within the hour to transport you to Shanghai for your much deserved contract payment. Once again, thank you for your inestimable service to the People's Republic of China."

Unable to fathom the lack of hospitality, the second mate from *Antilles* picked up two champagne glasses from the table and belatedly offered them to the father and son, who in turn immediately raised them up in a toast.

"Gentlemen, my son would like to say a few words in Mandarin."

Zhang Wei held his glass high. "*Zhù nî mâ daō chéng gong.*"

The father translated. "Gentlemen, my son wishes you all *Horse arriving success*. It is a compliment, I assure you. But as you are well aware, exact word translations never truly carry the nuance of the expression they are meant to convey."

There followed a faint chorus of *Hear!—Hear!* And a few clinked glasses, which were quickly emptied. Voss remained seated during the toast, preferring the company of semi-conscious drunken officers spread about the wardroom's overturned and broken furniture. Those who could stand eventually staggered back to their cabins to pack for their rail journey to Shanghai.

* * *

Newly promoted Admiral Phong and the PRC's special interpreter Qu Xing, stood side by side on the extreme end of the starboard bridge wing of *Leviathan*. Towering 470' above Lu-Shun pier, it gave them a panoramic view of all the activities of the shipfitters and welders that now swarmed aboard the many tankers. Despite the frenetic work beneath them, their attention was fixed on the line of two-tone green and red trimmed railway carriages on the pier's middle track. A line of men waiting to board included the tall figure standing next to a shorter one, holding a clipboard to check off their crew. Both observers easily recognized Voss and Het.

"Did he believe you?" asked Phong.

"Yes admiral, I'm quite sure he did."

Phong pressed further. "Quite sure or sure enough? The fates of our *Yin* deceptive *Lóng Pán* and its counterbalance *Yang* mission *Yôngbào* are relying on your persuasive guile."

"Admiral Phong, Captain Voss is a Dutchman. The Dutch are a congee soup of decadent French liberalism and barbaric German precision. His flawed occidental ethos is incapable of seeing a pathway other than the rabbit warren I have taken him down."

"Your enthusiasm is encouraging, Qu Xing, and your loyalty to the party is exemplary. Yet we must be sure Captain Voss voluntarily boards one of those foreign vessels and not that train. There must be no delay in him finding a stage to perform the role we have cast for him. So, we must give the good captain another incentive in that direction—a push so to speak. Therefore, you yourself must perform the next act for the love of our Chinese people."

Distracted by the clatter all around, Xing never saw the marines disguised in worker's overalls who crept up behind him. In one quick lunge, the first pinioned his arms behind him, then the others grabbed legs and arms and lifted him. With a last second go-ahead nod from their admiral, the marines heaved Xing over the bridge wing railing! His anguished death screams went unheard; drowned out by louder, heavier industrial noise from all over the pier. For the briefest of moments Voss caught sight of the chilling specter of flailing arms and legs of the falling body for the six seconds it took to impact the reinforced concrete pier. The result was an uneven gory sunburst pattern of extruded bloody trunk organs, cartilage and bone splinters.

Voss was first to run to the scene.

He had seen men mangled by machinery before, but what remained now looked like a butcher's block of assorted offal. What disturbed him most was a blood splattered box of cigarettes visible under an arm.

As with any liquid that seeks its level, the flowing rivulets of blood channeled towards one of the pier's numerous storm drains that emptied into the Yellow Sea. Captain Voss looked up at the lone figure who stood at the edge of *Leviathan's* bridge wing. The distance was too great for the two captains to read the expression of the other. In smoldering rage, he turned around and walked away.

Without a word to his crew, he picked up his suitcase and stepped aboard the waiting railway carriage. Instead of locating his sleeper compartment however, Voss crossed the front vestibule and descended the steps on the opposite side. He then headed directly towards the gangway of the icebreaker.

Admiral Phong put down his binoculars and smiled. For a moment, he thought he would be forced to order a derailment of their luxury train when it crossed over the Great Liao River Bridge. But Xing's sacrifice had paid off. Tonight, he would burn an incense stick to venerate his memory. *Qu Xing truly did love the Chinese people.*

* * *

Upon approach of a large man with four gold stripes on his sleeves, two Russian petty officers in standard blue and white uniform shirts, each with an AK-47 and a fixed bayonet, snapped to attention. Voss returned their salutes and was allowed to ascend the gangway steps without challenge. Once aboard, the officer of the deck also showed him all traditional naval courtesies befitting his rank. He was at once escorted to the ship's spacious officers lounge. Its interior of tawdry red hanging drapes and faux art deco light fixtures resembled a second class ballroom. No sooner was he offered a table when a white jacketed steward placed a glass of tea in a silver cage before him. The animated tone in the lounge became hushed; its few occupants discreetly began to file out. Except for the steward who went back to the galley, he now had the room entirely to himself, but not for long. The man who next entered matched his size and demeanor.

"Captain Voss, welcome aboard the Russian icebreaker *Krasin*," said an aristocratic looking man with deep blue eyes.

Not one to be intimidated, even by a seaman as formidable as himself, Voss asked the obvious question. "How is it you have the advantage of knowing my name?"

The hulking, broad-shouldered man smiled and affected the disarming persona of a lovable Russian circus bear who politely didn't hear the question. "My name is Captain-Lieutenant Vladimirovich Kovalev of the Federal Security Service. I understand you just witnessed an accident on the pier." The captain snapped his fingers.

The steward reappeared, holding a silver tray with two glasses and a bottle of Ketel One vodka, distilled exclusively in Schiedam, Netherlands.

"Captain Voss, before we empty this bottle imported from your homeland, you look like a man who has a story to tell. Where shall we begin?"

Chapter 7

POTUS Almost Posthumous

President Alexander Atwater leaned back in an ergonomically designed chair in the flying oval office on the newest version of Air Force One: a Boeing 747-8. A well-liked president in the second year of his first term, he was enjoying his popularity. The American people, exhausted by legacy families, rich community organizers never living in those communities and abrasive-mannered business men, this time voted in a man of science. In his youth, Atwater had graduated *Egregia cum laude* from Rensselaer Polytechnic Institute. After a post graduate degree in thermodynamics, he served six years as engineering officer aboard the nuclear submarine *USS West Virginia*. Pundits were effusive in making comparisons to former President Jimmy Carter, a comparison he always loathed because to him, #39 was a living definition of the ancient adage: *You never, ever, put a saint in charge of the church.* Once his tour of naval service ended, so did the rest of the similarities to the gentleman farmer president.

President Triple A (Alexander Archer Atwater) didn't pray on his knees, if he prayed at all. He did take his old chemistry professor's advice and invested every dime of his trust fund in speculative platinum mining shares that made him a multimillionaire on the precious metals commodities exchange by age 30. With that equity he founded an R&D company, filed several patents on the practical and inexpensive means of harnessing geothermal energy applications, and in the process added three more zeros to his net worth by the age of 35. To stave off the effects of being a bored self-satisfied billionaire, constantly besieged by importunate politicians, he opted for a career change. He then applied his scientific background and financial success to intuitively master the alchemy of politics, which allowed him to achieve the governor's mansion in the Excelsior State on the first try by 40. His Earth-friendly entrepreneurship of harnessing geothermal clean energy made him the poster boy of the environmentalists movement, and confirmed his *bona fides* with the Green Party. At the same time, his reputation for business acumen gained him the support of the center wing of the Republican Party. Further endorsements came from academia. All of these attributes dovetailed with the next generation sentiments as well. After completing only one successful term as governor of New York, and by unanimous consent, he was drafted by his party, and handily won the presidency. Two years later, Americans felt no buyer's remorse. Such a fast rise based only on academia and ownership level business transitions left Triple A's hidden weakness a secret … for now.

For the depleting ranks of the war baby generation, this handsome president and his elegant first lady offered them a fondly remembered twilight glimpse of Camelot's second coming. The few blue collar workers left after the surge of automation could now pick and choose decent manufacturing jobs. College students envisioned a future of innovation and exploration. Of course, there were always threats to national security. Terrorist organizations were still lurking about wanting to kill Americans as a way of manifesting their right to interpret the word of God. But as Atwater gazed out the pressurized window watching one of two F-35A Lighting fighters flying escort, he felt reassured. America's vast array of killing machines was ready for a surgical strike anywhere in the world, including using nukes, and the world knew it. Strategically, President Atwater feared neither The Bear nor The Dragon. With over a billion Chinese on Russia's southeastern border, neither country could afford to expose their 1,000 mile flank to the other. He likened the current situation to the Hitler/Stalin non-aggression pack of 1939; this time with America as the third party to keep the other two off balance.

Vice President Francis Lejeune, former senator from Louisiana, was entirely another matter. Put on the ticket as a garden variety politician, he was strictly a regional vote getter. The real Lejeune was an old school southern Christian gentleman. Nevertheless, such public softness didn't stop the pundits from assigning the Vice President his own moniker–The Crawfish.

The third member of the Atwater Triumvirate was Chief of Staff J. Carl Dunlap. A few years older than the president, Dunlap looked upon him as an adopted younger brother, reminiscent of the one who died when the south tower of The World Trade Center collapsed in 2001. His intense loyalty to the president came from guilt for having insisted his younger brother take a job headquartered in that south tower. Dunlap was on the phone with him that fateful day when the line was irrevocably disconnected.

President Atwater, with attention split between watching TV news and reviewing his upcoming UN speech, shifted his concentration to acknowledge a knock on his cabin door by a secret service agent stationed outside. The agent opened the door to permit Chief of Staff Dunlap to enter, then closed it.

"Mr. President, we'll be landing at JFK in 45 minutes. Is your speech on Blue Nile finished? Or should I send it back to the speechwriters for a final review?"

"No problem with the speech J, but have you seen this?" The president pointed to the TV set then unmuted the Newark, NJ, channel.

> "… rioting today in Paterson … abandoned Ramapo Valley police cruiser … heavy handed search of Muslims … locate its still missing officer … ethnic Egyptian Community known for their overt sympathies to the Muslim Brotherhood … police incompetence …"

"I'll go upstairs to the comm deck and get the why and wherefore on this story ASAP Mr. President," said Dunlap.

"Please do! I don't need to be ambushed by the press at JFK on something I don't have a clue about."

After Dunlap had been gone over 30 minutes, Atwater began to get anxious. When he didn't hear the customary announcement to prepare for landing, and when another glimpse out the window didn't reveal the New York City skyline, but instead the new bridge farther north at Nyack, the president became concerned. His chief of staff finally returned accompanied by the Head of Secret Service, Burton Rooks, along with the president's military attaché, Rear Admiral Langsdale. Atwater gauged the grim faces staring at him. "This looks ominous."

Dunlap spoke first. "Mr. President, we've received a flash cipher from the Chinese embassy in Washington. Ambassador Xiao sends greetings. He states the PRC has irrefutable evidence from back channels in Karachi that an attempt will be made on your life when we land at JFK. His government claims this attack will be carried out by the Egyptian group known as the Muslim Brotherhood. Ambassador Xiao urges you to take all possible precautions for your personal safety. Lastly, Mr. President, the ambassador does not mention any linkage to the minor events now unfolding in South Paterson, New Jersey, even though some of the same players are in motion and he smothered the message in platitudes."

"J, you know damn well I won't announce to the world the president of the United States cowers before terrorists! We need to stick to our schedule. What options do we have?"

"We knew that would be your response. Agent Rooks will brief you on the overlay, and Rear Admiral Langsdale on the specifics," said Dunlap.

Looking like a tree trunk in a business suit, Burton Rooks laid out the stark facts. "Mr. President, Ambassador Xiao states the attempt will be made at JFK during your transition from Air Force One to Marine One. Therefore, we cut that part of the transition. We land at Stewart International in the lower Hudson Valley, just north of the George Washington Bridge. There, we'll board helicopters and take a thirty minute flight to Manhattan. For additional security, the helicopters will land in Central Park where you'll be met by a reinforced detail of secret service agents with a reserve support of NYPD special event and SWAT teams. From the park it's a ten minute drive to the Waldorf-Astoria where you'll join the first lady now under maximum protection in the presidential suite."

"Central Park? Why land there?" Atwater leaned forward showing some irritation.

Rooks answered, "Sir, the heliports in Manhattan are all well-known and might be targeted. The unused one on the MetLife Building is walking distance to the Waldorf, but it's just too dangerous."

Dunlap interrupted, "There's precedent for landing at Central Park, Mr. President. For security reasons and helicopter size, President Johnson landed there to attend the funeral mass at St. Patrick's Cathedral for Robert Kennedy in '68. We'll also be flying in that same type of monster helicopter LBJ came in on. It is just too large for the standard Manhattan heliports."

Admiral Langsdale nodded and then took over. "At this time, three Sea Stallions from a heavy marine helicopter squadron based at Willow Grove have been activated and are en route to Stewart with a 50 minute ETA." There was a hesitation in the admiral's voice. "There is one major security concern, Mr. President. So as not to show we've been alerted, the Marine One helicopters will still be held on the tarmac waiting for Air Force One. That means the Bell Viper gunships that fly shotgun will be standing down as well. Our Air Force One fighter escorts can't loiter at helicopter speeds. Once they escort us to Stewart, and once we transition to the 53s, we're on our own for the 30 minute flight to Central Park. Stateside reservist helicopters aren't equipped with CHAFF countermeasures to decoy heat seeking stinger missiles if we're attacked."

"Your plan's sound. If I can fly for 30 minutes without an in-flight toilet, I can chance a 30 minute window of opportunity for a domestic missile attack. What about the Marine One crew and ground personnel just standing around at JFK? I want them safe!"

Rooks spoke to that concern. "They haven't been alerted about the situation, but we've layered concentric circles of SWAT teams now saturating the airport perimeter. We're hoping any attacker will get nervous by our announced delayed arrival at JFK and make mistakes, causing them to prematurely show their hand."

Atwater had other concerns as well. "Hope is not a strategy. In any case, lets land this bus. I have a noon appointment with the first lady."

Prior to landing, a call was put out to locate Vice-President Lejeune and sequester him at a secure location in case the best laid plans went awry. In the press corps section of Air Force One, secret service agents were busy collecting everyone's cell phones and ensuring that all window shades were lowered. The members of the press were then informed that they wouldn't be allowed to deplane until further notice due to the security nature of this unscheduled stop. Air Force One soon touched down at Stewart International. The transition went smoothly.

Three grey CH-53 Sea Stallions were waiting on the tarmac. Admiral Langsdale was lead escort, shepherding everyone on board into the two long rows of seats that lined both sides of the interior fuselage. The few members of the president's entourage who had never been aboard a military helicopter devoid of soundproofing and with exposed piping, were unnerved. The admiral reassured them all that dripping transmission and hydraulic fluid that oozed out was a good sign. After everyone was buckled in, the crew chief handed out ear protectors. Shortly afterwards, the seven bladed rotor started to turn. The crew chief gave a demo on the use of the on board relief tube since there was no restroom, but suggested they all wait if they could.

Admiral Langsdale commandeered the jump seat between the aircraft commander and the copilot. Still in dress uniform, he now wore a helmet. He was busy reviewing the plan with the pilots. The other Sea Stallions would carry no passengers and fly chase. This was designed to keep up a ruse that the three aircraft formation flying down the Hudson River was nothing more than a routine training mission.

After a final preflight check by the crew chief, they got a thumbs up. In unison, the largest helicopters in the American arsenal went airborne. The rear loading ramp was left extended to vent any accumulating fumes of high octane jet fuel. The flight was extremely loud and the vibration nerve-racking, but the rear view was panoramic. For the first ten minutes the experience was a noisy, riveting adventure.

As the formation flew over George Washington Bridge, the port positioned helicopter passed the New York tower side, the middle one over the center span, and the president's helicopter passed over the New Jersey Tower.

Suddenly——a flashing amber light signaled a collision avoidance proximity alarm!

Simultaneously, a warning tone pierced every crew member's headset.

The aircraft commander killed the sound by flipping the manual override switch. A human voice transmission followed:

"This is Westchester Approach Control to helicopter traffic over the George Washington Bridge—pleased be advised you have a fast approaching aircraft—altitude unknown and negative transponder interrogation just north of Teterboro Airport and south of Ramapo Valley—recommend you immediately alter heading and descend clear of terrain to helicopter visual flight rules minimum altitude. Do you acknowledge, over?"

* * *

Several minutes before that stark warning, in broad daylight, a straight winged jet with an H-tail configuration had inexplicably appeared from an abandoned airfield once known as Ramapo Valley Airport. At first it loitered just above stall speed over Interstate 80 so the pilot, unfamiliar with the terrain, could orientate himself on the lattice work steel towers of the George Washington Bridge. Once his bearings were set, it flew straight across the Jersey Palisades, banked a steep 60° right turn and headed due south, following the Hudson River. It maintained course for 30 seconds. Using a reference point of wooden masts rocking below which the pilot knew was West 79th Street's boat basin, the aircraft engaged in another erratic maneuver. It turned 180° north, back towards the bridge as the helicopters were just crossing the span.

The man who had impersonated the Egyptian exchange pilot was dreaming of being the first jihadist to assassinate a president of the United States using whatever ammo remained, then he planned to turn south again towards the Manhattan skyline to wreak havoc and rain down gruesome death on the streets of New York City. After the last shot, he would enter paradise where his rewards were waiting after he crashed himself into the glass façade of the United Nations Building. Knowing the president would be in one of the helicopters, the pilot advanced his throttle control to bear down on all three in an apparent head-on collision course. The Sea Stallions were there for the taking, and no amount of death defying aerobatic maneuvers could save them. The pilot raised the glare shield visor on his helmet and pulled off his oxygen mask. He keyed the button mike so they knew exactly what was coming, *"ALLAHU AKBAR!"*

With seconds to react, Langsdale turned in his jump seat, unable to shout a warning over the sound of the helicopter turbines, he frantically waved his arms to the president. With even less time to spare, five secret service agents instinctively reacted to the admiral's gestures and piled on top of the president to create a human shield for whatever was coming.

At that same instance—the jihadist pilot took aim and prepared to fire! He couldn't have missed even if he wanted to. He pressed the red trigger button on the left side of the control stick. For a nanosecond—nothing! Then his entire cockpit erupted in flames. There was a brief sensation of being stung by a thousand bees at the same time. Then a secondary explosion under the ejection seat blasted him into pieces. Due to the Thunderbolt's unique reinforced armor around the cockpit, nicknamed the bathtub, the force of the explosion went straight up through the ½ inch Plexiglas canopy. The free falling aircraft left a spectacular arching meteor trail as it made its dramatic impact into the smooth flowing waters of the Hudson. The Sea Stallions flew on to Central Park and completed their mission with a president acting as if this were a change in his schedule in order to press hands and see the masses; keeping a calm happy face was the best acting job Atwater had ever performed. He was shaken to his core knowing he had been seconds away from being blown to bits. Though he would be fully informed of the details of this failed assassination attack at a later date, the reality of his death started to sink into his scientific soul.

* * *

At JFK where Air Force One was originally supposed to land, the second jihadist action of the day against the United States of America began. This terrorist cell was completely unaware and independent of the first one's attempt to intercept the president's helicopter. Once these on-site jihadist realized the president's plane was overdue, they were forced into unprepared action. If they weren't able to kill the president, they were going to take out as many important Americans as they could on their way to death and fame. Airport security and SWAT teams were fast closing on the suspicious Newark airport shuttle van weaving around the police barricades trying to get as close as possible to Marine One.

The van suddenly swerved toward it and accelerated.

Sharpshooters immediately opened fire at the oncoming van, causing the driver to lose control and crash into a concrete barricade. As SWAT surrounded the van, the driver and front seat occupant detonated their suicide vests which bizarrely blew only their heads off their shoulders without causing any collateral deaths.

Warily, SWAT approached the van but were unable to see inside due to the blood splattered windshield. When they were able to investigate, they discovered suitcases packed with glyphosate fertilizer instead of the usual truck bomb weapon of choice, ammonium nitrate.

The headless bodies were sent out for forensic analysis. Immediate results revealed only the inept design of the jihadist's suicide vests and the make of their firearms. Subsequent press reports would label the terrorist The Headless Hezbollahs. What the press failed to mention was how the stolen shuttle van bypassed the first ring of defense so easily. There was also an unverified account that initially the van's driver was recognized to have had Asian facial features, and racially profiled not to be a threat.

* * *

Later that afternoon, President Atwater gave his anticipated humanitarian speech before the United Nations on his assured support for construction of the Blue Nile hydropower dam in Ethiopia. Prior to delivering it, he called the PCR embassy giving heartfelt gratitude towards the People's Republic of China in general, and toward the Chinese UN delegation in particular, for their vigilance in combating worldwide terrorism. During the UN gala that evening at the Waldorf-Astoria, President Atwater and First Lady Barbara Brooke Atwater entertained their dinner guests with charm. Though the president was laughing and circulating amongst all the dignitaries, a tight chill of panic was knotting in his stomach. Atwater couldn't wait for the festivities to end so he could learn what had happened and what was going on in regards to his personal safety.

Thirty-four floors above the grand ballroom, sequestered in a private suit, Chief of Staff Dunlap wanted scalps and lots of them! He was absolutely livid over the gross ineptitude of governmental agencies from the State Department to the US Air Force, to the FBI, CIA, and every agency in between. *How could they let this happen?* he raged as he paced across the rooms. A missing attack aircraft turns up ready to assassinate the president and carry out another 9-11 on New York City, and nobody tells anybody anything! Not a hint! But somehow the Chinese knew! *Now we're beholden to that glorified ant hill!* Dunlap planned to work well into the night to comprise a long list of departmental heads to send rolling.

In stark contrast, Chief of the Presidential Secret Service, Burton Rooks, was a happy man. POTUS was saved from almost certain assassination on his watch. Another gold star was added to his record when his security team at JFK eliminated a potential terrorist attack with no loss to American lives and well before they could attack Marine One.

The other great news of the day was that the missing Ramapo Valley police officer had been rescued safe and sound. When the FBI swarmed all over the Ramapo Valley Airport, the officer was found in an abandoned hanger. His accounts varied about his captors. The last thing he remembered was pulling over a suspected stolen van to run the license plate. Somewhat disoriented from a blow to the back of his head, he was certain he was assaulted by a gang of Arabic speaking men. When he regained consciousness, he found himself stripped of his weapon and uniform with a length of chain attached to his ankle, but with an ample supply of food and water. Carey also claimed that while coming to, and still pretending to be unconscious, he heard what sounded like Asian voices mixed with the distinct whine of a jet engine that echoed through the cavernous hanger.

In the euphoria of the moment, oddly, no one questioned why this cop was treated so humanely or why he didn't end up having his throat cut on a fundamentalist video.

It was time for some self-congratulations. Burton Rooks moved about the corridors of the Waldorf-Astoria's ballroom and complimented each agent posted at all the exits that ringed the president's reception. He extended discreet back pats, nods and handshakes. At the same time, he admitted to himself that the day's events were mostly attributed more to happenstance than to his professional intercession. With that caveat aside, Burton Rooks could not believe his good luck.

* * *

At the CIA's old headquarters building, ensconced in his third floor corner office, Head of The Strategic Analysis Department Robert Brown, did not believe in luck. He too had been monitoring the extraordinary events of the day. His own analysis coupled with an imaginative Trojan horse hypothesis put forth by Val Parrott, and supplemented with Johnny Cirrus' detailed desert report, all tended to disabuse the latest running accounts now being served up by the mass media for pedestrian consumption. To Brown's analytical mind, none of the details interlocked to make the slightest bit of sense. Neither the botched JFK terrorist attack nor the bizarre event over the Hudson River. Obviously, they were both red herrings. He was sure he had the pieces, but how much time did he have to complete the puzzle? Brown decided it was time to shine some light on theories of his own. He stepped outside his office and walked past several rows of cubicles until he buttonholed one of the East Asian audio network monitoring analysts, Peter Chan aka Peter Pan. A bestowed nickname for no reason other than lazy co-workers couldn't come up with anything else.

"What mischief have your twice removed mainland cousins been up to today?"

"The chatter is—there isn't any chatter. All cell traffic along the Sino-Indian border went off grid; dropped to zero like a fucking rock. Same with tactical military bases scattered all over China. The strategic nuclear bases are putting out their normal volume of housekeeping transmissions, though," answered Chan

Before he had a chance to consider that latest little piece of the puzzle, Brown was interrupted by Parrott.

"Mr. Brown, this just came over the threat board in real time—the Muslim Brotherhood is claiming responsibility for a suicide truck bomb attack on the Chinese embassy in Cairo. Initial reports say it's eighty-plus casualties—all Egyptians! It's obvious the Chinese had prior knowledge because the night before, embassy grounds were ringed with sand-filled dump trucks. The trucks were all driven by Chinese workers pulled from construction sites associated with their African belt and road initiative."

While trying to process this horrific bit of news, Brown was interrupted a second time.

Peter Chan just recalled a flurry of two week old intercepts. "There was mass cell traffic about a rather mundane subject, but the Ting Foos were really bitching about it," said Chan.

"Peter, it's not feigned modesty for me to say I cannot see around corners. What the fuck are *Ting Foos*?"

"Ting Foos, that's our code name for *Jiātíng Zhûfù*, Chinese mainland housewives. They were complaining all the manual can openers were gone from the shops and turned over to the government for some special project," answered Chan.

The CIA's current head of strategic analysis was forced to complete this jigsaw puzzle on the reverse blank side without knowing if all the pieces came with the box and without the luxury of time. "Can Openers?" he repeated to himself shaking his head, something this odd and wide in scale was important—but how—and **can openers?** In search of any advantage, Brown returned to his corner office, picked up his phone and requested a secured line direct to Cairo station. Seconds later, someone answered the call six times zones across the globe.

"I need confessions! Cast a wide net; ensnare as many as you can without raising the ire of the local magistrates and police. Offer each their virgins on *this* side of Paradise. For the obstinate ones that require enhanced interrogation, you're green-lighted to sub-contract the Alchemist. Never mind about chasing down the faux story behind that pilot. He's a construct. I need to know why the Muslim Brotherhood turned on their Chinese paymasters," emphasized Brown.

"I heard about today's assassination attempt. It's under total redaction. Displaced by the jihadist mess at JFK. How close was it for Atwater?" asked the Chief of Cairo Station.

"POTUS was almost Posthumous!"

There was a brief reflective silence, then both men simultaneously hung up.

Chapter 8

Year of the Monkey Sergeant

After being bounced around for over a week on an unscenic railway journey across central China in a jam-packed troop train, Lee Ji-Nan was nearly thrown out of his seat when the engineer abruptly applied the air brakes. This action subjected 15 passenger cars to a hard stop. Lethargic from a cramped train ride, he had to summon all his remaining strength just to stand upright and put on his backpack. He stepped off the passenger car into a pandemonium of disembarking soldiers. His senses were assaulted. Pushing his way forward, he caught sight of a line of berthed supertankers. They were the largest man-made objects he had ever seen in his brief 22 years of life. His nose inhaled delicious smells from a long row of mobile ovens. His ears were filled by shouts of orders from marines armed with rifles and fixed bayonets who greeted him as he lined up for muster with the rest of his platoon on the endless expanse of dock space that was the port of Lu-Shun.

This welcoming committee in starched camouflage wasn't sadistic or overtly mean-spirited. They were stationed there to enforce discipline and efficiently choreograph the large influx of troops. Due to inter-service rivalry, they were called dot heads by regular PLA soldiers to ridicule them by implying the blood red insignia of crossed daggers over an anchor on the front of their caps was like the red bindi mark of their enemies in India. It was a popular PLA ridicule, though rarely invoked within earshot of dot heads themselves whose motto was **A tiger on the land—A dragon on the sea;** and the marines in China were growing in prestige and popularity. All the more perplexing why they used the American title of marines for these better trained soldiers. Ji-Nan would be thinking of ways to use this to insult them, for now he was tired and still in the middle of chaos.

When one of these dot heads ordered Corporal Ji-Nan to sit and eat, he obeyed without challenge. He slipped off his backpack and randomly chose a seat from the long line of open-air tables. As he did so a young woman in blue overalls and white apron, with a tired smile to match his own fatigue, placed a covered terrine with mouth-watering aromas wafting up directly in front of him. He was both perplexed and pleased. Perplexed because the woman was aged beyond her youth and her pronounced oval cheekbones signified Korean ethnicity. Pleased because when she lifted the cover, he was presented with a Peking Duck—A whole Peking Duck! Brushed and baked in soy sauce, brown sugar and honey. He hadn't eaten one since his mother prepared his farewell feast when he left for the army almost two years ago. Alongside she placed a traditional rice bowl and a vegetable bowl with salted strings beans, carrots and mushrooms. He was allocated only one bottle of Tsingtao beer but had his own personal pot of black tea with unlimited refills.

At first, he ignored his chopsticks and used only his fingers. Ji-Nan was gorging himself on hot savory pieces of duck, eating like a pig. Only as an afterthought did he use the chopsticks to empty his rice and vegetables. When dessert came, he shoved the steamed sugar bun into his mouth in a one hand movement that forced both cheeks to bulge outwards. He licked his fingers clean. If his table manners were first class poleman peasant, his Korean server betrayed no sign of disgust and steadfastly maintained a fixed smile. Frankly, he didn't give a damn what she thought. He would rather be taken for a pig than a fool. Ji-Nan knew when the Chinese army gives you a feast, they expect to be repaid in dangerous work. Now, he just wondered what was next.

One of the hulking marines came up from behind and held his wristwatch in front of Ji-Nan's face. "You have twenty minutes!"

Silently, his Korean server walked over and took him by the hand. As he was being led back to his railway car, he spotted a member from his gun mount, Private Nguyen Diem also in tow behind a Korean server. He called out, "I thought you were saving yourself for Pearls of May?"

"My fiancée is part French. Those people understand this sort of thing," responded Diem with a smirk.

Once back on board, she began walking the length of the railway car searching for an empty space. A cacophony of grunts and groans of bestial ecstasy from those soldiers who consumed their prized ducks faster than he did came from behind the curtains of the occupied ones. Finally, she managed to find an empty compartment. She gently bid him to come inside and pulled the two large curtains closed behind them. With speed and dexterity, she had the fold down seat prepared and sheets retrieved from the overhead drawers. The detachable headrests were improvised as pillows. To improve the ambience, she reached over and pulled down the large window shade. Thus reducing both of them to silhouettes with barely enough light to distinguish each other's features. This proved to be a good thing. Now it was time for some physical therapy.

"What's your name?" asked Ji-Nan, unsure of how much Mandarin she understood.

"Yu Yan," she replied.

"No, No. Your Korean birth name," he demanded, not knowing why he cared, but somehow, he couldn't do this unless he knew; unlike his coupling with fancy whores in limos, he could jump right on one of them with not another thought but his cock. *Maybe I'm growing up.*

Alarmed that this soldier might be displeased with her, she responded in a supplicating voice, "Ji Su—my name is Ji Su. I am grateful to China for giving me sanctuary from the north."

Ji Su immediately began to demonstrate her gratitude by removing her clothes and sliding off her shoes. Totally naked she couched down to unlace his boots. Without wanting to prematurely start groping her, he merely placed his hands on her shoulders to keep his balance as she pulled off his boots and removed his socks. The sensation he felt on his fingertips unsettled him. He permitted his open hands to slide further down her back. The lattice-work pattern of ridged scar tissue confirmed his guess. What crime could this young woman have committed to warrant such a severe punishment? Ji-Nan's thoughts of anticipated sexual pleasures momentarily abandoned him.

In the meantime, the woman undid his belt and pulled down his trousers. Even in the semi-darkness of the compartment she saw he lacked an erection. For this remedy, she removed her dentures, carefully placing them in a small container for safe keeping. This gesture was not lost on Lee. It was surely the brutality of the North Korean regime that was responsible for this. Now he was playing the part of a brut master about to be serviced by a tortured slave. Disgusted, yet knowing he would still use her, he insisted on unbuttoning his own shirt and tossed it in the corner. Once her soft gums and tongue started to work their practiced oral routine, his baser instincts replaced whatever minor outrage and shame he felt.

After all, what soldier of any army in the world turns down an opportunity for sex?

Not wanting to expend his precious twenty minutes on oral sex, he eased the woman back and down. Totally docile in a prone position, she slowly opened her legs. Lee got down in between them and pushed them further apart. Before he mounted her, he slid his hands up the side of her strong torso. His right hand touched another scar, a smaller one. It was obviously a recently healed bullet wound. Then he worked his way up to her firm little breasts. Here he stayed. She wrapped her arms around the back of his neck to keep him there. He thrust into her deep, hard, and relentless until that point of no return—then collapsed back down on her warm but tortured body.

He was too ashamed to know how to even show her a small kindness.

His personal guilt was mounting fast. Lee wondered if he just gave to this poor Korean creature a momentary pleasure as well or inflicted one more invisible scar in addition to her physical ones. Perhaps in another life, a man could count himself fortunate to have such a strong woman of character capable of enduring such inhumanity. It was a relief when he heard whistles from outside the railway car to signal time's up. Sitting quietly in the nude, Ji Su watched him hurriedly get dressed. When she dutifully attempted to assist him in tying his bootlaces, he slid his foot back from her hands.

Accustomed to such gruff treatment, ignoring it she asked, "What is your name soldier?"

Lee felt under such circumstances it would soil his family's honor and be a personal loss of face to give his real name. To transfer the indignity of it all, he substituted a name that belonged to a man he hated. "Woo Haung, Sergeant Woo Haung from the Southern Province of Yunnan," he lied.

"I wish you good luck Woo Haung," said Ji Su. Whether or not she could distinguish a southern Yunnan dialect from a Shanghainese one, or recognized the difference between sergeant and corporal stripes, Ji Su's farewell wish seemed sincere. Not waiting for her to finish dressing, he moved on ahead and stepped off the railway car and again was confronted by a marine.

This time he was pointed to a long line of soldiers waiting to enter a series of connected tents at the pier's end. Before Lee joined the file of soldiers, he glanced over his shoulder to spot Ji Su in service once again as Yu Yan working ovens, getting ready to serve another Peking Duck.

* * *

Entering the first of five enormous tents, Ni-Jan was taken aback. Its physical space could accommodate the Beijing State Circus with the entire troupe performing every individual act in its repertoire simultaneously. A sergeant ordered silence. All eyes focused on the lone officer standing atop of a raised podium in front of a microphone.

"Soldiers, my name is Major General Woo Sheng. The Communist Party of the People's Republic has entrusted me to lead you Patriotic Volunteers on an enterprise of vast consequences for the future of our Motherland. Today we board ships in an experimental training exercise unprecedented since the Ming Dynasty launched Emperor Zhu Di's great treasure voyages of discovery before the barbarians Columbus and Magellan were born. Our mission is to demonstrate China's freedom of navigation rights and ancient lawful hegemony over the South China Sea and Spratly Islands which are now infringed upon by the pirate navies of the United States and their puppets: namely Japan, Vietnam and the Philippines. Soldiers, our duties in such close confinement may at times be difficult, but such adversity is merely the weight of a feather compared to our duty to the Motherland and the Party, which is the weight of a mountain.

Therefore, it is my pleasure to announce upon successful completion of our thirty-day training cruise that will warrant the full love of the Chinese people, you patriotic soldiers shall receive a generous pay bonus and a shortened enlistment service." General Sheng thrust his right fist into the air. "Long Live China!"

On cue every soldier, minus one, responded with the same full-throated chant. Ji-Nan had the presence of mind to elevate his right fist along with the rest of the true believers but kept his mouth shut. Instead, he engaged in thought crimes. His friend Wen alleged China was going to invade an English-speaking country. His troop had mobilized from the Wujang garrison for alleged earthquake assistance and recovery. Now he was promised a pay bonus and a shortened enlistment for a mere 30-day voyage to the Spratly Islands? *Some bullshit is in the air.*

General Sheng waited for the collective third cheer to die down. "I shall now place you under the guidance of Sergeant First Class Gon Toy and his loyal detachment of marines."

The sergeant mounted the podium and saluted the general, then replaced him in front of the microphone. "Patriotic Volunteers of the People's Liberation Army—Listen up! Strip! Shit! Shower! Shave! **MOVE IT!**"

Ji-Nan was given a numbered bin for his clothes and backpack. For a second time in the same afternoon, he was naked. As fast as the tent full of soldiers stripped down, it was not fast enough for their guards. There was no let-up in their staccato bursts of obscene exhortations to hurry. After their belongings were bagged and tagged, everyone was issued a thin towel and a block of coarse soap. Next, this forest of naked men was unceremoniously herded into the adjoining tent in groups of 100. High-speed fans strategically placed about this second tent did nothing to dissipate its malodorous stench of hot steaming feces.

"Find a commode you like and sit on it!" was the collective order.

There was a choice of 100 portable field toilets arranged in military rows; the middle rows were back to back facing the ones along the sides of the tent. Ji-Nan had been in the army long enough to know it was best to approach one backwards and avoid looking down. He was unappreciative of the rim's relaxing warmth. Since all the other naked men sitting in concentration were mostly strangers from unknown units it was easy to detach eye contact and pass time staring up at the tent rafters or down at bare feet. Unfortunately, he was soon recognized by a fellow gun mount crew-member, the Mongolian Private Ba-Hui. The one who always boasted about his extra glandular endowment.

When the two did make eye contact, it gave the Mongolian another opportunity to brag about his one unique attribute. "Hey Lee, how was your duck and fuck? I gave my little Korean a sampan paddle to Heaven's Lake!"

Ji-Nan bolted to his feet. "Those poor Korean creatures risk what's left of their wretched lives to seek sanctuary under the protection of the PRC and what do we do? Turn them into comfort women! We're no better than the fucking Japs!"

With that outburst, group defecation stopped.

All heads swiveled toward the naked man standing there.

Everyone seated knew it was the truth. What made it dangerous was shouting it out loud. It was not too bold an outburst since the guards had voluntarily absented themselves from the shitter tent. It made him feel good to somewhat ease his conscience with a demonstration of real outrage. Still, not stupid enough to keep it up and risk getting informed on, he hurried to the next tent where he lost himself in the anonymity of clouding steam and other showering soldiers. As Ji-Nan soaped down, he wondered if he could ever get himself clean enough. *Why is that fuck bothering me? Her life is her own problem.*

The third tent was palliative.

A sundry kit of toothbrush, paste, razor and tiny mirror were placed on the side of each portable wash basin. It felt good to shave and brush his teeth properly after 11 days of fighting for five minutes of privacy in the railway car's closet bathroom. And it was refreshing to see a clean, healthy face in the mirror. Then the unpleasant thought of Ji Su and venereal disease crossed his mind. *How many soldiers does she service in a day, or for that matter, a week?*

This last tent also involved a medical inspection of sorts. Only eight field medics in pairs handled 25 soldiers at time. One medic operated a laptop and the other wore a stethoscope and blue latex gloves. Their assembly exam began straight away. He was given a cursory exam with the stethoscope on his back and chest.

"Heart rate—65—excellent—blood pressure—116 over 74—normal." A blue latex glove cupped his scrotum. "Cough!" demanded the medic.

Ji-Nan put his hand on the medic's shoulder. "Excuse me but are those Korean servers medically inspected?" He deliberately avoided the politically charged term of comfort women.

"They're supposed to be. When we have adequate staff. Next time test before going in. Squeeze a half a grapefruit over her pussy. If she has any infection or open-sores you'll find out quick enough, because after she stops screaming, she won't let you fuck her anyway. Okay soldier, we're almost finished here, bend over…"

* * *

Finally, back where he started, Ji-Nan collected his bin. His clothes had been laundered and pressed, even his boots were shined. Like it or not, he grudgingly marveled at the efficiency of the PLA.

Once again, shouted orders interrupted his thoughts. "Regardless of rank, form a single file outside on the pier to your left! If you speak or have any knowledge of the English language, report to Colonel Ming's table on the right. Move NOW!"

This last order put hundreds of soldiers in the left line and only five soldiers standing with Ji-Nan on the right line. When it was his turn to be interviewed, he was ordered in English to stand rigidly at attention. Colonel Ming was flanked by two aides. One of whom held up a sign in English and ordered him to translate.

"Sir, the sign says…."

"Drop the extraneous words corporal! Just a straight up translation without qualification or equivocation!" ordered the colonel in perfect English.

Ji-Nan stared at the three large yellow stars enclosed between the two thick yellow lines on the colonel's PLA shoulder boards, and translated, "Leave the city at once—you will not be harmed."

"What English language books have you read?" asked Ming.

"*The Last of the Mohicans* by James Fenimore Cooper and *The Old Man and The Sea*, by Ernest Hemingway," he responded with self-satisfied pride.

"Ever read anything by Orwell?" This question was to see if anyone read subversive material, some wouldn't see through the purpose, but Ji-Nan certainly did.

"No Sir! I've never read any book not on the party's approved list."

"Have you ever visited a country of English-speaking devils?"

"No sir! Not even Hong Kong sir!"

"Then why did you learn to speak the devil's tongue?" demanded Ming.

"It was an extra-curricular study course generously offered by the party at my school in Shanghai. It would have been a sign of gross ingratitude not to avail myself of the party's unselfish contribution for the intellectual benefit of its people to help defeat the foreign devils by using their own language as a weapon against them."

For the first time the colonel smiled. "Why corporal, you have the makings of a fine political officer, especially since we're short of one from the 312th Artillery Regiment. A Major Tone, you must have known him?"

"Yes sir, he personally promoted me to corporal."

"Did he indeed? Perhaps since he held you in such high esteem, you can enlighten us as to the confusing reasons why Major Tone would commandeer a Mengshi personnel carrier and suborn an enlisted man to cross the frontier with him into India without permission."

Blindsided, Ji-Nan stammered around to conjure up some plausible excuse but his mind just went blank. Colonel Ming, evidently in no great rush to hear what he plainly believed to be a perfectly innocent explanation, continued to smile while he lit a cigarette and drew a few relaxing puffs. It turned out to be a tranquil interlude of short duration. A couple marines were dragging Diem over. Dripping with blood, he had been savagely beaten about his face and body with rifle butt strokes and kicked and stomped with hobnailed boots.

"Excuse me Colonel Ming, we caught this traitor trying to stowaway aboard one of those Vietnamese fishing boats."

The colonel examined the semi-conscious soldier's identity tags. "Do you know this traitor as well corporal?"

"No sir!" lied Ji-Nan. Survival was paramount over anything or anyone else.

"Well, it seems your 312th Artillery Regiment is one big rat's nest of traitors. Obviously, you're not expected to know everyone in a 1,000-man regiment, not even the wanted criminal and a fellow Shanghainese named Ku Shen Wen. Now tell me corporal, should I execute this traitor or not?" he asked.

"Sir, any soldier from the 312th Regiment is a highly trained artillerist. If executed, all the party's specialized training investment dies with him. I believe the party would be better served if you impose a ten-year sentence of extra army enlistment service." Survival or not, Lee couldn't bring himself to the outright murder of a decent man.

"That's a very good answer corporal. Only cowardly traitors offer up their own kind for execution to save their worthless skins." Colonel Ming sat down and turned his chair to face the marines. "Wait for the next train, then execute this traitor in front of the new arrivals." Ming turned back to smile at the soldier whose advice he just ignored and saw Ji-Nan was making a superhuman effort not betray a terrified expression. "Oh, relax young soldier! Remember our old saying: *In order to scare the monkeys, you need to kill a chicken.* We're almost finished here, just one more question." Colonel Ming held up two fingers. "How many fingers am I holding up?"

"How many fingers do you want me to say you're holding up colonel?"

"Correct again! You're definitely going places young soldier. I hereby promote you to sergeant 4th class. You're dismissed!"

One of Ming's aides handed the newly promoted Ji-Nan upgraded shoulder epaulettes and an embarkation chit. After getting his papers stamped, he was assigned to his ship. He joined the moving columns of soldiers waiting their turn to board *Leviathan*.

The massive troop embarkation included gangway steps, but more went up the side via hull rope ladders. At a distance the hundreds of climbing soldiers resembled an upward creeping ant infestation overwhelming the ship.

The marines kept a wide gap between the bottom of the ladders and the columns of soldiers waiting to take their turns. This safety precaution prevented any unnecessary broken necks of the soldiers standing underneath from the one out of a hundred or so odd soldiers that lost his balance. This safe space insured that a soldier who accidently took the 180' fall struck only the concrete pier and not another soldier waiting in line to take his turn standing underneath. Ji-Nan realized all the troops were males for this mission. That didn't bode well; females in the PLA made up only 4% of the force and were highly valued, implying this was a very dangerous operation.

He stumbled forward from a harsh push to his back. "Okay soldier, spread your arms out! Grasp the vertical side ropes to hold on. Do not! I repeat—do not attempt to climb up hand-over-hand on the horizontal ropes, or the soldier above you will step on them! Ascend step by step at a normal pace keeping your feet on the horizontal ropes only! Stare straight ahead! Do not look up! Do not look down!"

With his impromptu lesson over, Sergeant Ji-Nan put his foot on the first rung of the rope ladder and pushed himself up. During his ascent he was as scared as the next man but knew no matter how scared the men above him were, it was comforting to know their bowels had been evacuated the hour before. Thereafter, he kept his mind focused on the climb.

By the time he assumed he was halfway up the side of this massive supertanker's hull, his hands started to get moist and slippery. Worse still, the soldier directly above him stopped moving.

A voice from above shouted out a warning, "He's frozen! Sidestep to the left and pass him! Don't try to help him or he'll latch on to you and you'll both drop!"

Not wanting to know how high above the concrete pier he actually was, Ji-Nan kept repeating to himself, *I mustn't look down—I mustn't look down.* He needed to summon courage before he attempted the next maneuver. Ever so cautiously, he made the lateral move to cross over and grab the nearest rope ladder and insert himself into another rising column of men to successfully bypass the panic-stricken soldier. By constantly looking straight ahead at the endless number of steel plates on the side of the ship's hull, he was unaware that his ordeal was nearly over.

Right before he reached the gunwale, two marines leaned over, grabbed him by his backpack and hoisted him aboard the main deck to the sound of a half a million clucking chickens and a few thousand grunting pigs.

As far as the eye could see, the whole length of the middle upper deck of the ship from the bow to the base of the island superstructure was taken up with chicken cages. Underneath them were never ending stalls of pig's pens. The endless number of parallel top deck intake pipes were unsealed, section welded open and pumped with sea water to convert them into live fish tanks. Atop this menagerie was a ship's length canopy of continuous panels supported by scaffolding welded to the main deck that he assumed were solar panels.

"Papers!" demanded the officer of the deck. After a cursory glance at his orders, Ji-Nan was handed a laminated ship's schematic and schedule. The officer pointed brusquely to those highchairs welded along the entire length of the ship's gunwale in a fashion that extended them with a 2' clearance outward from the edge of the hull. "Those are your toilets sergeant! Check your schedule for your main deck authorization time. We can't have the chaos of thousands of soldiers creating unruly mobs fighting for their place in the twice a day meal lines. Report to level B. You're in charge of Troop Section Four. Keep it hygienic and your men disciplined. Any problems you fail to contain call on the marine guards. Clear?!"

"Yes, sir!"

"We're stationed on every deck level stairwell. Remind your men we have no capacity for a stockade aboard. Any serious disciplinary violations will result in the asshole being tossed overboard. Clear?!"

"Yes, sir! Excuse me sir, what about that soldier frozen on the rope ladder?"

"Embarkation of this ship will not be delayed! At this time, we have 17 other weak-willed soldiers from our ship alone frozen on the ropes. If they manage to hold on until we get underway, they'll be hauled aboard like fish caught in a net. Now report to your compartment and take charge!"

"Yes, sir!" Ji-Nan descended by one of the newly installed doghouse hatches that was crudely spot welded into the main deck. Once below, it was three decks down before he located Troop Section Four. Like a giant bee hive curved at the top, the first quarter section of this massive redesigned oil tank had been form-fitted with submarine type coffin beds stacked 15 high and a staggering 100 beds across in a rectangle. In addition to the odor of crude oil residue, it gave the impression he was standing under a center atrium of a claustrophobic apartment complex. Ten corporals approached and in unison came to attention in a semi-circle in front of him and requested their orders of the day. Newly promoted Sergeant Ji-Nan knew he was in way over his head. "Where are our officers?"

The senior corporal pointed to a large speaker box with a wall phone underneath. "Our CO is Captain Pao. His quarters are in the ship's superstructure. I strongly recommend you don't disturb him. We're supposed to be assigned six lieutenants but so far none have arrived. Since you're our senior NCO, we've reserved the bottom bunk for you."

"Thank you. Please see to the men's needs until I get settled."

That last remark was a deliberate stall for time until he could figure out his next move. He wondered how he got from recently discredited low ranking private to trusted sergeant in less than two weeks. *Happenstance, Buddhist Yin and Yang, or because I was born clever in the Year of the Monkey as my zodiac sign foretold.* Then he remembered a Confucian quote Wen like to joke about: *If you are the smartest person in the room—then you are in the wrong room.*

"You should have taken a middle bunk," a voice called out.

Ji-Nan walked over to the lone marine sentry whose duties were to restrict unauthorized access of the ladder wells to the main deck. The marine clicked his polished boots together and came to attention. Unused to being shown such respect, Lee requested him to stand at ease and explain.

"We marines spend a lot of time aboard ships. The bottom bunk is where all the puke splashes down from the higher up seasick soldiers. Though if this convoy gets into a confrontation with the US Navy, where you sleep will be the least of your problems. The military geniuses insisted on squeezing in 5,000 soldiers per deck. To do that, contractors had to cut multiple passageways though the watertight bulkheads. Because these massive oil tanks have been cut open, their watertight integrity is compromised. Prior to all this construction, all 41 of these holding tanks acted like giant life preservers because of the air sealed inside. Not anymore! We get holed below the waterline? This ship will sink like a rock! Once we start taking on water, go lie down in your bunk. Best to make yourself comfortable waiting for the vortex then be trampled to death by thousands of panic-stricken soldiers all rushing for the exits at once."

Woo Haung would have called that defeatist talk. Ji-Nan thought otherwise.

"By the way sergeant, there are approximately 25,000 troops aboard, and I haven't seen one life jacket stored anywhere."

"I see." Ji-Nan was at a loss for words and it wouldn't have made the slightest difference. The marine's dour assessment of the facts confirmed it, he was neither lucky, born a clever monkey, nor the smartest man in the room. They were all pawns and had no idea of what they were being pushed forward into.

Momentarily thrown off balance, he sensed a jarring, pulsating vibration underneath his feet. *Leviathan's* three-story high steam turbines four decks below came to life and began gathering momentum.

I'm definitely going places, but this is ridiculous.

Chapter 9

Revelations

In the anteroom of the West Wing at 1600 Pennsylvania Avenue, three people huddled in conference. Now and then they momentarily lifted their heads to catch a phrase about war in the words of raised voices coming and going from inside the Oval Office. Two of them sat grim faced but their junior member was grinning in thought.

"If you find something amusing about all this Parrott, please do share," said CIA Assistant Deputy Director Lawrence St. John Lowell.

"Sorry sir, it's just the idea of General McMackinaw stalking the corridors for years with a loaded gun concealed in his cane. He was a bit of an eccentric. I guess we should all be thankful he never went postal," Parrott said.

Robert Brown shrugged. "I had that weapon's firing pin secretly disabled the day after he first hobbled into my office. Give me some credit Val. If my job is to keep a running account of the world's nefarious psychopaths arrayed against our God-fearing, peace-loving people, don't you think I have a handle on the multifaceted personality disorders of my own staff?"

Lowell looked impatient and ignored them. "Don't be goaded by the Chief of Staff into self-incrimination or a confession. Once inside the Oval Office, we keep strict adherence to our CIA guideline protocols. We touch nothing domestic."

"Shouldn't that be amended to the strict adherence to the *verisimilitudes* of CIA guideline protocols?" suggested Brown.

"You know Robbie, your team gives me grey hair. So, let me spell it out for you. You, me, Parrott here, and the fucking four walls of this anteroom have no knowledge of, nor have heard of, any rumors that are germane to the

Thunderbolt that went missing. Our Sonora Desert exhumation is, for the record, externally abridged and internally redacted. Have I made myself understood Mr. Head of Strategic Analysis?"

"Let's be precise as a German about this, Mr. Assistant Deputy Director. You are ordering me either to shovel some bedizened bullshit upon POTUS or make a demonstrable flat-out denial of the absolute facts as they exist?" asked Brown.

"I guess when all is said and done, it was a gross oversight on my part. I should have just provided you with a memorandum of understanding to deceive POTUS in an open and notorious subterfuge with my name prominently at the bottom. Robbie, nobody appreciates your years of inestimable service to the company more than myself. In fact, the CIA couldn't possibly manage without you for more than three days. I would personally hate to see your life's work shredded and carried out in a burn bag to the old Fort Meade crematorium. Now let's go in to see POTUS and then let's see if you still have a career when we come out."

As they were ushered in by Burton Rooks they passed several glum-faced USAF generals, senior FBI agents and Homeland Security agents. When their turn came, they were treated like wayward students sent to the principal's office and lined up in front of the large oaken desk which harkened back to Teddy Roosevelt's time. In attendance was Vice President Lejeune, Chief of Staff Dunlap, and off in a corner, military attaché Rear Admiral Langsdale.

President Atwater had previous dealings with Lowell. Brown was known only by reputation; but the tall woman was a blank page to him as well as a pleasant distraction.

"Where's Maulehouse?"

"Mr. President, Director Maulehouse is secluded somewhere along the Aroostook River at his Elk Hair Caddis Rod and Reel Club, exercising his trout fishing rights," answered Lowell.

Everyone in the Oval Office sensed a storm about to break. A question was then put forward as to the whereabouts of Assistant Director Reginald Cairncross. This elicited an uncomfortable pregnant pause. The only man in the room with nothing to lose broke the silence with the unvarnished truth.

"Mr. President," said Lejeune, "I believe Assistant Director Cairncross is entertaining Mrs. Beatrice Van Arnam at her estate in College Park."

"What?! You mean he's with my cousin Bee-Bee? That fucker is pretty damn sure of himself!" Embarrassed and doing a slow burn, the president stared straight at Lowell. "How would you like a promotion?"

"Sir, in the interest of national security and public faith, I would advise against a *coup de main* within the CIA at this time," Brown replied for his stunned boss.

"Nobody asked you to advise us on a damn thing!" snapped Dunlap as he turned from Brown, facing Lowell. "Do you want the fucking promotion or not?" Then he deferentially turned to face the president. "Pardon my French, sir."

"I serve at the pleasure of the president," responded Lowell.

The president shifted his attention, knowing he was being emotional and was just called out on it by Brown; he needed to make a gain quickly for his own ego's sake. So, he left the firing and promotion issue hanging. "Your reputation as an analyst precedes you Mr. Brown. Everybody tells me you're the brains of the outfit. I'll make the reasonable assumption you're a smarter man than myself."

"Mr. President, your methodology of governance, albeit successful, is still subjected to the confines of a rigid engineering construct, though my fallible analysis could simply be dismissed out of hand as a parallax view from the standpoint of our incongruous academic disciplines," responded Brown.

President Atwater smiled and turned to face his Chief of Staff. "Did you hear that J? Mr. Brown politely just said the President of the United States is incapable of thinking outside the box. How come you never council me with such admonitions?"

"Because I'm not a cultural anthropologist anymore then I am a bullshitting unlicensed psychologist, sir," Dunlap retorted.

"That's why I need you J, to keep me anchored in the reality of absolutes." Next the president turned his attention to Valentine. "And what's your story?"

Intimidated for the moment, she just stood there like some child. Her brain was whirling with the pressure to say the right thing.

Lejeune interceded. "Mr. President, Parrott here was my assistant in Louisiana. Her tireless campaign efforts helped put me over the top on my second successful senatorial race. She was also the brightest student I ever taught when I was a professor at LSU."

"Now I'm familiar with your name. You come from a long line of naval heroes," said the president.

The momentary spell of presidential intimidation was broken and she found her voice. "Mr. President, my Louisiana ancestors served in every armed conflict since The War of 1812. My namesake relation, George Fountain Parrott was the only naval officer killed in the First World War. They christened a destroyer in his memory, the *USS Parrott*. Unfortunately, it was sunk in a collision off Norfolk during the Second World War."

"I don't mean to be too personal, but is that why you didn't take your husband's surname?"

"No Mr. President, I did it for my father's legacy. He has no male heirs."

"Felt it was bad luck to follow in your family's naval traditions then?"

"No sir, I found my talents have advanced enough to decide I would do my country more service in the CIA than as a token on a ship's bridge."

The president had a full plate of worries and needed to keep things moving along. "Now as you all may have guessed, I didn't convene this meeting to chat about personal family issues. Therefore, kindly be seated, we have very important actions to discuss."

Atwater waited for everyone to be comfortably seated. Only his Chief of Staff remained standing. "I've tail ended you CIA people in here under the guise of another wholesale reprimand that was administered to all culpable state, military, and domestic agencies for their gross incompetence regarding my near miss assassination attempt and failed attack against New York City, which I have been informed was narrowly averted only by intelligence sharing from China. Before we begin this meeting, indulge me for a moment. Back when I was a serving officer in the U.S. Navy, we heard atomic bomb doomsday tales passed down from the 1950s. One was about an early warning radar operator on an old propeller Lockheed AWACS on a routine patrol in the south Atlantic. New at his job, and due to cold war tension at the time, he was understandably alarmed when his radar screen suddenly lit up like a Christmas tree with multiple sonar blips. Convinced the entire Soviet Fleet was heading for the eastern seaboard of the United States, he initiated attack warning protocols that advanced so far up the chain of command as to get President Eisenhower out of bed. By a hair's breadth America survived an attack from the Azores; the islands were misinterpreted as an invading Russian armada. I wonder if the ambassadors from the Netherlands and India have requested crash meetings today for a similar overreaction. Both countries claim to have unique intelligence of a bizarre and calculating subterfuge underway by the very nation we owe an indeterminable debt of gratitude to. Before I inform the joint chiefs and members of congress what is about to be revealed, I need the analysis of the most astringent mind in my Central Intelligence Agency—that means you Brown. I need to know if I am facing another potential Cuban Missile Crisis or just islands causing a radar blip?"

President Atwater motioned to Dunlap. "J, can you kindly escort the Dutch ambassador and his guest into the Oval Office."

Dunlap stepped outside and exchanged a few words with Rooks, who then escorted in two men who had been waiting in the anteroom even before Brown, Parrott and Lowell arrived. The most striking of the pair was the large bearded man in a naval uniform who contrasted with the average sized one in a Baroni pinstripe. Formal introductions were made by Dunlop.

"Mr. President, Mr. Vice President, Admiral Lansdale, and our CIA contingent, I have the honor to present his Excellency Cornelius Ver Der Zwain, His Majesty's Ambassador Extraordinary and Plenipotentiary of the Kingdom of the Netherlands. In attendance is Captain Voss of The Royal Dutch Maritime Navy."

After handshakes all round, everyone was seated. Ambassador Van Der Zwain came straight to the point in uncharacteristic bluntness. "Mr. President, through unimpeachable sources it has been revealed by the diligence of Captain Voss here, that a provocative and surreptitious military invasion of Taiwan is either in its advanced stages of preparation or already underway by China."

Langsdale interrupted, "With all due respect Mr. Ambassador, the PRC may have the world's largest land mass army but it can't march across water.

They simply don't have a navy adequate to transport and sustain logistical support for massive amounts of troops and materials for this level of seaborne invasion."

"Beg your pardon admiral," spoke up President Atwater, "I'm incredulous too, but I believe this captain is here to validate some facts."

"And I believe the captain is going to scare the hell out of us with a tale of supertankers reconfigured into Trojan horses," said Parrott, remembering her son's comment about the supertanker's potential of moving whole communities all over the world.

"You are quite perceptive," responded Captain Voss. "Furthermore, I can't overemphasize that the circumstances of acquiring this information were obtained at the cost of a man's life. He was a friend who was literally murdered at my feet."

"Just what were those circumstances?" inquired Brown. "Was he a crewmember of your ship?"

"The man was the official PRC's language interpreter aboard the three-ship convoy of tankers I was contracted to deliver to the port of Lu-Shun. He divulged the invasion plans for Taiwan under the code name *Lông Pán* or its translation: Dragon's Coil. For taking me into confidence, he was thrown from my former ship's bridge, four hundred feet above the pier," related Voss.

"Captain, you called this interpreter your friend. In that context, are you simply referring to him as that due to a shipboard courtesy?" asked Brown.

"The man's name was Qu Xing, and he saved me from going permanently deaf when I misplaced my ear protectors during a maintenance procedure in the ship's machinery spaces," answered Voss.

"There is not the slightest doubt in your mind this interpreter might not have deliberately misplaced your ear protectors on the pretext to ingratiate himself with you? Then once he planted his scripted false narrative, your so called *friend* was unfortunately hoisted on his own petard? A victim in a stage-managed death by his own government to enhance his credibility and your own gullibility? Furthermore, I find it highly suspicious that a low level interpreter would be privy to such a military operation, especially since you were all isolated in Norway for over a year." Brown tapped his fingers in thought.

"May I ask in what capacity are you interrogating me sir?"

"As head of the strategic analysis department of my country's Central Intelligence Agency."

"So, making me out to be a fool is doing your job? You're quite the professional."

"With respect, your expertise is commanding the world's largest ships on the high seas. Mine is completing puzzles. Your piece doesn't fit captain," answered Brown calmly.

President Atwater decided to table this meeting. "Mr. Ambassador, time constraints now force me to investigate this through our military and national security venues. Thank you for bringing it to our attention. Can Captain Voss be available for a briefing at the Pentagon with the joint chiefs?"

"Of course, Mr. President, but Captain Voss has been in transit for nearly ninety-six hours; from Vladivostok to Amsterdam to briefings in The Hague and now here to Washington. Will he have time for a few hours rest before the joint chiefs meet?" asked the ambassador.

When Brown heard the word Vladivostok, he violated protocol and raised his voice over the president and ambassador. "Captain Voss! Did you talk to the Russians!?"

Before he had a chance to respond, Parrott followed suit and raised her voice. "Captain Voss! Did your convoy sink a Namibian gunboat?"

Alarmed by the two questions, Ambassador Van Der Zwain interceded at once. "His Majesty's government has no knowledge of, and abstains from, all questions along this line of inquiry."

"I understand completely Mr. Ambassador and once more thank you for coming," said the president who seemed as perplexed as the Dutch ambassador was distressed by those quick questions. Nevertheless, they both shook hands to formally end the meeting.

Captain Voss, ever his own man, defied his ambassador and loudly spoke out in the doorway, "Yes, to both your questions!"

Langsdale followed the Dutchmen out of the Oval Office and closed the door behind him. Afterwards, there was a moment of reflective silence until the president said, "You know, nothing irritates the shit out of me more than that *faux* term Pennsylvania Dutch."

"Quite correct Mr. President, it should be Pennsylvania *Deutsch*. It was the writer Henry Miller who said, *Germans make bad Germans but they make good Americans*," responded Robert Brown.

"And I have a sneaking suspicion the good captain is going to be dry-docked for the foreseeable future when he gets back home," commented Dunlap. "What were you thinking Brown? And you Parrott? Both points hit home, so clear it up for us."

"Enough! Whatever depth of crisis is coming our way the window of opportunity for dealing with it is closing as we speak!" said Atwater. "Just get the goddamn Indian ambassador in here now!"

Before the ambassador of India was escorted into the Oval Office, he thought he caught the words *goddamn Indian ambassador* but diplomatically kept a neutral expression. Mr. Raghavan maintained strict protocol by shaking hands with only the President and Vice President. The four others in the room were obviously below the rank of a credentialed ambassador. When you grow up within a rigid caste system of one billion people, social equality is not an ingrained ethos and placement before others is paramount.

"Mr. President, let me first convey that this impromptu meeting to which you have generously allotted me is most appreciative by Prime Minister Arjun Naidu. Prime Minister Naidu does feel the intelligence I will share will more than validate my government's post haste imposition on the good offices of your presidency, and by extension the government of the United States and its people."

"Thank you, Mr. Ambassador. Rest assure the concerns of Prime Minister Naidu are my concerns as is the welfare and safety of both our nations' peoples," said President Atwater, though he sensed that welfare and safety may soon be in doubt. Furthermore, whatever was about to be revealed, the previous ambassador had laid down some somber groundwork indicating the seriousness of what was going on.

Ambassador Raghavan felt the need to preserve his reputation as a sound diplomat not given over to precipitous and alarmist tendencies, even at the behest of his own government. So, to reinforce his role as mere intermediary, he opened a leather dispatch case and played mailman. Removing the enclosed communiqué, he read it in a dignified cadence:

"From Army Chief of Staff, General J.J. Singh to Prime Minister: Top Secret--your eyes only--approximately 03:35 hundred hours Saturday April 26ˢᵗ last. Commanding Officer Colonel Doogal Vidal Kumar of the Gulmarg High Altitude Acclimation School in the Northern State of Himachal Pradesh reported two Chinese soldiers from the People's Liberation Army of the 312ᵗʰ Artillery Regiment from the border outpost of Wujang unlawfully crossed the disputed area along the Sino-Indian frontier in a stolen personnel carrier and surrendered themselves to the Officer of the Guard Post. Both soldiers whose names and ranks were redacted for their own personal safety have subsequently submitted statements—"

"Excuse me Ambassador Raghavan, time is of the essence, may we get to the damn point!" interrupted Atwater in uncharacteristic temper.

Shaken, the ambassador blurted out, "Massive troop landing—code named: *Yôngbáo. Translation:* Close Embrace, using tankers to transport soldiers to the west coast of the USA."

Incredulous, the president began to laugh out loud. The CIA agents were looking at each other in alarm, not laughing at all.

"Mr. Ambassador, where are these two soldiers now?" asked Brown.

Caught off guard at that question, the president abruptly tamped down his mirth. The very fact his CIA analysts took this communiqué seriously was more than unsettling.

"To avoid any further antagonizing diplomatic incidents with our Chinese border rival, the two soldiers were quickly spirited out of India to the country of their choosing."

"And what country was that?" Val asked.

"Luxembourg. Where these two had private bank accounts. There, they have since caused further consternation. They have hacked hundreds of their ex-compatriot's hidden accounts and redirected the assets to their own accounts! They went from being common soldiers to billionaires with just a few keystrokes. Our intelligence reports the two plan on chartering an investment bank. The Chinese businessmen who had their accounts drained have no redress to Luxemburg authorities because doing so would expose their financial theft to Beijing which prosecutes economic crimes as a capital offence. The government in turn cannot make any legitimate claim to these assets as stolen revenue belonging to the Chinese people without causing a national scandal involving their party members who were many of the account holders. Such a revelation could bring down the CCP. Lastly, Luxemburg stands to gain higher tax revenue from an investment bank than the paltry quarterly fee charged for each individual account. These defector thieves were very clever," summarized Ambassador Raghavan.

Brown had heard enough. He quickly stood up. "Mr. President, you must mobilize the First Marine Division at Camp Pendleton at once. They are the only significant military force we can deploy on such short notice. The Second Marine Division is stationed aboard ships in the Mediterranean and the Third is scattered between Japan, Okinawa, Guam and The Philippines. Equally useless to our immediate defense is the 82nd Airborne squatting at Fort Bragg in North Carolina and the 101st Air Cavalry at Fort Campbell on the borders of Kentucky and Tennessee. We must repel this invading force before it lands; destroying it at sea!"

"Now just hold on a goddamn minute!" exclaimed Dunlap. "Mr. President you can't seriously consider throwing the country into wholesale panic on the hearsay of two Chinese from some god-forsaken shithole outpost on the other side of the world?!"

After being initially laughed at, Ambassador Raghavan looked to salvage some diplomatic honor by voicing his support of Dunlap. "Mr. President, I second your chief of staff's skepticism. Though I was ordered as a servant of my country to present the aforementioned communiqué, I believe it's blown out of proportion."

"Of operatic proportions," interjected Dunlap.

"Mr. President," continued the ambassador, "we have a steady stream of Chinese soldiers who routinely cross our frontiers to escape the harsh drudgery of military life under an authoritarian regime. Every one of these deserters come predisposed with embellished tales of planned invasions of my own country. They will say anything to make themselves credible just to guarantee their asylum. Take for instance the latest batch of deserters from two weeks ago. All four of them complained of being forced to eat English cans of pet food. All come with wild rumors, perhaps even planted ones to sow confusion among China's enemies, but rumors nonetheless."

"And the Chinese are sewing confusion right here in the Oval Office amongst ourselves. Mr. Dunlap, your loyalty is not lost on anybody in this room, but there are no enemies here," pleaded Brown, uncharacteristically endeavoring to make a supreme effort to show good manners.

President Atwater started to feel he was losing control of this extraordinary meeting and the balanced judgment of his staff and advisors. His first order of business was to courteously show the Indian ambassador the door as rapidly as decorum permitted. "Mr. Ambassador, I am, of course, less than pleased with this disruptive communiqué Prime Minister Naidu has passed on to us. He naturally wished to error on the side of caution. Nevertheless, if your advanced intelligence is instrumental in the thwarting any acts of war against the US, India and its people will forever enjoy our eternal gratitude and respect. Thank you for coming sir."

With no further ado, the middle-aged man was ushered out the door. Whether he was out of earshot or not was the least worry of the chief of staff. He jumped right in and let his outrage get the better of him. "Well Mr. Head of Strategic Analysis, how and where is this Chinese army going to descend upon us? In a two-pronged pincer movement across the Aleutian Islands, down from Alaska like the Japs in '42? Or are they coming up Baja after, of course, they seize the Panama Canal?"

"No! They're simply going to sail right through our unlocked backdoor. Those supertankers are five football fields long. The maximum amount of human beings you can squeeze into one football field is six thousand people. Multiply that by five decks multiplied by the number of supertankers they have. Do the math! Once this landing force comes ashore and gains a foothold inside a major west coast city and holds it hostage—it's the classical Chinese army strategy successfully employed against the Japanese in Manchuria they called The Close Embrace! Didn't you hear the Indian ambassador reveal the operational code name: *Yôngbáo*? You lock horns with your enemy in such close quarters an adversary cannot bring their artillery and air force to bear without endangering their own troops and/or civilians. Once these Chinese soldiers either capture or hold hostage a major American city—how do you extract them?"

"*Close Embrace*? Are you trying to explain a war strategy or a love story, Brown? If the Chinese dare invade America, we'll just envelope it in a cloud of sarin gas to exterminate them all like cockroaches and save the infrastructure from any real collateral damage," mocked Dunlap.

"Well, that would certainly solve *half the problem*," interrupted Lejeune.

Stunned to find the Vice President had turned against him, Dunlap looked towards the only friend he had left in the Oval Office. "Alex, you can't possibly entertain this preposterous bullshit scenario?"

Undeterred, Brown pursued his hypothesis. "Mr. President, the PRC's strategic long term goal is most certainly Taiwan, but with its infrastructure intact! Not destroyed in the carnage that would surely result between any invading and defending forces."

"Not if we get the Seventh Fleet there first! Ring the whole damn island of Taiwan similar to the 1962 blockade of Cuba," exclaimed the frustrated Dunlap.

"Is everybody not understanding what I'm saying?" shouted Brown.

President Atwater answered for the group. "As I understand your theory, you're emphatically trying to convince us that the Chinese government is planning to blatantly seize and occupy an American city! Then hold it hostage until we agree to their terms of a negotiated Taiwanese surrender."

"Exactly Mr. President; like Czechoslovakia was handed over to Hitler in the Munich Agreement, which failed to stop the outbreak of the war anyway."

"Well just suppose for the purpose of argument we acquiesce to their demands. China's annexation of Taiwan goes off smoothly. After Chinese troops occupy and hold hostage an American city, they expect us to let their invading fleet just sail unmolested back to China?"

Lejeune spoke up. "Suppose for a minute they don't give a rat's ass about the soldiers they send on this mission. Taiwan is high stakes for them. Once that island co-op is *a fait accompli* why wouldn't the Chinese consider their expeditionary force expendable? Their current population is one billion point four people. What's a loss of a few thousand troops to that?"

Brown bolstered the Vice President's argument. "I totally concur. The assessment is brutally true. It is worth remembering during the Korean War Mao Zedong threw away his entire 204th Army Division by ordering them to make a full frontal assault on the US's entrenched positions at the battle of Heartbreak Ridge simply because he thought them disloyal. Mao was beside himself with joy when our B-29s carpet bombed what was left of the survivors."

With all eyes calming down and now on him, Brown added, "What we haven't considered is the desertion factor. Once those troops manage to gain a foothold ashore, I seriously doubt the troops sardined in those supertankers have any idea where they're going or their true mission. This opens an opportunity to flip them."

Lowell spoke up to raise the dreaded final option. "I hope we can rule out nuclear blackmail? Suppose each of those tankers contains nuclear weapons?"

To everyone's relief, Brown said, "If such weapons were concealed inside the hulls, why bring massive amounts of troops to accompany them? Besides it's just too dangerous. If one of those supertankers were to sink, regardless of safeguards, the low quality nukes China builds would all pressure detonate at 80 fathoms. Also, Beijing must know if they let one go either by design or accident, we would blow China back to the Pleistocene era and survivors would have to start from scratch."

"Suppositions, nothing but suppositions and ill-defined ones at that," exclaimed Dunlap. "Mr. President, let's haul Ambassador Xiao's ass in here right now for some enhanced interrogation."

"That is a colossally stupid, time-wasting idea Jerome!"" said Lowell who, despite the gravity of the situation, enjoyed cutting the chief of staff off at the knees in calling him by his off limits Christian name. "Chinese diplomats are sure to lie and continue to sow discord. They are trained for this; whether they know a damn thing about Dragon Coil or not, they will feed us a load of crap."

Then he turned to his senior analyst. "Tell the president what you know Robbie! Tell 'em every goddamn thing!"

Released from his gag order, Brown held nothing back.

"Mr. President, your recent assassination attempt was an elaborate two-fold hoax against you. First, by being informed of the attempt on your life by the Chinese themselves, you would naturally feel indebted to them and blindsided to their true machinations. Second, it was not a too veiled threat to let you know that you and any American city are not immune from the long reach of the PRC. It's an admonition not to interfere with their global designs. They are the puppet masters who organize, finance and dispatch or in this most recent demonstrable event, restrain and even thwart the fanatic missions of their Islamic terrorist proxies. The Chinese are the ones paying the pipers, and the Chinese are the ones calling the tune."

"Mr. Brown, if my life is in such easy reach and depends on China's good will, maybe I should just dismiss my secret service and go into hiding," said Atwater.

Brown ignored the president's look of doubt. "Through our own independent investigation, we can directly link Beijing to the intrigue around the whole missing A-10 aircraft affair that attempted to attack your helicopter, and the Chinese were the ones that sabotaged it at the moment of attack. The leaving of a witness sure to implicate Muslims, and the reason you are more important to the PRC alive right now, rather than having Lejeune assume your role; these are all planned out. As I said, Mr. President, it was an elaborate hoax to deflect you from their true intentions."

"Now wait just a goddamn minute!" again interrupted Dunlap, unable to flex enough to embrace a theory that would rock his world view, so he attacked on process and not facts. "So, the CIA bypassed every lawful governmental agency and kept them out of the loop, not to mention breaking all manner of federal statutes and your own CIA guideline protocols involving domestic ventures?"

"Through the work of our diligent field agents at Davis-Monthan Air Force Base, we identified the body as Huang Li, a low-level cryptography specialist attached to the Los Angeles Chinese consulate. He was probably coerced into their plans to facilitate the theft and disappearance of the aircraft. A postmortem indicates he suffered death by electrocution. Not surprisingly, within twenty-four hours a Chinese national with that identical name stamped on his passport passed through customs at LAX and hopped a Shenzhen airline flight back to Beijing." Brown finally leaned back to assess the others.

"And this is the sum total of your in-depth analysis Mr. Brown? The rational on which I should convince the joint chiefs to take us from DEFCOM-4 to DEFCOM-2?" queried the president who was now so over-whelmed with the idea he could be assassinated easily that his brain was overriding logic.

Brown made one more attempt to totally convince the president. "Over the last year the PLA has undergone intensive English language training to identify canned food labels. You heard the Indian ambassador say as much. When they invade their intended city, it will be a onetime surprise landing. The Chinese troops that successfully come ashore must know they'll be on their own with no support or supplies forthcoming. No second wave after their initial one. How long do you think one hundred thousand or so Chinese soldiers are capable of logistically sustaining themselves?"

Nobody in the Oval Office, not even the acerbic Dunlap dared crack a joke about these invading soldiers ordering from a Chinese takeout, but it did float through some minds.

Lejeune was clearly becoming alarmed. This worst-case scenario was beginning to sound all too plausible to him; and worse, he was seeing Atwater start to crumble.

"Do you have any more revelations?" Dunlap asked.

Out of patience, Brown's response was abrupt. "Locking in rings!"

"What?!" asked the President.

"Locking in rings! The radar operator who mistook the Azores for an invading Russian fleet. He simply neglected to fully insert his oscilloscope— locking in rings that would have enabled him to accurately determine if the blips on his 1950s era analog screen were reflecting a moving or stationary object. Due to the operator's procedural error, he thought the islands were moving along with the AWACS aircraft."

"Thank you, Mr. Brown. The US Navy has been trying to clear up that mystery for over seventy years. At the first opportunity I'll inform the navy of your due diligence," remarked Atwater.

Then the special red button linking a landline directly to the Pentagon began silently flashing. Atwater lifted the receiver and listened. After a five-minute one-way conversation, the president's only response was, "Yes admiral, tell the joint chiefs we're on our way."

Atwater put the phone down and solemnly addressed the group. "Events have forced our hand. The Pentagon has received NSA satellite confirmation that three Batillus supertankers with troops jam packed on their main decks have departed the port of Lu-Shun. NSA has no way of confirming the number of troops that might be concealed below decks but high-end estimates could be as much as thirty thousand per ship. This convoy is expected to rendezvous with China's navy in the Korean Bay. Coincidentally, the South Sea fleet is now sailing northwest, presumably to position their power inside the Formosa Strait."

"Mr. President, does the NSA have any reports of supertanker convoys in the Sea of Japan sailing due east?" asked Brown.

"None, except for an unusually high concentration of fishing vessels, container ships and ferry boats. But no tankers in that area of the Pacific Ocean. So, we needn't worry about a west coast invasion of the United States. As we speak, Admiral Olendoft has sent our Seventh Fleet at flank speed with orders to protect and defend Taiwan and if need be, blockade, challenge or sink any ship with hostile intentions entering the Formosa Strait."

"Mr. President! For the Love of God—it's a fucking feint! At this very minute an unknown number of supertankers using the latest application of satellite countermeasures is heading toward our shores! Technology sold by the Pakistanis when they salvaged the stealth Blackhawk helicopter that was lost during Operation Geronimo to kill Osama Bin Laden. I'm positive there are troop-carrying supertankers embedded in that Jackson Pollock seascape shit-show that are California bound! Just confirm the speed of those three supertankers that recently left the port of Lu-Shun. I bet they're not making anywhere near their top speed of 16 knots. The Chinese are giving us all the time in the world to denude the Pacific of our Seventh Fleet and lure them into the Formosa Strait which was China's deceptive plan all along. It's classical Sun Tzu: *We must make the enemy believe we are far away. When far away, we must make him believe we are near, attack him where he is unprepared, appear where you are not expected.*"

"We've all had enough of your Dr. Fu Manchu inscrutable East subterfuge theories!" yelled the exasperated chief of staff.

"Why does every US President look for every opportunity to imitate that overrated JFK blockade of Cuba and then claim he saved the world from nuclear holocaust?" said Brown quietly, deliberately ignoring Dunlap's taunts; staring directly at Atwater.

"Overrated JFK blockade? Care to explain how avoiding World War Three was overrated?" Atwater felt he had lost all control of his CIA agents; all control over forcing an invasion of California and his own assassination into the shadows. Atwater was losing focus. He was becoming weak and confused, feeling like Jimmy Carter; a comparison political pundits always brought up.

"In 1962 World War Two was only 18 years settled. Russia had lost over 25,000,000 of its people! Mr. President, do you actually think Soviet Premier Khrushchev who had personally experienced the first hand devastation of his country in that war was going to ultimately destroy it all in a third? For some fucking flyspeck island in the Caribbean 6,000 miles away from Moscow?" responded Brown in an almost pleading tone.

"Okay we're done here!" said Dunlap. "Come Mr. President, Mr. Vice-President, the limousine for the Pentagon arrived." He turned to face the three CIA antagonists. "You can all show yourselves out after we leave. In fact, you can all leave your resignations behind when you do."

After that last remark, Parrott made deliberate eye contact with Lejeune whose facial expression telegraphed subdued contempt. Parrott interpreted it to mean the chief of staff was talking rot, engaging in impotent scorn, and full of bullshit. Reassured she still had a job; Parrott was first to come to her feet followed Lowell then Brown, the three standing shoulder to shoulder out of respect until the country's top executives exited the Oval Office.

After a decent interval of time, Lowell smiled. "I believe within a week or two the president is the one who's going to be out of a fucking job. When this national debacle unfolds, Triple A will be lucky enough to secure a posting as a second-class office clerk."

Val nodded, feeling back on steady ground with Brown leading the way. They would keep doing their jobs, just as the institutions were set up; and the weakness of the president and the foolishness of the chief of staff would be overcome by the processes set in place to safeguard this country. Or she very much hoped so, for the sake of her children.

Lowell spoke up again. "Personally, I think it would be most propitious for the agency if The Crawfish of St. Bernard's Parish, and Parrott's special friend, is put in charge of things. In the interim, I suggest we should all return to Langley and send a coded flash to Major-General Heimiller and suggest he cancel all leaves and activate an emergency base recall for his First Marine Division. Then I'll have to interrupt our Doyen of Beacon Hill, Director Maulehouse, from his holiday of trout fishing and inform him of the likelihood that the US is about to be invaded for the first time since the War of 1812. Now, as to the immediacy of our dilemma. It would be a futile attempt to countermand the president's order sending the Seventh Fleet on their fool's errand to encircle Taiwan. I'm sure once I explain the dire situation to Director Maulehouse, he'll sign off on activating our deep cover Mr. Hydes in naval operations to cut some priority orders for a squadron of fast frigates out of Bremerton Naval Base currently in transit for the Panama Canal. We must turn those ships around and make all possible speed to take station along the California coast."

With Lowell's nod at this plan of action, they started to file out of the Oval Office. As an afterthought, he asked, "So where are they coming in at Robbie? LA? San Diego? Or San Fran?"

"Probably the city by the bay; its harbor is deep enough to accommodate Batillus supertankers. Plus, the natural geography of the city makes it ideal for encirclement and isolation," answered Brown. He stopped to open his briefcase and removed an old-fashioned typed letter, slightly yellowed and encased in a clear plastic cover. Brown placed it squarely on the president's desk.

Out of curiosity, Lowell leaned over to give what turned out to be an 80 year old confidential document a quick perusal. "Jesus Robbie! That's below the belt for our ex-navy president. I guess the penalty for ignoring your warnings is to remove a layer of skin!"

CONFIDENTIAL 10465

From: Chief of Naval Operations
To: Commander-in-Chief, Pacific Fleet
Office of the Chief of Naval Operations Op16-F-2
(SC)A16-3/EF37 Serial No. 09716 Feb. 1, 1941

Subject: Rumored Japanese attack on Pearl Harbor

1.   The following is forwarded for your information: Under date of 27 January the American Ambassador at Tokyo telegraphed the State Department to the following effect: "The Peruvian Minister has informed a member of my staff that he has heard from sources, including a Japanese source, that in the event of trouble breaking out between the United States and Japan, the Japanese intend to make a surprise attack against Pearl Harbor with all of their strength and employing all of their equipment. The Peruvian Minister considered the rumors fantastic. Nevertheless, he considered them of sufficient importance to convey this information to a member of my staff."

2.   The Division of Naval Intelligences places no credence in these rumors.

Furthermore, based on known date regarding the present disposition and employment of Japanese naval and army forces, no move against Pearl Harbor appears imminent or planned for in the foreseeable future.

    Jules James, Op-16F By Direction, Op-16-F-2
    Dictated Jan. 31, 1941
    Lieut. Comdr. A. H. McCollum typed by K. E. Morse
    CC – Com 14 10466. (SC)A16-3/EF37

Chapter 10

The Sea Dragon

Approximately 232 nautical miles mid-point from Japan's southernmost island of Kyushu and directly north of Okinawa, the Japanese destroyer *Hamagiri DD-155* was vigilantly patrolling her home waters. During a calm non-typhoon season, this area of the western Pacific seemed to be inexplicably pockmarked with floundering Chinese sailors and commercial fishermen. The ocean seemed to be overcrowded with lifeboats and desperate survivors clinging to makeshift rafts. The night sky had become a virtual meteor shower from the arcing trajectories of multiple firings of distress flares. Luckily for a number of these hapless drifting seamen, Petty Officer Megata was assigned night watch due to his uncanny night vision. Standing watch as starboard bridge lookout, as soon as he spotted another arcing flare shooting across the horizon-line he spoke into the microphone harnessed to his chest. "Bridge—starboard lookout reports distress flare zero-two-zero relative."

Immediately the officer of the bridge ordered the chief bosun's mate to turn on the topmost beacon searchlight. He deftly manipulated the joystick which in turn rotated a servo arm that directed a hybrid halogen/xenon cone of 2,500 Watts of light 750' in length with a 50' swath. The full incandescence of the searchlight's powerful lens created the optical illusion of a shooting comet tail in a low Earth orbit. To the overjoyed men in the water, the beacon of light that materialized out of the black void heralded their salvation.

"Easy, chief! Aim the searchlight slightly off center to the survivors' last known position," said Lieutenant Shinohara. "Let's not save their lives only to risk blinding them in the process."

"Aye, aye sir," responded the bosun.

"Bridge—starboard lookout identifies what seems to be a floundering life raft with a dozen or so men aboard," reported Megata, whose voice came through the bridge loudspeaker.

"Very well," acknowledged Shinohara as he hung up the intercom mike with one hand, and with the other picked up the bridge phone and buzzed the combat-information-center two decks below to notify Captain Kunikata.

Instead, his call was intercepted by the harsh speaking and highly annoyed XO Lieutenant Commander Azuma who responded with utter distain. "Again!? That's the third group we've fished out today! Listen to me! All survivors are to be hosed down on the fantail. They are to be allocated only tea and rice. You're authorized to issue one blanket each. Furthermore, these witless Chinese swine are to be confined inside the helicopter deck under armed guards. Under no circumstances are they to be permitted below decks. That goes for any injured as well. All medical assistance is to be administered topside. You have your orders Shinohara! And don't bother Captain Kunikata or me again!"

In response to the questioning looks of the sailors, Shinohara said, "Don't disturb them. The captain and XO are focused on monitoring events around the confrontation between the American and Chinese build up around Taiwan. They're disappointed to be sidelined from such a defining historical event." He ordered the bosun to set the searchlight on automatic and pipe ship's company over the intercom to brace for a short radius turn and head for the raft.

Within 15 minutes of *Hamagiri's* new course and speed correction, the raft and its occupants were close. The beacon was shut down and the ship's portside floodlights kicked in. It was at this point Megata was almost bowled over by a drifting, sea-level cloud of sulfur dioxide. A rotten egg smell, only it smelled like there were millions of them. Either that, or his destroyer had inadvertently sailed into a sea of unflushed toilets. Megata began to cough violently but remained at his station. This smell was even more pronounced in the area where the rescue party had mustered.

Once the destroyer's hull came alongside the exhausted men struggling to hold onto their overcrowded raft, an all engine stop order was given. Now it was a simple matter for survivors to haul themselves up and grasp the gangway handrails. The smell was followed by the disgusting visual of floating shit that coated the ocean's surface.

Assisted by the boat crew up the short gangway steps, the rescue went smoothly. Survivors pulled from the sea are expected more or less to have a ragged appearance but the condition of these fishermen was downright repellent. Master Chief Yutaka had to direct the rescue then interrogate the feces-covered survivors with his less than 50-word Mandarin vocabulary. In addition, he established a makeshift triage for those suffering from dehydration and exposure. Trying to maintain a semblance of military order despite the miasma that surrounded him had one beneficial effect. It kept him too busy to succumb to vomiting himself.

Shinohara thought it best to come down from the enclosed bridge and give himself a first-hand progress report of how the rescue efforts were proceeding. Immediately, he found himself utterly repelled by the vile odor emanating from the portside deck. When Yutaka saw the queasy facial expression on the approaching officer, he gave a short salute, then offered him a lemon wedge.

"Chew on this sir. It's more effective than Dramamine." Shinohara eagerly accepted, and bit down to get every ounce of the acidic juice to coat his stomach.

"These Chinese all tell the same story sir. Beijing ordered all available ships to sea regardless if they were seaworthy or in need of repairs from small to major. That's why we see such an inordinate number of shipwrecked survivors floating about. Quite a few of them have been making wild claims other boats were lost with all hands. They say in the dead of night, supertankers with no running lights, not blasting their fog horns, just plowed right through their trawling nets and dragged them under. Look over here, sir." The master chief leaned over the ship's handrails and pointed to the sticky brown strip that traced along the waterline for the entire length of the 450' hull. "Captain Kunikata would commit *seppuku* if he knew the side of his ship was painted with shit. The whole ocean around us as far as the eye can see is filled with floating turds. It must be the Chinese or the North Koreans. If we assume they're responsible, then they're waging biological warfare against us to poison our fishing grounds. I've served 23 years in the Emperor's Navy and I've never experienced anything like this."

"Neither have I," said Shinohara. After he received Yutaka's parting salute for the last time of his life, he turned to seek refuge inside the climatized bridge. He never made it.

AAW – AAW – AAW – AAW- AAW– Sounded the ear grating collision alarm. Out of the night void an immense bulbous bow bore down on the Japanese destroyer's starboard side. For a split-second Shinohara felt the deck shift under his feet. Then a horrendous impact radiated shockwaves throughout every compartment and space of the ship. The full kinetic impact of thousands of tons of raw steel from the two colliding ships attempted to overcome the laws of physics by both occupying the same space at the same time. In the first catastrophic impact of grinding and buckling the *Hamagiri* was upended on her starboard beam by a tanker 100 times her size. The destroyer instantly heeled over past her center of buoyancy to the point of no return. The collateral violence of the supertanker's bow crashing into the smaller ship had snapped Lieutenant Shinohara's neck which instantly caused his legs to collapse. He was already fast losing consciousness before the secondary aftershocks hurled him overboard. Then all 4,900 tons of what was left of the hull rolled over his body and that of Shino who had jumped into the putrid water in an effort to save injured members of his boat crew, as well as some of those twice ill-fated Chinese sailors.

In the maze of twisted metal that was once the starboard bridge, Petty Officer Megata was out cold. Several minutes prior to impact he had sensed something menacing approaching on the night wind. Unfortunately, his vision skills were insufficient to see around curves. The collision occurred on his blindside. Now conscious but disoriented, he blinked. He saw his feet where his head should be. It presented the illusion he was standing on top of a star-studded section of the night sky. That inverted image was rapidly blotted out as foul ocean water began to swirl around him from *Hamagiri's* final plunge. He succumbed to momentary panic because he was still harnessed to his bridge microphone. At an untold depth, in pitch darkness, he managed to untangle himself and broke free of the harness. Saved from death, he ascended to the surface, pushed up by enormous geysers of air bubbles escaping from one collapsing bulkhead after another.

Shock would set in later, survival training necessitated finding debris to keep himself afloat. When rescue came three days later, Megata in no way felt lucky, only cursed when informed that out of his 219 shipmates, he was the sole survivor of the Japanese *Hamagi DD 155*.

Chapter 11

All Ships At Sea

The stately north portico image of the White House with its four classical Greek Ionic columns, accentuated by subdued lantern and garden lighting, was projected on a large wall monitor. After a brief introductory voice over, the next image was that of the Oval Office. In an uncharacteristically grim demeanor, President Atwater faced his nation.

"Good evening my fellow citizens. First let me categorically assure you that the latest television and social media reports being spread about concerning the belligerent events leading to war with China do not in any way constitute a physical threat to the security of our United States. Nor do these actions constitute a threat to our own personal safety, to our economic stability, or to our overseas military bases and other interests—" Atwater droned on for nearly an hour, mostly glorifying American culture and the importance of protecting Taiwan. Then ended with, *"God Bless America!"*

After the screen was turned off, the lights in Admiral Phong's stateroom aboard *Leviathan* were turned back on. Sitting next to him, Major-General Sheng lifted a small iron teapot packed with steamed fujian green leaves and poured an aromatic blend into a decorative porcelain bowl.

"Congratulations admiral, it appears *Yôngbáo* is becoming the interlocking deception you predicted, not to mention the anticipation of making the President of the United States out to be an utter fool very soon."

"I second Major-General Sheng's congratulations," said Colonel Ming.

"Thank you, comrades, your whole-hearted support in the people's enterprise of *Yôngbào* will be eternally praised by our party which is the ultimate laudatory accolade we must all be worthy of attaining," responded Admiral Phong. "Colonel Ming, you are the most conversant man in my fleet in the nuance of the English language. How did you evaluate President Atwater's call to arms?"

"It's nothing more than a panegyric for the feeble-minded. The tone contained all the outraged clichés of American self-righteous platitudes layered with non-existent immediate dangers. A weak rendition of President Kennedy's speech in 1962 about the Cuban issue. It is obvious he never read Sun Tzu. The good news is, his piratical navy and our fleet of seven supertankers are sailing in diametrical opposite course headings. The deception is total," said Ming.

"Nevertheless, I'd like you to provide me with a close as possible Mandarin translation of President Atwater's speech. I'd like to draw my own conclusions. In an hour. But first, answer the telephone. It has been flashing since we turned the lights back on."

"Right away sir," said Ming who picked up the receiver and listened for less than a minute. The message wasn't propitious. "Admiral, Captain Wua reports he has taken repeated urgent requests from Captain Ping of *Transvaal* for permission to turn on his navigation and running lights as well as his passive radar reflector. Captain Ping further reports he just had a collision with a military ship of unknown nationality."

"No! He must not!" snapped Phong emphatically. "Colonel Ming, tell Captain Hua to transmit an encrypted message to our fleet at once. If even a single running light or open porthole violates the blackout, that offending ship's captain will be tossed over the side wearing a lifejacket so he can flounder for days before he succumbs to exposure or is eaten by sharks!" He furthermore demanded a conference call to be set up with all ship's captains immediately.

Colonel Ming forcefully relayed the order. Then deferentially excused himself to his two superior officers. He then retired to his cabin to translate the American President's speech into Mandarin.

After Ming left, a somewhat amused Sheng took the opportunity to line up a collection of nitroglycerin tablets, beta blockers, plavix vials and antiplatelets in a neat little row next to his teapot. "Now I'm convinced my decision to join the PLA instead of going to sea with you so many years ago was a fortuitous one. I've heard rumors, all unfounded of course, whispered about in the corridors of the People's Ministry of Maritime that the compassion of *Shui-Bào* has been known to humble many a comrade. Humor me admiral. When Colonel Ming completes his translation, will you have him tossed off the bridge as well?"

Sleeping Leopard was not appreciative of the tone this exchange was beginning to take. "Our expeditionary fleet is a mere five days from landfall. *Yôngbào* will be our crowning historical achievement since the Xía Dynasty."

"Whatever fortune awaits China in this century, I have not the slightest doubt you will be the one to write its epilogue," answered Sheng.

"Is the once young lieutenant who fought like a *seladang* and single-handedly destroyed three Vietnamese tanks during our 1979 border war with those little vermin now plagued with cynicism and choked with caution?"

"A mere six weeks ago I was serenely fishing with my grandsons at Lake Koko Nor right after the military physician gave me less than a year to live. The party insisted, not threatened mind you, insisted I take command of the landing force of *Yôngbào*. The party assured me my grandsons' future would not be affected in anyway if I declined. Now, not for a moment did I misinterpret the party's sincerity as a threat, but nevertheless, here I am. Your leukemia patient Captain Hua is a similar story. What leverage does the party have over you admiral? I'm sure that opium pipe displayed next to your small shrine and bronze incense burner under Chairman Mao's benevolent portrait is solely an historical curio."

Sheng discreetly stopped his words but his thoughts were creating answers. The merchant marines were their country's drug path to an emerging new empire. The vast coca and poppy fields from Valparaiso, Bogota, Karachi and Istanbul were their lucrative ports of call. From captain on down to deck hand, huge illegal fortunes were made. Just as long as they were shared with port officials and party members, the chance of prosecution was next to nonexistent, unless one got greedy. The CCP that professed to embrace the theory of communism recognized a cash cow when they saw one. Though Sheng had been a card-carrying CCP member for over 50 years, he also recognized a zealot when he saw one. He further recognized a rational and frank discussion with a zealot was futile and called into question one's own sanity for even making the attempt. So, he talked about the deception instead of the real mission.

"Admiral, our decoy supertankers *Hainan, Canton* and *Macau* are expected to confront the outlying US Navy frigates soon, if they have not done so already. How do you think Americans will react when they discover the invading force is comprised of nothing more than a top deck of unarmed college reservists engaging in Tai Chi to keep themselves from boredom?"

Not waiting for a response, he poured a second bowel of tea and placed it beside the admiral who had moved off his sofa and was now hunched over his desk studying a schematic print. Phong accepted the tea as sign of deference.

"When confrontation is made and *Hainan, Canton* and *Macau* do a 180° turn-about, it won't matter a melon seed what those devils think. I suspect they will be euphoric. They'll believe a great victory was achieved and be blinded to the staged non-lethal force they frightened away without firing a shot. It plays well on the American psyche. All will be in a Zen mindset right up to the moment when you, General Sheng, put ashore 15% of the entire PLA on America's west coast hopefully without firing a shot either. You know we are deliberately equipping our troops with rubber bullets to prevent unnecessary carnage and give the US military pause before they engage in blind retaliation which is what will assuredly happen if our troops have a high kill number in the first hour."

"I'm reminded of Admiral Yamamoto who said *you cannot invade the United States because behind every blade of grass is a gun*," responded Sheng.

"All the more reason for your marines to maintain iron discipline on our soldiers. We must give these Yankees absolutely no excuse for provocation so Beijing can begin Taiwan's negotiated annexation on day one of our landing."

"Quite a gamble Beijing is playing. You realize if *Yôngbào* ends up as one great debacle Premier Jian will claim we're all members of a renegade cabal of military officers who wanted to remove him from office. He'll most certainly admit to plans of invading Taiwan but wash his hands of invading the American mainland. Whether we're successful or not, some, if not all, of us are dead already, either militarily, politically or medically."

"Thank you for that dour assessment but I know you too well. You wouldn't turn this fleet around now if it was in your power to do so. Better for an old soldier to die as a legendary Chinese general who led the invasion against Fortress America than a forgotten and wizened old man gasping for breath in a urine-soaked hospital gown. What story about you do you think your grandsons would prefer to hand down to *their* grandsons?"

"I have always detested you, Phong. But my reasons were altogether unclear, like the morning haze. Though from this moment onward, I now bask in the amiable clarity of sunlight."

"Thank you for your honest expression of transcendence general. Is there anything else?"

"I can't help but notice our three Taiwan deception ships are comprised of supertankers named after two prominent mainland cities and another after our largest island, while our invading seven tankers retain their commercial titles?"

"Yes, other than an off-chance encounter with a passing ship, nothing has been left to chance. All must be deceived into thinking we're en route to the major oil area at Point Barrow. Such a story will check out as true since we shoveled millions on oil leases and redundant land tracks of frozen tundra in Alaska. Deception requires no half measures." Phong interrupted himself to answer his desk phone and pressed the speaker as a courtesy for Sheng to hear.

The captain of *Leviathan*, Hue, spoke with nervous apprehension. "Admiral, all captains are standing by with the exception of Captain Feng of *Malabar Princess*. We've been unable to raise communications with her."

"How long has *Malabar Princess* been incommunicado?" demanded Phong.

"Ten hours," answered Hua, now more nervous than ever anticipating the admiral's wrath.

"What!? You're just informing me now? What kind of fools do I have for captains?"

Another voice on the conference call broke in. "Admiral Phong, this is Captain Jian of *Queen Wilhelmina*. At one time we were beside *Malabar Princess*. We thought we heard the echoes of gunfire and just assumed it was a training exercise but ...."

"But what!?"

"In addition to the gunfire, we thought we caught shouts of *Allah Akbar* briefly transmitted over an open microphone. You understand admiral, there is nothing we could have done. One tanker can't heave to alongside another in a rolling sea and conduct an investigation. Even if we did launch a drone over the *Malabar Princess*, her anti-satellite scaffolding would blind us. That stealth covering prevents us from knowing what the mutineers, if that is the case, are actually doing or what future intentions their actions are signaling. With all due respect Admiral Phong, there is no way to ascertain the actual conditions. There is nothing we can do."

Another voice broke in. "This is Captain Shan of *Antilles*. I concur with Captain Jian. Just forget about *Malabar Princess*. The loss of one ship does not sufficiently degrade our troop integrity or jeopardize the mission."

"Captain Shan, the CCP has bestowed its trust solely on me as the admiral to faithfully execute *Yŏngbào*. I say when a ship is irretrievably lost, and I determine to what degree of circumstance the mission, if at all, has been compromised. Now the rest of you captains that have not done so, acknowledge your name and command!"

"Captain Ping of *Transvaal*."

"Captain Liu of *Zeelandia*."

"Captain Yi of *Suriname*."

"To all captains! Attention to orders! Our beloved party with the motherland's safety and future uppermost in our hearts paid 10,000,000 yuan renminbi to those rapacious and ungrateful Pakistanis whom China defends with her blood against their Indian enemies. For that extortionist money, China purchased state-of-the-art stealth technology to sail undetected by satellite reconnaissance. Those panels above your main decks cost 125,000,000 yuan renminbi per ship. Therefore, no deviation from fleet protocol will be tolerated. Especially when underway at night. As you were earlier admonished: no navigation lights, no running lights, no activation of passive radar reflectors. Violations will carry the penalty of a wartime capital offense. You are all in command of the world's largest ships. You have nothing to fear except a loss of nerve in the event of a collision. Resume your duties at once."

Sheng quietly approached the admiral who sank behind his desk lost in thought. He sorted through a stack of the seven portfolio binders that held each ship's manifest and statistical data. He selected the one titled *Malabar Princess* and flipped through several pages. After a cursory review, he placed the open binder in front of Phong and pointed. This indicated the geographic origin and ethnic concentration of the majority of troops assigned to *Malabar Princess*.

"We are the inheritors of the world's oldest ongoing civilization. That makes us the most cunning people on earth as well as the cruelest. These qualities preempt us from being a nation of a billion fools. Here before you is an act of sabotage, because collectively, we as a people do not possess the degree of ineptitude for such an oversight."

Phong took a long studied look and agreed. "Yes, the enemies of Premier Jian want to bring him down by bringing down *Yôngbào*. Who else but a saboteur would mobilize 25,000 troops from a Muslim province and assign them all to one ship? Any number of minor incidents from a ship's dietary oversight to a lapse in disciplinary enforcement could spark a mutiny. Captain Shan is right. *Malabar Princess* is lost to us. Thank you for opening my eyes to this act of sabotage. I hope it's not the first of many. Goodnight General Sheng."

"Goodnight admiral," *and may snakes and monkeys plague your dreams.* Sheng received a salute from Colonel Ming as they passed each other when Ming re-entered the stateroom. Ming deferentially placed a translation on the desk.

"There is a traitor amongst us," said Phong. The colonel turned his head toward the stateroom's open hatchway and the man who just exited. "No, Sheng would never undertake any deviant machinations that might jeopardize his grandsons' future."

"Perhaps he might attempt to alter their future by altering China's?"

"Perhaps, but he reminded me, China is not a nation of a billion fools."

* * *

Since the day Ji-Nan climbed aboard *Leviathan* it had been one wearisome task after another as head zoo keeper of his troops; from breaking up fist-fights to reprimanding peasant soldiers urinating on the nearest bulkhead. In addition, there was paperwork to be collated and schedules for going topside for a breath of fresh sea air and twice a day meals; all repeating and all overwhelming duties for one man.

Keeping up the shitting schedule around the meal schedule was a joke. Most toilet chairs near the bow were unusable due to the ship's forward momentum into headwinds. It was discovered when in use a soldier's feces tended to blow back amidships towards soldiers standing in a chow line or landed in one of the open fish tanks. Worse still, two anti-satellite surveillance panels detached in high winds and decapitated a soldier using one of the chairs, and flew on to severely injure others sitting next to him.

Ji-Nan's leadership role gave him no special priority on the chow. He stood for hours along with the other 5,000 men permitted on deck at any one-time for their breakfast ration of a sugar bun, boiled egg, a mound of steaming rice topped with a fillet of sea bass and a full canteen of hot tea.

The only difference at dinner time was pork substituted for fish. There was no middle meal.

This day's misery was further compounded when he spotted the pig farmer Yu-Shu now employed as a cook who insincerely congratulated Ji-Nan on his promotion. The cook then went out of his way to serve him a choice piece of pork with a lying smile. Suspecting some ingredient was no doubt added, he sought out his other former gun mount crewmembers. The boasting Ba-Hui and the obsequious informer Yi, to which Ji-Nan unselfishly offered up his savory piece of pork to divide evenly between them and which they both greedily accepted. All he needed now to have a perfect end to a perfect day was to have a chance confrontation with his hated previous gun captain Haung.

His depression was such, he even considered adding himself to the running statistic of a ship suicide per day by jumping over the side. Just when he thought things couldn't get worse, someone grabbed his shoulder. It was his absentee company commander, Captain Pao.

"Sergeant Ji-Nan, you are to accompany me at once! Fleet Political Officer Colonel Ming wants to see you!"

Filled with dread, he trailed after his new found commander like an obedient puppy on the way to the annual Yulin Prefecture Dog Meat Festival. Pushing his way past a crowd of soldiers and diverse odors from the never-ending mess lines, Ji-Nan kept pace behind Pao.

Ming was waiting impatiently for them in the 5th level wardroom. He gave both a cursory inspection. Without so much as a word, the colonel stepped forward and backhanded Pao across the face with such force he split his lip and sent his round garrison cap flying off his head. Then Ming turned his attention to Ji-Nan who waited for his own blow. Instead a strike he received the colonel's signature cruel smile.

"Oh, relax young sergeant! As I expected, I have heard nothing but satisfactory reports about you. For example, troop compartment Unit Five reports the gallons of piss that had been raining down on them has been curtailed to a small seepage since you took over above them. Plus, your troop moral indicates you now have the lowest average of weak-willed soldiers who have committed suicide by leaving the ship without permission. Still, that is no excuse for your commanding officer to present you looking and smelling like a wharf-rat!"

The colonel merely had to glance at his wristwatch before the chastened officer, still nursing bleeding lips, hauled Lee off to the officer shower stalls. Ten minutes later, a dripping wet Ji-Nan, wrapped only in a towel, was handed over to the ship's barber for a shave and haircut in record time. Meanwhile Pao issued him a new forest-green utility uniform, a fresh set of underwear with a clean pair of socks and a polished set of boots.

This time Ming was satisfied with the presentation. He ordered them both to follow him down a long passageway where another pair of marine sentries flanked an open hatchway. They were told to wait while the colonel stepped inside. In less than a minute Ji-Nan was called, stepped inside the spacious stateroom, and approached Major-General Sheng who sat behind his desk. At a respectful distance, Ji-Nan brought his boot heels together and rendered the general the sharpest and the most polished salute he had ever given anyone in his 16 months in the PLA.

"Stand at ease," said the general. "Do you have any idea what is about to happen on this mission?" Sheng felt there was no need to add to the young sergeant's anxiety by informing him that the troop level was now diminished by 25,000 troops from the missing *Malabar Princess,* or that this 15% of the nation's army would not be receiving support.

"No sir, all the wild claims I heard came from a traitor whose story I dismissed out of hand," he lied. Then wondered if he was actually fooling anybody. He dreaded being asked for the name of this anonymous traitor to trap him in his own tangle of lies. Luckily, Sheng was satisfied with the abrupt denial masking what was obvious feigned ignorance.

Sheng turned to Ming and smiled. "This young sergeant is everything you made him out to be," then he faced Ji-Nan again and told a tale of the Great Wall of China and Asian slaves building American railroads. Of the clever workers cutting inches off their shovels making their masters think they were working harder, getting paid the same. Ming forcefully gripped Ji-Nan's shoulder as he finished. "Our mission is to cut something off from their capitalist descendants until China reunites with all our territory and make us more prosperous. The part you must play is that of interpreter. You must be the intermediary for our soldiers and prevent any rampage and mayhem that will engender irreparable harm towards our negotiations with the Americans. Are you capable of undertaking such diplomatic duties for the motherland?"

"So, it's true then! We're invading America!" asked a stunned Ji-Nan in a momentary lapse of protocol.

"Not invading! Occupying a usurper's home territory until the usurper relinquishes Taiwan!" sharply answered Ming. For a brief pause, there was utter silence between all three men. Then Ming turned to address Sheng in a most respectful and supplicating tone. "Sir, for the exigency of his mission in dealing with what would be a fluid situation between different units and ranks, I recommend, with your approval, we promote Sergeant Ji-Nan."

"I've reviewed the sergeant's official disciplinary portfolio. Do you really think it's appropriate to promote a man to lieutenant who has willfully and salaciously been engaging in an open and notorious affair with a party member's mistress?"

"Thank you for pointing out my error in judgment. Who would this sergeant fuck next? Where would his fucking end?" replied Ming in a fawning manner, angry at being off balance and not know what Sheng wanted.

The old general was keeping all options open. "Then again, when a civilian manifests initiative at every opportunity, however questionable that opportunity, he deserves a captaincy for such audaciousness. Wouldn't you agree colonel?"

"Absolutely!" responded Colonel Ming, right on cue.

Ji-Nan answered with that safe-in-all-situations Maoist rote quote every adolescent pledges on his first day of middle school: "I am ready, willing and able to serve in any capacity that the motherland and the party requires of me!"

From his desk drawer, Sheng took out a pair of green shoulder boards with three tiny yellow stars on each. He stood up and handed one board to Colonel Ming to slide in Lee's epaulet shoulder flap while he himself did the other side. "Congratulations Captain Lee Ji-Nan. I'll leave you in the capable hands of our political officer to brief you on your first mission. Oh, and colonel, procure the new captain a pistol and leather belt so he'll at least look like a genuine PLA officer."

Dumbfounded, Lee said nothing. He took his cue from Ming and in unison both saluted. Together they made a sharp parade about face, and exited the open hatchway past the marine sentries, who in turn gave both officers an equally sharp salute. Then another salute from the waiting Captain Pao.

"Captain Pao, Captain Ji-Nan has been detached from troop Unit Four for a special assignment. Surrender your pistol belt to him and then resume your duties below decks. You're dismissed," said Ming.

After his humiliated loss of face, Captain Pao slowly descended the stairwell decks, his bootsteps fading out of earshot. Captain Ji-Nan hurriedly buckled on the brown leather holster and magazine pouch. Then he dutifully followed Ming to the command bridge.

A festive atmosphere of rousing cheers was what they walked in on. One by one all the ship's officers were taking turns to offer their congratulations to the short man wearing an old-fashioned chin beard. Back in Shanghai, elitist party members and urban snobs would laugh and scorn at such a man whose countenance was emblematic of centuries past. Though with just the briefest of scrutiny, Ji-Nan knew *exactly* who represented the power in this fleet.

What words and phrases he was able to catch and put together was that the American navy had intercepted three tankers in the Formosa Straits, and somehow this was a prescient for some great coming victory. Even with all the reign and reverie on the command bridge, Colonel Ming managed a brief introduction for the newly promoted captain. Fleet Admiral Phong was informed this young man was going to be the landing unit's first line interpreter. The admiral gave Ji-Nan a cursory nod and handshake and wished him a successful mission.

Thoroughly intimidated, Lee admitted to himself he had no idea what that assignment actually entailed. Ming gave his usual perverse smile and beckoned Lee to follow. He was led out to the middle of *Leviathan's* port bridge wing. Enthralled for the moment by the perspective of height above the main deck and the exhilarating rush of ocean breeze, he was handed a pair of binoculars.

"You'll be on the first assault wave to take that objective," said the colonel pointing straight ahead.

Adjusting the binoculars, the only thing Ji-Nan saw were two giant rusty towers supporting a truss and suspension span nearly a mile and a half long across a bay ringed by hills.

When it came into focus, his jaw dropped.

Chapter 12

Dark Angel of Justice

Admiral Phong looked down from *Leviathan's* bridge with the detachment of God. Unlike God, he couldn't see through the blue-black stealth canopy that covered the ship. The only soldiers he could see were the ones using the toilets hanging over the sea. Underneath was the first wave of 5,000 troops mustering on the main deck. The approach to the ten nautical mile marker buoy offered the last chance to abort *Yôngbào*. Once the six tankers passed under the center span of the Golden Gate Bridge and sailed into San Francisco Bay, there would be no turning back. Yet the daring of the undertaking, even at this late stage, caused him no apprehension. His confidence permeated inward as well as outward, enveloping him in a Zen calm from the knowledge that his name would be a legend in the glorious annals of the Middle Kingdom. Henceforth the legend of Zhao Ju Phong would forever be recorded as the admiral who launched a surprise attack on the mainland of the United States of America!

With his part of the naval transportation mission almost completed, formal command of *Yôngbào* was now transferred to Major-General Sheng. The slowly dying Captain Hua switched on the ship-to-ship intercom. He gave a wheezy preliminary standby for orders announcement to introduce the equally dying Sheng. Despite his infirmity, the general's voice boomed out without any hint of approaching mortality and resonated in every compartment bulkhead from bow to stern in all six tankers.

"Patriotic volunteers of the People's Liberation Army — attention! Beijing has notified this command of a belligerent and cowardly attack on our breakaway province of Taiwan by the piratical navy of the United States. These cowardly running dogs have

blocked our freedom of the seas and navigation rights in both the Formosa Straits and the South China Sea. Therefore, in answer to this grievous insult against the Sovereignty of the Motherland, and the Communist Party, the Chinese People have unanimously called for a limited war of punishment to oppose this theft. We patriotic volunteers are fortunate and honored to be uniquely situated to strike the first blow of redemption for our Motherland. Now soldiers, our mission must be one of occupier *– not invader! We must not mirror the barbaric Japanese beasts who raped and pillaged our beloved city of Nanking. On no account must we give the Yankee devils an excuse for a revenge nuclear retaliation on our Motherland. Consequently, our mission is purely a tactical one to temporarily occupy the city and facilitate the exodus of the population. The longer the American military is kept observing the streams of civilians fleeing the city, the less inclined they are to attack us. This will ensure our safety against being bombed or poison gassed. The long-term strategic end of our mission is the peacefully negotiated annexation of Taiwan for the unmolested return of their city intact, as well as our own peaceful debarkation back to China. Therefore soldiers, we must exhibit a discipline of the highest order. That is why you have been issued rubber bullets. You are to discharge your weapons only in the most extreme cases of personal safety. Our marine detachment will have live ammunition to neutralize any and all hostile gunfire. I repeat – your main mission is that of occupier! Your main duty is to escort the civilian population out of the city politely but firmly and as rapidly as possible. You may arrest and hold captive any military or police who stand in your way. Civilians are not to be harmed. While carrying out your duties, you are forbidden to enter hospitals, schools and places of worship. Do not stop fire-trucks or ambulances. You may enter private homes to impound food stocks only. There is to be no looting! Perpetrators of rape crimes will be executed. Soldiers—this harsh discipline is for your own safety. It is for the supreme love of the Chinese people we pledge our sacred duty and lives for the Motherland and the CCP – Long Live China!"*

Inside the command bridge Sheng could not quite hear or gauge the response. Unlike the indifferent Admiral Phong, it remained a matter of great concern to him.

"United States Coast Guard ship—dead ahead!" called out the starboard lookout.

Colonel Ming scrolled through a ship ID app. "Black hull, sea going buoy tender, large." He was able to see the name: *Aspen.* "Juniper class, length 225',

7 officers and 42 enlisted, armament two 50 caliber machine guns." Then as an afterthought he remarked, "I doubt those guns are staffed and ready to fire."

"Captain Hua order the fleet to alter course five degrees to port. We'll just ignore them and pass by," said Phong.

No sooner was the course correction transmitted to all ships, then a tense response blared out from the overhead ship-to-ship speakers. Captain Jian, commanding *Queen Wilhelmina*, as tail end in the line of ships raised a secondary alarm.

"Admiral, our surveillance drone has pinged a US warship 25 miles bearing west-southwest closing fast!"

Boxed in and soon to be confronted with a ship dead ahead and another at his stern, Phong ordered his captains to make all possible speed to enter the bay. Once there, he would locate their pre-assigned mooring berths and disembark the landing force as quickly as possible.

* * *

Lieutenant-Commander Lloyd Holman, captain of the USCG seagoing buoy tender WLB-208 *Aspen*, stood in the center section of the exposed catwalk that extended across his ship's 46' beam from starboard to port directly in front of his enclosed command bridge. He was engrossed in the dangerous and labor-intensive work between the forecastle and main deck as a crane boom operator hoisted aboard a 13,000 pound red harbor buoy. The rigger crew had their work cut out for them as they struggled to control the rotating motion of the giant buoy and the pendulum movement of the wide cement mooring sinker suspended underneath. It was during this point of the operation Lieutenant-Commander Holman gave a cursory glance at a line of several enormous ships a few degrees off *Aspen's* starboard bow. Having memorized today's vessel transit manifest, he couldn't recall any supertankers given permission to enter the bay area. Something was definitely wrong when the first tanker failed to give the international maritime signal of two short horn blasts when it passed by on *Aspen's* starboard side.

Even during the current national emergency dealing with Taiwan and seeing strange scaffolding above their main decks, in his wildest suspicions he couldn't conceive that the appearance of these tankers had anything to do with the confrontation unfolding on the opposite side of the Pacific. Holman was relieved to see the fleet's white Plimsoll markers way above their waterline indicating all were riding high and empty of crude. Since there was no immediate environmental danger to the bay area, he only made a mental note to notify base after completing the morning's maintenance. Holman went back to monitoring the progress of the rigger crew and ignored the second ship which also failed to give the passing horn blasts. Bizarrely, after the third tanker passed by as silent as the previous ships, it broke out of the convoy line and came about in a sharp 180° due west. It obviously had the intention of running back to the open waters of the Pacific.

This abrupt maneuver brought the tanker in dangerous proximity to *Aspen*. With the gigantic bow closing fast on his ship's starboard quarter, Holman at once sensed danger. Still standing on the catwalk, he barely had enough time to turn around and shout through one of the open bridge portholes. "Sound collision alarm!" Then he clutched the catwalk handrails and braced for impact!

It never happened. Inexplicably, with less than a cable's length separation to spare, the fast approaching wall of massive steel veered off leaving waves of choppy white water exposed between the two hulls. This near miss gave a false sense of divine providence.

Within moments of that reprieve, a good portion of the ship's crew died violently.

An anti-armor missile impacted right underneath the suspended harbor buoy. An explosive orange-white blast sent pieces of flying molten deck plating into the crew. Blue construction helmets with heads still inside and shredded pieces of life-vests strapped around blood-soaked body parts were swept over the side by the explosive force. The second part of the charge penetrated the weakened deck and went on to detonate in the enlisted mess area killing more crew enjoying their coffee break.

Due to the explosive effects and fire damage, foundation mountings and rivets melted through and snapped apart at the crane's rotation base. The 50' boom couldn't sustain the weight of the massive buoy suspended underneath. In utter helplessness Holman watched in horror as the buoy plunged through the burning deck which in turn pulled down the crane and instantly killed the fire-fighting crew working below. He remained in harm's way up to the last moments of his life shouting orders to clear the bridge and never saw the boom arm that crushed him. All three officers and four crewmembers of the watch made it out alive due to their captain's valiant efforts and self-sacrifice.

The survivors now stood bewildered outside the collapsed pile of twisted metal and smoldering electrical cables. One of them, XO Lieutenant Albert Gallatin, memorized the block letters on the stern of the retreating supertanker that just fired a mortal blow at his ship: Royal Dutch Maritime crude carrier *ANTILLES*–Rotterdam–Netherlands. Unfurled at the masthead was the incongruous blood red flag of China.

* * *

The sound, smoke and flames brought everybody from *Leviathan's* command bridge out to the starboard wing to gaze aft in alarm at the burning Coast Guard ship. Equally alarming, was the view of the receding stern of *Antilles* taking another 25,000 troops earmarked for the landing force back out to the open ocean.

"Do you still think I'm the traitor here Colonel Ming?" asked General Sheng.

"We have no time for this!" angrily voiced Admiral Phong. "That party traitor Shan has set us up for a possible bloodbath. Shan could have just turned and ran. Instead, he deliberately chose to fire on that American ship to paint blood on our hands for which our landing force will be held accountable. How will Beijing be able to negotiate now?"

"Not to mention we've been deprived of 50,000 troops before we've even taken a first step on American soil," said the general.

For the first time, Phong started to feel *Yóngbào* held the possibility of failure. Therefore, to evade all responsibility, he responded in the only way a long-standing party member knew how. Denounce another party member and deflect blame away.

"Defeatist talk serves up a meal to our adversaries," he said. "Furthermore, Chairman Mao says *The party worker assigned a task who bemoans his tools lacks initiative.*"

No amateur himself, Sheng understood what Phong was attempting. Also admitting in his mind *Yóngbào* was fast becoming the debacle he always envisioned it would; he became caustic. He turned to face Ming. "As our Chief Political Commissar, say something to restore my faith in revolutionary heroism. How about a quote from our deified insomniac leader who had a paternal fondness for pubescent ballet dancers? Something along the lines he used to blather on about like—*He who is not afraid of death by a thousand cuts dares to unhorse the Emperor.*"

Before the wary Colonel Ming could respond with an equally obnoxious answer, Captain Hua sounded another alarm calling all senior officers back inside to the command bridge.

"Admiral we're sailing into a trap!" said the excited Hua as he pointed to three large objects on the navigation screen. "Our surveillance drone indicates three large US Navy aircraft carriers are lying in wait for us!"

Ming in his dual role as both chief political commissar and senior fleet intelligence officer allayed all fears. "They are the Vietnam War era decommissioned *Ranger*, *Kitty Hawk* and the *Constellation*. You can't see yet that all three hulls are painted white. If you look closely, you can make out the large red cross as well. After their 1989 earthquake these were converted into floating hospitals, virtually earthquake proof. In addition, with all ships' engines on line, they could sustain the city's power grid as long as their stockpiles of oil hold out."

Not all fears were allayed. For a second time, Captain Jian's exasperated voice transmitted dire warnings about a menacing US Navy warship hurrying on their destruction. Fleet Admiral Phong had but one option. "Signal all ships!

Full speed ahead! And let's get ourselves under that damn bridge! Even the Americans are not stupid enough to sink a supertanker inside the bay."

* * *

The USS *Shanksville* was a variation of an LCS: littoral class combat ship. Fast, maneuverable and loaded with weapons. Her main propulsion blades were powered by three immense gas turbines. Though not the fastest ship in the US naval arsenal, the *Shanksville* was one of its most lethal. So named to commemorate the unarmed passengers aboard Flight 93 who heroically fought terrorists in the skies over Pennsylvania. Their sacrifice ended in an isolated field in Shanksville saving the Capitol Building.

The USS *Shanksville* had yet to fire a shot in anger. Though, weeks from the day she came down the ways at the Lockheed Martin shipyard, a word of mouth reputation soon developed that the navy engineers overreached by creating an anomaly. Conventional dinosaurs began to accuse marine architects of inadvertently letting loose a rouge shark in the family pool. *Shanksville* carried a Pandora's box of high-tech weaponry. The most lethal was the Forward Rim-116 Rolling Airframe anti-ship missile that rotated in flight like a bullet. That weapon system was augmented by both fore-and-aft secondary anti-ship and anti-aircraft Hellfire missile pods. *Shanksville's* close quarter combat lethality came from an old-fashioned, tried and true, Bofors 57mm main turret cannon. Her redundant defenses were six Phalanx Goalkeeper Gatling guns that had the combat record of never being successfully penetrated by a missile or aircraft.

Her human weapons came in the form of specialized mission crews. In addition to the normal compliment of 11 officers and 46 enlisted, there were 35 more specialized mission crewmembers. This included pilots and service crews for the Blackhawk and Viper helicopter gunships, as well as two MQ-8 Fire scout drones. Also deployed was a US Marine Corps sniper team and a squad of US Navy Seals. Unofficial and incognito was a CIA Black Ops section embedded as on-board naval contractors. These highly specialized intelligence and interrogation agents were results oriented; ultra practical for stealth operations that involved permanent solutions for those deemed enemies of the state.

Shanksville had other unique human resources as well. Several Muslim-American crewmembers were master linguists in Arabic and Berber. Had the ship been deployed to the Arabian Sea as her original orders intended, their talents would have been immeasurable. It was ironic for all the well-planned talent aboard *Shanksville*, none of her 92 plus crewmembers understood a word of Mandarin.

With the main bulk of the Seventh Fleet deployed around Taiwan, and the national emergency notwithstanding, the USS *Shanksville* was still a blank page in the annals of naval history. A ship like this required a hero captain; and there was none better suited in temperament then the perpetually pissed-off woman now in command. Captain Amber, The Archangel, O'Sullivan had an uncanny foresight to spot an infraction against the code of military justice before it was committed.

Twice passed over for admiral, Captain O'Sullivan, while in command of the Fast Frigate USS *Oliver Hazard Perry* accidently, on purpose, hull bumped the Russian guided missile cruiser *Admiral Grigorovich* while patrolling the Black Sea. Later, and still under reprimand, guarding the Straits of Hormuz, her ship accidently, again on purpose, collided and sunk an Iranian patrol craft and besmirched the hitherto sterling record of American altruism by not bothering to search for survivors. As Captain O'Sullivan's after action SITRAP explained:

> **During the Iranian vessel's erratic and hostile maneuvers, they openly transmitted obscene and disgusting invectives against the US flag, our president, and my ability as captain. Since they were probably jihadists anyway, I felt a religious obligation to help them arrange a meeting with their prophet.**

Again transferred and given command of the dock landing ship USS *Fort McHenry*, another incident occurred when a seaman apprentice, smoking a joint on his graveyard watch, found himself tossed overboard by a large shadowy figure.

Captain O'Sullivan's reputation became legendary (and secretly admired by her superiors) when a newly commissioned female ensign and a junior officer were caught cohabitating on the hanger deck inside a tied down CH-53 Sea Stallion helicopter. Rather than give them both a career ending court-martial, she invoked the ancient maritime rite as captain and married them at sea. Thereafter, the word was out—nobody fucks aboard The Archangel's ship without permission in writing.

Now almost 50 with a colorful but stagnant career, and passed over for flag rank, she had only two options remaining. Sail on to an early retirement or sail into harm's way.

The Archangel was not in a very angelic mood. Chief-of-Naval-Operations, Admiral Olendoft, had personally intervened in the interest of national security to keep her away from the volatile situation surrounding Taiwan and the Formosa Straits. Then, to add insult to injury, she received last minute esoteric orders countermanding deployment to the Arabian Sea where at least some adventure might show up.

The data stream of real-time information about the Sino-American confrontation brought only barely contained bitterness about being sidelined from the world's momentous events. *Shanksville's* captain did not relish being reduced to a floating sentry post. And the damnable thing about was, it was her own fault; the higher ups wanted to promote a woman up the ranks, she was qualified, but her Irish temper and brash actions in handing out justice seemed to flare up at just the wrong moments.

Deliverance was at hand.

One message directly to the ship's comm deck from the Chief of Naval Operations in Washington D.C. and one received by the on board "naval contractors" with a cipher link direct to Langley changed everything.

Radar screens in CIC were painting some sort of over the horizon anomaly. Comm deck just intercepted ominous Coast Guard radio chatter and cell traffic from the Yerba Buena Island base in San Francisco. The CIA communiqué was specific: *Aspen* was on fire, dead in the water with major casualties!

On *Shanksville's* command bridge Amber O'Sullivan, Executive Officer Benjamin Ben-Ezra, and Jordanian born, American raised, Lieutenant-Junior Grade Fara Hamdan faced each other, nodded and engaged in their duties. Hamdan, as conning officer, pushed forward a black handle which in turn increased the turbines to surface battle speed.

In silence, the XO followed his assigned protocol. He reached over to the console. He first lifted the special red safety latch cover to press the button underneath. Instantly every loudspeaker throughout the USS *Shanksville* blared out with a pre-recorded trumpet call followed by a series of attention-grabbing klaxon gongs, followed by the words: "General Quarters—General Quarters—All hands to your battle stations—This is not a drill!"

* * *

The menacing shark bow of the special warfare ship and the blunt one of the moving steel mountain were rapidly converging at 61 knots. A very calm but heavily accented Mandarin-English message came over the open international frequency on *Shanksville's* command bridge speaker.

"To the approaching American warship—This is Captain Shan of the People's Republic of China. We have no hostile intentions. I repeat—We have no hostile intentions! We desire only to peacefully return to our Chinese mainland unmolested. We were duped into an attempted invasion of your country by traitors who at this time have fellow conspirators launching a coup d'état on the Chinese people and its lawful government. It is most exigent you intercept, deter, or close with and destroy the five troop-carrying supertankers invading the city of San Francisco with 125,000 misguided soldiers, led by a treasonous cabal."

The message was repeated three times until acknowledged. Captain Amber O'Sullivan was unaware it was the approaching *Antilles* that actually fired on the unarmed *Aspen*. She also had no way of knowing the truth or motivation of that message. The clincher that left no time for a bridge consultation with her officers was the revelation of 125,000 soldiers invading San Francisco. If true, that tidbit was the priority.

"Proceed!" was *Shanksville's* single word transmitted in response.

As *Antilles* sailed passed the port side of *Shanksville*, this time it gave the proper recognition signal of one long horn blast and observed the honored tradition of dipping her red flag to the American warship; the courtesy was not reciprocated.

Captain O'Sullivan was taken aback when she saw odd scaffolding and thousands of uniformed soldiers as the ships passed by each other. She wasted no time ordering *Shanksville's* two MQ-8 Fire Scout unmanned helicopters into the air to assess the threat of the hostile forces she was now up against. The details of *Antilles* were recorded by Hamden; they could follow up with that mess after the main event was verified.

The two grey drones were quickly dispatched ahead as the ship charged at full speed toward San Francisco. Soon they were hovering over a line of five heat signatures. Telemetry readouts were utterly confusing to *Shanksville's* CIC radar operators.

The ghost readings were the direct result of the anti-satellite scaffolding. After consultation with the bridge, the sedentary pilots descended their drones from a safe 10,000' altitude to sea level and conducted a lateral search. This exposed the $18,000,000 a piece drones to small arms fire, but the invading tankers were now exposed as well.

The full revelation of this unimaginable threat to San Francisco caused the Archangel to crash down in her chair with her brain racing. The fact USS *Shanksville* was the only lethal military force available left one course of action. *Neutralize the threat immediately!*

But it was in American territory. Civilian collateral damage would become the restricting variable that O'Sullivan had never bothered to concern herself with before. Nobody raised the idea of simply firing a warning shot across their bow or offering the Chinese terms for surrender. Her righteous temper demanded a lesson must be taught to these invaders for such an egregious and reckless violation of American sovereignty. And the penalty would be severe!

"We can't launch hellfire anti-ship missiles into the bay area. With so many ships in the harbor a missile might mistarget on a liquefied natural gas container ship," said XO Ben-Ezra.

"I concur with the XO sir. Let's engage the old fashion main battery cannon instead of launching those quarter million dollar hellfire missiles. It's safer to use the Bofors to accurately take out their propellers. Sodomize those Chinese right up their sterns; good and hard!" said conning officer Fara Hamdan pushing back the side of her blue hijab with a predatory smile.

O'Sullivan agreed with her bridge officers and grasped a black spiral transmitter and keyed the speaker button, "CIC–Bridge!"

Several decks below and aft in the most hardened compartment of the ship, the weapons officer responded, "CIC–Aye!"

"This the captain speaking. Calculate a seven nautical mile down range firing solution for the Bofors gun on that last tanker heading for the Golden Gate Bridge."

The weapons officer rotated two oversized dials as if he were aligning the tumblers on a safe until the white crosshairs on his HD screen were superimposed over a 3D hologram of the targeted ship. This enabled him to quickly factor in the heading, range and observer-to-target parallax correction. "CIC – Bridge! Captain I have a solution."

"Commence firing! And don't stop until I tell you."

The weapons officer flipped up a red safety guard on the firing grip handle and began squeezing the trigger. As the first of many 13 lb. fragmentation shells of depleted uranium blasted out the barrel of the Bofors 57mm cannon at 3,400' per second, three new American history pages were inscribed. Not only did the USS *Shanksville* officially log its first shot in anger, but it was the first time a US Navy ship fired on a hostile surface vessel in defense of home waters since Captain Perry aboard the USS *Niagara* during the War of 1812, and it was the first time a ship at war had women as two of the top three executive officers.

Queen Wilhelmina, due to her ill-fated position of being tail end in the convoy was soon to experience death in a myriad of unimaginable ways, and would do so without ever knowing their American historical connection. *Queen Wilhelmina's* doom came unawares.

First to die were two stern watch standers who were both eviscerated by impacting salvos at five and a half times the speed of sound long before they heard the whistling, then the eardrum splitting thunderclap. An unrelenting barrage of shells hideously disfigured the back of the ship's island superstructure down to her waterline. The massive rudder was fragmented. The vertical coupling that kept the rudder attached to the hull split apart. Then all 230 tons of the huge rudder came crashing down on a rotating propeller. With one end of the drive shaft jammed and the opposite end connected to the gear case still turning, the immediate result was a catastrophic stress failure midpoint in the drive shaft. When that happened, the giant elongated cylindrical shaft violently twisted itself apart. Hundreds of kinetic shards perforated the engine room personnel. The screams were soon drowned out by an inrush of seawater through the jagged holes caused by *Shanksville's* cannons that had now mercifully ceased firing.

It was a small mercy indeed.

The abrupt loss of propeller movement transmitted a different kind of reverberation throughout the ship–panic!

By the sudden stillness under their feet, all troops above and below decks sensed danger at once.

The lowest deck occupants heard and felt the hurricane rush of air turbulence displaced by the incoming deluge of ocean. Due to structural modification, the ingress of seawater was irreversible and irreparable. The contagion of panic became a stampede. For the troops below decks it was a surge toward the stairwells to get topside. Marine sentries stationed at those critical exits to prevent just such chaos were first to be trampled. In a matter of minutes every stairwell became a choke point. Hundreds of soldiers were crushed to death or slowly suffocated by the press of bodies in those narrow steps or into the handrails.

Once the engine room was totally under water the lights went out.

That left thousands more in rapidly flooding compartments to blindly scurry around in futile desperation to locate breathable air pockets and cling to life for an extra five minutes.

The rising water was a relief to the grotesquely crushed soldiers who had not yet lost consciousness.

The end came for *Queen Wilhelmina*; she started to show a pronounced stern-first downward angle. Once the tanker's bow started to rise out of the water, discipline simply dissolved into a vicious state of animal survival.

Some of the ship's crew who were foolish enough to appear on deck wearing lifejackets were mobbed by soldiers who pulled them apart limb from limb then fought among themselves for what was left of the bloodstained, torn shreds. After witnessing that spectacle, anyone left with a lifejacket had the presence of mind to furtively ease themselves into the water unobserved.

With *Queen Wilhelmina's* stern slipping below the waves, it became next to impossible for the mobs of soldiers to stand upright. Tumbling backwards, a few fell into the open pig pens and were ferociously attacked. Their desperate cries added to the overall chorus of anguish.

As the Pacific Ocean began to crest over the ship's gunwales, none of the clinging survivors had yet noticed a number of circling dorsal fins just breaking the surface.

Right up until the last moment when the sea closed over *Queen Wilhelmina's* top radio mast, Captain Jian both pleaded and cursed Fleet Admiral Phong for assistance before the vortex of swirling waters engulfed the command bridge.

By the time USS *Shanksville* appeared on the scene, the tanker, despite its size, had sunk so far below the surface it in no way posed a hazard to navigation. Only a few hundred struggling bodies thrashing about and a few thousand still ones floating face down marked its burial spot.

"This is going to be one hell of a major biohazard to clean up. Let's hope our mako sharks do their fair share," remarked the practical XO.

The private opinion of the conning officer was even harsher than that, but she kept them private so as not to encourage the XO and thereby the captain into any reckless action.

Shanksville moved on, approaching the still burning *Aspen* to render assistance.

It was at this juncture that the communication officer hand-delivered to Captain Amber O'Sullivan sealed orders she had to sign for. Chief of Naval Operations Admiral Olendorf praised her initiative and timely intervention and gave orders for *Shanksville* to continue to keep station west of the Golden Gate Bridge and stand by for special orders.

The Archangel transcribed it in the ship's log and finally knew her service record would reflect the power of her commitment to law and justice.

Chapter 13

The Close Embrace

The echo of desperation from late Captain Jian was not lost on Phong, but ignored by necessity. He had done what he could—nothing! He now conferred with Sheng over a large schematic of San Francisco and the surrounding bay to discuss a landing site. Sheng gave a studied appreciation of their diminished resources. He first determined *Zeelandia's* intended mooring site at the western entrance of the San Mateo-Hayward Bridge at the southernmost part of the bay must be abandoned. Instead, that supertanker would be redirected to take *Queen Wilhelmina's* place at the entrance to the San Bruno Canal that strides along the main runway of San Francisco International Airport. The largest airport in the city had to be closed down at all cost. *Zeelandia's* secondary mission would be to deploy troops to intersect the adjacent Bayshore and San Junipero Serra freeways, stopping all traffic into the city. Captain Jingping of *Transvaal* would continue on as originally planned to shut down the Oakland Bay Bridge to incoming traffic along the Rincon Hill. Captain Yi of *Suriname,* instead of supporting *Transvaal* as intended, was issued new orders to berth at Fisherman's Warf and fan out his troops throughout the city. With the loss of two ships, two critical objectives were abandoned. The Dumbarton Bridge in nearby east Palo Alto Airport had to be left totally operational as well as the northern bay's San Rafael Bridge. It also meant no resources were left to spare for shutting down the Oakland International Airport at Alameda.

General Sheng began to entertain the possibility that he might go down as the most ill-fated general in Chinese history. Whatever destiny had in store for him and thes remaining hapless volunteers, the point of no return had been crossed. By the time he issued amended orders, *Leviathan* had just passed under the Golden Gate Bridge. She immediately turned sharply to starboard utilizing powerful bow thrusters to maneuver alongside the pier that ringed Old Fort Point.

The fort itself was a Civil War era three-tiered fortress once built to defend the entrance of the bay. Long denuded of its original cannons, it stood as a toothless sentinel. A tourist attraction since 1934, Fort Point had been covered over by the arching steel lattice of the Golden Gate's southern tower. Seizing the bridge and sealing off the incoming south bound vehicular lanes was *Leviathan's* primary objective.

Living in an authoritarian regime for so long had totally blinded admiral and general of the possibility Americans would use the *outgoing* lanes to drive rescue and military vehicles *into* the city.

Ji-Nan was on the main deck to observe *Leviathan's* marines drop rope ladders over the ship's gunwale. Then they lowered themselves down the berthed side where the ship's crew had just secured the mooring line to iron bollards on the pier. Its parking lot was wide open this early in the morning; perfect for mustering troops. The Chinese marines came down the ladders armed to the teeth with automatic weapons and shoulder draped bandoliers of ammunition along with pouches of grenades. After them came a reluctant first wave of 5,000 army regulars. These less disciplined troops were equipped with short barrel carbines designed to fire only rubber bullets. Only their officers were trusted enough to be allocated four stun grenades per platoon and two 8-round magazine clips for their side-arms which was understood to be used on their own men if engaged in looting and rape.

As the first wave descended, the next 5,000 swarmed up from multiple stairwell hatches but didn't follow them over the side. Instead, these soldiers lined up for breakfast or headed directly towards the chairs on the seaward side of the hull. After filling their trays with the usual portions of fish over rice, to save time, hundreds of them mounted an unoccupied toilet and defecated while they ate. This routine was replicated for all decks on all four tankers. It was late afternoon before the last man disembarked.

Captain Ji-Nan followed the other officers in a civilized manner, walking down the steps of the outboard gangway, finally feeling some of the privileges of his new rank. When he planted his feet on American soil the thought never occurred that he was a hostile invader with only 24 live rounds for his pistol against a country internationally known for its gun carrying population.

Things began to go right—right from the start. Private Zheng was assigned to his marine detachment. This was the sentry who alerted him about the vulnerabilities of lower bunk placement and the possibility of sinking. During their time at sea together Ji-Nan came to rely more and more on Zheng's practical experience in overseeing troops. Both were still unaware of the sinking of *Queen Wilhelmina*. That sinking was now a closely guarded secret by the top three commanders of *Yôngbào* for reasons of morale. When the troops witnessed the turnaround of *Antilles*, it was announced over the loudspeakers it was joining up with the end tanker *Queen Wilhelmina* to make an independent landing at the port of Long Beach.

Ji-Nan approached the commanding officer of the specialized marine unit he was assigned to. It turned out be another captain named Ying. Lee introduced himself as the senior unit interpreter and gave respectful assurances his assistance would only be given if called upon. After a roll call and head count, there followed a mission statement. It ended with three full throated chants of "Long Live China." Thereafter, the first objective was executed. The marines began to double time towards the southern entrance of the Golden Gate Bridge.

It was the commencement of *Yôngbào*.

Americans were soon to experience the Close Embrace.

While the marines went off to accomplish their first mission, some soldiers not yet assigned to any specific unit caused problems the minute they climbed off the ladders. A mixed-language heated confrontation developed with the fort's park rangers who objected to the flag being pulled down and replaced with China's. Most of the tourists were clueless but took out cells to livestream the argument and the massive supertanker. That all changed quickly enough when soldiers yanked the cells from their hands and attempted to call family members in China. After a couple of sharp, painful butt strokes to any tourist who resisted, the rest ran back to their cars.

Terrified families were pulled from their cars; keys and fobs snatched as large handbills were thrust into their faces—*Leave the City at once you will not be harmed*. Every vehicle was immediately refilled with soldiers forming a convoy into downtown San Francisco.

From above the crenellated roof of the fort, a solitary park ranger watched in bewilderment as a foreign invasion played out right before his eyes. The roof of the fort was an ideal location to be a forward observer. He ran to the roof access doors and barricaded them closed behind him, then made frantic calls to Miramar Marine Corps Air Station in San Diego.

The rest of the world's major intelligence services (Russia, England, France, India) and NSA spy satellites all picked up the same spike in calls by homesick invaders to their mothers, wives and sweethearts. The airwaves were humming with activity.

Double timing along scenic Bay Shore Road from Fort Point to the toll entrance of the Golden Gate Bridge, Ji-Nan and his company halted at the foot of the welcome center's Welcome Steps. Each of the 20 steps was individually stenciled with a single work from 20 different languages. The very first step had a simplified Mandarin character: *Huǎnying*—Welcome. Everyone smiled. It was understood to be a good omen. At the top of those steps, the invaders began to split up.

A small detachment headed for the red and white art deco Round House café. It resembled a glass-enclosed carousel. Their assignment was to rouse the patrons eating breakfast and send them north towards Sausalito via the bridge walkway. As soon as the startled patrons finished choking on their pancakes and eggs, they didn't have to be told twice. Their secondary assignment was to assess the amount of food stocked inside the restaurant and estimate shelf-life before spoilage, which they did while finishing the abandoned plates.

Another detachment surrounded the two story brick welcome center and frightened the hell out of the tourists inside. Several managed to make incoherent calls to incredulous 911 operators. Once everybody read the handbills the fierce Asian were passing out, and realized the uniforms and guns were not part of an immediate attack, those tourists rushed away like the others. Two marines and a third with a radio backpack were detailed to set up an observation post on the center's open air second deck.

Fantastic 911 calls began to trickle in. Then it became a deluge. Soon police sirens were heard in the distance. Ji-Nan heard those same sirens, and for the first time since leaving *Leviathan* he felt a deep sense of foreboding.

The marines were too busy completing their mission to be concerned. They were permanently shutting down southbound bridge lanes and walkways into San Francisco. Troops stationed themselves along a line of toll booths. They couldn't abruptly halt traffic. The risk from multiple collisions might result in possible fires, jackknifed trucks and possibly spill over to the critical northbound lanes as well. To avoid this potential danger, marines tossed glowing flares all along the roadway at 50' intervals. This brought traffic to a crawl, then the desired full stop. At each toll booth a soldier knifed tires, ignoring the yelling which always stopped as soon as the driver noticed the uniform and firearm. Soon every toll line was jammed with a car unable to move forward with the terrified drivers extracted at gun point. In short order a bumper to bumper jam stretched back miles. It took no more than 20 minutes to shut down the highway. The cacophony of irate drivers mashing their horns drowned out the ever approaching police sirens from the fast moving lanes on the northbound side.

Then something odd began to happen on those lanes to Sausalito County. The flowing heavy traffic began to thin out, then disappear altogether. Ji-Nan heard his name called by Ying. He shouted over the relentless honking from drives who had not yet had a Chinese assault rifle pointed in their faces accompanied with the flyer.

"Captain Ji-Nan, the local police have used their vehicles as a barricade across the north bridge lanes. The success of *Yōngbào* is wholly dependent on the American government observing the mass exodus of its people from San Francisco. This buys Beijing negotiation time and keeps the US military from coming in and annihilating us. Take this white flag and talk some sense into those fools blocking the roadway. Tell them they have 15 minutes to move their police cars and let their people leave or I'm sending my marines down there and regardless of consequences, will move them ourselves."

Handed a stick with a white rag, Ji-Nan headed down a quarter mile of empty three lane blacktop toward a barricade of black and white cars with flashing lights. For all his language expertise, he had never actually spoken to a native English speaker. His life now depended on how coherent or stupid his use of nuance came across. *What tone should I adopt? Threats or Confucian cajolery?* The idea of threats was dropped immediately because as he got closer, he realized the cops were aiming shotguns right at his chest. Then he realized he forgot to leave his sidearm with Captain Ying. One out-of-place gesture and the police had every right to blow him to bits. He raised his flag arm as well as his empty one as high as he could and slowed his pace to half steps.

"Freeze Asshole!" came blaring out of a loudspeaker.

Ji-Nan stopped! *Freeze!?* He only knew that English word had something to do with cold water. Two uniformed cops stood up from a crouched firing position and cautiously advanced toward him. Unable to move, he just starred at the huge shotgun barrels and the large Americans wielding them.

"Officers stand down! I say again—Stand Down! Orders from city hall command center!" This came from a roof mounted speaker.

The wary officers walked backwards, all the while anticipating any sudden moves by the perp in their sights. Only after securing themselves behind their bulletproof vehicles did they lower the shotgun barrels.

With flashing roof beacons and sirens wailing, suddenly they all made a rapid U-turn heading away. Ji-Nan had barely enough time to drop his white flag and scramble over the lane barriers before the newly released flood of escaping traffic almost ran him down. Walking back he received cheers from the marines.

Zheng was first to give him a salute. "Congratulations, you single-handedly sent those white devils scurrying back to their rat holes even if you did upset our unit betting on which of us would be the first to shoot one."

Lee ate up the praise. Ying approached and smiled, then whispered in his ear, "You're a brave man, but I know you said nothing. After I sent you, I received an urgent call from Ming. It seems our wise colonel's first objective was to surround and capture the San Francisco city council or whatever the hell they call it. He extracted terms from those sniveling cowards that in exchange for our passive occupation they would open the lanes outbound. They promised total collaboration in evacuating their citizens. We both know that is only temporary but it bought Beijing negotiation time and ourselves a stay of execution." After seeing the expression on Ji-Nan's face, Ying smiled again.

"You don't actually think the Americans are going to let us leave California alive, do you? The world's most vaunted power can't afford to lose face. If they let us sail away with a promise of safe conduct who's to say the North Koreans or Iran won't imitate our success, or try? No, America must destroy or imprison every last one of us. Thereafter, other nations with hostile intentions toward the US will be hard pressed to find thousands of average soldiers to volunteer. *Yôngbáo* is our sacrifice for the Love of the Chinese People. Through our deaths, Taiwan will be annexed to the mainland and become the beating heart of our new economic revitalization. Our insignificant lives are a small price to pay for an era of prosperity for the Chinese people. Wouldn't you agree Captain Ji-Nan?"

After listening to that patriotic explanation of his impending fate, Lee showed no emotion. Instead, he let his thoughts wander. They traveled to the far off principality of Luxembourg and his fellow Shanghainese, Ku Sheng-Wen.

Though it had nothing to do with Lee's apathetic blank stare, Captain Ying's demeanor changed to a demonic scowl. He pointed to what appeared to be a giant caterpillar creeping up the bridge's western Pacific side. It was slowly moving to the top of the 746' south tower. A pair of binoculars revealed 10 men were carrying some sort of rolled tube over their heads which exposed only the leg movements of this human centipede.

"Zheng! What is going on?" shouted Ying.

"Sergeant Feng is taking his squad up the tower to unfurl the People's glorious red banner!"

"You knew this and didn't inform me?"

"Sir, the whole unit knew Feng's plan was to honor you with this tribute to your command."

"Feng just signed our unit's doom sooner than planned. If this misguided patriotic act does not provoke the Americans into a rallying call to arms, nothing will."

When Feng and his squad reached the platform atop the south tower, the soldiers below broke into riotous cheers. The sole exception was Ji-Nan who wandered off to the café to scavenge an American breakfast. Meanwhile, atop the tower, there was as much jubilation as there was below. For Feng's squad there was time for a short respite to relax and enjoy the breathtaking view. Then they did what they came for. The immense flag and the red-orange steel structure blended magnificently. It was a spectacular sight. The effect was immediate on all who witnessed its unfurling.

This effect included the captain of the *Shanksville* over a mile away holding station on the Pacific Ocean side of the bridge watching the stars and stripes floating away on the morning breeze and the red one flying in its place.

The squad photographed each other for posterity. Without the benefit of a safety harness Sergeant Feng took point to start the precarious 500' descent along the cable arm to the roadway. Had they known about the maintenance elevator, it probably would have saved their lives.

Standing on the roof of the *Shanksville's* helicopter hanger superstructure, a United States Marine spotter for a sniper team raised a handheld anemometer to check windage. Adjacent to him were three snipers in prone firing position. Each peered through their scopes fixed to a semi-automatic M107-50 caliber rifle and focused on their targets. The snipers patiently waited for their enemy to descend an estimated 200' down from the cable arm. That way, once the shooting started, there would be no escape—up or down—before a second round of shots could go off. With that margin soon calculated, the team leader ordered his snipers onto their targets starting with the highest man and working downwards. The human targets were now aligned inside the crosshairs; the command to fire was given.

Three triggers were squeezed in unison sending three 50 caliber shells with a velocity of 2,800 feet per second on their way. Two and a half seconds later three men collapsed with grapefruit-sized holes in their chests and silently tumbled to the roadway below. In quick succession, the second volley had the same gruesome results. One targeted invader slipped down knocking off the man below him. This caused both bodies to drop together with the live one screaming all the way down.

Feng, confronted with the inevitable, paused, then whirled around to salute the glorious red banner of China one last time. He hastily bid his last two squad members farewell, then lunged from the cable arm with such force he cleared both roadway and walkway to swan dive into the swirling depths of the Pacific Ocean. The remaining Chinese were summarily dispatched, but their flag was still there. The heroics of Feng instantly became legendary to the invaders.

* * *

San Francisco Police Sergeant Theodore Tao was a happily married father of two, an Iraqi War veteran, and a Chinatown community activist who liked to start each morning's shift with a tranquil green tea and a low carb red bean muffin. In silence he looked askance at his partner behind the wheel of their Ford Interceptor. Officer Johnny Lee always started his shift tour with a coconut guava Twisted donut washed down with lukewarm coffee diluted by half-and-half plus multiple packets of chemical sweeteners. Officer Lee balanced his morning's elixir in one hand and dexterously fingered the touch-screen of his iPhone with the other to read Facebook messages.

"Hey Sarge, did you know I have a Facebook friend who's a cop in Beijing? He just sent me a private message. He's never used Han characters before. My grandmother is the only one left in my family who speaks the language, but in Cantonese. Can you translate for me?"

Reluctantly Sergeant Tao took the cell and read out loud in Mandarin, "*Dóngbian de Hóng tàyáng sheng qî, xibian de shi tàiyáng,*" and then translated into English devoid of emphasis, "*the red sun rises in the east and shits in the west.* By the way, the name of your so-called cop friend is Officer Generic. *Zhóng Guó Rén* which really means Mr. Chinese Man—you idiot! By now Beijing has tracked your badge number, social security, bank account, and captured your facial ID. Any day now you can expect the mainlanders to come over, kidnap and kill you. Then the very next day I'll find myself partnered with a replicant programmed to look like you—talk like you—act like you—but sure as shit won't think like you! Which, *hum,* might not be such a bad thing after all. Now turn that fucking thing off!" snapped Tao, as he tossed the phone in Lee's lap.

"Okay, first send a message in Mandarin for me. Tell 'em I have bullets in my gun for any fucking Maoist running dogs that comes over here."

"No! Don't let them know you're aware of being played. From now on just feed them bullshit . . . on your own time."

"How about we go raid Madam Yin's House? We can pump our arrest numbers with more tourists."

"Much too early in the morning for that. I see a more tempting target. Pull up behind that blue Escalade parked in front of that Italian restaurant. Then get out and ticket that Vietnamese bastard Lam Dang."

"Sarge, he's legally parked."

"His tires are bald."

"Everything is brand new. Even has legit temp tags."

"They look bald to me, and if that shyster lawyer offers you a Benjamin, we'll cuff him right here."

Officer Lee did what he was told and drove behind the Cadillac. He got out and started writing a summons for bald tires and another for an expired parking meter that was showing an hour left on the timer.

Sergeant Tao lowered the front passenger side window and leaned his head out to interrupt the conversation Mr. Lam Dang was having with two Mafia types in front of the restaurant doors.

"*Chào Bạn!*" sang Tao in a Vietnamese accent.

"And hello to you too, Sergeant Tao," Mr. Dang reciprocated. "I should think it respectful when two ethnically diverse fellow Americans greet each other they should at least do so in our national language."

"Then you must have obviously cheated on your naturalization exam because America doesn't have an official national language," snapped Tao not happy that he hadn't shaken up his mark, the cool response was not what he was after. What this creep did disgusted Tao to his core, and he needed to rattle him to keep Dang off balance.

"If your fellow officer is not planning to harass me further with more non-moving violations which will cost me an afternoon in traffic court to have dismissed and another few hours in civil court to file a Title 42 Harassment charge against you, I'd like to assume our morning's salutations are concluded."

"You won't be filing a damn thing counselor. Every judge, even the ones you bribe, know you for the human trafficker you are." Sergeant Tao abruptly halted his righteous accusations to listen in incredulous disbelief to the radio.

"Central Station to all units—10-32 men with guns--10-34 multiple riots in progress—10-35 major crime alert! The city is being invaded by a Chinese army—I say again—the city is being invaded! All units respond to Central Station—ASAP!"

"Lee get back here now!" he shouted, then slid over to get behind the wheel himself. Once his partner got in, Tao floored the accelerator deliberately sideswiping the beautiful new Escalade which lost a taillight as a result of the glancing impact.

"Jesus! What did you just do? We're leaving the scene of an accident! That lawyer is going to have our badges!"

"Priorities Johnny! Priorities! It seems the mainlanders are coming for you sooner than expected. Central Station is reporting a Chinese army invading."

"What? Bullshit! The *Red Dawn* movie couldn't come to life here in a big city. Whose says it's the Chinese? You think the white devils know the difference between our people and North Korean balloon heads? Not to mention the Japs," said Lee in disgust.

"True, but it's hardly likely the Japanese are going for a second round. So that pretty much narrows the field," answered Tao.

"Where'r we headed then, and why?"

"Telegraph Hill, Coit Tower! The highest point in the city. I have to figure out what we're up against."

Barreling north through the Italian section of the city on Columbus Avenue, Tao kept his eye out for signs of panic. Seeing none, he began to wonder if it was an elaborate hoax at the station. Or maybe a sick mind or a calculating one setting off diversions and confusion for an elaborate crime. In any case, he was forced to reduce speed to take the turn up Greenwich Street and pass rows of multi-million dollar homes before slowing to a crawl to negotiate the hairpin curves of Telegraph Boulevard to reach the Coit Tower parking lot. Once there, he grabbed binoculars and ordered his partner to sit tight and monitor the radio. The transmissions were chaotic. It seemed like every SFPD patrol car was calling in sightings of Chinese soldiers.

The 210' tower of fluted white concrete resembled a straight version of the leaning tower of Pisa. Some locals also fondly refer to it as Coitus Erectus. Built on the site of an original fire tower, it had the highest vantage point in the city. Inside the marble octagon lobby, Sergeant Tao rushed past murals of working class people. He made straight for the observation deck elevator. Since the place was not yet open for the day, it was silent and gloriously empty.

Sergeant Tao peered out from one of the open portals near the top. He made a binocular sweep from east to west.

This is no hoax!

The veteran didn't know much about ships, except he was positively certain that behemoth oil tankers were never permitted to berth on the shoreline of the city proper. Yet here they were. Their top decks overflowed with what looked like swarming ants crawling down the side of the ship's hulls. He judged the reason both the Oakland Bay and Golden Gate Bridge's incoming lanes were jammed bumper to bumper was part of whatever the attackers had planned. His speculations were again confirmed when he spotted a Chinese flag flapping on top of the bridge!

That sight slammed the situation home.

He felt a tightening in his stomach. He knew the stories of oppression under a dictator and an elite ruling group. He knew it wasn't really possible that they could take over the whole United States, but they were starting with his city, and the damage that could be done in just a day when the city was totally caught off guard was incalculable. As if his skin color hadn't been problem enough for some idiots, if the invaders took over this city, the life of Asian-Americans was going to get a lot more dangerous ... Feeling the crush of a two-prong pressure and the future of his family and friends hanging by a thread, Tao forced emotion out and let training take over.

Assess, then act ... then rip their assholes apart.

Tao witnessed panic beginning to break out among early morning tourists on the wharf. Raiders formed up after a bit of confusion and marched down Van Ness Avenue in military columns handing out papers to everyone. Tao rotated the central focus knob on his binoculars for maximum range. This enabled him to spot one more supertanker anchored parallel to San Francisco International Airport. He assumed the airport was already seized. That would account for the last ten minutes of not hearing any jets coming in for a landing. His thoughts were interrupted by static from his radio. It was followed by the desperate voice of his partner calling out his name. Tao pressed the transmitter clipped to his shoulder. "Go ahead Johnny.""

"Sergeant Tao, Central reports the Levi's Strauss company is being looted. Some reports say invaders are stripping off their uniforms to put on jeans. Another report says shots fired! Levi's Plaza at Battery Street is down the hill from us. Should I acknowledge a 1-4 to Charlie-Sierra?"

"No! Stay put! There's nothing we can do until reinforcements arrive. I'll be down in a minute."

Tao fished around in his pockets to retrieve his cell. When his wife answered, he was abrupt. "Sweetheart! Just listen to me! There's an emergency. I want you to keep Teddy home from school today. Then I want you to take him and the baby to the basement and lock yourselves in."

Understandably alarmed, Susan asked, "What in the world is going on?"

"I don't have time to explain. Take the extra Glock and a portable radio and some food and water. Secure yourself in the basement, barricade the door and stay there until I come home."

Tao ended by simply, with wholehearted devotion, telling his wife he loved her for all eternity before ending the call.

Down from Coit Tower, Sergeant Tao opened the trunk. He took out the two Mossberg 590 pump shotguns and loaded each magazine tube with nine cartridges of 12 gauge shot plus one more in each chamber. He double checked the safety before placing them upright in the seat rack between himself and his partner.

"Get us to Commercial Street—NOW!" ordered Tao.

In his haste, Officer Lee missed their turn and drove straight on through to Battery Street and Levi's Strauss Plaza. This landed them right in the middle of a fire-fight with both groups wearing the same identical uniform of jeans. With fighting at such close quarters, mistaken identity was a moot point. They also saw green uniformed bodies of Chinese soldiers leaking red stains on the pristine white marble of the plaza's public space. In such close proximity, it was inevitable a few stray live rounds began to puncture holes on the side of their police cruiser and rubber bullets started bouncing off the windshield.

"Jesus! Get us the hell out of here!" shouted Tao.

Officer Lee made a tire smoking 180° turn back to Greenwich Street, and this time found the correct exit toward Montgomery Street and the city center.

"Something triggered a mutiny! Why else would officers and soldiers shoot at one another? It can't be over Levis—can't it?" asked Tao.

"I dunno! But it saves us the trouble! Then again, it's embarrassing to witness just how fucked up our mainland relatives are. Damn glad I'm an American!"

Driving on, they saw isolated units of soldiers and developing signs of panic from citizens. Operators simply abandoned their street cars and trolley buses to the utter bewilderment of passengers. Grippers walked away from cable cars leaving lines of waiting tourists eager for their first ride. Locals knowing something was very wrong were in a mad rush to round up their families and run. Every car Ted and Johnny saw was heading towards the Oakland Bay Bridge to escape to Sacramento.

As panic gathered momentum, every block in the city had at least one fatality: from sudden heart failures to careless accidents. Some lucky fools got immediate medical assistance, while others were stepped over where they collapsed, some getting the added insult of being robbed while they were down. It all depended on the chance collapse near a Good Samaritan or a thief.

It would later be confirmed the first recorded instance of a native San Franciscan who fought back against a Chinese invader happened on the infamous 300 block of Hyde Street, in the Tenderloin District. A man with full body tattoos leaped from his cardboard box and proclaimed himself the King of Easter Island. Then plunged a used syringe in a passing soldier's neck with such force it tore his carotid artery. His fellow soldiers avenged him by unloading rubber bullets point blank into the homeless man's face. Designed to break bones, they drilled into his eye sockets making a hideous mess. With no time for screaming, both the King of Easter Island and the Chinese peasant invader were dead within minutes, left on the feces-covered sidewalk.

After that incident no more safe conduct handbills were given out on Hyde Street. A few angry soldiers amused themselves by setting fire to homeless tents whether they were occupied or not.

In the meantime, Sergeant Tao and Officer Lee, after fighting traffic for nearly an hour, reached their destination at Commercial Street. It was the location of the popular All-A radio station – Asian-Americans Answer All. The only network broadcasting exclusively in Mandarin with a social media platform as well. Again, Tao left his partner with orders to stay put. As he bolted up the two flights of stairs to the main lobby, he rushed by the receptionist to seek out the daytime producer Daniel Song who was anything but surprised to see him. In his capacity as a Chinatown community activist, Tao was a frequent guest commentator and no stranger to the studio executives and technical staff.

"So, it's true then? You rushing here in uniform … Should I take down the portrait Dr. Sun Yat-Sen in the reception area and replace it with that of The Great Helmsman?" the incredulous station producer tried to joke, but it fell flat with fear.

"The first thing is to stop scheduled programs in Mandarin! It's giving inadvertent advice to these mainland invaders in their own language. Broadcasting about police activity and telling our people rescue is at hand by where the military will most likely be entering the city only helps the invaders. Even simple weather reports and supermarket commercials with locations gives them aid and comfort. This is some real shit, we got to stay focused! Let's record an announcement in English. Afterward, keep my speech on a continuous loop 24/7. That is, until our armed forces liberate us or the invaders bust in your front door! If it's Mao's minions—then sabotage the transmitters!"

"Whoa there, Ted. Those transmitters are five mil apiece," explained a horrified Daniel Song.

"If they take over this station, money is going to be least of your problems. Now let's get our script ready and get this going."

With no time to write and re-write the perfect speech, Tao bullet pointed a few things, and hoped he could be inspirational enough to make a difference; the first version was going to be going out live, then the recorded version would be looped.

"My fellow Americans, my name is Sergeant Theodore Tao of the San Francisco Police Department. Like most of you, my family immigrated from Canton and Guangdong provinces to find work and a new life here. Today I must address you in the English language not Mandarin. It is with an angry heart that I confirm today's rumor

*to be fact. That the tyrannical Maoists who have long plagued our ancestral home as parasites, now are trying to control the world. They have sent an invading army right to our homes and families. This elite run dictatorship devoured our ancestor's freedom, now it seeks to devour our children's future. We must never let this happen! Because of our culture and our ethnicity, **WE** must be the ones to push them back! At this very moment, thousands of Caucasians, Blacks and Hispanics are fleeing San Francisco in panic. We Chinese-Americans are the ones most betrayed by these mainland invaders and, make no mistake about it, we will be the ones most likely to suffer for it once our military kills them. The other ethic races now abandoning San Francisco will not distinguish between us and them! Or worse! They will accuse us of helping set this attack up. It is imperative we must strike the first blow. If we Asian-Americans hesitate, then we as a people will forever suffer the same shame and indignation that the Japanese-Americans unfairly endured after Pearl Harbor. And I, for one, as a patriotic American, will fight to the death any Maoist mainlander who causes us to be branded with that mark of collaborator. Therefore, I call upon every Asian-American adult within range of this broadcast to arm themselves with whatever weapon is available, and report to the Central Station Police Headquarters near the Chinatown Dragon Gateway. This is a call to battle not just against an enemy who seeks to enslave us. Their actions would forever eradicate the good our ancestors have done and worked for in the U.S. Their spirits must continue to guide us like a star, their honor and their hard work—our grandparents and parents sacrificed for us to be free Americans. **This attack will fall heaviest on us.** For that reason alone, we must not only destroy these attackers but we must make a show that it is* **us** *who are doing it for all of our neighbors. We must show no mercy! Death to the invader by a thousand cuts! Long live the United States of America!"*

As soon as the live lights went out, Song opened the soundproof door with a look of dread.

"My speech was that bad?" asked Tao.

"Our staff was debating whether to interrupt your broadcast or not. If we abruptly halted your speech mid-sentence live–it would have frightened the listening audience. More chaos."

"Well?" asked Tao

Daniel Song took a deep breath and picked his words cautiously. "Sealed inside here, you were isolated from the sounds of gunfire from the street below."

"Johnny!" exclaimed Tao making a dash for the exit.

He ran down two flights of stairs to the double doors of the entrance. He had to force the door open with all his might to push aside a body in a green uniform jammed against it. Once outside, Ted saw half a dozen more sprawled on the sidewalk.

Where the hell is the police cruiser? I told him to stay put!

Frantically, Tao looked up and down Commercial Street. He was about to press the transmitter button on his shoulder when he spotted a ribbon of blood on the sidewalk. It led up the street to another pile of bodies. To his horror, one of the bodies had a black uniform. Too angry to be shocked, Tao shoved aside bodies.

Officer Lee's badge, utility belt, wristwatch and academy ring had all been stripped away, as well as his cell phone. Tao knelt down beside his partner's almost unrecognizable bludgeoned face and removed the rolled up paper shoved down his throat. *Leave the city at once—you will not be harmed.* Tao stood up and with a sickened heart was about to transmit that abhorrent of all police codes: 10-54—Officer Down.

Interrupted just as he touched the button, he heard wheezing noises coming from one of the prone bodies. The wounded soldier's mumbling Mandarin was too difficult to interpret. Anyway, he was in no mood for conversation. He unholstered his gun to check to see if he had a fully loaded magazine. Then slid the safety off. As Tao stood over the semi-conscious Chinese soldier slowly choking on his own blood, he ad-libbed some lyrics: *If you're going to San Francisco, you're NOT! going to meet some gentle people here.* Sergeant Theodore Tao precisely, with extreme malice and forethought, fired three rounds point blank into the invader's head to make sure he was dead.

* * *

Squad cars circled the fallen officer, Tao gave a verbal report and knowing there was nothing further to do here, he said he was breaking for an early lunch. This brought gapes of surprise to the faces surrounding Officer Lee's body. Tao just growled that he would be back and stalked off.

Tao was still in a towering rage over the murder of his partner. Even after spending lunch with Susan and knowing she and the children were out of harm's way, Johnny's death tormented him. Since the Tao family lived on one of the steepest hills in the city, wandering bands of marauding soldiers hadn't bothered to attempt such an exhausting climb. Most of the invaders seemed to be controlling public buildings and not harassing civilians. Assuming the same would hold, at least for a while, he headed to his precinct after instructing Susan to keep a watch on the neighborhood and be ready to barricade in the basement again if things changed for the worst.

On the way back to the station Tao was surprised by how thinly dispersed these PLA soldiers were. This reduced unit cohesion and mutual interlocking support. It was not much of an effort to control or patrol now that the initial surge was over. Tao thought they were either leaderless, lost, or simply inept. *Why would China send a second rate, poorly trained army instead of crack troops to launch such an important mission?* Then it dawned on him. The best troops we being held back to protect the rulers. This was an act of desperation.

If football had been China's national sport instead of table tennis, this invasion would be their fourth quarter Hail Mary pass.

The station house that patrolled the borderline between Little Italy and Chinatown was a wreck. With great difficulty Tao managed to push his way through an angry crowd of Asian faces. Tao was glad to see the majority of them had hunting rifle cases slung over their shoulders. Most others had some sort of blunt instrument that could be an effective weapon in close quarters. Sergeant Tao even recognized members of the Tong gang by their cheap suits that ineffectively concealed shoulder holsters. Crammed to capacity, the six story edifice of the city's iconic police station was swamped. So much so, it spilled over to swell nearby Portsmouth Square Plaza. As Tao worked his way through the human morass, he could see the watch commander, Sergeant Jiee, had lost crowd control. Jiee stood on his large reception desk with a bullhorn and shouted for order but to no avail.

Tao knew the situation was volatile and about to explode when he heard a threatening voice say above the crowd noise, "You chinks threw us Japanese-

Americans under the bus for Pearl Harbor to get ahead! Now it's your fucking turn!"

Then a fistfight broke out.

Tao saw Japanese and Koreans mixed in with Filipinos, Chinese, Vietnamese and many other small regions in this Asian-American melting pot. He mounted the reception desk to stand alongside Sergeant Jiee and wrestled the bullhorn out of his hands.

Jiee, who was yet unaware of Tao's partner's death, accused him of being responsible for all this furor by making that totally irresponsible radio broadcast. Ending with a sneering, "Okay Paul Revere! What the fuck are you going to tell 'em all now!?"

The older cop at first said nothing. Then reached around with his free hand and inserted a blank cartridge in his Glock 9mm. Tao aimed at the ceiling and pulled the trigger. The non-lethal blast reverberated off the marble walls and echoed about the corridors. The sound was a classic when needing attention in an area where civilians could be hit by a live round; it worked perfectly here.

"Listen to me! All of you! We must get organized!" Tao bullhorned over them.

Tao needed to motivate them fast before the cacophony started again. Above all, he needed them focused. He racked his brain on what to do next. An idea jumped out at him when he spotted the oldest Asian face in a sea of youthful and middle aged ones. Tao gestured for the old man to come forward. With the help of those up front, they lifted the senior citizen onto the large desk between the two sergeants.

"Sir, can you tell us your name, and explain that button pinned to your jacket?" asked Tao who feigned ignorance. He knew exactly the symbolism behind it, as well as most of the older generation of men in the crowd. The not so frail old man was handed the bullhorn and spoke proudly.

"Yes, so, my name is Harry Kang. I'm ninety-four. It was on December 7th in 1941, I was just six. For weeks after Pearl Harbor my father and older brother were beaten up by roving bands who couldn't tell Chinese from Japanese but beyond that, they figured anyone of Asian descent was a spy. The US government issued these buttons with Dr. Sun Yat-Sen's blue and white

Chinese Republican flag with words declaring the wearer a loyal Chinese-American. These we could show, it worked sometimes, but—"

An angry voice yelled out, "That didn't stop you Chinese from denouncing your Japanese-American neighbors. When my ancestors were shipped off to their internment camps, you people bought up their homes in enforced foreclosures for pennies on the dollar. This time the shoe's on the other foot!"

Harry knew, as well as Tao who had stepped nearer to him, that this had to be handled fast before all hell broke loose. "I understand your frustration young man, but let's not double down on injustices. We have to rise above them. And this is OUR chance, we ASIANS, to show just what we are made of. Remember how your honorable ancestors behaved under the pressure of national scorn and vile racism. Your Japanese-American ancestors doubled down on their patriotism and organized themselves into the hardest fighting unit in World War Two—the 442nd Nisei Infantry Regiment. Now everyone of every color is fleeing our city; only knowing Asians have invaded. Be aware, when this current crisis is over, your fellow Americans will only remember they were attacked by Asians! I've lived through this before. They're not going to differentiate; the suspicions and animosity will drag on for decades. Hate crimes against anyone looking even slightly Asian will increase. We must all act now and our response must be a united one! And some of you young punks need to video our fighting back on your stupid phones!"

Tao saw the room was in thought, not needing the bullhorn now, he stomped his foot. "Harry is right!" He stomped again. "All the other ethic and color groups in San Fran are running for safety. We Asian-Americans have been handed a once in a lifetime opportunity by throwing these invaders back into the sea and shutting down 150 years of race prejudice! Every time one of those bastards opens their mouth again we will yell for them to remember San Francisco. God Bless America!"

Central Station erupted in a riotous cheer echoed by the lines of people all the way into Portsmouth Square Plaza. It was several minutes before the patriotic cheers dropped low enough to hear Sergeant Tao's next instructions. He began by asking all the people with military training to step forward so they could lead groups. They started to cluster in groups of 15 to 20 people: old grannies, basement computer nerds, retired military, lesbians, angry teen boys, and female and male teachers—all grouping up and sending their leader to Tao to get assigned to areas in the city where they were going to patrol and push back.

Tao faced the watch commander asking for the keys to the basement armory for which he was promptly denied.

"I've just heard about the death of your partner, our brother Officer Lee. Still, the answer is no! Martial Law hasn't been declared! I'm responsible for their safekeeping! I have no orders from the mayor or governor!"

The crowd started to mumble—threatening to grow back to a chaotic roar soon.

"Give him the keys Sergeant Jiee. I'll authorize it," came the voice of Precinct Commander Philip Chin as he bent over the watch commander's day log to make his verbal order a written one. After he signed the order, he smiled up at Sergeant Tao. "I was quite fond of Officer Lee. He reminded me of one of my sons; always on that smart phone, always cracking jokes. Anyway, arming these civilians will probably cost me my pension. I guess that's the price I'll have to pay to drive these fuckers from our shores. I quite enjoyed your radio speech. When this crisis is behind us, I'll have to call my brother-in-law. He owns a body shop in Palo Alto. I'm sure he can always use another welder. Carry on sergeant."

"Thank you, sir," was Tao's respectful reply, relieved and guilty that his own pension had just been covered since he could now be shown to be following orders. Then Tao turned back to the crowd. "Before we issue any of our Mossberg shotguns, you must all be deputized. Raise your right hand and repeat after me …"

* * *

The hills of San Francisco were glowing with the last golden light of the day. A magical few minutes when the air seemed both calm and metallic, with the sky purpling to night behind it. Any locals who had not been able to get out of the city locked up their homes, kept the lights out and prepared for a very restless first night. Radio and TV broadcasts were assuring everyone that the invaders wouldn't harm anyone, that the president and military were in deep negotiations, that help was on the way … all promises heard before in some version … all lies.

Despite the uncertainly and fear, since the invaders weren't actively shooting people, the first night of this war settled into a mistrustful stillness.

* * *

During the early hours of the second morning of *Yôngbào*, Fleet Admiral Phong and Land Force Commander Major-General Sheng breakfasted together in silence. Sheng had a feeling it was going to be the last day of his life. His apprehension was not shared with the man of stone sitting opposite of him in *Leviathan's* wardroom. Sleeping Leopard never dwelled on mortality; his own or anyone else's. Besides, he had other worries. Prominent among them was the US Navy warship lurking like a rogue shark on the Pacific Ocean side of that famous bridge. Its menacing presence seemed poised to savagely maul and sink another one of his ships. If it did attack, at least the invasion force was finally completely dispersed throughout the city. Even though it had taken ten agonizing hours to disembark all 100,000 soldiers, they were now tactically deployed at the major choke points throughout the city.

Deliberately sinking four tankers within the confines of the bay area would effectively shut down the port. Since money was king to Americans, and a closed port would cost them billions, this must be the reason that no attacks came from the warship yet. Convinced he was no longer a sitting duck to be shot to pieces, the fleet admiral had other worries to solve.

He was immediately plagued with the biological hazard of decomposing bodies. Some bodies had been trampled or fallen while getting off the ships. Some bodies were carried in by ocean currents——ripped and torn by sharks. This caused a near mutiny. Some of the crew members even made the reasonable assumption they might be next. There were rumors that the accursed American captain rescued some survivors for enhanced interrogation and torture, that the rest of the floundering men in the water had been used for live fire exercises. It was a gruesome price to pay in lives and debilitating morale connected to this single warship that shouldn't have been in the area.

It was within this psychological setting that both admiral and general apprised their situation and what this second day would bring. Both knew they were soon going to be held responsible for an unmitigated disaster; but only one admitted to it, the other was in denial. The general had no illusions and he had taken the precaution to have his grandsons removed from harm's way with the covert assistance of an unlikely source. He was betting everything he cared about that this covert help wasn't a trick, but had no way to check on his family when Phong was always within hearing distance.

The admiral would never admit, least of all to himself, he had chosen to lead a naval expedition that might escalate into World War III just to avoid opium trafficking charges and escape the misery of domesticity with an unhappy, tiresome wife.

Despite the initial heavy loss of life and internal political treachery, *Yóngbào* had achieved utter surprise on the inhabitants of San Francisco and subsequently the rest of the US.

The silence from the White House was deafening; and for the Chinese it was perfect.

* * *

The silence from the White House was a cause for concern for manys. The US military alert status was at defense level readiness 2; not a joke because DEFCON 1 was nuclear war. As it was, at level 2, every branch of the military was in readiness to deploy within 6 hours of receiving orders. President Atwater and Vice President Lejeune sealed themselves deep inside the bomb shelter at Mount Weather Emergency Operations Center in Bluemont, Virginia. They were strategizing over the short list of doomsday options. Though the president had been vehemently warned by CIA staff about this exact Chinese deception less than a week ago, he nevertheless sent the entire navy's Seventh Fleet into the Formosa Straits; only to confront a paper dragon. Bitterly humiliated, he was more determined than ever to undo this monumental blunder. Yet he was also more determined than ever to stay out of reach of any new assassins, this fear had been a slow growing panic that was taking over his thoughts.

Atwater was further pushed onto the verge of apoplexy when he received Beijing's overtures to legitimize their claim on Taiwan as the *quid pro quo* for abandonment of San Francisco.

Premier Jian and his hard core expansionist CCP leaders were willing to bet the lives of nearly two billion of their own people that the United States would never go to DEFCON-1 and launch nuclear weapons; and in this assumption the politburo was correct. They knew the US was willing to surround Taiwan with warships and risk some skirmishes, but launching nuclear missiles against mainland China was something only simulated in war games.

Conversely, American leaders were praying and feeling entirely dependent on the behavior of 100,000 poorly trained soldiers roaming freely on the streets of an American city. If military discipline were to deteriorate, who knows what could happen—including a war on both continents. To complicate matters further, the president steadfastly refused all calls from Beijing or via others trying desperately to end this insanity.

This non-response was misinterpreted by the CCP; they were thinking time was on their side and President Atwater was out of all options but one: acquiescence. They were now sure the annexation of Taiwan would soon be the bloodless *fait accompli* they all envisioned. Especially with the sanguine first day progress reports of the victorious invasion of an actual city in America. With the exception of a few ugly incidents, 20% of the population was evacuated with fewer than 100 reported civilian deaths. The majority of which were listed as stress related natural causes that the Chinese government would argue they could not be legitimately held accountable for in later diplomatic negotiations.

Friends or foes; within 24 hours of an invasion of the USA, the smell of blood and profit was in the air. No nation but China thought they would be successful in the long run; in the short run there was massive money to be made and positioning to be done.

Russia mobilized along the Manchurian border to procure a bit of resource rich new territory while the current owners were occupied.

India was strengthening their mountain posts with the same goal in mind.

Filipino marines were surrounding the Luzon Straits.

Vietnam, Laos and Thailand were in joint preparation for a punitive expedition into China's soft underbelly at the southern boundaries of Yunnan Province.

Japan was calling up her military reserves.

Only South Korea kept its forces in place. It had to stay on hair trigger against the north.

Even the North Koreans sensed a seismic shift in their relationship with China and the continuity of its largesse. Rumors abounded that hordes of starving North Korean peasants were gathering just outside of the barricades of the newly constructed Great Yalu River Bridge ready to cross over and swarm China's Dandong Province.

African countries were seizing and nationalizing all Chinese financed factories and mines.

The European Union, not to be outdone in tearing off their piece of the carcass, declared themselves solvent of all liabilities to Chinese banks; Wall Street played follow the leader on that self-interested move.

* * *

Between Phong's stoicism and Shang's disciplined tranquility, not so much as an eyebrow was raised by grim reports listing out country after country massing against their homeland's borders. They certainly weren't the reports they had wished for to start off this second day, but there was no going back now. Both knew these reports, if accurate, portended hard fighting ahead. A regime change was certainly in the making, but there was always the next century, and an another one after that. Admiral Phong ended his silence when he held up a special document affixed with the official red banner seal of the politburo.

"Premier Jian demands to know the optimum date you can conclude your exercise and return this fifteen percent of the People's Liberation Army now urgently required for mainland duties."

"*An exercise?* Now they're calling a blatant act of war against the United States an exercise? Well, I'm a land force commander. Unlike you admiral, I've not been given the onerous responsibility of transportation," answered the general.

"Once the soldiers disembarked my ships, they're under your leadership," said Phong.

"Then you can explain in writing to both Premier Jian and our politburo masters what became of the other 75,000 troops that simply vanished along with three of your ships before coming ashore here," he responded without a trace of irony in his voice.

"As these reports indicate, the motherland may suffer a thousand cuts by the piratical nations now encroaching on her sovereignty, and you manifest an attitude found to be wanting in your duties to the party which shall be reported."

Just as Sheng was preparing a retort about elite desperation, Marine Captain Ying first knocked, then approached quickly. "Admiral, general," he nodded briefly, "that American warship has transmitted a message."

"Read it!"

"*Leave the city at once—You will not be harmed*, signed Captain Amber O'Sullivan USS *Shanksville*. Is there a reply admiral?"

"Get out!" he snarled.

"Hold on captain," spoke up Sheng. "I'm going on a troop inspection this morning. I'll need vehicles and escorts. Kindly see to it. And here is paperwork to settle the promotion of my new assistant."

"At once general," replied Ying.

The old general finished his breakfast. He got up to leave the wardroom but hesitated, then turned to confront his joint-commander. Exhausted of animus, he went out of his way to be sympathetic for a parting he alone knew was a final one and adopted a tone of serene Confucian understanding.

"When I was offered the commission to command land forces for *Yôngbào*, I undertook some private research on my own. I investigated all the ill-fated invasions by a foreign power against the United States. One attempt struck me as the most prophetic. During the Second World War, Japanese Admiral Hosogaya led a surprise landing in Alaska. At the time, America's main battle forces were scatted across Pacific islands or fighting in North Africa. All other military troop concentrations then, as now, were deployed along the eastern coast. The entire west coast from Alaska to Canada down to California was vulnerable."

"Your point?"

"This Admiral Hosogaya had scarcely put ashore ten percent of his landing force when colored shells exploded near his battleship from a small flotilla of puny American destroyers. He mistook the shells for bombs and panicked. He lost his nerve, choose caution over daring, and abandoned the landed soldiers and ran. All perished except a few prisoners. Then, like now, somebody, somewhere, has lost his nerve. *Sayonara* admiral!" he said with deliberate emphasis on that Japanese word.

Phong gave no response. There was none to make. It was understood between them that the ultimate outcome of *Yŏngbào* was the responsibility of a politburo apparatchik made 6,000 miles away. They had so much power, and no control at all.

* * *

Eardrum splitting sounds of jet afterburners and trailing sonic booms reverberated throughout *Leviathan's* lower decks and passageways. Raised from a much needed sleep from the exhausting previous day, Ji-Nan stumbled around dressed only in underwear and holding a flashlight. He spotted Ying also walking around. Ying snapped his fingers and hurried over the second he saw Lee to calmly tell Lee the F-18s were only reconnaissance aircraft getting a photo op. The bombs would come another time. Ying was holding up two PLA green epaulettes, each with a singular large gold star. With a grin.

"Major-General Sheng has honored you to be his aide-de-camp. It comes with a promotion; congratulations Major Lee Ji-Nan! Now get dressed. We have an important assignment."

The new major stood at confused attention alongside a Lincoln SUV parked opposite *Leviathan's* outer gangway steps. Yesterday he was tasked to commandeer vehicles. Since the southbound lanes of the Golden Gate Bridge were jammed with abandoned cars from the previous day, he was able to accumulate a connoisseur's collection. Twenty-five of the most luxuriant SUVs and pickup trucks were now loaded with armed and ready troops.

The overall commander for convoy security was Captain Ying. As he portioned his men out, eight were squeezed into the SUVs and 10 in every truck. Ying wondered if his forces were adequate. He was certain that lone warship was behind the disappearance of six of his marines. Only residue pools of blood remained where they once stood sentry post during the night along the Golden Gate's walkway. The flag that cost him ten good men was also gone. He suspected there were Americans spying on his every move yet he didn't know the city well enough to send a strike force out to find spies; and really, there could be just one or a dozen of them. They should take out all cell and radio towers. But the general had other things on his plate.

Standing like a fool by the general's SUV, Ji-Nan wondered if his latest promotion fulfilled the second of the ancient Chinese five blessings—Prosperity. The third blessing—Good Health—he took for granted. The fourth blessing — Good Morality, was questionable from his birth until now, but he would contemplate that blessing when an opportunity for soul-searching redemption showed itself. It was achieving the most important first and fifth blessings— Longevity and Natural Death—that in present circumstances, seemed wishful.

Sheng descended *Leviathan's* gangway past Major Ji-Nan and Captain Ying in frozen salutes. Zheng was holding the SUV's passenger door open. All received the general's signature benevolent smile with his returned salute as he slid into the middle row. Ji-Nan got behind the wheel with Captain Ying in the passenger spot. Zheng and two other enlisted men occupied the last row with their weapons locked and loaded.

Before the convoy got underway, Sheng leaned forward and handed his assistant an address. Afterwards, he gently rested his hand on Lee's shoulder and whispered, "When my grandsons reach manhood, I hope their gonads match the size of your pair."

Lee smiled, but knew he was just being pulled along the flow of life by fate, fate which seemed to look on him kindly for some reason.

Initially, General Sheng's 25 vehicle convoy took Highway 101 which passed by the beautiful Promenade Causeway. A rolling ocean breeze helped dissipate the smell of unwashed bodies closely confined inside the SUVs. The rush of sea air was a palliative, especially for the soldiers that rode in the open beds of the pickups. Unfortunately, this offered easy targets for a sniper. The convoy didn't stop or fire any retaliatory shots, they just tossed any bodies over the side as they rolled along.

The turn onto Lombard Street was less dangerous, but the scenes were shocking. RVs lined the curbside with waste tubes drooling out brown liquids and solids. Midpoint between the motor home area and a homeless camp was Moscone Health and Social Center. With the wholesale departure of its staff along with the scarcity of everyday drug dealers, the street was erupting in a violent collective episode of withdrawal. The desperation of addicts abandoned by their suppliers and medics caused them to scavenge needles off the sidewalk and out of trash bins hoping for a teardrop of heroin left in the syringe.

"This would never be tolerated in the public spaces of our motherland. Decadence and debauchery are private matters best kept within the confines of a family home," lectured Sheng with a straight face.

On the final leg of the journey, the convoy turned onto the broad thoroughfare of Van Ness Avenue. Unlike the filth left behind on Lombard Street, it was a scenic vista worthy of a postcard. Situated at the avenue's end was a two block long monochromatic building that supported the light blue and gold dome of city hall. At first glance, it could easily be mistaken for *Les Invalides.*

As the lead vehicle pulled up in front of the six columns of city hall the view instantly turned grotesque. Startling the occupants was a thumping that caused Sheng and the back row to look up and see dangling boots.

The body of one of their own soldiers was suspended above their heads. Sheng swung his door open, getting out first. He was further outraged when he saw all four flagpoles in front of city hall had a soldier hung with a large sign in Mandarin *—Qiángjiān fàn* (rapist). The general stormed up the steps, ignored the salutes of the posted sentries, and latched onto the first officer he saw.

"Who is responsible for this lieutenant!?"

"Colonel Ming," answered a frightened man.

"Have them cut down at once! Captain Ying shoot this officer if he fails to immediately comply with my order!" Then he entered the rotunda with Ji-Nan fast at his heels. Once inside the grand building, he stopped short before the palatial marble staircase. It was like being inside a castle.

Upstairs, they were acknowledged by an inner security detail. Then they were escorted past huge doors and announced. This brought everyone inside to their feet. The enormous room had pillars of rare wood and suspended French Limoges crystal chandeliers; it was the seat of San Francisco's municipal government known as the Board of Supervisors Chamber. It was now commandeered by the armed forces of The People's Republic of China. That gave Sheng a flush of pride.

The conference table was covered with occupation plans: large scale city maps and engineering schematics were displayed. TV screens and rows of laptops were monitored by technicians. Among them were five armchair pilots keeping drones sweeping the city to alert for any military response. Colonel Ming, with his insincere yet practiced smile, made it plain he was not overjoyed about this no-notice inspection. Luckily for him, Sheng controlled his steaming rage in front of all.

"Welcome general, may I escort you to your command desk on the next floor? It belongs to the mayor but it's vacant at the moment," laughed Ming.

"You may."

"Excuse me colonel," spoke up one of the drone pilots. "I've detected an airborne anomaly. Low altitude. I suspect it's a stealth helicopter."

"It's daylight! Is everybody blind? Tell the perimeter guards to open their eyes!"

Distracted for the moment, the colonel made a mental notation of the anomaly. Primarily, he was more concerned with getting General Sheng out of the operations area into the secluded office upstairs and out of his way. All three men ascended another flight of stairs to a smaller but no less ornate chamber.

After a cursory inspection of what was meant to be his gilded isolation, Sheng turned to Lee. "Major, would you kindly excuse us for a moment, and bring me a pot of tea if you please."

For some reason he always spoke courteously to Lee. As Lee hurried to find a way to get tea prepared, Lee figured he must remind the old man of a grandson somehow; that was the only explanation he could come up with.

Ming couldn't hold back cynicism. "*Major* Ji-Nan? From a pimp driver to thinking-for-himself private to field grade officer in less than a month? The PLA has advanced light years in the class struggle for the proletariat."

"Is that a surprise? I believe *you* had a hand in one of those promotions," Sheng said, his voice trailed off but his anger was simmering. He leaned over the edge of the large ornate desk in the center of the room. He lifted the receiver off a multi-button phone and began playfully tapping it on the table-top. "Am I giving your spies an earache?"

"I doubt it. Our equipment is the most advanced," Ming answered back.

At such insolence Sheng's anger became volcanic. Regardless of the stress he was inflicting on his failing heart, he smacked Ming across the face with the receiver. Then he picked up the entire phone base and flung it against the nearest wall. "Don't you dare play with me! Explain that grotesque spectacle of our hung soldiers!"

At first Ming remained stoic, then he spit out a glob of blood on the floor. "It was necessary!" he shouted back exposing bloodstained teeth. "Discipline was failing! Our soldiers started to disobey orders the moment they disembarked. They're a bunch of peasants that think they're in a theme park without rules. This invasion was thrown together out of desperation. The army should have been trained for over a year for such a complex operation—not three weeks. Which is why you, General Sheng are no longer held in a position of esteemed trust by the Chinese people and are forthwith relieved of command. Beijing's latest communiqué has appointed me powers to implement extraordinary measures for the successful resolution of *Yôngbào*."

"Which means you're going to do something drastic and stupid!"

"I intend to maintain the current exodus from the city for another twenty-four hours. By which time if President Atwater fails to respond to Beijing's demand for Taiwan's peaceful annexation, I shall begin taking hostages and publicly execute them. I'll replace the Chinese with Americans hung from those flagpoles."

"You're mad!"

"I find your attitude both baffling and squeamish. How many comrade corpses did you step over? Do you remember? Do you even care to remember?

For the moment though, I'm sure as land force commander you're anxious to carry out your limited duties. Therefore, I needn't detain you any further."

With Sheng effectively reduced to a figurehead, which was his plan all along, Colonel Ming, without taking formal leave, abruptly turned his back on his once superior officer. Before he closed the door, he noticed Sheng lift a magnifying glass off the large desk and pocket it. Also, the way the old general didn't push back and also kept glancing at his wristwatch was altogether suspicious. For a brief moment, Ming speculated a connection between the general's out of character acquiescence of command and the stealth blip on their radar, but dismissed it out of hand.

Still, doubts lingered. Sheng was planning something.

Equally suspicious of Ming, Sheng gave himself a full ten minute interval from Ming's departure before he made his move. Lee must have gone all the way back to China to fetch his tea, so he would have to do without it for now. Time was slipping away too fast.

The most important meeting of his life was about to take place. He made sure to lock the double doors of the mayor's office. Then he walked into a smaller private side office and went up another staircase; locking all the doors behind him. At the top he walked down a dimly-lit corridor and searched for a specific numbered door. He felt secured in the knowledge no curious Chinese soldier would wander up to the unlucky fourth floor, much less dare enter a conference room numbered 404. Nevertheless, he drew his pistol.

An American-accented Mandarin voice came from the darkness. *"Ni hui shô yingyû ma?"*

"Yes, I do speak English," Sheng answered back.

When the light switched on, it revealed two Americans, both in business suits seated side-by-side at the end of a long conference table. The one in a grey suit with gold flecks matching hazel eyes was a woman. That surprised him, though he knew it should not have. It was too hard to overcome his years of power in a male dominated party structure. The Americans were different, if someone had the skills for a certain job, for the most part the most skilled person was awarded that job. "To whom do I have the honor of speaking with?"

"My name is Valentine Parrott. I'm a senior analyst at the CIA. This is my colleague and interpreter Peter Chan. We're the designated agents sent to privately negotiate with you Major-General Woo Sheng. I must emphasize we are not an official delegation of the United States government. We're not empowered to make guarantees as to the fate of your invading army."

Still with pistol drawn in his left hand, Sheng advanced to extend his right in friendship.

"That's close enough! I won't shake the hand of the leader of an invading force against our country," warned Parrott.

"Quite right. You are serious negotiators. If you did shake my hand, it meant you would have insincerely promised me anything—and I would have had no choice but to shoot you both to cover my subterfuge."

Peter Chan cautioned, "We've also come prepared to destroy a platoon of your best soldiers or take you out in one shot; or both."

"Where are your ancestors from young man? I detect Cantonese inflection in your voice, even when you speak English."

"Promontory Point Utah, May 10th 1869 is year one for the House of Chan. That is all I ever trace my ancestral lineage back to," he boasted.

"Yes of course, the completion date of the Transcontinental Railroad across America. You're from a coolie-class," the general taunted.

"*Hún Dàn!*" Chan growled.

Those two words were an ultimate Mandarin insult that roughly translated meant scumbag egg. It implied someone wasn't born in natural human childbirth. It further implied the mother who raised you was not your mother.

"Enough!" snapped Parrott. "We all know why we're here!" She placed a large envelope on the table and slid it over to the uniformed old man still brandishing a pistol.

This action finally caused him to re-holster it. He eagerly pulled out a 9x12 family photo which he examined in detail. *Yes, my son, daughter-in-law and two grandsons all look healthy and happy. Yes, the backdrop is the Taiwanese seven story Dragon and Tiger Pagodas in Kaohsiung. This means my family has been smuggled safely away.* There was only one more critical test to verify he was not fooled by a photoshop. Sheng took out the magnifying glass and focused it on his daughter-in-law. This scrutiny gave him a totally relaxed inner Zen. On her ring finger was the oversized jade stone he had given her as a wedding present. Li-ling vowed she would not wear it again until they were safe.

"Well, you've kept your side of the bargain. Unfortunately, events have overtaken our agreed upon timetable to sound an emergency shipboard recall. I've been relieved of command," said Sheng.

"Then who the hell is in charge?" Parrott demanded standing and pacing.

"Colonel Ming. I can see if I can push the command through to get…"

As Sheng was about to explain further, he cut himself off in mid-sentence to withdraw his pistol while whirling around and pointing it towards the door at the sound of boot steps in the corridor.

He crouched down and watched the doorknob turn.

The minute Sheng and Ming made eye contact bullets went flying.

The old general never had a chance to fire a shot. Bullets were flying in only in one direction. The firing came directly from sharpshooters; riders in the stealth helicopter from *Shanksville* that delivered Parrott and Chan to this meeting. A full load of 7.62 NATO rounds penetrated Ming's healthy, beating heart. None came anywhere near Sheng's deteriorating one.

Ji-Nan was behind Ming. Bullets hit the black iron teapot; the force knocked him down. He did suffer first degree burns from the scalding water over his arms, but it made an opportune substitute for body armor.

Sheng leaped to his side, extended his arms outward like a traffic cop, calling, "Hold your fire—he's no threat!"

The shooting stopped as abruptly as it began.

After a cursory inspection of his ADC, Sheng tapped Lee's cheek and pronounced him fit for duty. Next, he went over to the body with a fist-sized hole in its chest and removed a chain with a computer key from around Ming's neck. After close scrutiny for any damage, Sheng carefully slipped it into a pocket. Then he turned to face the Americans, unsure if they were his enemies, allies or just convenient neutrals.

"Mrs. Parrott, we haven't much time. The soldiers must have been alerted by your gunfire. I suggest you get to safety and leave everything to me. I'll initiate the ship's recall within the hour. By this time tomorrow, all the PLA soldiers will be gone from American soil. I only ask your military allows our troops to return to China unmolested," implored Sheng.

Without handshake or further words, Parrott ordered everyone to their pre-arranged fallback position. It was a reinforced panic room. Once there, they would hunker down to wait extraction by *Shanksville's* Blackhawk hidden and waiting about a mile away. Just as Parrott and Chan managed to close the heavy door, a mass of soldiers were heard clamoring up the staircase.

Sheng confronted them with shouted orders. "Be careful of random sniper fire!" as he stood over the half-dazed Major Ji-Nan.

Ying caught sight of Ming's prone body and open chest cavity; shrugged it off and reported to Sheng. "There are alarming reports of hundreds of armed hordes of Asian-Americans charging down Van Ness Avenue killing every soldier they can lay their hands on. They're not taking prisoners either. We have only rubber bullets, it's only a question of time before they overrun our operations here."

Sheng just grunted, concerning himself with his tea stained ADC. "Are you fit to drive major?"

"Yes general," Lee replied.

Only then did Sheng address the report. "As of this moment I'm terminating *Yôngbào* by sounding an emergency ships' recall. Captain clear out the operations personnel downstairs. Tell them to abandon their equipment and order the drone pilots to crash them. All personnel are to return to their ships as quickly as they can in any way they can." Ji-Nan was about to follow Ying and his troops downstairs but the general took hold of his arm. "Don't you have something to ask me?"

"Those Americans didn't shoot you? They even obeyed your orders to spare my life and cease fire?" Ji-Nan suspected he knew the answers to his own questions.

"You have family in Shanghai?"

"Yes general, an extended one."

"This commander dead at our feet intended to take men, women and children hostages today. Twenty-four hours after that he intended to hang them from flagpoles and traffic lights. Knowing the American temperament, soon after that, Shanghai would be a radioactive shadow land. Now get ready to fall back to our ship."

"Thank you for deeming me worthy of an explanation."

After Sheng received the last military courtesy salute of his life, he watched the young man until Ji-Nan had descended out of sight. Sheng then turned around, stepped over the dead man in the doorway, and once more seated himself at the long conference table.

He took out a box of cigarettes and lit one. He retrieved the photo still on the table for a final treasured smile. Then ignited a tiny flame to the edge of it. When its only trace was a minute pile of ashes, he went downstairs to the operations area. The place was now devoid of the frenetic activity of a mere 30 minutes prior; he had a choice of empty computer consoles. While still working on his cigarette, he chose one of the large screens and logged in to bring it back to life.

Despite the sound of shots fired, the occasional death scream and chaos emanating from outside the building, the general remained indifferent. He had heard those same collective cries of humanity in his days of youthful party ardor. After 50 years of faithful party service, his only loyalty now was to his family.

He inserted the security drive. At once the silhouettes of all seven tankers appeared on screen. This included the four berthed around San Francisco, the two missing ones, and the sunken one. He moved the cursor to select the button for a five horn blast to repeat for 30 minutes. It would take time for the onboard crews to override or physically disable the system. When soldiers (minus the ones killed, lost or deserted) started streaming back to their ships, there was nothing Admiral Phong or the crews would be able to do. Shooting at them would deter some, but not all. They all knew this was the emergency recall; and by now they would be nervous and very glad to be getting out of America.

Sheng took a final drag on his cigarette, then pressed Enter, sounding the death knell of *Yôngbào* and China's daydream of an economic revitalization. In unison, *Leviathan*, *Transvaal*, *Zeelandia* and *Suriname* instantly erupted with horn blasts generating in excess of 190 decibels and would continue to do so at an unrelenting five second interval for the next 30 minutes. Every Chinese soldier, drunk or sober, understood the sound. Native San Franciscans didn't, and feared a bombing raid. So most rushed indoors. The homeless milled around in confusion. The lucky ones sought refuge below ground in the rail stations.

As expected, Phong was blind with rage when the alarm couldn't be immediately turned off. Maintenance was working on it, but there would be no quick fix.

The design of the uplink satellite was connected to each supertanker.

Malabar Princess was given religious asylum in Surabaya, a predominantly Muslim country in Indonesia. When this ship's emergency recall was inexplicably activated, the horn blasts interrupted prayer time. For the next half hour thousands of the faithful were distraught from the noise and confused soldiers either hid from guards they thought were coming to arrest them or rushed back to the ship out of habit.

Captain Shan of *Antilles* was sailing over the Marianas Trench, six days out from Malaysia when the horns on her twin stacks blasted out to the bewilderment of everyone.

Only the ghost ship *Queen Wilhelmina,* 400 fathoms down, failed to respond to the satellite signal.

Inside city hall the acoustic echoes of the horn blasts reverberated. General Sheng was deep in thought. Dismissing the immediacy of events, he thought about the long view; deciding his actions just saved more lives of his countrymen then Chairman Mao Zedong had killed, either directly or through governmental ineptitude. He even dared to consider himself equal to the great unsung hero of the Chinese people, President Nixon, who personally prevailed upon Soviet Premier Brezhnev not to use nuclear weapons against China during the Sino/Soviet border conflict of 1969.

Finally, with such a mountain of responsibility reduced to the weight of a feather, secure in the knowledge his family had a future, it was time to resign from life. He stood up, adjusted his uniform, straightened his cap, and calmly pushed open the main doors to look out at the ongoing scene of slaughter of those unlucky soldiers who failed to make good their escape. He hoped his ADC was not among those victims being shot and clubbed to death even as they pleaded for their lives. It was only a question of time before he was spotted by the mixed crowd of police, military and civilian Asian-Americans rushing around brandishing shotguns, hunting rifles, baseball bats, butcher's cleavers and even axes. Sheng smiled to himself as they did spot him and rushed up the stairs. He took pride in the fact that these brave people of Asian heritage were hurrying on his destruction. After being subjected to 150 years of American decadence they had lost none of their ancestral savagery.

Tao was in the mad mix and realized too late their target was an elder and a leader. The mob pushed past his shoulders to butt-stroke and hack-down the stoic uniformed figure. Tao shouted for them to stop; it was too loud and chaotic so he raced up and threw himself over the old man's prone body. His attempted rescue almost cost him his own life; he was struck accidentally during the wild melee. The bludgeoned victim gazed up at Tao's sympathetic face. With his last bit of strength, he clutched Tao's shirt and pulled him down to whisper into his ear. The old man spoke slowly once in Mandarin, then repeated in English until Tao nodded in understanding. Only after that acknowledgement did Woo Sheng allow himself to breathe his last.

When Tao finally got up and stood over the body as the mob rushed on to find other invaders in the building, Tao caught sight of two civilians and a squad of military soldiers in full combat gear walking down the staircase.

A women spoke as they walked closer. "My name is Val Parrott. We're from the federal government," she deliberately avoided saying exactly which agency she was from. "We just negotiated a total troop withdrawal with this man. He is, was, Major-General Woo Sheng. What were his last words to you?"

I can smell CIA a mile away, but she sure does seem to have this under control. "He asked me to someday visit his family and remind his grandsons to burn incense sticks to his memory," answered Tao with a layer of sadness knowing as a father himself how important that last request was.

* * *

Major Ji-Nan, Captain Ying and Private Zheng were ducking and weaving together, running for their lives toward the main doors. Just seconds before ahead of them a group of operations personnel tried to escape through the same city hall entrance and were torn apart by buckshot at chest level. Shattered, blood-stained glass and chipped pieces of stone fused with human flesh as the three skidded to a halt just in time to stay inside in the shadows. Suddenly, horn blasts sounded out, it caused a confused lull in the attack which allowed the three of them to do a rapid turnabout and find a side exit, then rush to their SUV with all body parts intact.

Once behind the wheel, Ji-Nan had the presence of mind not to drive along small alleys. A limousine driver's instinct to get where he needed to go kicked in. With a quick touch on the GPS screen the SUV zig-zagged through a maze of interlocking side streets around the city hall area to reach the broad Laguna Avenue with a straight route to Fisherman's Wharf and the sanctuary of *Suriname's* steel hull. That was their one and only contingency plan at this point. Attempting to drive seven miles through a gauntlet of shotgun-toting Asian-Americans back up Van Ness Boulevard to reach *Leviathan* was certain death.

There was no fallback plan nor surrendering to the mercy of their English speaking, twice removed, cousins. The defensive situation was bad; Zheng had the only weapon with any meaningful firepower. It was a standard issue Bullpup assault rifle with a 30 round banana clip magazine plus four spare ones he carried on his belt. In contrast, the two officers only had their puny pistols with 24 rounds between them. All combined the three of them could lay down somewhat of a defense but it would not last. Ji-Nan began to have other worries as he drove. If and when they safely made it to *Suriname*—then what? He recalled Ying had offered a dour assessment that these Yankee devils would never let any survivors escape alive.

Added to his list of anxieties was their speed being restricted to 30mph on Laguna Avenue due to the obstacle course of abandoned and wrecked vehicles, a direct result from the first day invasion chaos. There were more ominous signs ahead when they spotted billowing smoke drifting across the avenue. As they drove further, the GPS announced, "Geary Boulevard."

To their right was a fortress-like building with two imposing marble lions totally indifferent to the flames spewing forth from the ornate entrance they flanked. In Han and English characters, a bilingual sign stated: Consul General of The People's Republic of China, San Francisco. From inside their SUV, they saw bodies lying all around the garden courtyard. The red banner was missing from the flagpole. In its place, was a man in a business suit they assumed was the consul general swaying in the breeze.

"These Chinese-Americans are barbarians! They have absolutely no respect for diplomatic protocols," said Captain Ying.

A split second later their luck changed three different ways!

The first was the windshield erupted into a hailstorm of crystal shards, the Lincoln Navigator went airborne, and the airbags deployed. When Lee regained consciousness, he was still sitting in the driver's seat and the SUV was lying on its side, driver's side down. He panicked when he felt his uniform soaked in blood. When he saw where the blood was raining down from, he added a coat of vomit to the mix. He hoped the body with a buckshot-shredded face of dangling meaty tissue suspended above him by the seatbelt was out of its misery. He was mercifully distracted by movement stirring in the back seat.

"Those shooters left us for dead! They went away to look for other soldiers to randomly attack. Are you okay?" asked the only other survivor.

"Zheng! Get me the hell out of here!" he pleaded.

The determined marine somehow managed to force open the back cargo hatch and crawl out unseen. Under the cover of smoke from the building and car fires, he made his way to the front of the vehicle and extracted Ji-Nan by way of the missing windshield. Once he got to his feet, Ji-Nan realized his rescuer was covered in blood.

"It's nothing serious sir," Zheng said in response to the look of concern on Ji-Nan's face.

Yet Ji-Nan could see the wounded man was getting weaker by the minute. Despite the horrendous crash, except for a few bruises, he was not bleeding much at all, unlike the man who just pulled him to safety. They both agreed there was nothing they could do for that red leaking pile of rags still strapped in the front passenger seat. Instinctively he took Zheng's right arm over his shoulder, while the private steadfastly kept a vice grip on his assault rifle with the left one. The two men looked up and down the streets of this accursed city for the nearest suitable shelter.

Deliverance was at hand!

Right across the street from the consulate was an overseas branch of the Shanghai Maritime Investment Bank.

In his desperate naïveté Lee expected a sympathetic reception.

They struggled up to the entrance, also flanked by two statues, except these were an ostentatious gilt-painted pair of Foo dogs. As they pushed through the glass doors, a macabre scene of bodies lying about the main entrance greeted them. All were bank employees in business clothes. Also scattered about were packs of red stained American money with the anti-theft dye packs blown apart. Obviously, it was a botched robbery—but by whom? American criminals who took advantage of the chaos, or those murderous Asian-Americans? Perhaps even his fellow soldiers seeing an opportunity?

A woman's scream echoed across the lobby.

Lee eased the wounded man down with an order to cover the main entrance while he went to investigate. There were more screams, these muffled, then men's laughter. The source was easily located to a corridor side office. Ji-Nan walked in on two PLA soldiers standing over a third who struggled to control the woman he was on top of. The instant he surprised the two gawking soldiers with dye-stained faces and uniforms, they came to rigid attention.

Ji-Nan's large gold star on each shoulder still carried the illusion of authority. Without hesitation, an outraged Ji-Nan reached down and grabbed the would-be rapist by the back of his collar and yanked him off the woman who was putting up a vigorous defense of her own. Then the man sliding away on the floor began to laugh uncontrollably while Ji-Nan's jaw hung open and his brain froze in shock.

"Who the fuck made you an officer?" mocked his hated ex-gun captain from Wujang, Sergeant Haung. He looked around and barked orders at his two soldiers. "Don't you stand at attention for this Shanghainese Pi Yang puppet!" Then he ignored everybody except his intended victim. Haung crawled back in an attempt to reclaim his prize. "We have some unfinished pleasure my little Vietnamese *Cô*."

As he reached out to grab her ankle the young woman delivered a swift snap kick to his face with predictable results.

"The bitch broke my nose!" he squealed, then cupped his face to contain the bleeding. His second motion was to reach for his holster and draw his pistol.

It was not much different from the type Major Ji-Nan was now pointing directly at him. "Don't make me do it Haung!"

"I'm going to shoot this bitch! In fact, I'm going to shoot both the bitches in this room!"

Having known this Karma was long overdue, Ji-Nan aimed and pulled the trigger. He was stunned when the pistol made only a latching sound but failed to fire. Ever since he was promoted it had only been worn as a status symbol; there had been no time for practice shooting. He had no idea how to release the trigger safety or even load the weapon.

Haung gave a mocking laugh all the while trying to stem the flow of blood drooling down his chin and throat. "I told you he's a phony officer!"

The two soldiers that were first intimidated by the gold stars on his shoulders were no longer standing at attention and began to raise their weapons. Even though they had only non-lethal rubber bullets, at such close range it would be a painful death by being pounded into a pulp by solid rubber bullets from both guns. Haung raised his weapon as well. He taunted the young woman teasing about who he would shoot first. It was a testament to her courage she showed no sign of fear—only contempt for the lot of them.

All three soldiers suddenly began jerking in time with eardrum blasts of repetitive muzzle fire. Thirty rounds of 5.8mm bullets penetrated their bodies as neatly pockmarked entrance wounds then as crater-sized exit ones.

Shredded in seconds, the three of them were dead before they hit the blood-drenched carpet. Due to the claustrophobic office space, the initial gunfire left the living with eardrums ringing like church bells.

Unfortunately, the shooter was suffering.

Zheng slowly dropped his weapon and succumbed to a loss of blood increased from the kickback of firing. Still cupping one of his ears in order to relieve the piercing pain, Ji-Nan leaped to the aid of the man who just saved his life. One look told him it would have required a full surgical team and an untold number of plasma packets to save him. He resigned himself to the brave man's death.

As Ji-Nan stood up, he faced the prospect of his own death yet again.

The woman now pointed Sergeant Haung's pistol right between his eyes, and unlike himself, he was sure she knew how to use it.

"You killed your own soldiers just so you could jump in front of the queue you *Ba Tau* invader!" she shouted contemptuously.

Of the few words of Vietnamese he knew, he knew she just called him a cheap chink. Even with a gun in his face, all he could think of was his mother's warning to avoid all Asian-American women. They were vain creatures obsessed with their skin tones, white teeth, and social power in all forms. They were actually men lurking inside female bodies, beautiful Lotus Blossoms soaked in insecticide. Nevertheless, he needed to say something to allay her fears—damn quick!

"I would never harm a woman! That would be a violation of the fourth Chinese blessing I'm so desperately trying to achieve—Good Morality. I'm a virtuous Buddhist like yourself," he stammered.

"I'm a Vietnamese-American Roman Catholic and you're a fucking invader. I should do my patriotic duty and shoot you dead here and now!"

"I was forced on those invasion ships! The army first told us we were needed for earthquake recovery. They changed their story again to a simple cruise to the Spratly Islands. Then it was all about the US Navy's blockade in Formosa Straits."

"That's a touching story *Ba Tau* but I can't turn my back on you," she said and prepared to squeeze the trigger.

"I would never dishonor my mother by violating a beautiful young virgin. You must believe me! All I want to do is meet up with my fellow Shanghainese in Luxembourg," he pleaded.

At those incredulous words, the woman swiftly raised her arm and fired into the ceiling getting perverse pleasure watching him cringe in ear ringing pain for a second time. Strangely, the sudden blast seemed to have no visible effect on her. *This woman is a devil*, he thought to himself.

"Are you fucking serious? What kind of a son are you to drag his mother into this discussion? This is California! So shove your ideal virgins up your ass. Now just who the fuck do you know in Luxembourg?"

He was willing to give up all he knew, and more. There was something honest about her sharp language and bold self-assurance. "My fellow Shanghainese Ku Wen once worked for your bank. He told me he had a secret account there as did many officials."

With weapon still at the ready, she did turn her back on him. She stepped over the three dead soldiers to riffle through a desk drawer. She removed a booklet, opened it to the introductory page, and with a marker blotted out the names underneath the bio pictures.

"This is a portfolio we received the day before all you *Ba Taus* decided to visit us unannounced. Identify these men. Your life depends upon it."

Though he had never seen either man in business suits before, they were both easily recognizable. "The one on the right is my old political officer Major Tone. The other is my friend Wen."

The woman was visibly intrigued. "So, you know who they are. Do you have any proof of a real friendship?"

Ji-Nan took out his wallet to remove a small photo of them in front of their 155mm howitzer in the frigid mountains. "Why is this so important to you?" he asked.

She pointed back to the brochure. "This man is the president and CEO and your friend is Senior VP and CFO of this newly chartered bank. Both men are overnight billionaires. Since one of those billionaires is a close friend of yours, lucky for you I'm no longer going to kill you. In exchange for your life, you get me out of this mess. We will have to pretend to be married. I can get us quick passports made. Let me introduce myself, I'm Nancy Cà Nguyen. What's my fiancé's name?"

"Lee Ji-Nan," he answered. His facial expression begged for clarity.

"Is my future husband really this stupid? Don't you understand we have to travel as a long time couple to escape San Francisco in order to make it through US and European customs? As a result of your country's invasion, every Chinese man will be stopped all over the western world. So, we'll be a married couple traveling on Vietnamese passports. They can't distinguish the difference between Chinese and Vietnamese. Plus, I speak French like most Vietnamese, which will get us through passport control when we land in Paris. We grab a train at the airport directly to Luxembourg. I'm in the mood to give you a big fucking kiss for making me rich, but you smell like a three day old bowl of rotting eels."

He was about to mention Americans smelled like greasy cheeseburgers but thought better of it. Instead, he watched her sit down and enjoyed the pleasing shape of her bare legs as she put her shoes back on. His eyes followed every delightful move. The opened-eyed corpses draped around the office in no way distracted from his enraptured feelings for his new found female companionship.

"What are you fantasizing about?"

"It was a pair of shoes and set of lovely legs that landed me into my present circumstances," Lee lamented with a sheepish smile.

"Why am I not surprised? Take off that filthy uniform before I throw up!" Nancy ordered. Her fiancé obeyed and began to undo his buttons. "Not in front of me you perverted pig! We're not really married! Take it off down the hall in the bank president's executive washroom. There's a shower stall in there. I'll get you some fresh clothes, hope I can find some that aren't soaked in blood. Now hurry up before more idiots come through the door because I won't be able to save you if they do."

Once she heard the shower running, Nancy started to multi-task. The front doors of the bank had to be locked and alarmed. The teller drawers had to be unlocked and dye packs carefully removed so some banded 50s and 100s could be swiftly loaded into a luggage carry on. A quarter million each would be sufficient for immediate needs. She felt the Chinese owned American money she was walking away with was grossly insufficient for the trauma of attempted rape inflicted upon her by the soldiers of that country.

The next item on her agenda required a presentable fiancé. For an impromptu wardrobe of business attire, she guessimated his size, narrowing choices down to three lifeless co-workers. Then she stripped the bodies to lay out suits, shirts and ties to pick out the least amount of dried blood to make a fairly matching set of it. Shoes of different sizes were unlaced and pulled off as well, but she left it for the next wearer to peel off the style of socks he preferred. It was also his choice of underwear to pick, choose and remove.

Ji-Nan soon emerged refreshed, wrapped only in a towel. The new dominant woman in his life gave him some privacy to dress. He skipped the bloodstained choice of ties altogether. Deciding on a pair of socks was bad enough but he absolutely refused to put on any dead man's shit-stained underwear. He hurriedly tried on what was available but none of the pinstriped trousers completely matched any of the suit jackets. There was not one complete suit that didn't have bullet holes. Ji-Nan's debut as an Asian-American came off as a fashion oddity, and it showed. One glance by his streetwise fiancée and she wrapped him in an overcoat that ended her embarrassment and any potential scrutiny from the wrong people asking the wrong questions.

"Put this on and keep it buttoned up," demanded Nancy. "It belonged to our president. That pig lying dead over there. He was a mainlander who used to offer me the bank's money to go to bed with him. When I refused, he couldn't fire me because these Chinese banks are required by US law to hire a certain quota of Americans. I wound up getting my sex money anyway when I threatened to denounce him to Beijing by way of an exposé in the San Francisco Examiner. That's our town's most influential newspaper. Not that it matters now, but any negative press with his name connected to misuse of Chinese funds would have warranted him a recall, then a death sentence. Everyone else here is dead but I was spared for that shit scene you walked in on; I'm sure they would have shot me when they were done."

"Our soldiers were under strict orders to avoid harming Americans. Nobody would care if any mainlanders were killed. These soldiers knew exactly what they were doing by not leaving any witnesses who could tell tales back to Beijing," he said.

"You don't say!? Now we have to go out on the street. Follow me and keep your mouth shut! If those vigilantes hear your accent—you're dead! Grab your pistol, this time undo the safety. Shoot anyone who comes between us and our luggage. It's got enough money to give us a fresh start."

She led him out the rear door through the loading dock. Luck favored them. Cool ocean breezes rolling in from the west mixed with the land temperature and pollution causing a drifting curtain of iconic San Francisco smog. In this soup, they were just another pair of shadows trying to escape the city. North was the chaos of small skirmishes; the sound of PLA soldiers being hotly pursued towards Russian Hill where *Suriname* was berthed.

The pursuers were recently deputized and calling themselves the Asian-American Rescue Squad. Afterwards they settled on the A-Squad in media interviews. A band of the squad now chased down scattered remnants of soldiers who tried to escape across Mission Street in an effort to fall back to relative safety inside *Transvaal.*

Sounds of fighting and dying were coming from all around, groups of the A-Squad were spreading out evenly; taking back their city. Mothers in the A-Squad were especially vicious when catching an invader trying to enter anyone's personal house, especially if there were frightened children.

In this dense smog, Ji-Nan could hardly see the woman in front of him. He literally blindly followed her down unknown streets due south. At least it was in the opposite direction of the sound of most of the gunfire and screaming (both of pain and anger). Except from the light click of her heels on the sidewalk, they were silent. She gestured for him to follow into a more commercially congested part of the city. This area made up the bulk of San Francisco's small business community known as Hayes Valley.

These merchants all felt the same apprehension about the city's foreign invaders. With more to lose than most, they were resolved never to abandon their property to looters until tanks with big yellow stars rolled through the neighborhood; and so far, none had appeared.

For this walk into a spot with more people, Nancy handed him a pair of black sunglasses. After another five minute trek the two crossed a much calmer Van Ness Avenue. Five more minutes and she smiled and broke into Vietnamese. "*Sai gon Nho,*" she proudly announced.

He needed no translation. The yellow banners draped from the Eddy Street lamppost all proclaimed **Welcome to Little Saigon.** The beautiful, thorny woman knew her way around this city blindfolded. Now she led him right to a three story office building. The chauffeur in him noticed a new blue Escalade with a smashed taillight parked out front.

As they were buzzed passed the front lobby, Lee also noticed a tri-lingual sign in English/Vietnamese/Mandarin: **Lam Dang, Attorney at Law & Notary Public.** Not at all sure why they were at a lawyer's office, he was absolutely sure after looking at the Vietnamese man in an expensive suit sitting behind a large desk. He was starkly reminiscent of a mainland party commissar. He exuded the same unctuous self-importance of the party apparatchiks he used to chauffeur around to the seedier parts of Shanghai night life. *This is a gang boss for sure, I have to be charming.*

"Why, if it isn't the beautiful Ms. Nancy Cá Nguyen. I haven't seen you in my office since you turned down Philip's marriage proposal," said Mr. Lam Dang.

"That prospect ended the day your secretary brought a paternity suit against Philip. Frenchmen may claim a wife and a mistress, but you should have reminded your son what country he's living in. Where is Ms. Tam?"

"On a generous paid vacation visiting her infirmed mother in Seattle." He raised his voice, "Now kindly tell me why you brought this *ba tau* into my office? You know the current situation! Where is your pride woman!"

"*Puh-lease* spare me!" she retorted.

"Get out! Both of you! Have fun dodging those axes!"

Ji-Nan understood by the insulting tone of this heated exchange these two were having a squabble but the nuances were way over his head.

Nancy wheeled around to face him and firmly demanded the small photograph in his wallet. Then she confronted the sleazy attorney with it. "Before you contemplate pulling out that snub nose .38 in your drawer—know this! His best friend is the number two man at Cathay Maritime Investment Bank in Luxembourg."

After a quick studied glance at the photo that matched an individual that had been all over the world's financial news the past two weeks, Mr. Lam Dang had a genuine epiphany.

"Of course! You're here to purchase Vietnamese passports so you can travel to Luxembourg. They're ten times easier to duplicate than the chip embedded in US ones. Leave everything to me. My firm will take charge of all travel arrangements. As you are well aware, my dear Miss Nguyen, international boundary crossing is my specialty. I think it best to accompany you both just in case you'll need legal assistance along the way. Immigration officials can be an obnoxious lot." The now animated Dang didn't wait for a negative response from his two new *pro bono* clients. He had already calculated the gratitude of a billionaire for helping a friend would lead to a handsome thank you. *At least,* he told himself, *I don't have marry this* ba tau *like this little bitch will have to act like she did.*

For the moment he needed to keep up an enthusiastic façade. "So, here's my plan. Due to the current crisis, all west coast travel is over-loaded or nonexistent. I'll use my mules who normally smuggle refugees out of Vietnam and into the US on a reverse course to shepherd us out of San Francisco to Los Angeles at midnight tonight. From there we take first-class sleeper berths on the Amtrak Sunset to New Orleans. The next step is an Air France flight direct to Paris. Then the TGV to Luxemburg. Let's hope this *ba tau's* friend, excuse me, I mean your 'husband's' friend, will show us some largesse for our efforts in saving him from certain death at the hands of our Asian-American vigilantes. Now if we're all agreed, how about you play the dutiful little Vietnamese fiancée and bring your intended a bottle of my best *Bau Da* rice whiskey served along with a traditional pot of tea, and show him how a truly civilized Asian race behaves."

It wasn't long after that offer of hospitality that Ji-Nan was euphorically drinking himself into a warming bliss from several shots of whiskey chased down with half a pot of amber tea; it felt transformative. He sat there oblivious to the machinations being set in motion by others on his behalf, grateful to have a moment of safety.

After a few shots of soul warming rice whiskey, a much calmer, sexier Nancy sat herself down and cuddled up next to him; he certainly was a good physical specimen, no matter what he may lack in other areas. She whispered in his ear, "Have you ever made love on a moving train before? The man and woman stay coupled together for hours with the rocking and rolling motion of the journey doing all the work!"

"My mother was wrong," he vaguely mumbled thinking that they may actually get married instead of just pretending as they escaped to Europe and a wealthy life. What a lovely life he could have as an idle rich man with a wife to deal with any problems in her no-nonsense way.

* * *

Phong was a man alone. Random sniper fire cracking against the portholes kept him off the bridge and confined to the wheelhouse. The sounding of the fleet's recall horn left him powerless. The officers of the watch kept their distance. They neither asked questions nor sought his consultation, but conspired among themselves for an opportune moment to put an end to this lost cause.

However, there was one uncommitted exception. The terminally ill Captain Hua. Since he was a walking dead man with nothing to lose, that made him either a formidable opponent or an unassailable tower of support for Phong and his position. The conspiring officers made the initial miscalculation to simply dismiss Hau as an impotent bystander, unable to be a part of the intrigue and kept him out of the loop of their plans.

Admiral Phong's isolation was further compounded by the fact his land force commanders, Sheng and Ming, were incommunicado. He would never learn their true fate, and only began to speculate on options for his own. The admiral may have been a party zealot, but he was no fool. He knew *Yôngbào* might become another legendary fable in the Middle Kingdom's history to facilitate the destruction of current politburo leaders. Still, he was hesitant to order the fleet to weigh anchor. His decision was based on the uncertain reaction of the US warship keeping station on the Pacific side of the Golden Gate Bridge. Except for constant back and forth helicopter traffic, it hadn't moved since the day it showed up and sunk one of his ships. Yesterday, the American captain did signal, though in a duplicitous tone, To *leave the city at once—you will not be harmed*. He decided to wait a little longer before he offered up his fleet to the mercy of that Mother Tiger. He hated that it was a woman who held the power to pin him down.

Phong resolved that if amended orders from Beijing were not forthcoming in 24 hours, then regardless of the number of troops still ashore, he would order the fleet to sea. He would make sure to take the precaution of keeping *Leviathan* as the second or third ship of the line, not the first or last.

The bulk of the panic stricken PLA soldiers concentrated in San Francisco sensed their surprise party was over. These were the ones who had enjoyed three days of free reign of looting supermarkets, jewelry stores, bars and a few barbaric back alley gang rapes. Not all soldiers imitated their ancestors like Attila the Hun. The better educated soldiers sensed retribution was in the offing for the bad behavior of their fellow soldiers. They began to question the stated purpose of *Yôngbào* and the wisdom behind it. There was also the mystery behind the ferocious attacks by Asian-Americans and why they didn't embrace their mainland brothers as liberators. It was interpreted as a curse. Some soldiers actually began to feel guilty for battling with their reincarnated ancestors in American form. It took only one soldier in ten to believe this to affect morale.

Defeat was a foregone conclusion when the well-disciplined Chinese marines, originally there to provide lethal support, abandoned them. The marines obeyed their last order first. When the emergency recall was sounded, that is exactly what they did. No longer encumbered by ill-trained soldiers, the marines took minimal casualties regrouping in a fighting retreat back to their respective supertankers, including the two most distant ones, *Leviathan* and *Zeelandia*.

The few army officers who kept their heads during the recall confusion understood they had only two routes of escape. Head north towards *Surinam* at Fisherman's Wharf or east for *Transvaal* berthed near the Oakland Bay Bridge whose steel towers were plainly visible.

On the third day of occupation there were simply not enough cars to be found to transport thousands of troops the seven miles north to *Leviathan*. *Zeelandia* was equally too far south for a daylight dash to safety. Especially while being hotly pursued by 30,000 highly motivated and armed A-Squad fanatics.

Adding to the general demoralization was a circulating rumor a US marine division was on their way from Camp Pendleton with M1-Abrams battle tanks supported by helicopter gunships. That last rumor had the most damaging morale effect on *Zeelandia*. US Marines would be coming straight north on the Bayshore Freeway—liberating the airport as a first priority.

In no way looking forward to that reception, Captain Liu and his deck officers surreptitiously abandoned *Zeelandia* to her coming fate. They roused no suspicion when they left the ship. They noted in the log they were going to make an inspection of airport buildings. The captain and five deck officers at first wandered about the terminal taking salutes and asking innocuous questions of the soldiers ordered to keep departing flights on schedule. The standing order was any civilian who showed up was put on a plane, no tickets or security check necessary. The catch was they were put on the next available flight. They had no choice of destination. When Liu deemed the opportunity right, he and his officers hurried up a passenger loading ramp with pistols drawn to hijack a Japan Airlines Boeing—757 about to seal its cabin doors. The hijackers knew a non-Chinese aircraft with an unknown number of civilians aboard would not be shot down.

Shortly thereafter, another scene of collapsing morale hit the invaders. This time by a group of junior officers who were successful in hijacking both a Qantas and Korean airplane. When the lower ranks got wind of these desertions, they wasted no time putting guns to the heads of a United Airlines and an Air Canada regional carrier crew. Despite mixed language exhortations they managed to get aloft. Ill-equipped for a long-range transcontinental flight, both aircraft soon ran low on fuel. One glided safely to a landing in Anchorage. The other disappeared from radar over the Polar Cap with 243 passengers.

Once word got out about the rash of hijackings, every commercial pilot, including those of Air China, made themselves scarce. A few male flight attendants in uniforms were mistaken by soldiers for pilots and captured at gunpoint. Then they were herded into an abandoned flight deck of the nearest available parked aircraft. When these uniformed men refused to attempt a main engine startup, they were either summarily executed or mercifully just butt-stroked unconscious. From that moment onward, the constant stream of departures which had safely evacuated 180,000 people in three days abruptly shut down.

* * *

Unlike the dereliction of duty on *Zeelandia*, on the bridge of *Leviathan* there was no lack of candidates anxious to take command. Chief among them was First Mate Bohai. Phong, who normally inspired fear, was now held in contempt. The first mate and a small contingent of bridge officers corralled Phong demanding to know his intentions. Equally contemptuous of them, Sleeping Leopard cowered to none. During this prelude to a mutiny, a third party forcibly intervened. Captain Hua entered the command bridge and in a weak, rasping voice ordered this gathering of mutineers to stand down. Normally the last person on the ship to intimidate anybody, he was accompanied by a squad to back him up. Most intimidating was an officer who wore a leaking bandage covering one eye. It was obvious to all; these battle-scarred marines had just endured a hard fight, street by street from the city center to the sanctuary of

Leviathan. Still on edge, they were ready to fire on anybody they were ordered to. When Hua had the mutineers' undivided attention, he merely nodded in the direction of the troublesome first mate. Off that cue, the wounded marine raised his service revolver and pressed the business end of the barrel hard against Bohai's forehead with such force it made a red circle.

"Who is captain of this ship?" politely inquired Hua.

Silence.

The marine officer expedited the answer by cocking the hammer.

"You are sir!"

With that satisfactory answer, Hua again nodded, the gun barrel was pulled back; the red mark lingered.

"Since you're anxious for a ship of your own, I have congratulatory news for you First Mate Bohai. A captaincy has become available aboard *Zeelandia.* You and your friends are to take command immediately. As Admiral of the Fleet, my orders are as follows—"

"Excuse me captain!" loudly interrupted Phong. "Have you become the supreme mutineer? Lieutenant, arrest this man at once! In fact, arrest every officer on this bridge!"

The marines not only ignored the order but instead pointed their weapons at the old man. Then looked to Hua for an order to pull their triggers.

"Comrade Phong please be discrete. I'll attend to you in a moment." Hua began giving new orders. "*Leviathan* is to weigh anchor immediately and head south deeper into the bay area until we can heave alongside *Surinam* at Fisherman's Wharf. *Surinam* is under heavy siege by American mobs. We must assist her crew in rescuing as many of our soldiers as possible. *Transvaal* reports only light resistance and requires none. After rendering *Surinam* all possible assistance, *Leviathan* will again sail deeper into the bay, and this time heave alongside *Zeelandia.* There our newly promoted Captain Bohai will assume his first command, and Captain Bohai, please feel free to pick and choose any of these loyal bridge officers you wish to have under your command. After the fleet has rescued as many of our soldiers as possible, all of our ships will make a dash for the open Pacific. Our brave Captain Bohai will lead us out. Captain Bohai will have the singular honor to ram and sink that warship blocking our escape. This will ensure the safety of the rest of us who sail in your glorious wake. These orders are clear; therefore, I shall not be open to consultation or changes. Now make all preparations for getting underway. Good luck comrades. You're dismissed."

As an afterthought, Hua turned directly to confront his predecessor. "I've spent the entire afternoon on the communications deck. I have to admit Beijing's mixed signals indicate a government in crisis. The last one our cryptographers were able to decipher before a loss of satellite signal relives you of command. How timely. You no longer have the love of the Chinese people or the confidence of the CCP. That communiqué also includes the indictment of Major-General Sheng for military malfeasance and nefarious counter-revolutionary plots. Your son has been arrested as well. Mahjong tiles are falling all across the motherland. I'm assuming overall command of *Yôngbào*, and it ends now!"

Sleeping Leopard had heard enough. "Your sickness has rendered you a mere hourglass of a man whose sands of time cannot be inverted. Since you will never live to suffer the long term consequences of your actions, I find your inopportune power grab cowardly. You're no better than our ancient princes who, when they failed to overthrow the emperor and afterwards were condemned to death by a thousand cuts, swallowed opium to nullify the pain of the swordsman's slice."

"Confucius says, *There is always one maneuver the master swordsman deliberately neglects to teach his novice.* Was it purely because of your contempt of me, and my expendable mortality, no lesson was ever held back?"

With no answer except a stare full of contempt, Phong was escorted off the command bridge. One would be dead in a day, the others in two.

* * *

Leviathan's primary rescue mission as planned by the Admiral Hua was disastrous. Her secondary one, a complete failure … *Leviathan* skillfully pulled alongside *Surinam* at Fisherman's Wharf in the midst of a hailstorm of unrelenting gunfire. It was no mean feat to maneuver one of the world's largest man-made moving objects alongside another in semi-darkness without the benefit of running lights which would draw small arms fire like moths to a flame. Yet they still found themselves under heavy fire.

A-Squad groups converged from all directions to Fisherman's Wharf after receiving citizen reports of increased activity there. Their ferocity increased into a mob mentality as they found more and more gruesome discoveries of raped and murdered Americans of all ages and types, many left stuffed in dumpsters.

The emergency recall, though meant to save the lives of the invading force and expedite their escape, turned out to be a tactical blunder; a prelude to slaughter. When the recall sounded, the marine presence evaporated. Now thousands of deputized A-Squaders were free to attack PLA soldiers who had only rubber bullets and fists. Outnumbered and overmatched, shooting and bludgeoning ensued along every inch of Fisherman's Wharf, including its centerpiece: the brightly colored carousel. It made for a macabre spectacle of mutilated dead soldiers draped over rotating unicorns and sea horses while organ pipes played on.

Bodies were tossed off the boardwalk's upper tier, thumping near sea lions who roared their disapproval and dove off for quieter spots to sleep for the night.

Soldiers hiding in the arcade behind pinball machines and antique booths of Zoltar were flushed out pleaded something in Mandarin with their hands up. No mercy was being shown on this day, no prisoners could be taken by the A-Squad anyway.

During all this mayhem on the wharf Admiral Hua came to the rescue. With the aid of his ship's bow thrusters, he maneuvered *Leviathan* alongside the besieged *Surinam*.

Leviathan's marines clambered aboard *Surinam* and rained down suppressing fire from on high. The automatic weapons instead of fists temporarily caused the A-Squad to seek shelter while troops then made a mad dash to board *Surinam*. While the troops escaping the bloody slaughter on the wharf were boarding *Surinam,* sailors and officers on *Surinam* realized they would be not only over-crowded, but hemmed in until the other tanker moved out. While stuck in place they would be a target, again. They abandoned military discipline and started crossing over to the less crowded main deck of *Leviathan*.

It was during the organized chaos of transferring thousands of officers and troops from the over-crowded dark ship to *Leviathan* without the benefit of spotlights that Hua, unprotected by marine guards, mysteriously disappeared from the starboard bridge wing.

Unconfirmed rumors said he was brought down by a sniper round like Lord Nelson. Another said Bohai pre-arranged a bribe to have a marine toss him over the rails. Another said he slipped away in the confusion to the wharf and disappeared to a hospital for a cure and a new life.

In any case, none of the bridge officers questioned Captain Bohai's opportune assumption of command; they just didn't care, they only wanted to get the hell out of there. Since his first order was to break away from *Surinam* and head for open waters, he had full cooperation.

Without warning, *Leviathan's* massive bow and stern thrusters engaged pulling her away from *Surinam*. In semi-darkness hundreds of soldiers who had been struggling to climb over the gunwales to reach *Leviathan* suddenly plunged into the ever-widening crevasse between the slowly separating hulls. There was hardly time for screaming. Soldier after soldier was pushed forward by the momentum of the panic stricken ranks behind them. Untold numbers fell 180' to the water line, with more landing on top of them. Any who managed to stay conscious and able to tread water were then sucked under into the thruster blades.

When *Surinam's* captain grasped what was happening, he panicked, he hadn't realized all his officers had slipped away. Then he likewise ordered his ship's fore and aft thrusters engaged. As soon as he had enough momentum to steer, *Surinam* pulled away from the dock. In his haste, Captain Yi showed no concern for the troops being picked off by sniper fire still struggling to hoist themselves up rope ladders along the now moving hull. Either in undue panic or gross lack of seamanship, he neglected to cast off the mooring lines. When *Surinam* finally ripped free heading into the bay channel, a good portion of the pier was dragging in tow.

Dawn broke over San Francisco the following morning.

The A-Squad and about a third of the population that had not yet left or never planned to, wondered where the US Marines from Camp Pendleton were since they had just suffered two full days of occupation! There were estimates shared by Tao that between 15,000 to slightly less than 20,000 PLA soldiers were still roaming throughout the area, with groups at the Presidio and Golden Gate State Park. And far too many were reported as holed up in private homes which could lead to some very dangerous hostage situations.

Some dispirited soldiers even sought out unarmed non-Asian-Americans civilians to surrender to. The more determined abandoned soldiers traveled in menacing bands trying to reach the last remaining tanker in a vain hope *Zeelandia* might soon put to sea.

Dawn also revealed a partially collapsed Fisherman's Wharf with hundreds of floating corpses mutilated by both man and machine being feasted upon by cawing seagulls. Pockets of resistance still fought a last stand to their inevitable conclusion.

Doomed PLA soldiers were trapped in this seaside abattoir. West coasters soon had a new phrase for any bad or lost situation—*Chinese Chance At Pier 39*.

* * *

In the pre-dawn hours of the 3rd day of the grandiose gamble for a bloodless annexation of Taiwan, the remnants of the invasion force were aboard escaping tankers making all possible speed from the city they once occupied. All ships were at sea with the exception of the abandoned *Zeelandia*. She remained berthed near the city's main airport. Her planned rescue by a replacement crew that never materialized left the few thousand isolated soldiers aboard staying below decks to avoid relentless sniper fire. They were fully abandoned.

Down to three ships out of seven and less than 45,000 of the original 100,000 troops, the convoy salvaged what it could from an ever deteriorating situation.

Also, just before dawn broke, making for the open Pacific at flank speed, was *Shanksville*. Before doing so, she took on two guests: US Coast Guard

Lieutenant Albert Gallatin, temporarily detached from the damaged *Aspen* and CIA East Asian Audio Network Analyst, Peter Chan.

Shanksville put to sea under sealed orders and strict radio silence.

Hours and nautical miles behind in *Shanksville's* wake were the three escaping supertankers.

Underway for 18 hours at 16 knots, the golden gateway to America's back door had long faded from the three tankers' stern view. The collective thinking of all three captains was to deliberately keep no specific sailing formation to avoid being one large target. The ships kept themselves miles apart but all sailed roughly the same course home: straight for the western horizon, now showing the setting sun creating a pink and purple ocean. It had been a tense day of sailing, hoping the warship didn't blow them out of the water. Knowing they had put 18 hours between them and the last known position of the warship; the troops finally started to think they might make it home alive.

Mutineer Captain Bohai doubled the stern watch and ordered every remaining drone aloft. He was as paranoid as he was prepared for *Shanksville* and her bloodthirsty pirate captain. To save his own skin if attacked, he had a lifeboat already loaded with US currency, PRC Yuan Renminbi and gold coins he had emptied from the ship's safe. At the first sign of trouble he, and he alone, would escape in this 24' lifeboat. Designed and equipped for 55 survivors, Bohai would shoot anybody who attempted to share. Whether the convoy was revenged attacked or not, he had no intention of sailing back to the chaos China was now enveloped in. One way or the other, *Leviathan's* fourth captain in as many months was determined to abandon his ship. For the moment it was a tossup for Malaysia, Tahiti or hiding out on one of the many islands of Micronesia. Bohai would make that decision when they were closer.

A volcanic flash followed by a faint acoustic echo, then a funnel-shaped plume of grey smoke shattered the picturesque purpling ocean view. Whether it was *Transvaal* or *Surinam* that was struck, Bohai didn't care. The American ship was now downrange! Not where it was expected. A major cause for alarm. He ignored the approach of his bridge officers and their panicky questions, and concentrated his attention on the oceanographic chart on the navigation table. Ironic that he had just been thinking about his final destination; his decision now needed to be made in seconds. After a hasty but intense study, he felt his hopes crushed. The nearest land mass not under American jurisdiction was French Frigate Shoals! That was over 2,000 miles from *Leviathan's* present position. He bitterly cursed that American captain. Bohai understood he would have to solo navigate his lifeboat at least two to three months to reach those shoals.

Certain his ship, crew and the thousands of soldiers milling about above and below decks were living on borrowed time, he gave out his last and totally inane order. He ordered all bridge personnel to search for the lurking American warship and for the communications deck to contact them on the international hailing frequency and offer to surrender. After those orders were given, the last captain of *Leviathan* took cowardly advantage of the frenetic activity which he deliberately caused to furtively go to the boat deck. He unsealed the hatch of the lifeboat. Once he shimmied himself inside, he resealed the hatch and prepared to launch the lifeboat that resembled a miniature submarine.

While he strapped himself in for the rollercoaster launch down guard rails for a six second plunge, an enormous explosion erupted from inside *Leviathan's* hull. The lifeboat violently shook. Emergency rations and money satchels were tossed about. Though he could see no daylight breeches in the fiber hull, he did see billowing smoke and felt baking heat all around him.

An anti-ship Hellfire missile had struck the edge of *Leviathan's* port quarter directly in front of the island superstructure and directly underneath the boat deck. It penetrated five decks before it detonated a 20 pound warhead below the waterline. Normally a supertanker could absorb ten Hellfire missile strikes if the watertight bulkheads and holding tanks had not been redesigned into one open system.

Without a moment to lose, Bohai prepared to abandon ship and pulled the large release ring. To his utter horror the lifeboat failed to advance an inch. He speculated the missile blowback must have twisted the launch rails. With time still available to locate another lifeboat, he attempted to unseal and push open the hatch but found that impossible. It just would not budge. From tiny portholes, he could just make out some overhanging metal debris from the blown apart main deck that had landed on top of the escape hatch. The pieces were huge; they would need a crane to move them! As his skin began to blister from scorching heat, he drew his pistol and fired at one of the small portholes in a vain attempt to call for help. The bullet cracked but failed to penetrate, then ricocheted back to break his arm. Now in extreme pain, he heard the bulkheads began to groan under stress as the ship took a pronounced list to port.

Out of options, the last thing he wanted was to be baked alive inside a melting fiberglass lifeboat. Bohai put his pistol against the soft tissue palate at the roof of his mouth and blew his brains out.

* * *

Still under arrest and confined to his fifth deck stateroom, Phong was serenely brushing calligraphy to record his defense of all charges he might face. Though there was never an expectation of acquittal, fate now denied him even a trial. When the initial missile struck, the reverberations from the aftershock overturned most of the small objects in his stateroom, including the inkwell on his desk. Aware this portended *Leviathan's* doom as well as his own, he manifested his distain by not even bothering to wipe off the indigo ink that stained the rice paper of his once meticulous calligraphy. Instead, with fatalistic calm, he synchronized his wristwatch against the increased angle of the wall mounted inclinometer. It was a quick habit to calculate the amount of list declination over positive buoyancy. After eight minutes, the 8° port list stabilized back to an acceptable 3°. Once he calculated the flooding and rolling force to capsize, he stopped monitoring.

Leviathan was fated for a slow death.

With time to prepare, Phong walked around his spacious stateroom unsealing and bracing open all the portholes. He gave a cursory glance out of the last one but couldn't see the panic of the hapless soldiers, and wouldn't have cared if he could. When the end came, he wanted the room to flood quickly. Even a stoic such as himself was not willing to gratuitously suffer the agonizing death of exploding eardrums if his stateroom remained sealed until crush depth. Choking as seawater filled your lungs would be considered a mild form of euthanasia compared to a slow crushing death.

With that task out of the way, he went over to his bed to make himself comfortable. Above the head rest was a dour portrait of Mao Zedong; it was uninspiring. He reached up and retrieved the only two items of any value to his old soul, his bamboo opium pipe and the accompanying bronze tray with its centerpiece miniature oil lamp. When it was lit, its glow became a seductive beacon in the ever darkening area. Phong placed a sticky black ball inside the ceramic bowl at the tip of his pipe and allowed it to begin to vaporize over the flame. The smoke knew him and embraced him as a long sought after friend. For the connoisseur, a single ball of opium expertly ingested could make the euphoria seem to last a million years. Phong leaned back in preparation to leave this world for another one of more enhanced dimensions; one that honored and adored him.

Events intruded after less than an hour of bliss; the Pacific revived him to a minimal level of consciousness. Saturated with cold water already claiming half the stateroom, he leaned up on his elbows to witness torrents of white water pouring through all ten portholes. Ex-Admiral Phong only wondered with serene detachment, *Will hell be loud?*

Chapter 14

Whiskey & Chanel

At CIA headquarters Valentine was called to the Director's 6th floor office. Even after the protocol of entering the building at street level, she passed through another metal detector and three security guards. One of which politely ask her to sign into a visitor's log.

Val signed where instructed. Though she detected an English accent, it was the grotesque calloused knuckles on the man's index and middle fingers that she found unsettling. Obviously, the man had been in more than one fight or sparing match and rather recently by the look of some healing scabs. Parrott also made out the same bruises on the other two guards who framed the entrance to the office. A decent martial artist herself, she ran through scenarios of her having to fight them off; none of which realistically came out in her favor.

The next step was to be buzzed passed the protective door of the outer security ring. Inside a plain and utilitarian room sat a man with heavy black eyeglasses, whose personality reflected the décor. Pale and aggressively repugnant, with a receding hairline to confirm his age, he never once looked up from his desk to acknowledge the intrusion. Val felt just as invisible to the tall female assistant wearing a dark business suit in matching heavy black eyeglasses. A ceiling to floor bookcase swiveled open to reveal another office; this one rich and looking like an old boy's club with brass and emerald lamps and wooden paneling, heavy velvet green curtains topped off the look. Val took a deep breath and entered thinking, *the only thing missing is a fog of cigar smoke.*

Two more guards of the same physical make up stepped away into the modern office to give Val and the men inside privacy. They were like the director's personal guard dogs.

"Come in further Parrott."

Them?

Her quizzical expression prompted him to explain. He nodded toward the door as it was clicking shut behind them. "I call them my Baker Street Irregulars. They are proper retired English special forces veterans. Totally off the radar and answering only to me, they keep me safe and I use them for special tasks."

The term *special tasks* jogged her memory. Its origin was old Soviet KGB, something about doing anything Joseph Stalin wanted done. It gave her spine a cold chill. That kind of power never flowed to a good ending. Val knew Director Maulehouse was a Mayflower descendent, he and others in power considered him an elite. She wondered how a man who could trace his lineage back to the Founding Fathers, then back even further to Plymouth Rock, had off the books personal guards right in the CIA building. Then it dawned on her; Vladimir Lenin similarly used the Cheka to hunt down enemies to torture and kill those he felt were a threat to his power.

Val walked toward the lengthwise conference table where Brown and Assistant Director Lowell sat with Maulehouse. *Oh my god, the top three old white men of the CIA have called me in here, I'm about to be fired. I have to keep my cool. I will not cry. I will not cry.*

Maulehouse, in an immaculately tailored three piece suit who wore a miniature rose boutonniere in place of the standard American pin flag, was the first to come over and proffer his hand in greeting, exuding all the *noblesse oblige* of his class to an inferior.

"I understand you're the young woman with the prophetic dreams that helped knit our clues together. Welcome Ms. Parrott. We meet at long last. I must admit though, I prefer your married name of Mrs. Valentine Regnault, it has an Orson Wells *The Third Man* intrigue to it."

After they shook hands, the director unhooked a silver key from a vest chain and handed it to the only other person in the room, he was wearing a white jacket. "Colin, go into my private reserve, you know the bottle I require. Everyone, we have events to celebrate and lament."

Val sat down, unsure now what was going on; this wasn't a dressing down, demotion or firing. She opted for silence until she knew more. Lowell and Brown just leaned back and also were quiet.

Colin, position and rank unknowable to Val, soon returned. He carried over, then presented, a large silver tray with four tumblers, a pitcher of tepid water, a glass pipette water dropper, and the *pièce de résistance*, a 50 year old bottle of Macallan single malt. The men all leaned forward, nearly drooling. Maulehouse performed a ritual: thumb tapping on the pipette for precisely three droplets of water placed into each tumbler of scotch.

Well, that's odd, feels like an initiation. They're acting like I'm one of them.

The director offered his first toast. "Kindly raise your glass to our newly promoted Assistant Deputy Director, Ms. Valentine Fountain Parrott. *Slan-ge-var!*"

Nothing but pure instinct kept Val's face from showing the shock. She did tuck one brown curl behind her ear to give that hand something to do while the other traced the top of her glass. She managed a stately nod. She realized she was making history; on this side of the ocean no woman had ever been a part of this top cabal; in Europe maybe queens had been, but then again, it was more likely they had been used rather than welding the power.

With their first toasts downed and refilled, the tumblers were again raised. This time Assistant Director Lowell offered his idea of an effusive congratulation which ended with a backhanded insult to the university she attended.

Maulehouse took immediate exception to having his decisions challenged in graceless humor; and was able to land a jab at Yale while calling on Brown to sing the praises of Cornell.

After the ivy league pissing match died down, the director pointed out that Vice President Lejeune may be president soon if stirrings of impeachment went forward. If that happened Parrott's connection would prove very valuable. In addition, her husband's position as a professor would also allow them to have contact with and gather information about a wide variety of questionable people, including everyone at the French embassy. Including

Ambassador François Delattre, with whom Claude had been students together at the prestigious École Normale Supérieure in Paris.

"Ms. Parrott, our intentions are not to be intrusive with your husband, we would only ask for his consultation after other intelligence was verified about a target. We are, after all, an intelligence gathering agency in constant search of sources," said Maulehouse.

"I quite understand sir." The response of the new assistant deputy director was as polite as it was *pro forma*.

Lowell mentioned something about being guided by angles, and the conversation bounced on about cardinals and saints and religion's place in government; much to Val's relief since she was still trying to digest and own the new situation she was in.

"Well, I hope that flushed our minds clean," said the director. "Colin, re-flush everyone's drink and see that we are not disturbed. In an hour, assemble my Baker Street Irregulars in preparation for a special task."

Colin nodded, turned and left; having never let an expression of any sort cross his face.

The director balanced his scotch in one hand, motioned them all to stand up, and with his free arm around Val's shoulder, he led them all over to one of his prized exhibits. Underneath an aquarium-sized glass case was a three foot long highly detailed model of a US Navy WWII destroyer. "She's a beauty, isn't she?"

When Val saw the white decaled letters and numbers on her hull – DD-218, the significance finally broke into her frozen mind. "It's my family's namesake ship, the *USS Parrott*. Beautiful model sir, but inaccurate. Clemson-Class destroyers were nicknamed four pipers. Your model has only three smoke stacks, you're missing one."

After three full tumblers of 50 year old scotch, the director was mellow. "Technically you're correct Valentine."

The use of her full first name startled her. She had assumed these old guard white men were uncomfortable with women, and used her last name (or Val) in order to allow them to keep up some sort of denial. Being sexually neutral and blending in had allowed her to rise in the ranks. Seeing the frown on Lowell's face, she decided she was mostly correct; now she was nervous about what this use of her feminine name could mean. Was the arm slung lightly around her shoulders going to turn into a creepy advance? It would ruin all she had worked so hard to achieve; because it would be Val leaving the power group, and certainly not as the newly appointed assistant deputy director the CIA.

The director seemed oblivious. "When they were built during World War One, they had four funnels, so that is your four pipers. This model is the World War Two version. The contractors removed her aft stack and converted one boiler room into an extra fuel tank to give her an unprecedented range of 4,900 nautical miles at 15 knots. This is the same ship my grandfather Josephus Brinley Maulehouse served on. He quit his freshman year at Harvard a month after Pearl Harbor to join the navy. His father, my great-grandfather Matthias Maulehouse was absolutely livid his son would involve himself in Franklin Roosevelt's War. They both hated each other since 1904 when they shared a dormitory at Harvard. Great-grandfather was instrumental in keeping Roosevelt out of the Porcellian Club. To make matters worse, during the war Matthias flooded the White House with telegrams demanding President Roosevelt halt those B-17 bombing raids on the I.G. Farben factory in Frankfurt. At the time, the Maulehouse family owned $2,000,000 worth in shares of the company. A substantial amount of money in 1943 dollars."

"Wasn't Farben the chemical company that produced Zyklon B for the camps like Auschwitz?" Val naively asked, getting caught up in how interlocked and deep into the past these power lines went.

The director abruptly pulled back his arm from her shoulder. "*Pharmaceuticals* Ms. Parrott! Pharmaceuticals! Let's not be accusatory! Haven't you ever heard of Bayer aspirin? Besides, any international company like Farben can't possibly be responsible for the unscrupulous actions of every single one of its subcontractors."

"I see your point sir," she acknowledged, keeping the eye rolling under control.

"I sincerely hope you do Ms. Parrott," repeated the director. "We must always look at the big picture, we must always work toward the maintenance of good order of the state."

Val took the hint and wisely dropped the subject of chemical by-products and ethical trans-national responsibilities; there would be other places and other times to push forward this battle. She steered the conversation back to her family's namesake destroyer. "The *USS Parrott*'s end was tragic. Did your grandfather survive or go down with the ship?"

"That is a convoluted but heroic tale all by itself. It's for another time under different circumstances," and with that remark the matter was closed.

Parrott dutifully followed the director back to the conference table, puzzling out why Brown and Lowell had stayed quiet during this whole time. As she looked over his shoulder, she caught a glimpse of a horribly disfigured human skull preserved in a large bubble of clear resin. "What happened to him? That left ocular orbit is crushed in."

"Yes Ms. Parrott, those 5.5 NATO rounds worked as designed."

She leaned in close to read the brass inscription on the wooden base. *Presented to CIA Director Marshall Maulehouse — acquired by Seal Team Six with extreme prejudice: Abbottabad, Pakistan May 2nd, 2011 — For God and Country— Geronimo— Geronimo—Geronimo.*

"Yeah, that's him, or what's left of him."

Val raised her eyebrows. Obviously intrigued.

The director smiled and told one of his favorite agency stories: "The one who got the janazah funeral aboard the aircraft carrier *USS Carl Vinson* was the son, Khalid Bin Laden. His was the body buried in the Arabian Sea. The father's body was secretly handed over to some unidentified Arkansas hog farmer. Out of gratitude, Seal Team Six was kind enough to present me with this touching trophy." The director picked up on Val's thoughtful and slightly frowning expression. "You seem perplexed Parrott? What is it you think we do here at this agency? Sit around and debate humanist virtues? Our commission is the United States of America and to maintain it as a going concern sometimes requires the latitude of open-ended missions. In brief, our job is to tell the US military who to kill and *why*. We leave it up to them to execute the *when* and *how*. Now let's sit down and let me hear your report Parrott."

All four settled in around the conference table. Parrott never carried notes beyond her desk on top secret things so spoke off the cuff yet with certainty. "This Chinese invasion became unavoidable when President Atwater refused to accept our—"

Lowell rudely interrupted. "For God's sake Parrott! I fully apprised the director of our discussion at the White House! Stick to your brief!"

"Lawrence! Don't interrupt like that again!"

Brown finally spoke up. "I would appreciate it if you refrain from your caustic repertoire of cheap shots. As motivational tools, I find them as useless as a prophylactic on a seed bull."

The director tried to disguise his laughter by clearing his throat. "Parrott, it's my fault for not stating the specific topic I wanted briefed on. Since you just returned from San Francisco, I want a tactical, on the ground, sit-rep. We're well aware of Atwater's ineptitude, that will be addressed later. Continue."

This time Parrott cut to the chase. "The Chinese invasion of San Francisco was with four supertankers out of an original seven, they were still able to surreptitiously appear at our western coast and land an estimated force of one hundred thousand men. In a week's time though, three factors have brought about its utter and complete failure. By far, the largest unforeseen element was a spontaneous uprising by the Asian-American community. It was organized by a local San Fran police Sergeant, Tao. These Asian vigilantes performed bravely to defend their city. Their lack of clemency was a shock to the average PLA soldier. Regardless of their patrolling the streets, I believe the whole underpinning of the collapse was due to the CIA's master plan having Major-General Sheng prematurely initiate the emergency recall. From that moment onward *Yôngbào* deteriorated into a debacle. Another determinant was the retributive actions of Captain Amber O'Sullivan. The *USS Shanksville* sunk one supertanker prior to the invasion and three post-invasion as they were trying to escape. Loss of life has yet to be determined. The last three were sunk in contravention to President Atwater's stated assurances to the new government in Beijing that they could safely sail home."

"Is our hero captain still under our orders without her knowledge?" inquired the director.

"Yes sir," replied Parrott. "Captain O'Sullivan believes her war orders are coming directly from the Chief of Naval Operations in the Pentagon. At this moment *Shanksville* is headed towards Malaysia to hunt down and extract retribution on Captain Shan. He is the one responsible for destroying the Coast Guard ship and her crew."

"This retribution, and the fear of more in the future, always saves more lives than it cancels out," added the director. "Unfortunately, we can't save O'Sullivan from President Atwater's punishment for willful disobedience to his idiotic orders without exposing ourselves and jeopardizing our guardianship over the state. The good captain may have to go down without her ship."

Val frowned at the injustice of this. Brown noticed and tapped his lips in thought.

Lowell said, "We still have one supertanker berthed in San Fran that has to be sunk once it puts to sea. We need to make Captain O'Sullivan's last mission that attack, and she can't be sacked before she gets that done."

"There's no danger of that, is there Robbie?" asked Maulehouse."

"No. We have enough of our Jekyll and Hyde operatives aboard to prevent just such an eventuality. The communications deck is manned by our people to intercept the wrong signal from reaching the command bridge," assured Brown.

"So, for carrying out *our* orders we're going to throw a patriotic navy captain to the sharks after she's done her duty for God and country?" spoke up Parrott feeling the slight to her pro-navy bones.

"Once the dust settles and as time passes after Captain O'Sullivan's court-martial, we can restore her to the senior officer retirement list. Perhaps even award her the Medal of Honor as a guilty-minded congress did to General Mitchell," answered Lowell.

"Years after her *death*," snapped Parrott.

"Posthumous honors are still honors, assistant deputy director," cut in Maulehouse. "Now just what is the story with that last supertanker? Is it abandoned or not?"

Val flared her nostrils, then took a deep breath and continued, she promised herself she would revisit this issue soon. "Sir, from my last observance aboard one of *Shanksville's* Blackhawk helicopters *Zeelandia* was still anchored near the two main runways of SFO. Her captain and primary deck crew deserted the ship on day two and hijacked an Air Nippon back to China. I have reason to believe there is still a skeleton crew aboard competent enough to navigate the tanker back to the mainland or at the very least out into the Pacific. Once at sea it can be easily intercepted by *Shanksville* on her return voyage from Malaysia. For the moment, *Zeelandia* is sort of acting as a beacon and a last stand fortress for the remaining PLA soldiers. Their aggressiveness is limited to foraging for food and holding their small section of real estate. Regrettably there have been isolated reports of murders of rape victims. It's understood as soon as those scatted about in private homes and other shelters manage to board *Zeelandia*, she will put to sea. Lastly, as for the street level morale of the average San Franciscan—"

"The average San Franciscan?" Lowell piped up. "Are we referring to the Tenderloin dwellers with a syringe permanently in their arms or the beret wearing bughouse poets who bop around with two cigarettes in their mouth? Surely you can't mean the only four normal nuclear families left in the city?"

"Enough Lawrence!" The director cut off his assistant from a theme often repeated. "Stop your social sermonizing. If you wish to continue working here, you don't have to be normal, just *act* normal and keep your ideas to yourself!" Maulehouse steered the conversation away from his obnoxious assistant. "Okay Val, take me back to the streets where cable cars climb halfway to the stars. What is the morale of the brave citizenry who didn't turn tail and run?"

Back to Val again, well that's a good sign. "Where are the Camp Pendleton marines, is the common refrain," she answered.

"Director," called out Brown. "I believe I can find that answer to that question. Though the protocol will be embarrassing and reflective of the oftentimes ill-disciplined democratic way my analysis department functions."

"Robbie, we are first and foremost results oriented—embarrass me!"

Brown dialed a number while saying, "The man who picks up the phone can enlighten us as to why the US Marines 'First to Fight' motto is fast becoming an anachronism."

An irascible voice belted out from the speaker, "McMachinaw, third floor! What do yeah want!?"

"Mannus, I have good news for you," said Brown who raised his voice in case the senior citizen had his hearing aids out.

"Fuck you, Robbie!"

Brown immediately matched the adversarial tone and responded in kind. "Shut up and listen to me you old fool! I'm speaking on Director Maulehouse's private line who is monitoring this conversation. So, unless you wish to be prematurely interned in your reserved niche next to your father at the Arlington National Columbarium by sunset taps tomorrow, you better show a little supplication."

"You mentioned good news?" McMachinaw responded in a noticeable lower octave.

"For your past record of honorable service, and with my full recommendation, the director will overlook that fiasco you instigated at Davis-Monthan Air Force Base and reinstate you back to colonel so you can retire with full pension," said Brown.

"What do you really want?"

"You septuagenarians are sharp. Now the director needs to know—"

"Bullshit! First, you're going to do *me* a real favor. I want that punk's ass. That Air Force officer that filed the complaint against me," demanded McMachinaw.

After an affirmative nod from Maulehouse, Brown responded, "Okay, in 72 hours he'll be on a C-17 transport to Iraq."

"No! In 24 hours I want the little bitch to freeze his ass off in Greenland. I want him tending the frozen meat lockers at Thule Air Base."

After another affirmative nod, Brown got right to the point. "Request granted. Now I understand you graduated Marine Corps OCS at Quantico with Keith Heimiller back in the day. Why is he holding back his marine division from entering San Francisco? Why is he imitating that dilatory Civil War General, McClellan, and refusing to fight?"

"Because Heimiller hates the people of San Francisco and its past counterculture. In '68 his older brother came back from Vietnam missing a leg. While passing through the airport his brother was mobbed by anti-war protesters who overturned his wheelchair. Believe me! Heimiller won't lift a finger to clear out those Chinese from *that* city. He'll make up some excuse about collateral damage. If you want immediate action, you'll need to replace him."

As soon as the line disconnected, Assistant Director Lowell sensed an angle. "Heimiller is a godsend! By not sending in the First Marine Division, he's giving the Chinese stragglers more than enough time to reach that last supertanker. If his marines did attack, they'd wind up killing some PLA soldiers but most would surrender out of desperation. Then Triple A would play the humanitarian fool and ship them all back to China after first class medical attention with full stomachs to boot, all on our dime."

"Excellent point Lawrence," concurred the director. "Need I remind you all that President Atwater is returning from his self-imposed exile at Mount Weather today. We're charged with a scheduled briefing at six this evening. Afterwards he'll address the nation at eight. Need I further remind you all, the idiosyncrasies of Heimiller are not to be raised. We'll advance the creative narrative he's the American mongoose slowly circling the Chinese cobra." Maulehouse then directly spoke to Parrott. "After this evening's White House briefing, I need you back on the agency Gulfstream on your way to San Fran again. You're to liaison with this vigilante police sergeant. What was the name again?"

"Tao."

"Convince Tao to focus all his militant resources on pulling back to the edges of the city then driving the remaining Chinese soldiers towards that last supertanker instead of dispatching them on the spot. Offer this patriotic police officer all our agency's resources. Whatever he needs: money, weapons, trucks, Mandarin interpreters. I'd send you off this very minute, but I need you at tonight's briefing, we can always tame Lejeune with the announcement of your promotion. The man's half in love with you anyway. You would probably be America's second lady if the French professor didn't get you first."

Then Maulehouse slapped the table and turned to Brown.

"Now we have to discuss what I was informed will be the end of our Glorious Republic as envisioned by our senior head of strategic analysis. Tell us professor, how much time does the American Empire have left before we implode into a Red Dwarf Star?"

The smartest man in the room cleared his throat. "We are all in concert China's *casus belli* invasion of San Francisco, though still ongoing, is an unmitigated disastrous misadventure earning the qualification: tactical failure.

A failure that has brought about the unintended consequence of the collapse of the Chinese Communist Party. Their Close Embrace, their *Yôngbào,* may be envisioned as a great strategic opportunity for whatever government fills the void. The longevity of the American Empire is contingent upon the type of replacement government China settles on. If they adopt a sham democracy of billionaire oligarchs like their Russian neighbors, a neighbor, I might add, that now has troops occupying northern Manchuria, the US can survive with its empire intact. Totalitarian governments are by nature malignant. Their inherent paralysis on the body politic always prevents a nation state from reaching its maximum potential. The other alternative is for China to become a republic again. That's the real danger for us! If they become like us—they can over take us! They out number us five to one. Imagine the unlimited resources of one billion four hundred million educated, free-thinking Chinese. All those people free to act upon their unrestrained creativity and entrepreneurship without party oversight or restraint."

"What most concerns me," interrupted Director Maulehouse, "is that Chinese banks hold over a trillion dollars in US treasury bills. Suppose this new government, for whatever reason, wants to liquefy those assets? If we just null and void the account because their former regime attempted an invasion of one of our cities, there will be heavy blow back. Other foreign countries hold five point six trillion and the American people and domestic institutions hold twenty-three trillion in treasury bills. If we simply refuse to pay the Chinese, it could trigger a margin call and collapse our economy. If you see a solution out of this potential financial ruin Robbie, let's hear it now!"

After a few taps on his smart phone, Brown had an answer at the ready. "If this new government is foolish enough to want their T-bills cashed in at once, we first notify them the post-traumatic stress of their previous government's invasion on the 884,000 San Franciscans has been assessed at one million per citizen. This will reduce their worth to a downsized two-hundred-fifteen trillian. Once we attach bproperty damage, criminal conduct retributions, and individual lawsuits, it will further reduce their principal to a negative. That's when they'll begin to owe us money. If nothing else, the sheer number of lawsuits will have the Chinese in the United Nations world court until the end of this century."

Lowell felt he had to make up for his earlier outburst and prove his worth in front this woman who had only seen him at his worst so far. "Irrespective of what new system the Chinese adopt, their people will be proud of it. A China worth fighting and dying for. We all know what follows next. New waves of patriotism, jingoism and expansionism. The precedent is in their own backyard. They'll construct something like the 1930s Japanese Greater East Asian Co-Prosperity Sphere. They have the infrastructure to do it; and ours barely has a production factory in each state. The Chinese will turn Japan, Korea and the rest of Southeast Asia against us faster with a cornucopia of jobs rather than a military threat. We'll have to introduce some sort of countermeasure."

Maulehouse drummed his fingers, looking at Val who at this point had nothing to offer since this was the first she had thought beyond the attack to the complex repercussions.

That thought embarrassed her a little, she knew better than to get emotionally caught up in one focus like that. *Mental note to not make that mistake again, I'm running with the top dogs now, not much room for overlooking anything.*

The director leaned back. "Right. So, what I'm coming up with is having America enter a NATO-like alliance with the Indian Bengal Tiger and the Russian Bear against the Chinese Dragon."

"Exactly!" confirmed Lowell. "What say you, Robbie?"

"On the face of it, a sound idea. But at the moment it would be a maelstrom of deadly intrigue to enter a defensive treaty with two member nations already technically at war with China. As previously mentioned, Russia now has troops occupying parts of northern Manchuria. India has driven out the Chinese from Tibet. It remains to be seen if they stay and become new occupiers. One thing is certain, now and forever India is determined to keep the Tibetan plateau a neutral buffer zone. You've all reviewed the latest NSA satellite photos that show Vietnam, Laos and Thailand have troops entered into a joint punitive expedition along the southern border of Yunnan Province. As long as any belligerent doesn't bomb Chinese cities, the nukes will most likely remain cocooned in their silos. The adoption of a tripart treaty must be contingent on the form of government that emerges from the ongoing mainland chaos. Where there can't be any comprise is our navy's hegemony over the western Pacific. That is absolute to the maintenance of our empire," concluded Brown.

"I keep hearing you saying, 'American Empire.'" Val shifted, hoping she was not going to say something stupid. "Just exactly when did America become an empire? At the conclusion of the Spanish-American War of 1898?"

"No Parrott, that splendid little war was only our prelude to empire. The American Century was officially instituted in January of '43 at Casablanca, Morocco," answered Brown. "At that specific place and time, the Imperial Head of the ossified British Empire, Prime Minister Winston Churchill and the crumbling French Empire both came to grudgingly pay fealty to President Franklin Delano Roosevelt. Since then, there hasn't been a Third World War. Can we forecast the same if a Chinese Empire overwhelms the world?"

Dramatically a mantle clock chimed for the top of the hour.

"There is one more thing," said the director. "We have a small threat to neutralize. Your predecessor Lawrence, Reginald Caircross, is about to bring disgrace upon us and the White House. He's been writing a tell-all book about his affair with the president's cousin. Beatrice has deep ties to money that keeps us all afloat. I've already spoken to Colin who assures me the Baker Street Irregulars will attend to the matter." The director faced Val looking for any signs of dissent. "Are you on board with us Parrott?"

"So, you intend to deprive Mr. Caircross of life without the benefit of clergy but want my blessing? Isn't that eating our own?" she asked keeping voice and expression deliciously neutral.

"Get with the program Ms. Assistant Deputy Director!" said Lowell. "Do you *really* think former U-2 pilot Powers, who spilled his guts to Soviet intelligence, bad-mouthed the CIA, suffered a fatal helicopter *accident?* That Vince Foster *actually* shot himself? That former CIA Director Colby had a canoeing *accident?*" As an afterthought to that last historical footnote, Lowell looked up to reassure his boss he was only blustering for effect. "My words are for Parrott alone, director. It's certainly not meant to be taken as a veiled threat to your personal legacy."

"That will do Lawrence," interrupted Maulehouse. "Thank you for your reassurance. Parrott, do you want to see the president humiliated? A scandal whose blowback will tarnish our agency too. Just so a disgruntled ex-employee wants to make money? Have some pity on Atwater. The poor man has been humiliated by the Chinese. Let's not add insult to injury. Let's make him grateful to our agency."

"You mean indebted." Val immediately felt she may have overstepped in this first meeting. She knew this was the tight group that discussed with similar groups in other countries—the groups that actually ruled the world and she was pushing back! She knew she had to ease up, no matter what her gut reaction might be.

"What difference does it make!?" snapped Lowell. "If it was up to me, I'd shove Caircross into the Fort Meade crematorium head first kicking and screaming at low gas psi levels just to make it last!"

Val mentally gave a sigh of relief at Lowell's input, it took all attention off of her, allowing her time to get it together. Discussing assassination plans hadn't been on her list for today. And by the look on Maulehouse's face, Lowell was the one treading on thin ice, not her.

"Jesus Lawrence, you've must have been Lucifer's protégé before you were mine." The director looked a bit guilty at the mention of a secret crematorium. "Now what say you Valentine Fountain Parrott? Are you in? You can wash your hands of this distasteful affair, but this is what it takes to play on the varsity team."

"I understand, and I'm all in, sir." Val had full intentions of working her way up to the director position and changing some of these barbaric missions, but she had to get there first. This unexpected promotion and inclusion in this meeting was an indication her hard work and the mentorship of Brown were paying off.

"That's a good fellow Val. Do you like to fish?"

"Of course, catfish from the stern of a Cajun flatboat."

"Next spring at my Elk Hair Caddis Rod and Reel Club you'll be invited for two weeks, a working vacation so you keep your accrued time for family holidays. Now before you thank me and we all head out to finish our day, there's something we all need to know. Why does Claude refer to Robbie as Spaghetti Man?"

"It's an abstruse French nuance lost in translation. It sort of means if you have a mouthful of spaghetti a person can't talk. It's a Gallic roundabout way of telling someone to shut the fuck up."

That was the perfect way for Val's first big meeting to end; they were all laughing as they walked to the office door.

Maulehouse said, "I expect all of us to celebrate our great victory over the Chinese in San Francisco by ordering a uniquely Asian-American meal of savory chop suey in a few weeks."

"I agree," said Brown walking out. "There's precedent for a victory meal. The precedent comes from Austria when they celebrated their great victory over the Ottoman Turks at the Battle of Vienna in 1683. The Viennese bakers introduced a celebratory crescent roll in mock reference to the Turkish Flag – The Croissant."

"I thought croissant was French?" questioned Lowell.

"So, did I," responded Val, "until my husband informed me Viennese born Marie Antoinette introduced it to Paris in 1770. Another thing, a French Bistro is of Russian origin, but if I kept on going, we'll be here all day."

Val remembered something, and seeing that Lowell was the one in the dog house she felt bold enough to ask. "Mr. Director, I'm still curious to know how your grandfather survived when the *USS Parrott* was accidentally rammed by the cargo ship *SS John Morton*. Naval archives record that most of her crew below decks were boiled alive from the ruptured steam lines. The topside sailors were crushed to death or drowned."

Director Maulehouse responded with pride. "Grandfather was in jail at the time of the *Parrott's* tragic loss. After two years of relentless combat in the Pacific, his ship returned to base in Norfolk. He was given shore liberty and took a bus with the intention of attending a football game at William & Mary University. An elderly black woman got on. Without hesitation grandfather gave up his seat for her. Well, his seat was up front across from the bus driver. Now mind you, the time was pre-Rosa Parks 1944 in the Old Dominion state. Well, all hell broke loose and a fistfight with the driver ensued. Luckily, grandfather was a white man in uniform so he wasn't beaten up by the police, just arrested. While detained in the local jail for a few days waiting for shore patrol to spring him out, the *USS Parrott* left port without him to meet her predetermined fate. God's Elect, Parrott! The Maulehouses are God's Elect! Oh, by the way, I've been meaning to ask you Madame Regnault, what social clubs do you belong to?"

Chapter 15

Ancient Mariner / New Masters

Dawn was just breaking over the quaint seaside village of Harlingen in West Friesland. If all the parked cars and bicycles along Nooderhaven Barge Canal were removed, the village could exist anytime in history.

An arctic white Rolls-Royce parked along the canal causing people to turn to stare at the graceful car. The two Asians inside stretched the good manners the locals were so proud of: keeping stoically to their own business.

Ji-Nan and Wen watched a bright wooden door. Wen was relaxed and happy to wait for their target, Ji-Nan was fighting to keep down an overly rich breakfast. He would not vomit in a car as perfect as this one. Ji-Nan had a new outlook on life now; he appreciated fine things—this car—his new Vietnamese-American wife.

For Lee it all started less than six months ago on the Amtrak Sunset Limited from California to Louisiana, when Nancy Cá Nguyen, the type his mother vociferously warned him about, drove him to a wild orgasm. Lee had been putty in her hands since that day. He soon learned the pleasing discipline of letting his little Nancô, as he privately called her, being the one in charge, and it suited her just fine. He did save her from rape when he could have joined in; and that refusal proudly earned him the fourth Chinese blessing-Good Morality. He felt worthy of this great life now. She was the one who proposed they marry for real. With no prenup, a thing unheard of in the mainland. Later, when Wen was told the happy news, he remarked he would be standing in line to purchase tickets to that performance of an Ancient Chinese mother greeting her future California girl Vietnamese-American daughter-in-law.

Now Ji-Nan was VP of the bank's fleet of vehicles, including this crown jewel. His precious Nancô, due to her triple-language skill set, was made VP of public relations. Thinking of this reminded Lee of what she insisted he bring up with Wen on this outing. "By the way, did my wife mention that California lawyer? Lam Dang? She says his actions are alarming our more reputable European clients. It is reflecting back on us, and we are just building up our reputation in the finance world."

"It might be too late to sack him. Our CEO, Tone, seems to like him; and he really likes being in charge. Tone saved me, but being able to use his millions has changed him. I know for a fact he's running a money laundering business in the Caymans. I don't want any part of crap like that; I barely got out of China alive, *we* barely got out alive!"

Lee nodded at that, then felt queasy again.

Wen paid no attention. "I had this feeling, so when we set up the bank's charter, there is a moral character clause in there … we will be running it all if Interpol gets him for something like that. And as for Dang, I figure he's still making his money human trafficking and lawyering for the guys that get caught transporting girls. Those two scum are tight as shit."

Wen tapped his lips in thought. Then he slowly turned toward his friend. "We could, just maybe, send an anonymous clue with plenty of details to Interpol or for that matter MI-6 or the French Deuxième Bureau."

Ji-Nan nodded again and was about to speak when his stomach rolled violently. He bolted out the door and toward the canal just as the door opened and a very tall, very blond man stepped out. The giant of a man stood high over his wife and teenaged son; embraced her good bye and started down the stone steps with his son.

The Rolls caught his eye at once, the gagging from the canal too. "Son, go meet up with your Uncle Lukas. Tell him I'll join you both on the barge shortly. Let me go check on these rich foreigners, they must be lost."

He was about to grab the sick man's shoulder when the passenger door of the Rolls opened.

"My friend is okay. He's just having some indigestion from your fine Dutch cuisine. Peking Man is used to lighter fare," laughed Wen. "Captain

Voss, I presume? Kindly come into my mobile office. May I offer you a cup a tea?"

Voss raised his eyebrows but didn't move an inch.

"Okay fine. I'll get to the point. The reason this white whale of a beauty is here is to offer you a job. I'm Ku Shen Wen. I'm the Senior Vice-President and Chief Financial Officer of Cathay Maritime Investment Bank in Luxembourg City. We have *no* affiliation with the People's Republic of China or whatever it chooses to call itself today. Please come sit for a quick proposal and salary offer."

Voss, now no more than a barge sailor, slid into the back seat and Wen went back joining him with some papers in hand. "We were both previously employed by the Shanghai Maritime Investment Bank. I'd like you to be inspector of dry docks and VP of shipping. We lack any board member who holds Master Mariner papers."

"The Dutch government has cancelled my papers," said Voss.

"Sure. But a phone call from corporate to the Hague will have you reinstated within a week. We want to offer you a signing bonus of 250,000 Euros plus a salary of 800,000 Euros."

While Voss started to spout the usual about checking with the family and his brother-in-law who gave him a job, Wen smiled. He knew the giant's Achilles heel. "We understand your son, for whatever reason that is none of our business, was kicked out of Leiden University. If you're so inclined, another call from corporate will have your son back to start their next semester."

Voss watched his son walking down the lane to his uncle's barge, then turned to look at Wen directly. Without further ado, Voss demanded to know where to sign.

Wen wanted to engage in small talk as Voss skimmed and signed the paperwork but was distracted when Ji-Nan opened the driver's door and sat down behind the wheel. Lee asked Wen to pass up a bottle of Vichy water from the Rolls' mini bar.

Voss handed back two signed copies of his contract keeping the third for himself. Now the gregarious Wen was able to get to the silly chatting he loved.

Lee Ji-Nan turned around from his chauffeur's position. He put down his bottle of stomach settling Vichy water and loudly belched for which he profoundly apologized. Then he joined the conversation in which Voss had just ask if they knew Xing.

"Never heard of any interpreter named Qu Xing, and I was a military one once myself. However, I was once presented to a fleet Admiral Phong who shook my hand on *Leviathan's* command bridge right before the start of that ill-fated mission they called *Yôngbào*. As far as I know, he's still on board."

That ended the meeting with the three men laughing in relief.

Nothing like coming out filthy rich from a near death mission.

Chapter 16

Operation Coda

At two bells of the graveyard watch Captain Amber O'Sullivan observed her flight deck personnel going about their routine of preflight preparations on two UH-60 stealth Blackhawks. Tie-downs were undone, <u>Remove Before Flight</u> red streamers were un-sleeved, fire tanks were moved into position under the main intake ducts. Inside the cockpits, overhead toggle switches were flipped on and the fuel boost pump unit was engaged. Next, the auxiliary power units were started. The pilots monitored green columns on all engine panels. Then the main blades slowly began to windmill. The crew chiefs completed their final walk around visual checks and hand-signaled the pilots with thumbs outward to indicate wheel chock removal. Then they climbed aboard and made a safety belt check on the Seal Team detachment along with the two other specialized crew members. The first Blackhawk lifted off and disappeared into the void of the moonless night with no lights visible. Mission integrity and lives were not to be solely dependent upon technology. To avoid the remote possibility of a collision under blackout conditions, a five minute differential between launches was set. Once both helicopters were on their way, they skimmed just above the waves. The helicopters were like hovercraft riding smoothly on their own cushion of air.

Kill mission Operation Coda was now in progress.

Coda was organized to kill one man: Captain Shan of *Antilles*.

In China there was no price on his head even though he had sided with one defunct party faction against another. He had done so not for patriotic principles, but for money. His death sentence was decreed by the CIA during that off the record meeting.

Shan's crime was the unnecessary attack on *Aspen*. By taking it upon himself to needlessly fire on an unarmed vessel, he would find no appeal to mercy to which a Navy Seal would give a flying fuck about.

Still, a straight forward kill mission didn't mean it was without complexity. Violating territorial integrity of a neutral nation was always diplomatically hazardous. How much blood the mission left on the street was exponentially connected to the diplomatic consequences.

The Archangel knew her success would be shared and her failure would be career ending. The pressure showed on her stone face as she stood over the navigation table and gripped both edges with outstretched arms. She moved aside the pencil compass, then repositioned chart plotter to the point of ingress where Operation Coda made landfall.

Captain O'Sullivan had the explosive temperament of a tyrant when interrupted. There was only one officer aboard with the mastery to break into her focus during such a tense situation; and the crew of *Shanksville* wasn't a ship of fools. Crew mantra had always been: *Go through Ben and save your rear end!* In fact, the XO had such a sterling reputation of competence and efficiency, that the second eye contact was made Captain O'Sullivan responded calmly because she knew the intrusion was warranted.

"Send him in Ben."

An officer in his late 30s wearing a sidearm and carrying a portfolio stamped **Classified** under his arm entered the command bridge. There was something about his countenance that put the captain on her guard.

"This is our new head of communications, Chief Warrant Officer Philip Gardner. He's Ensign Gilmore's replacement since he was unexpectedly ordered to Coronado. Gardner joined us at San Fran when we picked up our Coast Guard Liaison Officer and Chinese interpreter," said the XO.

"Yes, I know," said Captain O'Sullivan. "My apologies for not formally welcoming you. I've reviewed your SRB and see you've spent the last 11 years as an enlisted seaman in cryptology and information systems. So, tell me, who do you know to make this quantum leap from petty officer to CWO2 inside of 30 days?"

"Due diligence captain," he respectfully replied.

What a pair of balls to joke to his commanding officer, this fucker thinks I don't know? Fine, I'll play dumb for now. She reached out for the portfolio. "So, what do you have for me?"

After signing the captain's eyes only chit, she tore open the time-stamped folder and laid out the papers on the chart table. It was another straightforward interception mission. Right after Operation Coda, *Shanksville* was to head at top speed to the Marianas Trench. There to intercept and destroy *Zeelandia*. No mention about taking prisoners or rescuing survivors. The captain invited the XO to review the orders. Afterwards CWO Gardner gathered them up and prepared to transcribe them into the ship's log. Knowing she was in a dangerous game it was time for her next move.

"Mr. Gardner, everyone aboard is unable to send emails to their families. How long do you advise we keep *Shanksville* on electronic lockdown? We're running silent as a nuclear sub. You're our only effective set of ears to the outside world right now." Amber kept her face relaxed while she watched his reaction like a hawk.

"Captain, the minute we capture a satellite downlink we announce our presence and location to the outside world with all the vulnerabilities that entails. It's your prerogative captain, but I strongly recommend we maintain silent running until we sink that supertanker. After that we can light up *Shanksville* like it's a Christmas tree. In lockdown, we're invisible to ground sea and air defenses from both Malaysia and Thailand. The last thing we want to do is to alert them to our presence. It might jeopardize our Blackhawks who are in Thai airspace. At the last possible minute, the helicopters will veer south where the target is living exposed on the Thai–Malaysian border. This will also confuse any last minute Thai costal defenses in the off chance they have intercepted any random radio transmissions from fishing trawlers or pleasure boats about sighting low flying aircraft. To maintain mission integrity, we have to maintain our cone of silence." He went over to the chart table and for exactness pointed with the sharp end of the compass. "Here sir, shoreline ingress is just north of the Malaysian city Kota Baharu. This captain of *Antilles Shan*—"

"What? Excuse me Gardner, hold on a minute. Ben this tanker *Antilles;* is it the same one that kept reassuring us he had no hostile intentions? The one I let sail away unchallenged?"

"I'm afraid so captain. There was no way in the world we could know he was the bastard who fired on *Aspen* sir," confirmed the XO.

The Archangel burned with a slow rage. "Send word to the seals to take apart that son-of-a-bitch with a fork and a dull knife!"

At first embarrassed by his commanding officer's savage but understandable outburst, he knew full well the seal team was under radio silence. No communication was possible. Instead, Lieutenant Commander Ben-Ezra nodded for Gardner to continue. Still seething with anger against the Chinese captain Amber thought with bitter sarcasm, *Yes, by all means let's defer to this impostor communications officer sailing my ship anyway he wants to — anywhere he wants to! Thinking he's fooling me.*

"Sir, as previously stated our target was very easy to locate. Shen decided to spend his blood money on a luxury home right in the middle of a small hamlet of rice farmers. It's just below the Thai border. It's where he imports child prostitutes of both sexes; this was confirmed by an anonymous tip. He got asylum for a huge payment to the Malaysian government. They have their bribe; they won't stand in our way."

The captain remarked, "So confidence is high." *I want this target blown to hell too, so I won't push back on this…yet. But this fucker is not getting near my radio again, wonder what my punishment will be for holding him in the brig?*

"Sir, I think Operation Coda will come as a complete surprise to the target."

"Thank you, Mr. Gardner. You won't be resuming your duties on the comm deck. You can pick confinement to your quarters with no devices or the brig until we get back stateside."

All eyes rolled to The Archangel who was smiling sweetly over these steel words.

"After you leave my ship, send my compliments to your primary handlers, whoever they might happen to be."

Chief Warrant Officer Philip Gardner came to attention and saluted with an impressed expression. "I'll take my quarters sir," then emptied his pockets and walked under guard off the bridge.

Ben-Ezra cocked his head, questioning.

"Jesus Christ Ben! I'd expect a little more insight from a Rabbi's son. The guy's a fucking CIA spook!"

* * *

Where the gulf of Thailand merged with the deep unpolluted waters of Malaysia's eastern shoreline, the first Blackhawk touched down. Still at sea, the second observed the unmistakable bursting of a green flare—the LZ (landing zone) was secured. The second Blackhawk flew over 300' meranti trees. As hazardous as these thick top branches were to low flying aircraft, they helped muffle the stealth turbines to even lower decibels. Once the helicopter dropped below the rainforest canopy it touched down on a dirt embankment that cut across fields of squared off rice paddies laid out like a giant checker board. It was a testament to the pilots' skill that not a villager was disturbed. They immediately deployed the seals for a defense around the LZ.

Once the rotor blades spooled down to idle, it enabled the crew chief to assist his two special passengers out. Lieutenant Gallatin and CIA analyst Peter Chan were then rapidly escorted forward, both in camouflage and grease paint. As they sidestepped around a Blackhawk, inside they caught a glimpse of a drone operator in front of a circular green and white screen. He was concentrating on relaying any surface or air born anomalies in real time to the commander at the first rallying point up the embankment path right before the team's first obstacle, a high wooden fence. Its primary purpose was built to obstruct prying eyes witnessing lascivious behavior. Draped along the fence's midsection were exposed low voltage wires to prod away free ranging livestock. A second band of hidden black wires were installed to activate an intrusion alarm. By the time Gallatin and Chan arrived, a specialist had circumvented the electrical system. Long strands of jumper wires were spliced into the alarm lines to create plenty of slack to physically bypass them without setting it off. The rest was an easy crawl through the wooden fence's new hole.

Gallatin and Chan hunkered down and let the seals do their thing: reconnaissance, clearing, setting the path and keeping it all silent. This place happened to have guard dogs along with the men; an issue for the tough seals. The team leader passed the word—dart the dogs – shoot the men!

The nearest pair was targeted first. A paralytic dart was fired off to tranquilize the dog. Unfortunately, the large animal dropped quickly with its leash tightly wrapped around the guard's wrist. It pulled him down as the 8.6 mm round flew; it only parted his hair instead of his skull. In shock, the guard was still lying face down on the ground when four more bullets were fired off in quick, silent, succession. Each large bullet blew out spinal bone splinters from neck to hip. It wasn't a clean kill, but it was a painless death. The same mistake wasn't made again. This time man and beast went down together with timed shots. In an hour or so, only the beast would rise again.

Once security was neutralized, it took mere minutes to surround the two story mansion. The bad news was the main gate was open and the Mercedes was gone. The drone operator located the car speeding north. That spot on the Thai border was where whorehouses and bars were located. If a security guard was going for help, that would have been south to downtown Kota Baharu. In any case he could have used his cell to raise an alarm.

With less than four hours to sunrise, the seal team leader initiated the order to breach. From all compass points the mansion was penetrated. Once inside muddy jungle boots ruined the lush carpet. First floor rooms were rapidly cleared. Two female kitchen staff were woken up to the shock of their lives. Persuaded not to scream, Chan was brought in to calm things down but after a few phrases he gave up in frustration.

"I don't speak Thai or Malay, and these women don't speak Mandarin!"

Another member of the staff was frog-marched into the room dressed in pajamas and bathrobe. He turned out to be the chauffeur of the missing Mercedes-Benz. The man calmed the women down. He effortlessly conversed in Mandarin with Peter who in turn translated back to the seal commander that the third security guard habitually disappeared with the owner's luxury car and usually returned before daylight sexually satisfied. This chauffeur was exceedingly calm. He seemed to know the reason for this invasion and that staff was not a target, so cooperated in confirming the target's location upstairs.

The team members made more muddy tracks up the grand stairway. Shan woke to gun barrels aimed at his head from both sides. On each side of him was a terrified screaming pre-teen girl. The satin bed sheets were violently pulled back.

"Get some clothes on these kids!" shouted the commander.

The girls were hurried downstairs, Shan was grabbed by his forearm and violently yanked out of bed and thrown to the floor. Then grabbed again, to be pulled to his feet. Held fast, he was forced to stand naked for a DNA swab and photograph. As his hand was about to be pressed on a digital pad for finger printing, he managed to jerk it back and pointed to the picture on the wall.

"Ná qián! Ná qián! Túpiàn hòumiàn!" pleaded the naked man.

"He's begging for his life. He says to take the money in the safe. Look for one behind that picture frame," said Peter.

With two blows from their breaching tool, the safe was pried off the wall and chopped open. It contained $250,000 in US dollars plus plenty of Thai Bahts and Malaysian Ringgits. The seal team began to separate the cash by country of origin into three pillow cases. The team leader ordered one of his men to distribute two of the pillow cases with the Thai and Malaysian money among the staff and girls downstairs since they were about to be unemployed.

"A pittance as compensation for my murdered captain and crew," said Gallatin barely keeping his seething anger under control looking at the very murderer naked just in front of him.

"Chinamen always long to sleep over fortunes bed," mused Peter Chan quoting an old tale. "Let's flip it over and see what he's hiding there."

With that suggestion, the huge bed was hoisted up and tossed on its side. Sure enough, to the surprise of everyone except the Asian-American and to the utter horror of naked prisoner, a floor safe was at their feet. The team leader checked his wristwatch.

"We don't have all day to crack this beast. We may have to get creative."

Naked and afraid, Shan was pushed to his knees and the business end of a short barrel M4A1 pressed against the back of his head. No translation was necessary. Shan submissively turned the combination dial. The iron door opened on the first try. The contents were guesstimated to be around ten million in dollars, euros and francs.

"We're out of here in five. Pack it up!"

As Shan watched his treasure being scooped up and carted off, his helpless desperation blinded him to reality. His fear gave way to arrogance.

"Gěi wǒ yīxiē qián rang nǐ èmó!" he demanded.

"He wants you foreign devils to leave him some money," translated Peter.

"Devils huh!? That's rich coming from this killer!" said a seal. "Anyway, that's up to our officers."

The master chief had known all along the full reason why this officer was far more than just an observer of Operation Coda. The coast guard officer was intently watching and thinking.

As Shan's outbursts became shriller and more laced with old Chinese clichés about Yankee thieves and imperialist running dogs, Peter stopped translating. There was no purpose to needlessly antagonize the team so he just told the naked man to shut the fuck up, *"Bì zuǐ !"*

When the last of the money was stuffed into sacks approximately half a million apiece, Gallatin was now prepared to settle accounts. He spoke directly to Chan but pointed to the captain of *Antilles*. "Tell him I'm sending him on a journey to meet with the captain of my ship, Lieutenant-Commander Lloyd Holman, Commanding Officer of the United States Coast Guard Buoy Tender *Aspen*. He can explain face to face the reason why he fired on an unarmed ship and killed him and his crew."

Shan understood perfectly what was about to happen.

"Lieutenant," interrupted the team leader, "we can give you five minutes alone to settle accounts with your ship killer. More than that, and mission safety might be comprised."

"Thank you. I'll be at the LZ on time. Five minutes is all I need."

As the frantic naked man watch the seals walk away with his fortune stuffed inside red satin pillow cases, and before he could start another pleading rant, Lieutenant Gallatin slipped his fingers through four rungs on a brass knuckle hilt of a WWI trench knife secured under his garrison belt. With a lighting fast two step right jab (it earned him a middle weight boxing championship for the Coast Guard Academy) the trench knife was out of its scabbard, and its brass handle impacted Shan's chin and broke it apart. His lower face was a sagging, oozing mass of toothless gums and exposed bone splinters.

Shan crashed to the floor clutching his throat and thrashed about slowly choking to death as his own blood rapidly filled his lungs.

Being pressed for time to get to the LZ, Gallatin delivered the *coup de grâce.*

He at once drew back, and with all the force he could deliver, plunged the thick blade downward so it smashed through Shen's sternum and penetrated his heart like staking a vampire. The flailing arms and wildly kicking legs shook then stilled. Then US Coast Guard Lieutenant Gallatin slowly rotated the blade 90° to port and said with utmost pride, "A weapon forged in 1917 from solid United States steel is still working as designed."

The End

About the Author

Christopher Buonanno was born loving the globe and with a joy of learning. He got his pilot license before his driver's license! Right after high school he joined the U.S. Marine Corps for a four year tour of duty. After service he received an Associate Degree in Electronic Engineering.

Mr. Buonanno belongs to The Ernest Hemingway Society of Oak Park and is an avid collector of first editions of rare books. In addition to enjoying the classics, he has worked diligently for decades researching world history; much of which has been used in the creation of this novel.

Working from his Verizon office, he witnessed the horror of 9/11 directly. He immediately gave service at Ground Zero as a First Responder. This incident and work sparked the idea for this second novel (the first published in 1980-*Beyond the Flag*).

Love Books?

Support Authors - buy directly from independent publishers. This puts more royalty dollars into the pockets of your favorite author - and gives them time to write their next book.

Visit us for links to our other books as well as many other vibrant publishing companies to find the book for you.

These ARE The Books You've Been Looking For.

Vanvelzerpress.com